Critical acclaim for S

New .

"*Scorpio Rising* does for astr(
history." ~ *Suite101 Book Re*ι

"*Scorpio Rising* by Alan Annand, the first of his *New Age Noir* series, is a gripping murder mystery with a Hitchcockian twist."
~ *The Mountain Astrologer*

"Annand is a terrific mystery writer who weaves a convincing working knowledge of a metaphysician's world view into each page." ~ Steven Forrest

"Axel Crowe, the brilliant investigator of Annand's *Scorpio Rising*, is Agent 007 for the New Age noir set." ~ *Astrology Toronto*

"Annand has done a masterful job in creating a whole new type of hero - astrologer as detective." ~ *North American Jyotish Newsletter*

"Incredible power as a poet in prose - in the style of Hammett and Hemingway - to describe places and people." ~ Michael Lutin

"If you like detective stories featuring astrology and palmistry, this is a terrific read that will keep you flipping the pages."
~ *NCGR Newsletter*

"*Scorpio Rising* is an engaging mystery with a momentum that sends you rushing to the end." ~ *Horoscope Guide*

"A fascinating murder mystery, and a wonderful book for anyone with even a little knowledge of astrology and palmistry to enjoy!"
~ Ray Merriman

"For those with a mystical blend and more than a touch of Scorpio darkness, you're in for a treat." ~ *Dell Horoscope*

FELONIOUS MONK

by

Alan Annand

Felonious Monk

Published by Sextile.com

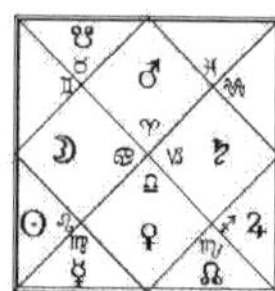

V.17032016

This is a work of fiction. Names, characters, places and incidents are the product of the author's imagination or are used fictitiously. Any resemblance to actual events, locales, or persons living or dead, is entirely coincidental.

ISBN 978-1-927799-02-4

Acknowledgements

Diane Plesz: editing and moral support

Anthony Bergmann-Porter: editing and fact-checking

Linda Tenenbaum: cover design

1

Friday, April 20

Barnet, Vermont

SETH GREER KNEW HE WAS ONTO SOMETHING BIG. With what he'd uncovered, he'd either write a story that would win a Pulitzer, or use the information to blackmail his subject for a million bucks. Maybe both. Either that or die trying.

It was day nine of a 10-day silent retreat at the Dharmapada Buddhist farm, a retreat for people seeking the ultimate pause in a too-busy life to find themselves. Along with 26 others at the ashram, he'd maintained a fierce silence thus far, but the tension was killing him. Like a pressure cooker left simmering on the stove, if he didn't let off some steam soon, he'd blow wide open.

A bell chimed. Greer opened his eyes, rocked his head from side to side and shrugged his shoulders. In the lecture hall of the converted barn, the other participants flexed their limbs to loosen up from the seated postures they'd held for an hour, mindfully observing their breathing. Thank god for the thick meditation cushions that made it bearable.

The bell rang again. On a podium at one end of the room, a coordinator hand-signaled them to go outside for the next phase of the program. By now Greer knew the drill and was thoroughly sick of it. From dawn to dusk were alternating hours of individual meditation, mindful meals, group meditation, lectures on the practice, walking meditation and mindful housekeeping chores - ten hours a day of self-introspection in silence. At least his sleep was mindless, else he might have gone insane.

Outside, the participants split into groups. Diehard devotees walked in slow motion to a circular maze, its path outlined by stones in a field that was once a cow pasture. There they spiraled in and out, like moths around a light bulb, seeking personal illumination. Others opted for a more vigorous walk, climbing a hillside trail along the rim of an old stone quarry. Others, for whom the middle way consisted of a straighter track and a leisurely stroll, followed a dirt road toward a river at the property's border.

Spotting Dean Bishop on the road, Greer set his sights on the man's back and adjusted his pace to stay twenty feet behind. It was only half a mile to the river, but if he walked like he'd just got out of the hospital after a horrible accident, he could stretch the return trip to just under an hour.

He kept his eyes down and honored the practice by observing nature as it unfolded before him - the grasses at the roadside, the occasional flower, the hum of insects - but it was hard to keep his mind off what had brought him here.

Few people had chosen the road today and, except for two women fifty yards behind, Greer was virtually alone with Bishop. They reached the river where the road ended. Judging by the remains of pilings and fallen timbers on either steep bank, there'd once been a wooden bridge here, but lack of upkeep or spring floods had spelled its ruin.

Bishop gave Greer a curt nod. Briefly alone, many a participant might be tempted to say something to break the monotony, but neither man spoke. After a few moments gazing at the river swollen with a late spring runoff, Bishop turned and began his slow walk back toward the house and barn that housed the admin office and lecture hall.

Greer gave him a twenty-foot lead and followed. In a few minutes they met the two women who looked like sisters, their short haircuts and plain clothing making them look like escapees from some nunnery. Brief nods of acknowledgement as they passed each other. Greer increased his pace to catch up with Bishop.

"I know who you are," Greer said as he came abreast of the other man. "Your name's Dean Bishop. You used to work for the CIA. You're now a security consultant but what you specialize in, using your old boys' network, is getting things in and out of a country."

Bishop gave him a wary look, no admission, but a silent regard that suggested, *Who the fuck are you and what've you been smoking?*

"Burma, Cambodia, Thailand - you've been to those places, right?" Greer paused a moment. "And you're a good judge of antiquities, maybe not for art's sake, but for the market's sake, no?"

The right hook caught Greer completely by surprise. He'd expected Bishop to deny what he was talking about, or ask who he was, or what he wanted to keep quiet. He thought Bishop would go on the defensive, but here he was in full offense, pivoting on his foot and driving his fist into Greer's face with some follow-through in it.

Reeling from the blow, Greer staggered off the road and went down in the grass, feeling short-lived gratitude as he crashed into the relatively forgiving sod. The sun swirled overhead as a silhouette loomed above him. He'd barely caught his breath when he took a sharp kick in the ribs.

"Hey!" someone yelled from a distance.

Bishop retreated to the road. Greer raised himself on one elbow. The pain in his face was incredible, as if someone had pressed a steaming clothes iron to his cheek.

A second silhouette appeared on the scene. The figure crouched before him. Greer blinked, his vision clearing enough to recognize Bryan Abbott, the chief resident of the Buddhist retreat.

"What's going on here? Did he hit you?"

Greer nodded.

Abbott stood and confronted Bishop. "Why?"

Bishop shook his head and made a zipper gesture with his fingers across his lips.

Abbott took pen and pad from his back pocket and handed them to Bishop. "Write it. Why were you fighting?"

Bishop turned on his heel and walked away, not pacing himself in a mindful way, but putting distance between them as promptly as possible.

"Pack your bags," Abbott called after him. "I want you

out of here, and you're not coming back. You're here to let go of your ego, not throw your weight around."

Bishop paused to give Abbott the finger, and continued on his way.

Abbott crouched beside Greer. "Why'd he hit you?"

Greer made the same zipper gesture as Bishop had done.

"Okay, I understand you don't want to break silence on day nine. But after we're finished tomorrow, I need to know." Abbott helped Greer to his feet and took a closer look at his face. "Let's go back to the house. You need to get some ice on your face and lie down for a little while."

2

Montreal, Canada

AXEL CROWE CIRCLED THE PODIUM and looked out into the auditorium. There were a hundred people in the audience - mostly university students with a few professors. He was at the end of his lecture, and had held their attention for almost an hour.

"...Despite hundreds of scientists who've signed petitions condemning astrology as bunk, its practice continues to this day. Nowhere is this more evident than in India, where a five-thousand-year tradition is rooted, not in a mundane desire to merely know the future, but to be in harmony with the natural order of things, and therefore, with God."

He paused, brought his hands together palm-to-palm at chest level and bowed his head toward his audience.

Although he did little to cultivate it, he had an athletic build implying a practice of yoga or martial arts. Whether it was his unkempt black hair or the five o'clock shadow hinting something of the primitive, he looked like he'd wandered off the beaten path, gone native in some exotic place, experienced things of which others only dreamed. The subliminal effect often aroused sexual curiosity in members of either sex.

Dr. Jack Skinner, a ruddy-faced Sanskrit professor with a pipe protruding from his jacket pocket, rose from his seat in the front row and mounted the podium.

"On behalf of the East Asian Studies Department, I'd like to thank Axel Crowe for a fascinating lecture on astrology in modern Hindu society. The Physics Department may not agree, but I for one will now see the planets in a different light."

The audience joined him in a hearty round of applause.

"Thank you, Dr. Skinner," Crowe said. "Always a pleasure to speak to the open-minded."

"Got time for a few questions?"

"Sure."

Skinner resumed his seat, took his pipe from his jacket pocket and gnawed on the stem. In the audience, several students raised their hands. Crowe singled them out at random.

"Mr. Crowe, what's your academic background," a young black man asked, "and how'd you train to become a professional astrologer?"

"In my undergraduate years I vacillated between physics and psychology. I did a master's in criminology and considered a doctorate preparatory to a career in forensics. Then I met my guru. Next thing I knew, I'd spent fourteen years studying astrology, palmistry, *ayurveda*, Sanskrit, and related subjects."

Another student, this time a blonde, asked the next question.

"You said astrology draws upon both left- and right-brain activities. You need a mathematical mind to do lots of computations in your head. You need a phenomenal memory to handle a complex system of rules. But every time you encounter a logical impasse, you invoke intuition to break a deadlock. How'd you develop that skill?"

"Years of practice under my guru's guidance," Crowe

said. "Some of it came from analyzing thousands of charts. Some of it was spiritual - yoga for the mind - using meditation and mantra. The goal is to achieve oneness with the situation. It's non-linear, therefore difficult to explain."

A professor in the audience raised his hand. Crowe nodded. "How's your intuition these days?" the professor asked.

"Pretty good."

"Could you quantify that for us, on a scale of one to ten?"

"Do you like baseball?" Crowe said. "I'm batting about .750 these days. Some days better, some days worse."

"Excellent. Can you tell me how many kids I have?"

A collective groan rose from the audience. Everyone squirmed a little in their seats. Intellectual debate was stimulating but nobody liked to see anyone humiliated.

"What's your name?" Crowe asked.

"Dr. Keehn."

"I assume you're faculty?"

"Mathematics."

"A recent import from Princeton," Dr. Skinner muttered around his pipe-stem, "and the epitome of academic arrogance."

"So why should I tell you something you already know, Dr. Keehn?" Crowe said. "Responding to your question puts my reputation on the line. But in asking, you risk nothing but your cynicism."

"Only if you're correct," Keehn countered.

"Cynicism is like scar tissue. Once formed, difficult to penetrate."

"Does that mean you can't answer my question?" Keehn challenged.

"I have a proposal," Crowe said. "Promise us you'll donate a thousand dollars to the Alumni Fund if I can tell you how many kids you have. Put something of your own on the line."

"Forget it. I think I've made my point." Keehn folded his arms across his chest.

"The only point you've made is that you lack the courage to put your money where your mouth is."

A titter rippled through the audience.

Keehn made a disparaging gesture, as if trying to scare away a bee that threatened to sting him.

Crowe shut his eyes and gently used finger and thumb to close his nostrils, first on one side, then the other. He opened his eyes again.

"You have three children," Crowe said, "Boy, girl, boy - in that order."

Keehn looked shocked. His failure to trumpet his denial drew everyone's attention. Dr. Skinner turned in his seat and looked back at Crowe's challenger.

"Is that true, Dr. Keehn?"

Nearly choking on the word, Keehn croaked a feeble, "Yes."

The audience broke into noisy applause. Sensing they'd witnessed the climax of the evening, people filed toward the exits. Keehn departed as well, shaking his head with incredulity.

After the last student had left the auditorium, Skinner mounted the podium, pipe clenched in a wicked grin, and pumped Crowe's hand. "Well done, Axel. Absolutely brilliant."

Crowe shrugged. "I came to provide a little infotainment, not to bloody anyone's nose."

"Never mind Keehn, he asked for it," Skinner said. "Can I buy you a drink at the Faculty Club?"

"Thanks, Jack, but not tonight. I'm visiting my mother and I promised I'd make an early night of it."

As Crowe folded a single sheet of speaking notes into his pocket, Skinner took his pipe from his mouth and poked him with its stem.

"Tell me, Axel. Your answer to Keehn's question - how'd you pull that out of the air?"

"You want the simple explanation or the complicated one?"

"Let me see if I understand the first."

"How many questions were asked tonight?" Crowe said.

"Three."

"Who asked them?"

"Let's see," Skinner reflected. "There was that black guy, then the young lady, then Keehn."

"Right." Crowe looked at Skinner.

Skinner tapped the stem of his pipe against his teeth. "Male, female, male." He stared at Crowe. "That's it?"

"Usually it's more complicated. Tonight it wasn't."

"I don't understand."

"You have a dog, don't you? Ever taught him tricks?"

"Sure."

"You teach a dog tricks with rewards. Every time he does a trick, you give him a treat, right?"

"Yes." Skinner nodded, and Crowe saw in his eyes how this discussion evoked his affection for his dog.

"But do you make him do a trick every time you give him a treat?"

"No," Skinner said. "Sometimes I just give him a treat because he's a good dog and I love him."

"Good man, good answer." Crowe patted Skinner affectionately on the shoulder.

"So, where's my treat?" Skinner joked.

"This is it," Crowe said. "For fourteen years my guru trained me to jump through hoops, open doors, climb ladders and sniff out hidden objects. I've become a good dog myself. And every once in a while, God tosses me a cookie. It's that simple."

3

Barnet, Vermont

SETH GREER AWOKE WHEN HE HEARD SOMEONE slip something under his cabin door. He lay there on his cot, digesting his reality. He was alone in the cabin, which consisted only of the cot, a rattan mat with a meditation cushion, and a small altar with a nine-inch Buddha and an incense holder. It was dark outside.

He turned his head on the pillow and saw something white on the floor near the door. He rolled off the cot and, not feeling steady enough to walk, went on hands and knees to see what it was. An envelope. He opened it and withdrew a note.

> *I know what you want. I was part of it but now I'm scared and I want out. I'll talk if you promise to protect me. Meet me up on the quarry trail at midnight. Come alone and I'll tell you everything. Destroy this note NOW.*

He studied the note. Just six cryptic sentences printed in what appeared to be a woman's hand. He had a hunch who it was. Bishop had a companion at the retreat, an attractive Thai woman named Kitti with a cabin near his. Each of the participants had a small cabin, of which there were almost thirty sprawled across the field behind the converted barn.

Greer crumpled the envelope and pushed the note into his pants pocket. He had no intention of destroying it. A journalist kept all his field notes. He never knew when he might have to answer to an editor, or a subpoena...

The room had no mirror by which to inspect his face. He felt his eye, still puffy, and winced with pain when he touched his cheek. He took two aspirin with water and lay down again, his head starting to pound as soon as it hit the pillow.

He pulled his old BlackBerry from beneath his mattress.

Books, iPods, games, writing materials or communication devices were forbidden at the ashram, but he simply couldn't have done without. He checked the time. Midnight was hours away. He set his alarm for 11:30 and groped for the gel-pack Abbott had given him. No longer cold but still cooler than his swollen face...

When the alarm vibrated, he rose and looked outside. Except for a light over the main house's back door, the grounds were dark. Taking his BlackBerry and the flashlight issued to his cabin, he stepped outside. There was just enough light to see his way among the cabins. He walked to the north end of the property where the hill began.

He found the trail and started up the slope. Not wanting to meet a skunk on the path, he turned on the flashlight and scanned ahead. In fifteen minutes he'd reached the summit. To his right was a line of Tibetan prayer flags strung on a cord supported by stakes. Brightly-colored, they formed a visual barrier on the east side of the path, warning walkers not to stray.

Six feet beyond the line of prayer flags, the ground dropped precipitously into a quarry pit that had been mined out and abandoned years ago. In daylight the old granite workings were visible but tonight, as Greer shone his flashlight into the pit, the beam wasn't strong enough to illuminate the floor fifty or sixty feet below.

He continued along the quarry's rim, past the hillcrest until the ground sloped to the north. The barrier of prayer flags ended and the trail looped around a tree to return the way he'd come. He checked his BlackBerry. Midnight. Where was that woman? He retraced his steps, expecting to meet her coming up the trail from the compound.

He looked up at the sky, cloudless and moonless. The stars were brilliant out here in the countryside. So different from LA, where he'd worked seven years at the *Times*, following a different constellation of stars, some of whom frequently crashed and burned on earth, much to the delight of the newspaper's readership.

Thinking of LA, he reflected he hadn't spoken to his brother Michael in months. Five years younger, Michael was a composer who eked out a living writing musical scores for B-grade movies. He'd had a bad spell with drugs a few years back, suffered a depression, then found religion with a West Coast spiritual group and got his life back on track. Ironic, Greer thought, that Michael would've enjoyed this silent retreat more than he did. Thus far, all he had to show for it was a black eye and a pile of anecdotal information that didn't quite weigh in as felony on the scales of justice.

He decided to give Michael a quick call while he waited for the woman to show. It was only a little past nine in LA. He tapped into his directory and connected to Michael's number.

Almost immediately, he heard someone coming through the bushes to the west of him. He held the forbidden BlackBerry behind his back and raised the flashlight.

A man emerged from the bushes and walked toward Greer, right hand behind his back. He wore a cap, its bill tipped so low that Greer couldn't make out his features. He put the light full in the guy's face, thinking it would blind him or halt his pace, but the guy just lowered his head and kept on coming.

"Where's Kitti?" Greer said.

"She couldn't make it." The man stopped an arm's-length away, crowding Greer's space.

"You're not part of this group. Who are you?" Greer cautiously backed away, mindful of the prayer flags and the rim of the quarry pit behind him.

"Just a guy who walks softly but carries a big stick."

"What do you want?"

"To shut your mouth, asshole. You stuck your nose into one too many places."

Without further warning, the man swung his arms up and over his head. Greer saw what looked like a garden spade in his hands. He tried to dodge it, raising his left hand with the flashlight to protect himself, but he was too slow. The blade struck him atop the head. He staggered backwards, snapped the line of prayer flags and tumbled into the pit of darkness below.

Even as he fell to his death, some primordial reflex made him flap his arms. The flashlight and the BlackBerry sailed free. A moment later he crashed onto the granite floor.

4

Montreal, Canada

AFTER THE LECTURE, Axel Crowe returned to his mother's house, a lower duplex in Notre-Dame-de-Grâce, one of the affluent boroughs on Montreal's west side. His mother sat reading in the living room, the TV on but muted. As soon as he entered, she set her book aside and looked up at him. She'd turned 60 just the day before, and he'd driven down from Toronto in order to attend a surprise birthday party thrown by one of her friends last night.

She was still quite beautiful for her age. She had ash-blonde hair to her shoulders, a good figure and a ready smile. On top of that, she was smart, and a generous soul. He imagined that her clients at the women's shelter where she worked as a psychologist loved her dearly. He knew he did.

"How'd it go?"

"Good attendance. About a hundred people."

"Did you get any clients out of it?" His mother could never quite believe that her only son, who could have had any other profession he'd wanted, earned a very good income as an astrologer.

"I left business cards on the podium. We'll see."

"Students don't have any money."

"There was faculty there too. Besides, some students have more money than you and me put together. Anyway, students become doctors and lawyers and corporate executives, you know. My future clients."

She rolled her eyes and stood. "Ready for a game of crib?"

"Sure." His mother was an avid card player. Throughout his grade school years, when she'd been in graduate school, it'd always been their routine to play three rounds of cribbage as soon as he came home. Over the years, she'd accumulated a 2-1 lead he'd never recover from. Despite his divinatory powers, this wasn't poker; cribbage was at least fifty percent luck, and the luck was all hers.

They played three rounds and she won them all, skunking him once. Defeated again, he decided to call it a night. He gave her a long hug and kissed her on both cheeks. "I love you, Mom."

She patted him on the cheek. "You should have shaved before your lecture."

"They dimmed the lights for my slide presentation."

"You'll never attract a nice girl if you look scruffy."

"When you're not fishing, you don't think of a lure."

She shook her head in dismay. Still single at age 41. If not for a mother's love, he was almost a write-off. "I put out fresh towels for you."

"Thanks."

"Good night." She turned out the living room lights and headed down the hallway to her bedroom.

He went downstairs to the finished basement, where there was a den with another TV and a computer desk and a sofa-bed. Adjacent it was a laundry room and a small bathroom. Clean towels were sitting on the laundry room counter.

He splashed some water on his face and looked at himself in the mirror. He needed a haircut. Perhaps he should start doing what Guruji had always done, and shave his head. But Crowe's excuse had always been that he disliked wearing hats in the winter and needed his full head of hair for protection. So what was his summer excuse, Guruji had teased him, vanity?

Crowe rolled a spare blanket into a cushion and sat for half an hour of meditation. As he came out of it, he reviewed his day, taking stock of his accomplishments and shortfalls, both spiritual and mundane. He acknowledged all the things for which he was grateful - his health, his parents, his friends, his work, but most of all, his guru, who'd made him what he was today.

Guruji was a Bengali *jyotishi*, an astrologer from Calcutta who'd been dispatched to Canada twenty years ago by his own guru to fulfill his karma. There in Toronto, the *paramaguru* had said, awaited a worthy student who would under his guidance become a detective, using knowledge of the Vedas to solve crimes. It had taken them awhile to find each other, but once they did, the magic had begun, if indeed the spiritual equivalent of boot camp could be called magic.

But so it had seemed to Crowe, and all those years of instruction and deconstruction, memorization and recitation, exercises and penances, mantras and rituals had shaped him irrevocably. To this day, he never lost sight of the fact that, without Guruji, he would scarcely have glimpsed but a shadow of his own self-realization.

Crowe undressed and read in bed for half an hour before he fell asleep. During the night, he dreamed he was back in Thailand, visiting one of the many large temples along the river in Bangkok. On the terrace were several gold-plated statues of *Kinnari*, a deity whose upper body was that of a beautiful young woman, the lower part bird. As Crowe stood looking at the row of *kinnari*, one spoke to him:

"The road to truth is long and crooked. But truth is a destination from which great vistas can be seen. There are no shortcuts, and those who promise them will betray you."

Having uttered these words, the *kinnari* struck a gong, which reverberated with a deep sonorous harmonic beat.

5

Saturday, April 21

CROWE AWOKE TO THE SOUND OF A HARP, the tone for his smart phone's alarm. He turned it off. It was five AM. He got up, shaved and showered. After drying off, he did fifteen minutes of yoga stretches and meditated for half an hour.

He'd just finished stretching his legs when his phone rang. He glanced at the time as he picked it up. A few minutes after six. Who would call at such an hour? He saw an 802 area code he didn't recognize.

"Hello?"

"Axel, it's Bryan Abbott. I'm sorry to call so early but I thought you'd be up anyway."

Crowe was surprised and delighted to hear from Abbott, whom he'd first met in India fourteen years ago. At Guruji's suggestion, Crowe had gone to Rishikesh for a month to study Vedanta. The course had been at the Dayananda ashram, right across the river from where the Beatles had studied with Maharishi Mahesh Yogi, founder of the TM movement. Abbott, an American from Vermont, had been Crowe's roommate in the austere ashram dormitory.

Over the course of many conversations and strolls throughout the area, the two had become good friends. One day, while walking in the neighborhood of the train station, Abbott had grabbed Crowe by the arm and yanked him off the narrow sidewalk. A moment later an air conditioner, which Abbott had noticed teetering from a third story window, smashed to the ground. Crowe had been shaken by the incident, knowing that if Abbott hadn't intervened, he would have died on the spot.

"What's up, Bryan? You sound upset."

"Upset hardly describes it. I just found one of my participants dead on the property. It might have been an accident but I'm suspicious. Just yesterday this fellow was involved in a fight with another participant."

Crowe quickly came up to speed. After having spent a few years in Seattle, Abbott had returned to his native Vermont and opened a spiritual retreat in the Green Mountains for frazzled city dwellers. Crowe had helped him get off to a good start by choosing both a name and a date for the official opening of *Dharmapada*. And he'd been among the first twelve participants in a 10-day silent retreat dedicated to Vipassana meditation, facilitated by Abbott.

"Have you called the police?" Crowe tapped his phone and opened an app for a Vedic astrology program, creating a chart for 6:05 AM, April 21, in Montreal.

"Once I open that door, things will never be the same again. Believe me, I've been struggling with my own conscience for the past half hour. You might find it ironic that I'm thinking of optics as much as ethics but the bad publicity could force the permanent closure of the retreat."

"I don't understand."

"I can explain later. Can you help me? I'd called your home phone first but after a few rings it went to voicemail. Where are you?"

"Montreal."

"Then you're only two hours away."

"I'm not driving Formula One, Bryan."

"Can you come?"

Crowe made a snap decision. He genuinely liked Abbott and knew him to be a man of true spiritual nature. And as a fellow traveler on a similar path, Crowe was sympathetic to his friend's dilemma and ready to offer what help he could. Bottom line, he literally owed Abbott his life.

Gratitude aside, Crowe also saw something in the *prashna* - the horary chart - that said this was part of his dharma, that it was the right thing to do, not only for Abbott, but maybe for something larger than both of them.

"Yes, I'll come."

"I can call you again en route to give you some background."

"In an hour."

"Thanks, Axel."

Crowe packed his bag and folded his bed back into the sofa. He unplugged his tablet from where it'd been sitting on the desk and put it in his bag. It was a Saturday and his mother would sleep in until seven, so he wrote her a note and left it on the kitchen table. He let himself out, locked the door with his own key, and went to the car.

Traffic was light and Crowe made good time. The speed limit in Quebec was 100 kilometers an hour but everyone drove 120, and some a lot faster. Crowe had his own driving style - fast, but never the fastest on any road - mindful of that old Japanese saying, *The nail that stands up gets pounded down*. He took Route 10 toward Sherbrooke, turning off at Magog to pick up Route 55 south. His phone rang shortly after seven AM.

"It's Bryan. Where are you?"

"Halfway there. Did you call the police?"

"I'll call them right after I get off the phone with you."

"Why are you delaying it?"

"Because I'm afraid the consequences will be immediate."

"You said something earlier about a permanent closure of the retreat. Why? Bad things happen in all sorts of places, but it doesn't demand their shutdown."

"It will in my case. Thirteen years ago when I was looking for a suitable property, I couldn't find anything affordable to buy outright. Except for this property in Barnet where the owner offered a thirty-year lease. But there were strings attached. He was a devout Baptist and leery of a Buddhist group taking up residence. So he had his lawyer include a clause that said, if any member of our community were ever involved in a felony, the lease would terminate immediately."

"Felony covers a lot of ground," Crowe said. "Arson, blackmail, fraud, theft, assault, kidnapping, and murder. Including conspiracy to commit any of those, or obstruction of investigation into same."

"I know, I'm already guilty. Except you and I are the only two who know. When I call the police, I'll tell them I just discovered the body."

"Tell me about the dead man. Was he one of your regular participants?"

"No, he's never been here before. His name's Seth Greer, from New York. He just popped up out of nowhere."

"You said he'd fought with one of the other members?"

"Yes, a regular participant named Dean Bishop. He's been here maybe a dozen times."

"When you say a fight, what do you mean - a shouting match?"

Abbott told Crowe he'd seen Bishop hit Greer and knock him down. They'd been alone on a walking meditation so there'd been no one nearby to witness whatever had provoked it. Bishop had refused to explain why he'd struck Greer, so Abbott had ordered him off the property.

"Did he leave?"

"He packed his bag and was gone in half an hour."

"What do you know about Bishop?"

"He's a security consultant in New York. He's been a regular attendee ever since we opened. A quiet guy, always kept to himself."

"Isn't everyone quiet on a silent retreat?"

"The first evening is sociable, so participants can get acquainted. And the last evening, after ten days of silence, we encourage people to talk about their experience. Bishop was always last to arrive, first to leave."

"It's a long drive to New York."

"Hasn't discouraged him. He's attended six sessions in the past two years."

"That's a lot of retreats."

"Maybe his job is very stressful."

"What do you know about the other guy?"

"I'm just looking at his registration sheet now. He's a writer."

"Next of kin?"

"A brother in LA."

"No discernible connection between Bishop and Greer?"

"None that I can see. I'm hoping you'll be able to figure it out."

"We'll see. I'll be there soon."

"Do you need directions?"

"I remember the way. Meanwhile, call the police."

6

Barnet, Vermont

AT THIS HOUR, THERE WAS NO LINEUP at the border crossing. After a glance at Crowe's passport and a few routine questions, the US Customs & Border Protection officer waved him through. It was quarter past eight when Crowe took the Barnet exit off I-91 and drove west a few miles on Barnet Road, eventually leaving it for a smaller road that crossed a river and brought him to the Dharmapada Buddhist farm.

He parked his car alongside dozens of others in the parking lot. Included among them was a Vermont State Police vehicle, a four-door Chevy Silverado truck with a king cab, dark green with a yellow stripe on the side.

He followed a stone path around the house and immediately came upon Bryan Abbott and another man standing with two police officers. Both officers wore the broad- and flat-brimmed hats that everyone associated with Smokey the Bear, except theirs bore the crest of the Vermont State Police. Their shirts were tan-colored, with dark brown epaulets and pocket flaps.

Abbott beckoned for Crowe to join them. He was fifty years old, looking healthy and fit, albeit a little pale at the moment. He had close-cropped dark hair with some gray at the temples, and a face that radiated kindness. Something about his brown eyes said you could trust him, confide in him, lean on him. He wore a nylon windbreaker over a plaid shirt, loose jeans and a pair of Wellingtons. In Barnet, he'd easily pass for a local farmer.

Abbott shook Crowe's hand. "Nice timing," he murmured as he gave him a hug. "Thanks for coming." He turned and gestured to the other civilian. "You remember my assistant, Neville?"

"Sure." Crowe shook hands.

Neville Webster was in his forties, a tall skinny fellow with a relaxed posture and thick graying hair. He wore matching khaki pants and shirt, giving him the appearance of a laid-back utility worker. As Crowe recalled, Neville was blessed with a folksy wisdom enlivened by a quirky sense of humor, a sort of hayseed guru.

With the two cops waiting expectantly, Abbott promptly introduced them. "Lieutenant Lynch and Sergeant Quaid."

Lynch was a big man who, despite an age Crowe guessed at early sixties, had retained the physique of a linebacker. He had a square head and a salt-and-pepper crew cut, a crushing handshake and a pair of blue eyes that looked like they'd been chipped from a glacier.

Quaid was in his thirties, a sleepy-eyed hulk who looked like he'd had a late night, or missed his coffee this morning, if not both.

"And who are you?" Lynch asked Crowe.

"A friend of Bryan's, just down for a visit."

"Down from..."

"Canada."

"Got some ID on you?"

"Sure." Having crossed the border less than an hour ago, Crowe still had both Canadian and US passports in his breast pocket.

"Dual citizenship?" Lynch examined both passports and handed them back. He turned to Abbott. "Okay, take us to the body." To Crowe he said, "You wait here at the house."

"Thanks, but I'd like to tag along."

"This is a police investigation. And you're not a resident of this property, so you have no business being present."

"Yes, I do." Crowe opened his wallet and handed a laminated card to Lynch.

Frowning, Lynch squinted at it. "A private investigator's license?"

"Issued in New York State," Crowe said. "I'm licensed to pursue investigations on behalf of clients in every state of the Union."

"Who's your client?"

"Me." Abbott extended a hand to Crowe. "Axel, here's your retainer. In order to protect my interests I'd like you to participate in this investigation as fully as the law allows."

"Done." Crowe accepted the single banknote from Abbott and put it in his wallet.

Lynch looked from one to the other and shook his head. He made a brusque gesture for Abbott to get on with it, and lead them to the body. Crowe fell into step next to Abbott. Neville trailed behind the two policemen.

Behind the house was a barn, refurbished with a new roof, and a small bell tower mounted on its peak. They threaded their way through a group of small cabins - over two dozen of them - scattered across a small field. The cabins were ten feet square, each with a single window and a small verandah with a chair.

"Is it my imagination," Crowe said to Abbott, "or are there a lot more cabins here than when I last visited?"

"A few years ago, we built some more cabins," Abbott said. "We used to have eighteen; now we have twenty-seven. We rearranged them too, just to provide more space between cabins. Some folks snore, you know."

"You said you have over two dozen attendees on site?" Lynch said. "Where is everyone?"

"After the breakfast period," Abbott said, "they all returned to their cabins for an hour of private meditation."

"And when they come out?"

"A walking meditation."

"We need to limit all traffic in the vicinity of the crime scene."

Abbott stopped and turned to his assistant. "Neville, maybe you should stay back. Can you make a sign telling people not to come up here? They can restrict themselves to the garden maze or the river road."

"You betcha." Neville turned and headed back to the house.

Abbott resumed his course, leading Crowe and the police to a dirt path that climbed a hill. Nearing the crest, a line of brightly-colored prayer flags formed a sort of fence to the right of the path. Crowe looked out into a deep quarry pit.

"We planted stakes and strung these flags along the edge," Abbott said, "to make sure nobody fell into the quarry." They neared the crest of the hill. "But when I came up here this morning, I noticed the fence was broken."

They arrived at the place where the cord was broken. Six feet off the dirt path, a pair of stakes were canted at a forty-five-degree angle and the string of flags lay draped over the edge of the precipice.

"What were you doing up here?" Lynch asked.

"I come up here every morning to meditate," Abbott said. "As you see, there's a great view to the east. It's a beautiful way to start the day. Most days, anyway."

"Where's the body?"

Abbott beckoned Lynch to the edge of the precipice and pointed down into the quarry. Amid a jumble of broken rocks and scattered vegetation at the base of the cliff, a body lay sprawled.

"Anybody else come up here this morning since you?"

"No."

"Go stand back there." Lynch directed Abbott and Crowe to a point on the dirt path about twenty yards back from the place where the victim had crashed through the prayer flag.

Quaid produced a camera and took pictures of the broken fence and the body below. He and Lynch spent several minutes scanning the ground in a ten-yard radius around the break in the fence, but appeared to find nothing. Lynch beckoned Abbott and Crowe to rejoin them.

"What's the best way to get down to the body?"

Abbott pointed further north along the dirt path. "Over the hill and then down to the quarry floor."

Lynch and Quaid took the lead. They walked slowly, scanning the dirt path ahead, peering into the grass on either side of the trail. Now and again Lynch squatted to look at something on the trail, then moved on.

7

THEY CONTINUED OVER THE HILLCREST until both the dirt path and the line of prayer flags ended. At Lynch's invitation, Abbott went on ahead and led them down a steep rocky trail to the quarry floor. Crowe looked around him as they approached the body. Underfoot was broken rock - the detritus of a quarry - ground incapable of bearing a trace of footprints.

The man lay on his stomach. A mass of blood had turned the ground dark beneath his head. He had curly black hair and from his profile Crowe guessed he might be forty years old, possibly Jewish. Judging by the clotted mass of blood, it looked like a fatal head wound.

"Did you touch the body?" Lynch asked Abbott.

"No," Abbott said, "but I recognized him. His name's Seth Greer."

Quaid circled the body and took pictures from all four quarters.

Lynch crouched beside the man for a closer look. He took a pen from his pocket and parted the dead man's hair. A bloody gash had split his scalp at the hairline just above his forehead. "Pretty deep gouge here," Lynch said. "Maybe an axe...?"

"There's a shovel over here." Quaid pointed to a garden spade that lay about twenty feet from the body.

"Don't touch it," Lynch cautioned. "It may have been the murder weapon." He and Quaid crouched to examine it.

Abbott and Crowe edged closer for a better look. Even from where he stood several feet away, Crowe could see what looked like a little gobbet of bloody scalp with several hairs stuck to the edge of the blade.

Quaid took more pictures. He and Lynch then returned to the body and searched the ground in an expanding spiral of twenty yards radius. Lynch found a chrome-plated flashlight and beckoned Quaid to take pictures of it too.

"The dead man's or the killer's?" Quaid speculated.

"It's his," Abbott said.

"How do you know?" Lynch said.

"We put cabin numbers on the butt end," Abbott said. "People sometimes misplace them. If they lose theirs, this way we know who to charge at the end of the course."

Lynch cocked his head to look at the flashlight. "You're right. It's number eight."

"That was his cabin," Abbott said.

Interesting, Crowe thought. Eight was the number of Saturn. Today was Saturday. Abbott had discovered Greer's body in the first hour of the day, even more specifically linked to Saturn via the concept of *hora,* assigning successive hours of each day to the seven celestial bodies. And Saturn was associated with death.

No sooner had this thought come and gone, a stiff breeze came out of nowhere. Crowe looked up at the rim of the quarry and saw the broken cord with the prayer flags fluttering violently in the breeze, the cord and its flags extended almost horizontally out over the precipice. With the flags acting as a weather vane, Crowe saw it was a west wind. In many world mythologies, the west was associated with strangers and death.

At the quarry floor, something different was happening. Perhaps due to the wind's passage over the hollow cavity of the quarry, the air down here had begun to turn in a tight circle, a whirlwind that appeared to be centered close to where the dead man lay.

"What the fuck?" Lynch said as both his and Quaid's flat-brimmed hats simultaneously lifted off their heads and went spiraling around. Lynch made a sudden lunge and snatched his hat from the air before it had gone too far. Quaid ended up chasing his halfway across the quarry before it fell to earth. Both officers jammed their hats under their arms and returned to where Abbott and Crowe had waited near Greer's body.

The whirlwind continued unabated. Crowe noticed it was moving in an anti-clockwise direction, never a good sign. Throughout history, wherever perambulations were required - around a monument or statue, church or temple, city or country - the requisite direction was always clockwise, the right-hand path. To turn in the opposite direction was to invoke evil. This was an ill wind that bode no good...

Lynch took a pair of latex gloves from his jacket pocket and covered his hands. Without turning the body over, he checked the man's back pockets. Nothing. Slipping his hand under the man's waist, he extracted a key from his right front pocket. It was on a keychain with a disk, a bas-relief of a smiling Buddha on one side, number "8" on the other. Lynch put the key in his own pocket.

He circled the body to get at Greer's left-hand pocket, from which he extracted a folded piece of paper. The wind devil suddenly increased its intensity. Perhaps because of the latex glove, Lynch's grip on the paper wasn't as secure as he'd thought. The wind ripped it from his hands and took it away. Crouched where he was, Lynch was prevented by Greer's body from lunging after the note. But in a few quick strides, Crowe caught up with it and plucked it deftly out of the air.

"Don't get your prints on it," Lynch barked.

"It's all right." Crowe had accidentally pinched it on the very edge of the paper.

Lynch came rushing up to him, but in those few seconds Crowe had time to glance at the note before the lieutenant snatched it from his hands.

"That's crime scene evidence."

"You're welcome," Crowe said. "If I hadn't grabbed it, the wind might have taken it into the woods." He pointed at a ragged cloud of dead leaves and grass, lifted from the quarry floor, that circled overhead, drifting eastward toward a line of trees.

Lynch studied the note a moment, then folded it and put it into his breast pocket. He returned to the body.

Crowe remained where he was for a few moments and closed his eyes to review the visual snapshot he'd taken in those scant seconds before Lynch had snatched the note from his hand. If he didn't commit it to memory, it would fade as quickly as a dream.

Aside from its brief message, there was something vaguely odd about the note. The words had been hand-printed, not written cursive style, but serifs here and there had lent the letters a feminine touch. Yet the overall look of the letters, small but bold, implied a man's hand. Curious.

Crowe rejoined Abbott and the two police officers at the body. "So what was that?" he asked Lynch, feigning ignorance.

Lynch had resumed searching Greer's other pockets. "A personal note," he said over his shoulder. "Our forensics people will analyze it."

Quaid stood off to one side, reviewing the photos he'd taken with his camera.

Lynch finished his search of Greer's pockets and used his cell phone to make a call. "Jenny, I've got a crime scene here in Barnet that needs forensic analysis. The Buddhist farm, off West Barnet Road. They'll see signs for the turnoff."

"What now?" Quaid asked his lieutenant.

"You wait here for the CSST," Lynch told him. "I'll go with Mr. Abbott and take a look at the victim's effects."

8

CROWE AND ABBOTT HEADED BACK to the house with Lynch. As they climbed out of the quarry and crossed the crest of the hill, the west wind was still trying to tear the prayer flags off the line of stakes.

"Where's your crime scene unit stationed?" Crowe asked Lynch.

"Waterbury."

Crowe did some mental math. "Over an hour's drive."

"Yeah, but the team was on a case in Montpelier last night, so if we're lucky, Dispatch might send them directly from there," Lynch said. "Could be here in forty-five minutes."

At the foot of the hill, they encountered a sign planted in the middle of the dirt path, a panel of cardboard stapled to a wooden stake. On it Neville had printed, *Quarry trail closed. Use the garden maze or the river road.*

Within the spiral of the garden maze, a dozen people were treading mindfully, their eyes down. Out in the field, another dozen walked along the road toward the river.

"What's with the zombies?" Lynch said. The wind had subsided down here, and he put his hat back on.

"It's a walking meditation," Abbott said. "The idea is to put consciousness into each and every step."

"Looks like they're going nowhere fast."

"That's the idea."

Abbott led the way to cabin number eight. Lynch unlocked the door with the key he'd taken from Greer's body. He paused at the threshold and said to Abbott and Crowe, "This may be a crime scene," he said. "Investigator's license or not, you can't come in here."

"Okay." Crowe and Abbott remained outside on the porch.

Lynch looked for a light switch, found none, and opened the window curtains. "No lights here?"

"Residents get a flashlight to find their way to the

communal washrooms," Abbott said. "There's no reading during the retreat so people do what our ancestors did - sleep or contemplate the nature of their existence."

Lynch had a quick look around. The accommodations were minimalist. The bedding of the cot was tucked in but rumpled as if someone had slept atop the covers. A suitcase lay on the floor. Lynch placed it on the cot and opened it. They saw him cautiously pick through Greer's clothing, which consisted of a pair of jeans, a pullover, some T-shirts, underwear and socks.

Lynch repacked the suitcase and left it on the cot. He stepped outside and locked the cabin door. He looked at Abbott. "You said you have information sheets on all your attendees?"

"In the office."

They returned to the house. The ground floor had been converted to accommodate a large kitchen, a communal dining area and two washrooms. Upstairs, the second floor had two bedrooms, a washroom and an office. The office had two old desks, one with a computer and a printer, and a row of three filing cabinets.

Abbott fetched a folder from a file cabinet. Lynch studied the single sheet of paper it contained.

"This all you got on Greer?"

"He's a writer, lives in New York. Next-of-kin, a brother in LA. What else do you need?"

"This is just a contact sheet," Lynch said. "Don't you have a registration form or something with a little more personal information?"

"Usually, participants complete a form on our website to book a retreat months in advance. That's where we gather information on their education and occupation, their email and postal addresses, some background on their spiritual journey or practice, and they get a chance to tell us what they hope to get out of the course. They also acknowledge they're not allowed to bring any reading or writing material, music or game devices, cell phones or anything that'll distract from their self-introspection during the ten days of silence."

"Sounds like a snore," Lynch said. "Why don't you have that information on Greer?"

"We'd had a cancellation two days before the retreat started. Although we have a waiting list, it was too short of a notice to contact them. Greer showed up here the day before the retreat, asking if he could participate, so I let him. We don't charge people that much but we do need all the revenue we can get."

"What day was that?"

"Wednesday, April eleventh. He showed up around mid-afternoon. In lieu of making him fill out an application form, we had a little chat and I judged him a worthy participant, since he'd already learned meditation in college. He signed the checklist of restricted items, filled out the contact sheet, and I charged his credit card for the course fee."

Lynch looked at the credit card slip stapled to the contact sheet. "You don't charge much for a ten-day stay."

"Our revenues are just enough to cover taxes, expenses and a modest stipend for me and Neville."

"Who else lives on the property?"

"Just me and Neville. We each have a room here on the second floor. The rest of the house is administrative or communal. When the courses run, we have two ladies from Barnet to cook food. Neville used to handle that, but nobody was eating, so we had to hire real cooks."

Neville shrugged. "Fasting is good for the soul. They can eat when they go home."

"Anyway," Abbott continued, "people started to arrive after six PM. They left their car keys with us and signed our checklist of restricted items. They filled out a contact sheet with any information on medical issues, next-of-kin, phone numbers, in case of emergency. We showed them their cabins, got them settled in, and gave an introductory talk outlining the ten-day program."

Lynch nodded and returned his attention to the page in hand. "So this guy was a writer. A journalist, novelist, what…?"

"I don't know," Abbott said. "He said he was interested in Buddhism. He'd heard of Vipassana meditation and was curious to learn more. But if he intended to write about his experience, he didn't say."

"He interact with anyone else on the course?"

"On the first evening, there's opportunity to socialize. After that, no talking, sign language, even direct eye contact for the ten-day duration. Up until yesterday, I assume he abided by those rules."

"What happened yesterday?"

Abbott told Lynch about seeing another participant, Dean Bishop, knock Greer down. When Bishop refused to explain himself, Abbott had sent him packing.

"What time was that?"

"Walking meditation is four to five PM, so it would have been around four thirty."

"Where's *his* file?"

Abbott pulled another folder from the file cabinet. Lynch flipped through several pages.

"This guy's a regular?"

"He's been here dozens of times."

"I'll need photocopies of both files." Lynch handed the two folders to Abbott, who passed them to Neville.

"Anything else?"

"I need to search Greer's vehicle. You have his car keys?"

From another file cabinet Abbott withdrew a large brown envelope with number "8" on it. He handed a keychain to Lynch. "White Volvo sedan. Want his cell phone too?"

"Whatever you got." Lynch waggled his fingers.

"That's it." Abbott gave Lynch a Samsung phone from the envelope.

9

LYNCH PUT HIS LATEX GLOVES BACK ON and unlocked Greer's car in the parking lot. He searched the interior and glove compartment, finding only an owner's manual, some CDs, maps of New England, a GPS unit, some dry snacks and a bottle of water.

Lynch went to the trunk. "Someone's jimmied this." He pointed to the trunk lid, where a tool had been inserted, damaging the rim around the lock. Inside the trunk were a tire iron and jack, windshield-washing liquid, a quart of engine oil, a six-pack of water bottles, a small tent and a sleeping bag.

"This guy was a writer. Where's his laptop?" Lynch turned to Abbott for the answer.

"Maybe he was on vacation," Crowe said.

"I told him the same as everyone, no electronics allowed," Abbott said. "If he had a cell phone, laptop, whatever, we'd keep them in the office, or he could lock them in his car, but we kept the car keys."

"So he could have had a laptop."

"Could have," Abbott nodded. "He never said, one way or the other."

Lynch got a roll of crime scene tape from the truck. He tied one end to the driver's door handle, wrapped the strip around the rear of the trunk and tied the other end to the passenger door handle. He tossed the tape back in the truck and gave the parking lot and immediate area a three-hundred-and-sixty-degree scan. "No security cameras here?" he asked Abbott.

"It's a meditation retreat," Abbott said. "No guard dogs either."

"You've got locks on the cabin doors," Lynch said.

"Single women participate. It's more for their peace of mind."

"Anything bad ever happen here?"

"Never. These are spiritual people. Theft and sexual

assault are the last things on their minds."

"Even so, Greer may have been murdered."

Neville came from the house with a large brown envelope. "There you go, chief. Copies of those two files."

Lynch tossed the envelope into the Silverado's front seat. He turned to Abbott. "I need to question your course participants."

"Why?"

"In case they saw or heard anything as to who might have killed Greer."

"There's nothing to hear at a silent retreat," Abbott said. "As for witnesses, I saw Bishop punch Greer. You want a suspect, start with him."

"I will. But other people might shed further light on Greer's activities."

"His activities...?" Crowe said.

"Maybe he provoked someone," Lynch shrugged.

"It's a spiritual retreat," Abbott said.

"You keep repeating that, as if it makes what happened impossible," Lynch said. "But a man's dead on your property, his car's been broken into, and he may've been murdered. I need to talk to your people."

Abbott looked to Crowe for help. "They won't want to break silence before the day's over."

"What's next on their program?"

"Group meditation starts in about fifteen minutes."

"So let's conduct a roll call then and tell them what's happened," Crowe said. "Maybe we can solicit their cooperation, without their breaking silence." Lynch was about to object when Crowe made a soothing motion with his hand. "Lieutenant, we're trying to help you. If you let us handle it our way, you might get what you want without alienating any of the participants."

Lynch bristled at the sound of this but Crowe ignored him and said to Abbott, "Why don't you prepare a complete list of participants for the Lieutenant - names, phone numbers, addresses, emails? We'll need it for the roll call anyway."

"Neville, can you run that off?" Abbott said.

Neville nodded and headed for the house.

Crowe called after him. "Bring it to the lecture hall. Along with some pens and paper."

Neville waved a hand to acknowledge he'd heard.

"Fifteen minutes, you said?" Lynch checked his watch. "While we're waiting for the zombies to come back to the barn, you can show me where you saw them fighting yesterday."

Abbott led them out the dirt road to the river. "You couldn't really call it a fight," he said. "Bishop threw one punch and Greer went down."

They met a few participants, still engaged in walking meditation, working their way back to the barn. True to their practice, the walkers kept their eyes down and moved in slow motion, paying no attention to the three men they met on the road.

Abbott stopped at the place where he recalled Greer having fallen. Lynch poked around in the grass for several minutes but didn't find anything. They walked back to the barn.

The lecture hall inside had been finished with a bamboo floor and drywall painted pastel green. Posters of Tibetan Buddhist deities occupied each wall. Dozens of meditation cushions were scattered around the room, along with a few chairs for those whose knees couldn't handle a cross-legged pose. At the north end of the room was a podium with an altar of incense, bells and singing bowls gathered around a stone Buddha.

Lynch brought a chair to the stage. People began to enter the hall, taking seats on cushions or chairs. Neville arrived with a list of course participants. He fetched a long rod with a hook at one end, and opened a pair of louvered windows, high on the wall beneath the sloping roof, to admit fresh air.

When it looked like everyone was present, Abbott told them, "I have an unfortunate announcement to make. This morning, one of our participants, Seth Greer, was found dead in the quarry pit. We don't really know what happened, so the police are here to investigate.

"Lieutenant Lynch solicits your cooperation in his investigation. First, I want to conduct a roll call to make sure everyone is present. As Neville reads out your names, please raise your hands."

Neville went through the list, leaving out Bishop and Greer. Everyone else was present.

Lynch stood. "Thanks for your cooperation. Now, I don't want to interrupt your routine but I do need your help. Did anyone notice anything out of the ordinary about Mr. Greer in the past nine days?"

His question was greeted with group silence.

"Did anyone here know Greer before this retreat?"

Again, mute response.

"I understand your need to maintain silence for the rest of the day, but we have pens and paper here. If you just give me some indication of what you know, we could discuss it more fully later...?" He looked to Abbott.

"After six o'clock."

No one raised a hand.

"Well, I guess that's it," Abbott said to the group. "We'll leave you with Neville to guide your next session. If anyone has anything to share, please speak to me at day's end and I'll give you Lieutenant Lynch's number so you can contact him in confidence."

Neville gave Lynch the roster of course participants. Lynch stuck it in his back pocket and looked at Abbott. "Got a restroom I could use?

Abbott lifted his chin in the direction of the house. "First floor, just beyond the dining room."

Lynch went inside. Crowe tugged Abbott's arm. They walked along the stone path to the corner of the parking lot where a bench sat under a birch tree. They took a seat.

"Do you have a lawyer?" Crowe said.

"Do I need one?"

"Even the innocent need legal counsel."

"At least you think I'm innocent."

"Of course I do."

They sat in silence for awhile. Aside from the circumstances, at least they were having lovely spring weather. Crowe noticed several bees working a row of rose bushes along the front of the house. "Are those new?" he asked Abbott.

"Planted them myself a couple of years ago," Abbott said. "Turns out I have something of a green thumb."

A van with Vermont State Police colors and markings, *Crime Scene Search Team* decaled onto its side panels, pulled into the yard.

Lynch came out of the house, saw the van and drew his cell phone. "Quaid, the CSST's just arrived. I'll go up there with them. You come back to the house." He holstered his phone and spoke to Abbott as he passed. "You're staying put, right?"

"This is my place," Abbott said. "I'm not going to run away."

"Just asking."

Lynch went to the van and spoke to the driver and his partner through the passenger side window. Someone opened the side door and he climbed inside. The van left the parking lot and trundled across the field.

Crowe watched the van disappear around behind the barn on its way to the quarry trail. "What is it about small town cops that always reminds me of the movie *Deliverance*?"

10

IN THE DINING ROOM Abbott poured himself a cup from a five-gallon urn on which was taped a label saying "CSF tea". Crowe took a cup too. Made of equal parts cumin, coriander and fennel, it was considered by ayurvedic practitioners as *tri-doshic,* capable of balancing the three essential humors of the body. Crowe suspected Abbott needed some balancing this morning.

Quaid showed up, carrying Greer's suitcase. Neville offered him some tea, which Quaid declined. But he did accept a cup of instant coffee and took it with the suitcase out to his truck.

Neville offered to make Abbott and Crowe some breakfast. In a few minutes they were eating buckwheat waffles with local maple syrup.

"So what do you think of my situation?" Abbott said.

Crowe shrugged and took out his phone. He opened his astrology app and displayed the chart he'd calculated when Abbott first phoned him. That was when the situation had come into his awareness and prompted his involvement. Even though death had occurred hours ago, he could still use this chart to pose the question, *Whodunnit?*

In the sidereal chart for 6:05 AM, Aries was rising. At dawn the Sun was in the ascendant. So was the new moon that had occurred only hours earlier.

Crowe's first thought was, *dharma* would rule and justice would prevail. The Aries ascendant, representing Abbott as client, was occupied by the Sun, Moon and Jupiter. All three were *sattvic,* or spiritual, planets. The Sun and Jupiter ruled the other two *dharma* houses, the fifth and ninth of Leo and Sagittarius. However ironic, this confluence of *dharma* lords suggested a crime interwoven with spiritual themes.

Crowe considered the facts. Abbott was a guru of sorts. Death had occurred on an ashram. The rest remained to be seen.

Whereas the ascendant also represented the victim, the seventh house showed the perpetrator. Saturn in the seventh occupied Libra, exalted with directional strength. Saturn was also retrograde, giving it a three-fold strength that implied an accomplished killer or someone of power, maybe both.

Since Saturn ruled the tenth and eleventh houses, the killer might occupy a position of authority, while profit was his motive.

Seventh lord Venus was in Taurus with Ketu, a point in the Moon's orbit where eclipses were enabled. Ketu was the headless one, associated with yogis, *sadhus* and ascetics who surrendered ego to pursue God. But Ketu was debilitated in Taurus, implying a phony yogi, like a corrupt evangelist who adopted a spiritual persona to profit from his followers.

He summed it up for Abbott. "I know you're a good guy, and this chart tells me Greer was too. I think his presence here wasn't so much a personal issue as it was some sort of noble quest, like a modern-day Don Quixote… But whatever he was looking for, he ran into opposition from someone powerful."

"Looking for…?"

"Maybe a story." Crowe considered the chart. "I think he was a journalist. Is there anything here that might have interested him?"

"How about threats to the first amendment and the free exercise of religion…?

"What do you mean?"

"I'm joking," Abbott said, "but it hasn't been easy these past several years. The locals didn't welcome us with open arms. Over the years we've received hate mail suggesting we join a real church. We've had road kill stuffed in our mailbox. Some yahoo with a rifle even took a few pot shots at our bell tower." He shrugged in resignation. "I know Buddhism might strike folks as a bit foreign, but I'd hoped for a little more acceptance from the local community."

"Did you advise the police of the harassment?"

"Sure, but they can't identify who's behind it, so there's nothing they can do. It's our problem. And Greer's death will take it to a whole new level. A criminal investigation could shut us down."

"You said the lease agreement threatened termination only if a member of your community was involved in a felony. Your discovery of a crime doesn't constitute involvement. Your lawyer should be able to argue his way out of that one."

"I certainly hope so," Abbott said.

"You said Bishop was a regular attendee. What do you know about him?"

"Very little other than what I have from his original application, plus a few brief conversations over the years. Aside from the subjects at hand - Buddhism, meditation, self-discovery - we discourage those '*What do you do for a living?*' conversations. We want everyone here to feel equal."

"Apparently he didn't feel that way about Greer."

Abbott shook his head. "I'm shocked and dismayed that someone with a spiritual practice would actually throw a punch at another attendee. I still can't believe it."

"Maybe you don't know Bishop as well as you thought you did."

"Obviously."

"And I'm still waiting to hear what you do know," Crowe prompted.

"Now you're starting to sound just like Lynch." Abbott rolled his eyes. "Okay, I know he's some sort of corporate security consultant in New York. Must pay well because he always drives a late-model high-end vehicle. This time around it was a BMW X6. He's traveled extensively in Southeast Asia. Seems knowledgeable about Buddhist art. I don't think he's married because he sometimes brings different women with him."

"You have his birth date?"

"Should be on his registration form. You want to do his chart? I can get his file."

"Later. How long's he been coming here?"

"Almost as long as we've been in operation. Since the fall of ninety-nine. He used to come once a year in the autumn.

Lately, he's been coming every three months."

"He have any friends?"

Abbott thought for a moment. "First time here, he came with a married couple from Bar Harbor. They all arrived in a camper van equipped with a satellite dish. Other guy was a bit of a kook. William Kinkelman, a writer. Haven't seen him since."

"What do you know about him?"

"A second-tier author who never made it. He gave me one of his books, a mash-up of sci-fi and fantasy. *Ripper Van Winkle*, it was called, about a sleeping zombie who woke up every seven years to go on a killing spree. Terrible novel - misogynistic, pornographic and violent. Ironic, considering Kinkelman was pretty mild-mannered."

"You called him a kook, though. Why?"

"He couldn't seem to keep his clothes on. Mind you, it was very hot that Labor Day weekend. Most of the time all he wore was a red Speedo and a leopard-skin tank top. It would've been funny if it weren't so ugly. He was a skinny runt, with long hair and a scraggly beard."

"What about his wife?"

"Completely normal as far as I could tell. Pretty woman."

"And they were friends - Bishop and the Kinkelmans?"

"They came together. They stayed in adjacent cabins. They ate together. They left together."

"But you never saw the Kinkelmans again?"

"They're still on our mailing list so they get our quarterly newsletter, but I never hear from them. Why are you interested?"

"Birds of a feather flock together. But Bishop is the real person of interest. You saw him knock Greer down. Twelve hours later, Greer's dead. It's a no-brainer to take a hard look at Bishop."

"I assume Lynch will follow up on that."

"You said Bishop usually brought a female friend. Which one was it this time?"

"There've been different women over the years, but the

past few courses, it's been Kitti Poornchai. Maybe you noticed her at roll call? Nice-looking Thai woman, back of the hall, wearing a blue yoga outfit."

Crowe closed his eyes and visualized her in the southwest corner. The image stimulated the pattern recognition faculty in his mind. The southwest was associated with Rahu, one of the lunar nodes associated with eclipses. Rahu was in Scorpio these days, exalted and powerful. In this morning's *prashna* chart, Venus lay on the Rahu/Ketu axis. While Venus indicated a woman, the nodes suggested the foreign and exotic.

This sparked an idea, however tentative, that Kitti Poornchai might be implicated in Greer's death. Crowe recalled the note he'd found in Greer's pocket. Although printed rather than written, it'd left him uncertain as to whether it had been penned by a man or a woman.

"They arrived together?"

"Yes."

"But he left alone and she stayed?"

"Participants take their commitments seriously. There's spiritual merit in completing ten days of silence as prescribed. That's why no one, even if they had something to tell, was willing to break their silence when Lynch asked for information."

"How's she getting back to New York?"

"Beats me. Maybe she'll catch a ride with someone."

"Maybe he's still in the area, waiting to pick her up when the course is over."

"I'll mention that to Lynch. He could intercept Bishop and question him about why he decked Greer. Where there's smoke there's fire."

Crowe nodded. That was true, but where there was smoke, there were sometimes also mirrors.

11

TWO WOMEN ARRIVED, a mother and daughter who took over the kitchen and started to prepare lunch for the course participants.

Abbott took Crowe up to the office and pulled the files for Seth Greer, Dean Bishop and Kitti Poornchai. He left Crowe to peruse them and went downstairs to help Neville attend to some mundane business. One of the washroom toilets was constantly running and the flush assembly needed to be changed.

Crowe examined Bishop's file. His original application form was there, dated August 1999. Under the section *Spiritual Journey to Date*, Bishop had indicated that in 1992 he'd spent a year in a Buddhist monastery in Thailand, and had taken vows as a monk in the Theravada tradition. But after a year's residency, he'd been obliged by family matters to return to America. One thing had led to another and he'd reluctantly resumed secular life.

Currently, Bishop now ran a security consultancy in New York with a 10012 zip code, which Crowe recognized as SoHo. The zip code numbers added up to four, the number for Rahu, associated with material ambitions, hedonism, intoxicants and foreigners. Not what one would associate with an aspiring monk, but how much weight should numerology play? *Meaning is in the eye of the beholder*, Guruji used to say.

Kitti Poornchai's file indicated only that her family were Buddhists and she'd learned to meditate as a teenager. She'd given her occupation as manager for an un-named New York talent agency.

As Abbott had explained, there was no application form for Greer. His contact sheet said only that he was a writer. Abbott had added a note that Greer had learned TM during university, and sought stress relief through mindfulness.

Crowe used the office computer to google Seth Greer. He scanned the first page of search results and saw Greer's name in the byline of several stories published by *The Village Voice*. So Greer was a journalist. Question was, had he come here just to rejuvenate his spirit, or had he been in pursuit of a story? And if the latter, was Bishop part of that story?

Crowe opened the astrology app on his phone and entered Bishop's birth data. He'd been born November 6, 1948. In lieu of knowing his actual birth time or location, Crowe entered noon in New York. The app displayed a sidereal birth chart.

Since he didn't interpret any chart without having first determined an ascendant, he looked around for anything that might trigger a clue to the rising sign. As he glanced above Abbott's desk, he saw a calendar for the month of April. The 11th was circled. So he used Aquarius as Bishop's ascendant.

The Moon and Jupiter in Sagittarius formed a *Kesari Yoga*, a classic combination for a consultant. Crowe took this to assume Bishop hadn't falsified his birth date on his application form.

Mars was strong in Scorpio. Mars often dominated the charts of people in control - military, police and security personnel. It implied a capacity for strong-arm tactics, like Bishop throwing a punch at Greer.

The Sun was debilitated in Libra, suggesting an unstable ego prone to over-compensation. Venus debilitated in Virgo often played out in unstable romantic relationships.

Finally, Mercury and Venus were in each other's sign, an exchange that implied friends becoming lovers or vice versa. Independently, it could also indicate a business that involved buying and selling art. Overall, the chart corroborated what Abbott knew about Bishop, but hypothesized more that remained to be discovered.

Crowe stared out the window, barely hearing the two women chatting downstairs in the kitchen as they prepared lunch. He stood and looked into the parking lot. In the Vermont State Police truck, Quaid was speaking on a cell phone. As Crowe watched, Quaid put the phone away, started the Silverado and drove away, headed for the highway.

Abbott came back upstairs to the office, rubbing his hands together in a satisfied way, as if he'd just discovered in them a talent for plumbing. "Find anything useful?"

"I'm intrigued." Crowe used the photocopier to duplicate all three files - Bishop, Greer and Poornchai. He told Abbott what he'd learned about Greer and Bishop.

"So what happens next?"

"We wait for the police to complete their investigation. Perhaps it'll turn out to be some sort of bizarre accident, in which case you can then forget about it and move on."

"Forget about it? Bishop knocked Greer down. Twelve hours later, Greer's dead. It's highly suspicious, don't you think?"

"Yes, but maybe there's an explanation."

"How do you explain Greer dead in the quarry with a shovel?"

"I don't know. Maybe he went up there on the hill to bury something. Or dig something up. There was no moon last night. Maybe he didn't see the line of prayer flags, so he walked through the barrier and fell to his death. Maybe his head struck the blade of the shovel when he landed."

"That's quite a far-fetched plot," Abbott said. "You should have been a novelist."

"I'm not entirely serious," Crowe was quick to say. "My point is, we can make sense of things if we suspend our disbelief and think outside the box. But in the end, it might just have been an unfortunate coincidence that Bishop's assault was followed by Greer's death."

"Do you really believe that was a coincidence?"

"Not when there's a note involved," Crowe said. "That's a link in a chain. And when I think chain, I think cause and effect, and that implies some sort of karma at work."

"You think this is my karma?"

"Just because it happened here doesn't mean it'll stick to you. This could be someone else's karma playing out, and you're just called upon to witness it."

"Being a witness is one thing, getting implicated is

another. I'm still trying to be optimistic about this, but I can't help but worry that, if it turns into a scandal, it could shut down the retreat."

"We're a long way from that. Take refuge in the teachings. You know what they say about being in the present moment. Regrets bind you to a past that can't be changed. Anxieties draw you into a future that doesn't even exist. Be here now. Take care of business."

12

CROWE PUT THE PHOTOCOPIED FILES in his car and went for a walk. It was a clear day and the sun was warm on his face as he followed the dirt road across the field. He removed his jacket and knotted the sleeves around his waist.

The road ended at a wooded gorge where a river ran through it. Some rotted timbers, remains of an old bridge, lay canted on the riverbanks. He sat and leaned his back against a tree, listening to the warble of birds in the bush. It was one of those beautiful spring days - sunlight slanting through the foliage, the sound of rushing water and birdsong in the background - that made him want to sell his house in Toronto and move to the country.

But that wasn't in his agenda, at least not yet. He'd trained many years with Guruji in order to hone his talent, and he wanted to help people. To some degree, that bound him to a city where the cross-currents of love and commerce pushed and pulled at people's lives, causing them in their confusion to seek answers.

He recalled his discussion with Abbott regarding the bonds of karma. It reminded him of many such discussions with Guruji.

Know karma and you understand the unity of all life, Guruji had said. *As your consciousness deepens, you'll see how everything you do interacts with everything else. Like stones dropped in a still pond, your thoughts, words and deeds produce ripples in the ocean of the universe. As these ripples spread, they create a field of interpenetrating energy where no part is separate from the whole. This field is Indra's net. To touch one strand is to touch all parts, for all parts are connected.*

A sudden sadness washed over Crowe. It'd been several months since he'd seen Guruji, and he felt his teacher's absence as keenly as a lover misses his paramour. There'd once been a time, a period lasting many years, when he'd spent several hours a day with his guru.

There'd been just the three of them - *guru, shisya* and *shastra* - in the classic triumvirate that had endured for millenia: teacher, student and scriptures.

Under Guruji's tutelage, he'd become *pukka* - cooked to perfection and ready to serve. Like lead in an alchemist's retort, he'd been transmuted, perhaps not into gold but silver - a metal that shone as long as he kept it polished with practice.

A bird landed in a nearby tree. It was two-toned - brown on top, white beneath - with a long tail and a yellow beak. It hopped from branch to branch, pecking at bugs, and made a call - a rapid *ka-ka-ka-kow*.

Crowe's mother had been an amateur bird watcher. For a brief period in his youth, when the family used to go on camping trips, Crowe had shared her interest. He'd familiarized himself with over a hundred species indigenous to Eastern Canada and New England.

This one was relatively uncommon but he thought he recognized it - a yellow-billed cuckoo.

He recalled Abbott's comment about Bishop's friend Kinkelman - whom he'd labeled a kook. There was an etymological link - kook being a derivative of cuckoo. Now here was one flitting through his field of awareness.

Crowe realized he'd neglected to pull Kinkelman's file along with the others. Out of sight and out of mind. But it was worth a look. As he'd said to Abbott, birds of a feather flock together.

He headed back to the house. Lunch was over and the course participants had taken up their walking meditation, some heading out the road his way. Rather than distract them with his purposeful stride, Crowe slowed and put mindfulness into every step.

He placed his feet with awareness, as gently as if he were walking on thin ice that might break if he lowered his weight too hard. Heel first, then the ball of the foot, centre of gravity shifting as he lifted his trailing foot and planted it in front of the other.

He continued to the barn and into the garden maze, joining other participants as they spiraled around a large stone that stood upright like a *lingam* - a ritual phallus - in the center of the maze. Although the gender distribution of the participants was equal, more women than men walked the maze. Coincidence, or primitivism at work?

When the group convened in the hall for their next sitting meditation, Crowe returned to the office. Abbott was absorbed in some paperwork. Crowe opened the file cabinet, found Kinkelman's folder and read his application form.

Raised a Baptist and having attended several years of Bible school, Kinkelman seemed an unlikely candidate for a silent retreat. But he'd become interested in Buddhism after visiting Southeast Asia. After a period of hospitalization following an accident, risking addiction to painkillers, he'd explored meditation as an alternative form of pain relief.

He'd listed his profession as retired, with an address on Mount Desert Island, Maine. Crowe assumed it was in the Bar Harbor area, as Abbott had recalled.

Crowe noted the birth date but didn't bother to calculate a chart. Kinkelman had nothing to do with Greer's death. It was only the appearance of the yellow-billed cuckoo that had prompted Crowe to retrieve his file.

He photocopied Kinkelman's forms and took them out to his car. He noticed that the Silverado had returned, and Sergeant Quaid was sitting in the truck, apparently waiting for something. But now there was also another Vermont State

Police vehicle, a cruiser blocking the driveway to prevent any car from entering or leaving the property.

Crowe added the Kinkelman material to the file folder of other forms he'd copied earlier. He'd just locked his car when the CSST van trundled around the barn, across the lawn and into the parking lot.

Lieutenant Lynch climbed out of the van, along with two of the crime scene officers. He pointed at the white Volvo with the crime scene tape. "I want that dusted inside and out," he told them. "Pay special attention to the trunk lid."

Quaid got out of the truck with a sheaf of paper in hand and walked to Lynch. The document exchanged hands. Lynch glanced at it and approached Crowe.

"Hello, Lieutenant," Crowe said. "Any developments?"

Lynch brandished a document. "I have a warrant here for Abbott's arrest."

13

LYNCH AND QUAID HEADED FOR THE HOUSE, accompanied by the two State troopers from the cruiser. The two crime scene officers approached the Volvo with their equipment. Crowe went over to speak to them.

"Stay away from the vehicle, sir," one of them said.

Crowe backed off a few feet. "Are you transporting Greer's body to the coroner?"

"The Regional Medical Examiner's Office," the officer corrected him.

"Which is where?"

"St. Johnsbury."

Crowe walked briskly to the house and took the stairs two at a time, arriving in Abbott's office just in time to hear Lynch reciting the formal charge:

"Bryan Abbott, you're under arrest as a primary suspect

in the murder of Seth Greer. This warrant gives me authority to take you into custody, seize your financial records, and search your property for further evidence."

"My financial records?" Abbott sputtered. "Why?"

Lynch read him his rights and Quaid handcuffed him. Under Lynch's direction, the two troopers pulled drawers from filing cabinets and carried them out to their cruiser.

"Axel," Abbott pleaded.

"That's the fastest warrant I've ever seen," Crowe said. "What do you have, a judge on speed-dial?"

Lynch handed it to Crowe. "You might think we're backwoods hicks, but we use technology. Fast as the CSST gathers information in the field, we can write a preliminary report and email it to the district attorney. With sufficient just cause, the judge can issue a warrant within an hour."

Crowe scanned the document. An affidavit was attached, giving the circumstantial evidence and justification for the arrest. "The preliminary crime scene analysis says Greer didn't die from the fall. He was likely killed by a blow to the head from a thick-bladed object. The garden spade found near the victim's body bore traces of scalp tissue and hair matching the victim's head and wound."

"Did you recognize that garden spade?" Lynch asked Abbott.

"You don't have to answer any questions," Crowe told Abbott, "until you have an attorney present."

Lynch turned to Neville. "You're not a suspect. Do you have any tools here on the property?"

"In the shed out back."

"Quaid, go take a look," Lynch said.

Quaid beckoned to Neville and they left the office together.

"What's Abbott's motive supposed to have been?" Crowe asked.

"I found a press card in Greer's wallet," Lynch said. "Turns out he's an investigative journalist for *The Village Voice*. So I called his editor, who told me Greer was working on a story about spiritual organizations and money laundering. He was probably here to investigate Dharmapada. Abbott must have suspected that, and killed Greer to stop him from writing a story. He knew that if Dharmapada was involved in anything illegal, his lease would be terminated."

"That's ridiculous," Abbott said. "There's no money laundering. We have a tax exemption as a spiritual organization. Besides, I'm no TV evangelist raking in millions of dollars. You've seen what we charge for our courses. There's barely enough revenue to run the place, never mind bank anything in the Caymans."

"Maybe you're hiding something else," Lynch shrugged. "That's why we need to examine your paperwork."

"You're fishing," Abbott said.

"You had motive and opportunity," Lynch said.

"Did you contact Dean Bishop?" Crowe asked.

"Yes," Lynch said. "I reached him at home in New York, where he's been since eleven last night. Remember, Abbott told Bishop to leave the retreat end of day? Do the math. Barnet to New York is a five-hour drive. Bishop emailed me PDFs of his receipts. He ate a meal and gassed up in Springfield, Massachusetts, at eight. And he paid a toll for the Henry Hudson Bridge in Manhattan at ten thirty."

"Did you ask him why he struck Greer?"

"Yes." Lynch smirked. "Greer said something offensive during their walk."

"What?" Abbott said.

"Apparently Greer said, 'Your friend is quite the beauty. I heard you together in her cabin the other night. Is that part of your meditation?'"

"Referring to Kitti Poornchai?"

"Yes, the woman who came to the retreat with him. I need to talk to her. Bishop asked if I could drive her to White River Junction to catch the New York bus."

"What about that note you found in Greer's pocket?"

"It was used to lure Greer up to the quarry. Whoever wrote it said they had something to confess, and they'd tell him about it if he could protect them."

"You think Abbott wrote that note when, according to you, he had everything to hide?"

"People try to cover their tracks and throw suspicion on others."

"I assume you'll fingerprint that notepaper?"

"Soon as we get it back to the lab."

"What happens to your theory if Abbott's prints aren't on it?"

"We'll cross that bridge when we come to it. And do you think I'll care, so long as we find his prints on that shovel?"

"I think answering a question with a question is evasive."

Lynch bristled. "You're not a lawyer and I'm not on the stand. Your friend will get his day in court."

Quaid entered the office, a little breathless after his quick ascent of the stairs. "There's a garden spade missing from the tool shed."

"That's what I thought." Lynch took Abbott's arm. "Okay, you're coming with us."

"Axel, can they do this?"

"It might be a bullshit charge, but they have sufficient grounds to take you into custody for questioning. Don't say any more. You need to call your lawyer."

Lynch allowed Abbott to make a phone call. His lawyer was on a picnic with his family on Lake Champlain but promised to see Abbott at the police station this evening.

"Can you cut me some slack?" Abbott appealed to Lynch. "The retreat's almost over. I'm supposed to address the group, give them time to talk about their experiences before they go their separate ways. Can you give me an hour's grace?"

Crowe spoke up. "You have to wait for Kitti Poornchai anyway, Lieutenant. And your men are still busy collecting documents."

As he spoke, the two troopers returned to pull another pair of file drawers from the cabinets. Lynch said, "Okay. I'll give you time to close up shop. But don't touch the computer, the desk drawers or the file cabinets. They're all covered under the warrant, and we're taking them."

At Lynch's nod, Quaid removed Abbott's handcuffs. Lynch left Quaid in the office to oversee the removal of anything deemed worth searching, and accompanied Abbott to the lecture hall.

14

CROWE SAT IN THE BACK of the hall with Lynch while Abbott congratulated the course participants on having completed their 10-day meditation. He invited people to talk about their experience and share any insights. Roughly half the people took turns describing a gamut of physical, emotional and mental shifts.

Abbott invited everyone to mingle and further compare experiences, but they were otherwise free to leave. He stood at the door and said goodbye to each attendee as they left.

Kitti Poornchai shook Abbott's hand and went outside. Lynch followed her. Crowe trailed after them. When Lynch caught up to Poornchai and spoke to her, Crowe saw her recoil from the cop. He wondered if the sight of Lynch's uniform had disturbed her. Many immigrants had suffered at the hands of the police or military in their home countries.

After a brief exchange, Poornchai headed off toward her cabin. Lynch turned and saw Crowe watching him. They held eyes for a moment, then Lynch entered the house, probably to check on the troopers' progress in removing Abbott's files.

Crowe lingered in the yard. Kitti Poornchai returned from her cabin a few minutes later, pulling a red suitcase on wheels. "Need help with that?" he offered.

"I can manage on my own."

He walked with her toward the parking lot. "I know Lieutenant Lynch offered you a ride to White Junction. But I'm driving to New York this evening. We'd be there in five hours.

Otherwise, it's eight hours on the bus."

"I'm tired," she said. "I'll sleep on the bus."

"You could sleep in my car too and still be home by midnight," he said, instantly regretting his choice of words.

"What are you, some kind of sex freak?"

"I'm a friend of Abbott's. I can help you."

"I don't need any help. Leave me alone or I'll cause a scene."

"Go ahead," Crowe shrugged. "Let's hear it."

But she had nothing more to say. She stepped up her pace and dragged her suitcase, bouncing across the flagstones of the walkway, to the parking lot. Crowe didn't pursue her. She sat on the bench beneath the birch tree and lit a cigarette, studiously ignoring him. He thought it odd that a person who meditated also smoked.

Abbott emerged from the hall, saying goodbye to the last of the participants. Lynch came out of the house with Quaid and the two troopers, each carrying a file box.

"Okay, we're done here," Lynch announced. "Abbott, come with us."

Crowe fell into step as they walked to the police vehicles. "Give me your lawyer's name and number," he told Abbott. "I'll follow up with him this evening."

"Never mind that," Abbott said. "I need you to figure out what happened at the quarry last night. Someone's trying to frame me for Greer's murder, but I have no idea who or why."

"I'll do what I can."

Abbott gave Crowe his lawyer's number anyway. They shook hands. Quaid cuffed Abbott and sat with him in the back seat of the cruiser. The troopers loaded the last file boxes into the cargo bed of the Silverado and closed its cover panel. They returned to their cruiser and drove away with Quaid and Abbott.

Lynch put Poornchai's suitcase in the Silverado's back seat and held the door open for her to climb into the front passenger seat. He climbed behind the wheel and started the engine. The Silverado turned, spun its wheels to fling some gravel in Crowe's direction, and followed the cruiser.

The crime scene officers were still dusting for prints, one inside Greer's Volvo and one outside.

Crowe entered the house and went back upstairs, where he found Neville surveying the gutted office. The filing cabinets had been emptied, the computer removed. Crowe was glad he'd made copies of a few files before Lynch had returned with his warrant.

"They won't find anything incriminating," Neville said. "Bryan's the most honest person I know."

Crowe looked at his watch, debating his next move. He intended to go to New York, but was in no hurry to drive down this evening. His offer to Poornchai had just been a gambit to get some time alone with her and ask a few questions about Dean Bishop. Now that she'd refused his offer and Lynch had whisked her away, Crowe's agenda was wide open.

He decided to call his father, who lived in Boston. The phone rang only twice before it was picked up. After an exchange of pleasantries, Crowe got to the point.

"Dad, I'm in Vermont, but I'm going to New York in a day or two. Are you up for a visit?"

"Absolutely. Any time."

"I'll be there in about three hours." As he hung up, Crowe reflected that he hadn't seen his father in a few months. It'd be good to catch up.

Crowe said goodbye to Neville and left the house. As he stepped outside, Bryan's last words echoed in his mind. *I need you to figure out what happened at the quarry last night.* Crowe decided he should take another look at the incident scene.

He walked through the scattered cabins. There was no pattern to their layout, just a loose sprawl across the field between barn and maze. He came to the footpath at the base of the hill. The makeshift cardboard sign was still there, asking people not to use the path, but there was no other barrier.

Crowe found it odd that Lynch hadn't strung up a ribbon of crime scene tape in case he subsequently decided to bring in a tracking dog or some other forensics specialist. Sloppy procedure, or just so convinced of Abbott's guilt that no further investigation was necessary?

Crowe climbed the path to the top of the hill where the broken string of prayer flags hung over the edge of the quarry. The wind had died to a breeze and the flags barely fluttered. Again, he wondered why crime scene tape hadn't been erected on the spot where Greer had breathed his last.

As he looked down into the quarry where Greer had fallen, he heard a raven call from the trees behind him. He waited. Guruji had trained him to pay attention to all natural phenomena in his environment. This involved noting the type, number and direction of birds in flight, the color of dogs and cats encountered, the activity of insects, and other things.

Crowe listened as the raven called five times. The number of Mercury. Siblings, the logical mind, communications, short distance travel. Crowe didn't see any immediate connection, other than having just phoned his father before embarking on a three-hour drive.

He followed the trail down the other side of the hill, the way Abbott had led him this morning, and crossed the quarry to where Greer's body had lain. He didn't expect to find anything because Lynch and Quaid had already searched the ground for twenty yards around.

He'd just arrived at that spot when the raven called again. He looked up and saw it fly overhead, then circle the quarry in a clockwise direction. It called again, four more times, almost as if it were drawing attention to itself. *Watch me.*

Crowe watched the raven as it landed on a ledge halfway down the face of the quarry pit. It dipped its head and pecked at something. An item the size of a credit card fluttered down the face of the cliff.

Crowe walked over and retrieved a piece of burgundy plastic. He saw *BlackBerry* on a molded panel with apertures for camera lens and flash. He looked up the cliff face. The raven looked down on him and cawed again. Almost as if saying, *Come see what I found.*

This is crazy, Crowe thought as he started up. Crazy but not difficult, as there were lots of handholds and footholds by which he was able to climb. The raven took off with a final caw long before he got to the ledge where it'd landed.

Crowe immediately saw a cell phone battery. A few feet away, protruding from a crevice, was the phone itself. It was one of the older BlackBerry models, a Curve, with the tiny chiclet keyboard.

Crowe inserted the battery and slid the cover back in place. He tried the power button but the phone was dead. He suddenly got a queasy feeling. Now that he'd handled it, his fingerprints were all over it. He pocketed it and carefully descended the cliff face to the quarry floor.

He walked back to the house, wondering what to do. Whose phone was this? Greer had surrendered his mobile upon arrival at the retreat. Abbott had given it, along with the Volvo's keys, to Lynch.

Crowe debated turning it over to the police, as he knew he probably should. Yes, it was potential evidence, but without having been secured with police tape, was this technically still a crime scene?

When he arrived back at the parking lot, the CSST van was gone, along with Greer's Volvo. Obviously the crime scene team had finished processing the car and transported it to an auto compound for safekeeping. He took it as a sign. With the CSST having vacated the scene, he was relieved of his moral dilemma.

Crowe was skating on thin ice, but justified it by thinking of his client first. If push came to shove, he'd argue he'd found the phone on neutral ground. But now that he had it, what to do with it?

The still bigger question remained - if this wasn't Greer's phone, whose was it?

15

Boston

CROWE STOPPED ONLY ONCE to gas up, where I-89 merged with I-93, and made it to Boston in two and a half hours. His father lived in Newton, within the ring road. His big house occupied a corner lot in a quiet tree-lined neighborhood. A black Mercedes GLK was parked in the driveway of a two-car garage.

Crowe rang the doorbell and walked in.

His father came out of his study and greeted him with a powerful embrace. "You're looking good!"

"You too."

His father had turned 69 the month before. Although graying at the temples, he had a full head of dark wiry hair. He appeared fit without having worked for it, one of those people who'd come out of the starting gate with good genes, an advantage in any race.

His father poured himself a glass of red wine and they sat in his study to catch up on news. Business was picking up again. His father owned a small software company that wrote apps for mobile devices of all kinds - smart phones, GPS units, product scanners and scientific measuring devices. Despite the economy's downturn over the past five years, he'd banked a few million.

"Can you do anything with this?" Crowe showed him the BlackBerry he'd found at the quarry. Briefly, he told his father the circumstances, and why he wanted to identify the phone's owner.

Having cut a few corners himself over the years, his father wasn't troubled by the gray zone of legality. He fiddled with the phone a bit before setting it aside. "One of my guys is a genius with phones. He'll revive it. How long are you in town?"

"I was on my way to New York, but I'm reconsidering

my itinerary."

"What's up?"

"There's someone in Bar Harbor I should talk to. I regret now I didn't go there directly from Vermont."

"That's a five-hour drive. Why not just call them, save yourself the mileage?"

"This kind of talk works best face-to-face."

"I could fly you up."

One of his father's few pastimes was flying his single-engine Cessna. The highlight of his year was the end of July when 10,000 light planes and half a million aviation enthusiasts converged on Oshkosh, Wisconsin, for seven days of air shows, demonstrations, workshops and aerobatics.

"Are you sure?"

"Sunday's forecast calls for clear skies and it's only two hours each way. I have a friend in Bar Harbor I haven't seen in a while. While you pursue your business, my friend and I can catch up."

"Okay, but you've got to let me pay for the gas."

"Is this a paying gig you're on?"

"*Pro bono,*" Crowe confessed. "My client's taken a vow of poverty."

"Like you," his father laughed. "Still driving that ten-year-old Saab?"

"Two hundred thousand on the odometer."

"Keep your gas money. You'll need it for repairs soon enough."

They chatted a while before calling it a night. Crowe fetched his bag from the car and went up to one of the second floor guest bedrooms.

He checked his phone for messages and read an email from Abbott's lawyer. Abbott was being held without bail, so the lawyer could do nothing until a bail hearing on Monday. But with no assets to his name, it'd be impossible for Abbott to secure even temporary freedom.

Crowe shook his head in dismay. Why'd such bad luck descend on a good guy like Bryan? The ways of karma were indeed mysterious. He felt frustrated, yet determined to help his friend.

He took out the photocopies he'd made from Abbott's files, and started the astrology app on his phone. He'd already calculated Dean Bishop's chart. Now he did those for Seth Greer, Bill Kinkelman and Kitti Poornchai too.

Kinkelman's chart immediately piqued his interest. Crowe had taken his birth date - March 28, 1948 - from his application form, but in lieu of knowing his actual birth time and place, used noon in Bar Harbor.

A conjunction of Mars and Saturn in Cancer caught his eye. The union of these two malefic planets implied violence at some level, sometimes within oneself, often with others. Mars was debilitated and unstable in Cancer, while both planets were retrograde and powerful to do serious harm.

Kinkelman's Moon was debilitated in Scorpio, exchanging signs with Mars. A troubled mind, perhaps bipolar? Stephen King had a Moon/Mars exchange too, and the famously morbid writer had confessed to having thoughts that might have justified placing him in jail or a psychiatric ward.

Intrigued, Crowe needed to establish a rising sign for Kinkelman's chart. In the absence of a birth time, there were several ways of deriving a substitute ascendant. He leaned back in his chair and let his mind drift. As he stared at the ceiling, he noticed the five-bladed ceiling fan. Possible, but not equitable. To level the odds for each of the zodiacal signs, he preferred numbers from a range of 12 or more.

He turned in his chair and his eyes immediately alighted upon a picture on the wall. His father posed before an airplane with a trophy he'd won 20 years ago in a Massachusetts rally. The plane's registration number was clearly legible on its fuselage: N757DA.

Using a numerology system that converted letters to numbers, Crowe added them all up to get 29 and expunged multiples of 12 to get a five. Ka-ching! The synchronicity with the five-bladed ceiling fan made him confident of applying a

Leo ascendant to Kinkelman's chart.

This placed the Mars/Saturn conjunction in the 12th house. The two malefics in the house of bondage made Crowe speculate whether Kinkleman had ever done time for a violent crime.

Regarding Greer's death, the irony was that Kinkelman looked far more capable of violence than did Bishop, yet he hadn't even been on the retreat. But could he have been in the area?

Crowe realized it was important to determine the owner of that BlackBerry.

16

Sunday, April 22

Bar Harbor, Maine

CROWE AND HIS FATHER HAD AN EARLY BREAKFAST and left the house at eight AM. Fifteen minutes up the I-95, his father took the Lexington exit and dropped off the dead BlackBerry at the home of one of his employees. They continued a few miles further west to Hanscom Field airport, where his father kept his Cessna 172 in a rented hangar.

After conducting the pre-flight check, filing a flight plan and getting tower clearance, they taxied out to a runway and got airborne shortly after nine AM. As the forecast had promised, the sky was clear, visibility five miles. His father took the Cessna up to 5,000 feet and set a northwest course that took them up the coast, well offshore from Portsmouth, Portland and other towns along the New Hampshire and Maine shores.

En route, his father confessed he'd jumped at the opportunity to make this trip, not just an excuse to spend time with his son, but to see a woman in Bar Harbor. He'd called her last night to confirm she was free today.

"How do you know her?" Crowe asked.

"I met her golfing in Myrtle Beach last January. We hit it off and spent some time together."

"You haven't seen her since then?"

"We've kept in touch via email. She's got an on-and-off boyfriend who lives in Bangor. Lately it's been more off than on so I thought it was time to rekindle our... friendship."

Crowe laughed to himself. He didn't know whether to consider it funny or pathetic that his father was acting like a college kid, all revved up for a hot date.

They landed at the Hancock County Bar Harbor Airport just outside Trenton shortly after eleven AM. Crowe's father taxied the Cessna to the small terminal and parked in one of the visitor bays.

In the terminal they were greeted by a tall and tanned brunette whose generous curves seemed trapped in her snug-fitting pantsuit. Crowe's father introduced them. Ursula had fantastic teeth and a mass of jet black hair that spilled down her back like a horse's mane. Crowe shook her hand, feeling heat and power in her grip, and noted a ruby ring on her left index finger, implying someone with a strong urge for self-expression.

"I'll see you later," Crowe told his father. "I need to get a rental car." He looked around for a kiosk.

"Don't rent a car," Ursula said. "You can borrow mine."

"Are you sure?"

"Absolutely."

She owned a late model Cadillac which she drove with careless abandon down Route 3 and into Bar Harbor. She parked in the driveway of a large house on a crescent overlooking the water. She and Crowe's father got out. As Crowe slid behind the wheel, his father held the door open a moment and leaned in.

"How long's your business going to take you?" he asked.

"Not sure. Probably be finished in an hour."

His father looked at his watch. "Maybe you want to do a little sightseeing while you're here, go for a drive around the island. See you back here, no earlier than one-thirty?"

"Sure." Crowe drove away, pausing at the corner to note the street Ursula lived on. He opened his phone and used Google Maps to plot a route from here to Bill Kinkelman's address. He put the Cadillac in gear.

17

CROWE CROSSED MOUNT DESERT ISLAND and picked up Tremont Road along its western shore. It was a heavily wooded area, with houses nestled deep in the trees, side roads accessing the headlands and coves along the rugged coast line.

Kinkelman lived near the end of Dix Point Road. When Crowe arrived at the address, marked only by a numbered wooden plaque on a tree, he noticed a surveillance camera near the property entrance. He followed a lane fifty yards into the woods, thinking this'd be a difficult place to access in the winter, before arriving at a two-story house of Scandinavian design.

A detached garage stood separate from the house, its open door revealing a black Dodge Ram parked inside. As he approached the house, he saw another surveillance camera under the eaves.

He mounted a wooden deck running the width of the house, and rang the doorbell. After a while, a woman with an aluminum walker opened the door. She was in her sixties, thin and obviously of frail health. She had gray hair cropped short, and wore loose jeans and a long pullover.

"Sorry to disturb you," Crowe said. "Is this the right address for Bill Kinkelman?"

"Yes. Do I know you?"

"No. I'm an acquaintance of Dean Bishop. Is Bill home?"

"Dean Bishop...?"

"You attended a Buddhist retreat with him and Bill many years ago."

"Oh, yes. Dean. I'm sorry. I haven't seen Dean in years and I just couldn't place the name. You must forgive me, I'm losing it."

"We all have our days."

"I have more than my share." She smiled at him. "What is it you're selling?"

"I'm here to see Bill. Is he home?"

"Bill? Yes, he's here. He's out on point."

"Excuse me...?"

"That's his expression. He's up on the lookout."

"Which is where...?"

She left her walker, steadying herself against the doorframe as she crossed the threshold onto the deck. Crowe offered his arm. She gripped it as fiercely as if her life depended on it. She pointed to a gap in the trees.

"Follow that trail and it'll bring you right to him."

"It's okay if I just walk out unannounced? He isn't carrying a gun, is he?" Crowe was mindful of venturing uninvited onto private property.

"I don't think so, but I'll call him anyway, let him know you're coming."

"I could do that. What's his number?"

She stared. "I don't remember. Maybe I have it on speed dial."

He guided her back to her walker. She shuffled to the kitchen counter, picked up a cordless phone and speed-dialed. "Bill, there's a fella here says he's a friend of Bishop Dean. Wants to come out and see you, okay?" She hung up. "He says alright. Go on out."

"Thank you." Crowe mused over her dyslexia with Bishop's name. Was it just a slip of the tongue, or a hint of Alzheimer's?

He followed a trail that climbed through the trees. The soil was thin atop rock and the trees were evergreen - spruce and fir and the occasional pine. As he approached the point, he saw the bay through gaps in the trees and beyond it the Gulf of Maine.

At the end of the trail stood a lone pine tree on the headland. At its base was a small wooden deck with two Adirondack chairs made of green PVC. Sitting in one of the chairs, a man warily watched his approach.

"Bill Kinkelman?"

"What's the nature of your business?"

"I'm an acquaintance of Dean Bishop."

"Oh yeah? How do you know Dean?"

"Met him on a retreat this past week. The Buddhist place in Barnet, Vermont?"

Kinkelman took a pack of cigarettes from a red plaid jacket and lit one with an old Zippo. He wore a bill cap low on his brow and had a scraggly beard and long hair down to his collar, giving him the vaguely unwashed look of a country bumpkin. Maybe the long hair was an attempt to hide his protruding ears, which still stuck out like an elf's.

Crowe walked around the deck and looked out over the water. From the cliff it was a fifty-foot vertical drop to a jagged shoreline. "Nice view."

"Usually."

Crowe turned and saw he'd blocked Kinkelman's view, prompting that touch of sarcasm. A sound drew his eyes upward. In the pine tree over Kinkelman's head, a cage embraced the trunk. It had a wooden floor about six feet square, and a roof. The space between floor and roof was enclosed with iron bars the thickness of pencils. Two owls sat on a perch.

"Unusual pets." Crowe noted the round faces, the brownish coloring with broad streaking on the breast, and the absence of ear tufts. Barred owls, common throughout New England. He wondered if it was legal to capture and cage birds of prey.

"Someone shot the mother," Kinkelman said. "I found them in their barn nest and raised them myself."

Crowe eased himself into the empty chair. "You never thought to release them?"

"Come winter, food's scarce. Owls are easily stressed and die of starvation. They're actually better off under my care."

Crowe doubted a naturalist would agree, but he wasn't here to pick a fight with someone from whom he wanted information.

"Dean told me you're a writer."

"Did he?"

"Said you'd written a couple of books. *Ripper Van Winkle*

was one of the titles? I haven't had a chance yet to pick it up, but I will. Sounds like something Stephen King might have written."

Kinkelman nodded at the compliment and tipped his cigarette ash into a coffee tin at his feet. "You read a lot of horror?"

"I'm familiar with the genre," Crowe said. Not that he read it, but occasionally he encountered it in cases he'd worked. "What I really enjoy is a good mystery."

"How is Dean?"

"To judge by his ride, life seems to be treating him well. Making big bucks as a security consultant in New York. Beemers don't come cheap. Plus which, he had a pretty nice looking woman in tow." Crowe hoped Kinkelman didn't raise more questions about Bishop, because Crowe had just used up everything he knew about the man.

"Dean always had an eye for the ladies," Kinkelman said. "How'd he happen to mention me?"

"First evening at the retreat, we had a get-acquainted period. I mentioned I wanted to write a novel. He said a friend of his was a published writer. One thing led to another."

"We're a long way from Barnet."

"Life is full of coincidences." Crowe told him about flying up from Boston this morning so his father could visit a lady friend. "I had time on my hands so I asked around and someone told me you lived up here on Dix Point Road. I just wanted to talk to a real live writer. I know Stephen King lives in Bangor, but I thought I'd have better luck meeting you."

"What kind of plane?"

"Cessna 172."

"Know it well," Kinkelman said. "I favor the Cherokee, but I've been up in Cessnas often enough. Hell, who hasn't? They built over forty thousand of them."

"You're a pilot too? Now that is a coincidence."

"Flying days are over, though. Last medical, my blood pressure was too high. Doctor wouldn't sign my health certificate."

"Sorry to hear that."

"Well, you do what you can with the time you've got, then you find other things to amuse yourself."

"Maybe quit smoking, get your blood pressure down."

"Tell me about it." Kinkelman took a last drag and dropped his butt in the coffee can.

Crowe got into character and asked Kinkelman a few questions about the writing life - where he got ideas, whether he worked with an outline, how long it took to write a book, how he found a publisher, how lucrative it was...

Kinkelman laughed bitterly. "For every Stephen King, there're a hundred writers who barely make a middle class living, and a thousand below the poverty line. If it weren't for my veteran's pension, I'd be broke."

Crowe's ears perked up. Finally, he'd heard something that clicked with Kinkelman's chart - the Mars/Saturn conjunction that often spelled acquaintance with violence. "You were in the military?"

"Tail end of the Vietnam war."

"Speaking of horror stories..."

"Wasn't so bad for me. I was in the Air Force. Technical analyst for aerial reconnaissance, nowhere near the gooks. Only thing I had to worry about was catching the clap from the local B-girls."

"That where you met Dean?"

"Did he say that?"

"Just speculating, on account of you're roughly the same age."

"Actually, Dean's younger than me."

"So, too young for Vietnam?" Crowe was still curious as to whether Bishop had provided his true birth data on Dharmapada's intake form.

Kinkelman looked at his watch, then took out a cell phone and pressed a single key. "Hey darlin', you up for some lunch today? No, don't start anything, I'll be down in a minute. We're just wrappin' up here." He closed his phone and gave Crowe a meaningful look.

"I should be moving on as well." Crowe followed Kinkelman's lead and stood. "Speaking of lunch, where could I get a good lobster roll around here?"

Kinkelman started on ahead with a limp that favored his right knee. He named a few places in Bar Harbor that weren't, in his words, overpriced tourist traps. They arrived back at the house without him saying anything further.

"Thanks for your time." Crowe offered his hand and the other man shook it hesitantly.

"Pleasure," Kinkelman said with little sincerity.

Up close, Crowe saw something he hadn't seen when he'd first met Kinkelman up there on the point. Something odd about his left eye. Whereas the right iris was blue, the left was two-toned, mostly green with a nugget of amber in the upper right quadrant.

"Did you get sick in Vietnam?" Crowe asked. "Malaria or dengue fever?"

"Hospitalized with dengue for two weeks. Why do you ask?"

Crowe shrugged. "I was thinking of taking a trip to Vietnam next winter. I hear it's beautiful but I'm worried about getting sick."

"Nothing beautiful about that place," Kinkelman said. "I was so glad to get back home, soon as I got off the plane, I got down on my knees and kissed the ground. God bless America."

"Amen, brother." Crowe gave him a salute and went to the Cadillac. When he got behind the wheel, he looked, but Kinkelman had already gone inside.

18

CROWE RETURNED TO THE HIGHWAY and parked on the shoulder where a bank of mailboxes serviced the residents of Dix Point Road. He used his phone to map the location of night clubs and bars in the vicinity.

On his way back into Bar Harbor, he stopped at every roadside bar he saw. In each, he asked the bartender if he knew William Kinkelman the writer. If yes, Crowe went on to explain that he was an aspiring writer who'd read one of Kinkelman's books and wanted to meet the guy. Was he approachable?

Out of four bars queried, Kinkelman was known to three, which seemed to imply he was in the habit of downing one here and there on his way to and from home. Because his wife wasn't very mobile, Crowe assumed Kinkelman probably did the household shopping himself. And given the look of the guy, there was little doubt in Crowe's mind he was tossing them back on a regular basis. Squirreled away in the woods, who wouldn't want an occasional foray into civilization?

It all fell into place at the Lompoc Café in downtown Bar Harbor. The name triggered something in Crowe. No stranger to California, he knew Lompoc was a military town an hour's drive from Santa Barbara, its proximity to Vandenberg Air Force Base lending a certain synchronicity to the fact Kinkelman was an Air Force veteran. Lompoc was also home to a low-security correctional institute for men. No connection there as of yet, but who knew?

As Crowe approached the café he saw, hanging over its front door, a carved wooden sign with a detailed etching of a barred owl. He was reminded of Kinkelman's caged owls. Another coincidence, or a sign?

Inside, a dozen tables looked out on a patio not yet open for the season. One wall was occupied by the bar, and the hallway to the washrooms was lined with poker machines. The place was mostly empty except for a few tables near the patio where a young waitress was chatting with one of her customers.

Crowe sat at the bar. He hadn't eaten since breakfast so he ordered a tomato juice and a grilled cheese sandwich. The bartender relayed the order through the kitchen window and resumed reading his newspaper. The sandwich came out promptly and Crowe began to eat. The bartender glanced up at the clock and flipped the pages of his paper, looking for something to capture his interest.

Crowe went into his spiel about Kinkelman the writer. The bartender heard him out, then shook his head. "Willy the Kink? He hasn't written shit in years. Why you wanna talk to him?"

"Willy the Kink?" Crowe echoed.

"That's what they call him."

"Why?"

"The guy's a bit of a freak. He was caught peeping in someone's back yard a few years ago. There're worse stories I won't repeat. Suffice to say, he was warned, and apparently he wised up a little. Now he goes to Bangor for his jollies. I'm not sayin' that's any better, but it's a dirty bird that shits in its own nest."

"What kind of jollies?"

"Unless you're a cop, none of your business."

"Private investigator." Crowe showed his NY license.

"Investigating what?"

"It's confidential."

"Rape?"

Crowe said nothing.

"I've got a young daughter," the bartender said. "Bad enough I've gotta worry about the boys in the next grade up, never mind some guy prowlin' the streets at night."

"I appreciate the information." Crowe paid his bill and left a large tip. "Where do I find the police station?"

"You can walk it from here." The bartender provided directions to Firefly Lane, literally only a few blocks away.

~~~

Crowe returned to the Cadillac and checked the street signs to make sure he could park here another half an hour. He walked to the police station, a two-story structure with four vehicle bays, to which a newer single-story structure had been appended.

He introduced himself to the desk sergeant and showed his ID. He explained his business - background investigation regarding an incident in Vermont wherein his client had been wrongfully charged.

"With what?"

"Murder, allegedly."

"What brings you to Bar Harbor?"

"William Kinkelman. Known associate of an alternative suspect, therefore a potential accomplice. Does he have a record or any charges against him? I could check the state database, but I like to pay my respects to the local authorities and get it from the source."

The sergeant turned to the computer screen. After some typing and mousing around, he said, "No record, but a handful of charges dating back almost twenty years. Couple of DUIs. Indecent exposure. Solicitation."

"All here in Bar Harbor?"

"Solicitation in Bangor."

"Charged but not convicted?"

"Lawyers did their job."

"Can I get a copy of that?"

The sergeant shook his head. "Not without a subpoena."

"Off the record, what can you tell me about the man?"

"He may be a drunk and a perv, but he's not the violent type. If you're looking for an accomplice to murder, I don't see it."

Crowe thanked the sergeant for his assistance, and walked back to the car. He checked his watch and saw it was quarter to two. Time to rescue his father from his *femme fatale*.
~~~

19

URSULA DROVE CROWE AND HIS FATHER back to the airport. His father was quiet en route, but maybe he was all talked out after two hours with a woman he hadn't seen in months. At the terminal, Crowe thanked her and bailed out, leaving his father to say goodbye in private. His father caught up with him a few minutes later at the plane. For the next half hour it was all pilot business, checking the aircraft and weather report, filing the flight plan.

They took off on the 04/22 runway, which took them southbound over the western half of Mount Desert Island. They were still climbing as Crowe picked out Trenton Road, Dix Point Road and the houses along the shore overlooking Goose Cove. Somewhere down there, in a tree on the point, two owls sat caged…

It wasn't until they were back at cruising altitude on a southwest heading that Crowe asked his father, "So did you have a good time?"

"Yes, it was nice."

"She seemed happy to see you."

"Yes, she was."

"Does she want you to come again?"

His father shook his head and laughed. "Well, she did but twice was all I could manage."

"Oh, I see. Are you bragging or complaining?"

"You know, with vintage airplanes, you can't put them through too many aerobatic maneuvers without some strain on the airframe."

"Uh-huh."

"And at my age, well, I need a little more than an hour to, um, refuel and get airborne again."

"I get it."

"So, it's a reality check. Maybe next time I'll have to pop a little blue pill, just so I can, um, stay aloft longer."

Concerned about the potential side effects of

pharmaceuticals, Crowe took some time to tell his father about dietary alternatives. According to ayurveda, *ojas* was the "sap" of one's life energy, a measure of the body's essential vigor. With sufficient reserves, it bestowed immunity, but if deficient, resulted in weakness, fatigue and disease.

To replenish *ojas*, he recommended his father eat organic butter, dates, almonds, avocadoes and basmati rice. Crowe used his phone to browse the web, found a good site for information on *ojas*-strengthening diets, and send his father the link.

An hour and a half later, they crossed Ipswich Bay and saw Boston sprawled in the distance. His father asked Crowe to take the controls while he made a phone call. It was just a matter of holding the control yoke steady to keep the plane level, occasionally applying rudder to stay on compass course.

"Jake, it's Daryl," his father said into the phone. "How'd you make out with that BlackBerry? Okay, that's probably good enough. I'll swing by in an hour to pick it up." He put the phone away and leaned back in his seat to stretch his arms overhead.

"He get it working?" Crowe asked.

"He got it powered up again to retrieve the directory and call log. But the main board's damaged, so there's no using it outside a laboratory setting. And it's not registered to any owner. It's on prepaid minutes."

"Can he email me the directory and call log?"

His father phoned Jake and made arrangements. A few minutes later, Crowe heard the ping of an incoming email. He gave the controls back to his father and checked his inbox to find an email with two attachments. The BlackBerry's call log contained only a dozen numbers indicating in or out calls, and a time stamp, obviously the last twelve numbers with which the phone had communicated. All were outbound calls.

The BlackBerry's directory contained less than 20 names. On first sight, seeing so few names, Crowe now doubted Greer was the phone's owner. Any journalist of even a few years' experience would have had hundreds of contacts. Plus which, all of these entries were nicknames, abbreviations or acronyms of some kind.

"Helpful?" his father asked.

"I'm not sure yet." Crowe told him how little data was contained in the two attachments.

"Maybe it's a drug dealer's phone," his father said.

"Why do you say that?"

"Didn't you ever watch *The Wire*?"

"Okay, I get it." In *The Wire*, the drug dealers used "burn phones" to avoid being wiretapped by the police on land lines. A burn phone could be purchased cheaply with prepaid minutes, with no requirement to register an associated name. After the minutes were used up, it could be tossed, saving only the SIM card if the user wanted to retain a personal directory. "But a BlackBerry's a little pricey to toss after a month's use."

"Not that phone," his father said. "The Curve's over five years old. That's practically an antique compared to current smart phones. So it wasn't worth much. And if you're making fifty grand a month, does it matter anyway?"

Crowe considered the possibility. What would a drug dealer be doing on Dharmapada's grounds? It made no sense. Unless Greer had been writing a story about the drug trade. Had he got so close to a source that his efforts got him killed?

They landed at Hanscom Field, stopped briefly in Lexington to retrieve the BlackBerry from his father's employee, and were back in Newton by five o'clock. Crowe used his father's computer to print out the BlackBerry's call log and directory files.

His father suggested they go out for dinner but Crowe told him he needed to go to New York tonight. His father was disappointed Crowe was leaving so early but he understood. The clock was ticking on the Vermont case and his friend Abbott remained behind bars.

Crowe checked the Amtrak schedule and saw a New York train leaving the Westwood station at six PM. He called the Washington Square Hotel in Greenwich Village and lucked out, getting a room whose scheduled guest had cancelled their reservation just an hour ago.

Crowe put the BlackBerry in a baggie, sealed it and stowed it in the glove compartment of his Saab. It was useless to make or receive calls, but he didn't want to lose it.

His father climbed behind the wheel of his Mercedes. They drove down I-95 to the Westwood station and arrived at the terminal ten minutes before train time. Crowe's father sprang from his seat and opened the rear hatch to take Crowe's bag from the luggage compartment.

"Thanks for everything, Dad. You've been a great help."

"Listen, you'll be careful, okay? If there's narcotics involved, you could be up against some really bad people."

"Soon as it's appropriate, I'll share what I've got with the police. Let them do the heavy lifting, right?"

"Good luck. Let me know if there's anything else I can do." His father shook his hand and gave him a bear hug.

Crowe waved goodbye from the curb as the Mercedes drove away.

20

New York

THE TRAIN ARRIVED, half full of college kids. Crowe found an empty seat, put his bag in the overhead rack and sat next to the window. The train departed on schedule just before six.

He studied the printout of the BlackBerry's call log and directory. Most of the outbound calls were area codes 212, 646 and 917. The first two were Manhattan codes but he didn't know the third. He looked it up and found it covered all five New York boroughs.

The BlackBerry's last call had been to a number with area code 323. He discovered it was a Los Angeles area code that spanned dozens of smaller cities in a ring around the LA core.

He debated dialing that last number to find out who it belonged to but part of him, probably his instinct for self-preservation, said it was a bad idea. If the BlackBerry's owner was associated with Greer's death, calling any of these numbers could trigger an alarm. The person could go into hiding or, if they felt threatened, come after Crowe.

In lieu of direct contact, he did a reverse number lookup and got an instant hit. The last call had been to an "M. Greer" in Culver City.

Crowe now assumed the phone belonged to Seth Greer after all, and his last call had been to a family member - parent, sibling, spouse or child. But it wasn't Crowe's responsibility to call the person and break the bad news. That was Lieutenant Lynch's job. Besides, he wasn't even supposed to have gained access to these numbers.

He put the sheet back in his pocket and called a number from his own phone. After three rings a young woman answered.

"Tracey, it's Axel. How are you?"

"Hey, stranger! Nice to hear from you again. What's up?"

He gave her a brief update on what had happened in the last 36 hours. His train was scheduled to arrive at Penn Station at 9:45. Did she have time to meet? She suggested he come over to her place after he'd checked into his hotel.

Crowe stared out the window, assessing his feelings. He laid three fingers of his right hand on his left wrist and took his ayurvedic pulse. Thus he gauged the state of his body's three *doshas* - *vata, pitta* and *kapha.* He wasn't amused to discover that, at a superficial level, his pulse was hopping like a frog. He pressed a little harder and found that, deeper down, it was more like a snake. Definitely more stable but still, somewhat stirred.

He'd met Tracey Lovegrove a year ago, on a case that had begun with the apparent mugging death of a prominent socialite, sister of his most wealthy client, Kevin Blaikie. Tracey was a forensic analyst with the NYPD. They'd become friends in the local phase of his investigation, before the trail of evidence had led him through San Francisco to the badlands of New Mexico.

Friends, but something else for which he didn't have an appropriate word. What did you call two people who were drawn to each other, yet restrained themselves from sexual intimacy? Had they exhausted the passion in a previous life? Been there, done that, no need to repeat? Had someone got burned, and was now afraid of the fire? Why did the thought of her arouse such feeling in him?

He'd seen her only twice since. On his invitation, she'd come to Toronto for a weekend in July, coinciding with a music festival in his neighborhood, The Beaches. She'd stayed at his place, sleeping on a sofa-bed in his office. For two nights they'd worked their way up and down Queen Street East, listening to the city's best blues, rock and jazz bands.

In the fall, he'd come to New York to see a dozen clients whose consultations could just as easily have been handled by phone or Skype. He'd stayed at the Washington Square Hotel, but in his off hours, he and Tracey had gone to the Museum of Natural History, hit a few blues bars, and had a wonderful time together.

Despite their compatibility, they'd been content to keep their relationship platonic. They talked on the phone once a month but it was more about keeping in touch with a friend than trying to worm a way into someone's affections with an end in mind. With Tracey it was all very relaxed and natural. Except for this anticipation of seeing her again...

He took a book from his overnight bag. Although he'd read an English translation of the great Hindu epic *The Ramayana* twenty years ago, he was now re-reading it in the original Sanskrit. Exciting as it was, full of demons and armed monkeys in flying chariots, he nodded off after an hour and didn't wake up until the train pulled into Penn Station.

He caught a taxi to Greenwich Village and checked into the Washington Square Hotel where he usually stayed. The desk clerk greeted him by name and checked him into a second floor room. As soon as Crowe entered the Art Deco suite, he felt like he was home away from home. He peeled off his shirt, washed his face and put on a clean shirt before going out.

Crowe walked to First Avenue and Ninth Street in the East Village. After almost four hours on the train, he needed the exercise and made it in a brisk 15 minutes. He entered the condo tower's lobby and buzzed Tracey's apartment. A few minutes later he was on the 12th floor. The door at the end of the hall opened before he'd even knocked.

"Hi, kiddo."

"Mr. Crowe." She held the door open and beckoned him in.

Her hair had grown out a bit since he'd seen her last. It now fell below her shoulders, a rich mass of dark tresses that framed a face with thick eyebrows, brown eyes and generous lips. She was tall - five foot nine - and their eyes at almost the same level made immediate contact.

She closed the door and locked it, leaning against it a minute as if to ensure it was really closed. She moved toward him. They embraced gently and she leaned her head against his shoulder, her arms around his waist. He rested his cheek against her hair and inhaled her fragrance.

They broke off after a minute. She stepped back to look in his eyes. He saw a question mark there and wondered if she was asking herself the same question as he was. As it turned out, she wasn't.

"Did you eat dinner?"

"No."

"Can I make you something?"

"It's too late for a meal. I'll just have some tea." Crowe fasted periodically so it was no big deal to go without food for 12 hours or more.

Tracey went to the kitchenette to make some jasmine tea. While the water boiled, she put a banana, an orange and a bowl of raw cashews on the counter. "Just in case you need a snack."

He wandered into her living room and immediately noticed an acoustic guitar in the corner. He picked it up. "When'd you get this?"

"Christmas."

"Nice." He didn't ask who it was from. It was a good one, a Gibson. He sat on the sofa and tuned it.

"I've always wanted to play," she said. "I'm learning lots of stuff on YouTube but maybe I'll take lessons too."

"Good for you."

"Maybe in a year, we can duet."

"Whenever you're ready," Crowe said, not oblivious to the *double-entendre*. He played the opening riff for Muddy Waters' *Catfish Blues*, and sang some lyrics he'd written.

"There's dridha *karma running, though it never runs my way,*
"But I have my mala *and I say my* japa *all night and all day."*

Tracey carried a tray with their tea and snacks into the living room.

Crowe finished with some vibrato on the E-note.

She applauded. "Sweet."

"Thank you." Crowe handed the guitar to her. "Your turn."

"Not until I've had more practice." She set the guitar aside. "I really liked your lyrics, but what's *dridha* karma mean?"

"That's fixed karma that supposedly can't be changed," he said. "As opposed to *adridha* karma, which isn't fixed, and can be tweaked by our intentions and actions."

"Good to know there's hope for us all."

She poured tea from a silver pot. Crowe was halfway through the cashews before he realized he was hungry after all. He peeled the banana and ate it.

"How's work?" he asked.

Tracey, who worked in the forensics unit at Midtown

North, told him about a few cases she was working on, sketching the broader picture, absent any details that could identify the principals. A double homicide, two black men shot on Eighth Avenue, the killer leaving a handful of shell casings and fleeing on foot. A letter bomb had blinded a diamond merchant on West 47th Street, third of a series whose *modus operandi* was starting to look like small-scale *jihad*. And the rape-murder of a young woman in Clinton Park by a perp whose size 12 running shoes had left impressions in soft earth near her body.

Crowe marveled at the workload with which police forces in major American cities were burdened. Given the volume of violent crimes and the difficulty of matching site evidence to suspects, no wonder so many went unsolved.

"And you?" she said. "Tell me more about your Vermont case. Where's the New York connection?"

Crowe told her about Manhattan residents Dean Bishop and his companion Kitti Poornchai. "Their connection with Greer's murder is completely speculative at this point, so I'm on a fishing trip. I thought I'd drop by the precinct tomorrow, say hello to Detectives Levinson and Rossimoff."

"Levinson's not with the 18th anymore. He was transferred to the 20th in the New Year."

"Where's the 20th?"

"West 82nd, between Columbus and Amsterdam."

"I'll pay him a visit anyway. I hope he remembers he owes me one."

"I'm sure he does. Last time I saw him, he said to say hello."

"He knows we're in touch? What'd you say about us?"

"We're friends," she said. "What else would I say?"

Crowe had no answer. He looked at his watch. "Hey, I ought to get going. It's already past my bedtime."

"It's not even eleven. You're such a boy scout."

"That's me." Crowe put on his jacket and went to the door. "A real straight arrow."

"Nothing wrong with that," she said. "It's the mark of a

good cop too."

"Speaking of which, are you having any luck finding one for yourself?"

She shrugged. "Not yet. But I'm keeping my options open."

They embraced again before he left. In the doorway he said, "I may be pretty busy the next few days. But if I get a break, you want to get together again?"

"You've got my number."

He left her condo and walked back to Washington Square. Along the way, he recalled what Guruji had taught him about archery. *With powerful arms you can pull the strongest bow. With an eagle eye you can see a distant target. With a poison-tipped arrowhead, you can kill the largest prey. But if your arrow is crooked, you'll never hit a thing.*

Crowe had understood immediately what Guruji meant. Without a moral compass, you were lost. That's why *dharma* – the right path – was so important, because when you knew you were doing the right thing, no obstacle could discourage you.

He reflected briefly on the chart he'd calculated at dawn yesterday morning. He'd seen something there that'd made him believe Abbott was innocent. Tomorrow he'd have to start proving it.

21

Monday, April 23

IN THE MORNING CROWE ATE BREAKFAST in the hotel and retraced part of the same route he'd walked last night. By a coincidence of geography, Cooper Square was halfway between his hotel and Tracey's condo. Having walked past it several times before, he knew *The Village Voice* occupied a seven-story brownstone building on the west side of the square.

Crowe remembered reading *The Voice* during high school in the eighties. Its coverage of the vibrant arts scene had made him want to catch the next bus to New York, there to roam the Village and SoHo with camera and notepad in hand. Since then, the alternative weekly had become the biggest community newspaper in the world, with a solid repertoire of investigative journalism.

Inside the newspaper building, the lobby was a scene of chaos. Dozens of people waited to have their bags checked and pass through a security scanner. A receptionist informed Crowe that no one was allowed in without an appointment. He showed his investigator's license and said he had information about the death of Seth Greer.

She made a quick call upstairs, then gave him a visitor's badge. "Sixth floor. Berndt Magnusson's the editor. He can spare a minute."

Crowe took a claustrophobic elevator to the sixth with three other people clutching bundles of files to their chests. He found Magnusson on the phone in a corner office. Crowe waited in the doorway while the editor extricated himself from a call, saying he was late for a meeting, they'd talk later. He put the phone down and regarded Crowe with controlled irritation.

Magnusson was in his fifties, a thick-set man with an unruly shock of red hair. He had a florid expression textured with the after-effects of severe acne that had pitted his cheeks and forehead. The bags under his eyes implied he hadn't slept much lately.

Crowe introduced himself and got to the point. He was investigating the Greer case on behalf of his client.

"Huh? I was given the impression it was practically an open-and-shut case," Magnusson said. "I got a call Saturday from a Lieutenant Lynch of the Vermont State Police. He said Greer had been murdered Friday night but they'd arrested a suspect." Magnusson retrieved a scrap of paper from his cluttered desktop. "Bryan Abbott, runs a retreat in Barnet, Vermont."

"That's my client, but there's no way he did it. Just for starters, this talk of motive is pure fantasy."

"Really? Lynch asked me what Greer had been working on these days, and I recited the laundry list. If you're acquainted with journalists, you know we keep a lot of irons in the fire. Among many topics, Greer had done some research for a story on spiritual institutions engaged in money laundering. For whatever reason, Lynch picked up on this right away. He said there'd been rumors Abbott was connected to a local grow-op. He said maybe they ought to seize his financial records for a closer look."

"Ridiculous! You're not going to repeat any of that, are you?"

Magnusson scowled. "Of course not. And I'm certainly not going off half-cocked on the basis of a phone call from someone I've never met. I don't even know if this guy Lynch is a real cop or not. You wouldn't believe the bullshit people try to run on us."

"He's real enough but, just between you and me, I'm beginning to wonder what his agenda is."

"I don't know about *his* agenda, but I knew Seth's, and he wasn't writing a story on dodgy spiritual organizations. That was a topic on which he'd done some preliminary research, but he hadn't got enough traction to make it worthwhile, so I'd told him last month to put it on the back burner."

"What was he currently working on?"

"A much hotter story about stolen Asian antiquities."

"Can you elaborate?"

Magnusson looked at his watch. "The ten-second synopsis? Stolen Asian art and antiquities represent ten percent of a billion-dollar annual market. A lot goes missing in wartime, disappearing into private collections. Iraq's a good example. Before US troops even entered Baghdad, the museums had been pillaged. Some of it may not show up again for decades, perhaps with authentic provenance, more likely forged. The FBI and Interpol have catalogued everything they're aware of, and appealed to museums to examine their collections. But for every law-abiding museum, a hundred private dealers would rather sell their holdings for profit than return it to the rightful owner, typically a third world country."

"Greer was writing this story?"

"Actively researching."

"In Barnet, Vermont?"

Magnusson shrugged. "I don't know. He was supposed to take some vacation time this month, but for Seth the line between personal and professional life was always blurry. Like a permanent busman's holiday, know what I mean?"

Crowe knew it well. He was programmed the same way. His work was a pleasure that seemed to require no downtime, and even when he was in vacation mode, he often dwelled on the same things.

"Has the family been notified?"

"In the process, I guess. Lynch said he'd tried to reach Greer's brother in LA, without any success. After we'd hung up I wondered why he hadn't called Seth's ex-wife. Things have been so crazy around here I haven't got around to calling him back."

Crowe nodded. Lynch had tried to phone Michael Greer because that's the only name Seth had listed as next-of-kin on his registration sheet. "What *is* going on here? It's like a war zone."

"Appropriate choice of words. We were invaded Saturday night."

"What do you mean?"

"There was a break-in. A lot of files were stolen."

"Don't you have a security system?"

"It went down at three AM Sunday morning. Our IT people are trying to figure out how it was done, but obviously a hacker penetrated our security system. He disabled the video cameras, motion detectors and alarms, and released the electronic locks. Burglars entered the back door by picking the physical lock."

"What was stolen?"

"Here's the weird thing. They cleaned out Greer's cubicle - all his paper files - and took the hard drive from his computer."

Crowe glanced out the window of Magnusson's office. Everywhere he looked, people rummaged through file cabinets, scrolled through directory listings on their computer screens, and conferred over cubicle dividers with other employees in their sections.

"Just Greer's files? This place is like an anthill with an anteater tearing down the door."

Magnusson rubbed his face. "Nice simile, I could use that for local color. For the time being, I think of it as twenty pounds of shit in a ten-pound bag."

"So there was collateral damage."

"After enabling the burglars' entry, the hacker moved on to bigger things. He put a worm through our firewall and set it loose in the network. It purged all the files in Greer's directory, searched out any he'd shared with other writers and editors, and deleted them too."

"So everything Greer wrote is gone?"

"From the digital domain. This hacker was thorough. The second phase of his search-and-destroy mission took longer, but his worm looked for Greer's name in every file on our network, and wherever it appeared, purged the file. Not only on our local server, but our backup too. Trouble is, Seth had contributed to several other writers' stories, some of which hadn't yet gone to print, and now those files are gone too."

"Sounds like a disaster."

"In more ways than one. Not only have we lost stories in active development, we've also lost research notes supporting stories already published. If we had to defend ourselves against a legal suit, say, defamation or libel, we'd be like a one-legged man running from a tiger."

"You must have paper copies."

"Of some stuff, not everything."

"What about Greer's current story on stolen Asian antiquities?"

"I have a draft but it's at home."

"Could I get a copy of it?"

"I'll bring it in tomorrow. You can have a look at it, but no copy."

"What time will you be in tomorrow?"

"Seven." Magnusson looked at his watch, gathered a few papers from his desktop and stood up. "Sorry, I've got to scramble. The editorial board is meeting to assess the full scope of this fiasco and initiate damage control."

Crowe blocked the door before the editor could rush out. "You said Greer was divorced?"

"It was in the pipeline. He initiated a trial separation six months ago."

"What was his wife's name? Got a number for her?"

"Selena Greer. My wife and I liked her. You can try this cell number, which is the last one I had for her." Magnusson checked his phone and read off a number. "If that doesn't work, try directory assistance. She moved into their condo in Boynton Beach, Florida."

Crowe stepped aside and Magnusson hurried off to his crisis management meeting. Crowe took the elevator down, surrendered his visitor's badge, and left the building. Contrasted with the hectic office scene he'd just left behind, the street seemed surprisingly serene.

22

CROWE FOUND A QUIET CAFÉ nearby and checked the time. He hoped Selena Greer would be up by this hour. He didn't want to wake her, but he wanted to reach her before Magnusson gave Lieutenant Lynch a heads-up. He dialed the number and a woman answered.

"Ms. Greer, you don't know me, but I'm a private investigator, Axel Crowe. I'm in New York now, but this past weekend I was in Barnet, Vermont, where your husband attended a silent retreat."

"Seth on a silent retreat?" she laughed. "That's a good one. How long did he last?"

"I take it you haven't been notified by the police?"

"What's he done now? If he expects me to bail him out of another bar brawl or trespassing charge, he's due for a rude awakening."

"I'm sorry to tell you this, but he died late Friday night."

There was a muffled gasp and a brief silence. "A heart attack?"

"He fell from a cliff on the property where he was staying. At this point, we don't know if it was an accident or foul play."

"Foul play?"

Crowe told her about the incident on the second last day of the retreat - Greer getting decked by Dean Bishop. "Do you know the name?"

"No. Who is he?"

Crowe told her what little he knew of Bishop, that he was a security consultant in New York, and was practically a regular at the ashram. And that he'd been in the company of an attractive Thai woman named Kitti Poornchai. But Selena didn't react to that name either.

"What was Seth working on these days?" she said.

"According to his editor, a story on stolen Asian antiquities."

"Maybe there's a clue. It wouldn't be the first time Seth uncovered something murky. Those people who live in the shadows can get pretty ugly. He's received threats before."

"From whom?"

"This was quite awhile ago. One was a property developer who violated, like, a thousand building codes and bribed inspectors to look the other way. But he died a few years ago."

"There were other threats?"

"One, but that was more than ten years ago. Something to do with the Chinese triads, I don't even remember the circumstances, except that the guy got a life sentence seven years ago, so he'll be there for another decade at least."

"Do you remember a name?"

"No, but the story would be under Seth's byline at *The Voice*."

"Did Seth have any other family?"

"A younger brother, Michael, in LA. His parents live in Albany." She broke up a little at this point and Crowe gave her time to compose herself and blow her nose. "I'm sorry. What were you saying?"

"Can you give me his brother's number?"

"Just a minute." She read off a number with a 323 area code. "But I don't think you'll be able to reach him for a few more days."

"He's out of town on business?"

"No, he's a music composer and his business is all in LA. But this week he's in Peru, on an *ayahuasca* retreat."

"*Ayahuasca*? The psychotropic drug used by South American shamans to communicate with nature spirits?"

"So you've heard of it."

"Yes," Crowe said. "Did Seth share his brother's interest in hallucinogens?" Perhaps Greer had tried to fly off the quarry cliff…

"No. He was strictly a scotch-on-the-rocks kind of guy."

Crowe hesitated. "Was he an alcoholic?"

"No," she was quick to answer. "But he was always

under a lot of stress, and he liked to drink. Sometimes he did foolish things under the influence."

"I'm sorry for your loss."

"Thank you. I guess I'd better phone his parents, and then start making arrangements. They're not Orthodox Jews but there are certain protocols."

"Let me give you the number for the police chief in charge of the case." Crowe retrieved Lynch's card from his wallet and read her the number. "I assume the autopsy's been performed by now. He should be able to tell you where the body is and when it can be released."

"Thank you. I guess I'd better catch a flight to New York, see if there's anything that needs to be done with his condo."

"You have the keys to his place?"

"Both the condo on the Lower East Side and this place here are still in both our names, pending the divorce going through."

"Could you let me have a look in his papers?" Crowe told her about the situation at *The Village Voice*, where all of Greer's files had been purged by a malicious worm.

"I don't know... Isn't this still an active investigation?"

"Depends on your perspective." Crowe was a little cynical. As far as the Vermont police were concerned, the case was already closed. "Maybe you should talk to Berndt Magnusson. I got the impression you knew each other socially?"

"Yes, we did. He and his wife came down here a couple of times to visit us and get away from those nasty New England winters."

"Speaking of getting away from it all, did Seth know his brother Michael was away in Peru?"

"I don't know. They had an on-and-off relationship. Sometimes they were best of buddies, other times they'd get all bent out of shape and not speak for months. It's ironic. Michael and I were never that close, but after things started to unravel last year between me and Seth, it was him I turned to. At first I'd just hoped he could talk some sense into Seth but later he turned out to be the most supportive friend I had."

At this, she had another little cry. After she'd composed herself, she told him she should let him go, she needed to go online and book the next New York flight she could get.

"Between now and your flight, do you have a friend you can talk to?" Crowe asked.

"No, it's all right. I did all of my crying six months ago. In a way, dealing with this will be easier than what I've already been through."

"There's a Sufi saying that's worth meditating on," Crowe said. *"When the heart weeps for what it has lost, the soul laughs for what it has found."*

"That's heavy," she said, "but I can carry it. Thank you for calling. When I get in later today, I'll give you a call and we can schedule a time for you to come over and look through Seth's papers."

23

CROWE RODE THE SUBWAY uptown to 79th. The 20th Precinct was of relatively modern construction, a three-story brick and concrete building on a tree-lined street. Crowe went to the sergeant's desk and called upstairs to see if Det. Levinson was in. Getting a go-ahead, he received a visitor's pass and took the elevator up to the detective squad section. Someone pointed the way to Homicide.

Levinson rose from his desk as Crowe approached. "Good to see you." He was a tall man with a dry powerful handshake, still fit-looking, albeit with more gray at the temples since Crowe had seen him last.

Crowe scanned the nearby desks but saw no one he recognized. "Where's your sidekick?"

"Rossimoff? Sick leave."

"I'm sorry to hear that. Nothing serious, I hope."

"Wake-up call from the doctor. Early signs for cirrhosis of the liver." Levinson cleared his throat. "He's taking a six-month sick leave to go through detox and try to turn his life around."

Crowe said nothing, but recalled the massive groove down the middle of Rossimoff's forehead. In the physiognomy of ayurveda, it was a leading indicator of bile duct or liver issues.

"Please give him my best," Crowe told Levinson. "Maybe his dietitian will cover this, but to restore liver function, he should eat lots of onion and garlic. And drink licorice tea, preferably made from fresh root."

Levinson seemed on the verge of saying something but bit his lip. He gestured for Crowe to take a seat. "So, what's it been – a year since the Janis Stockwell case?"

"Right." Despite initial skepticism from the police, Crowe had brought his unique insight to the crime scene evidence, teasing out a theory that had changed the case from a local mugging-turned-fatal to a three-way murder conspiracy spanning a continent. "Is the husband in prison yet?"

"Just going to trial this month." Levinson shrugged. "The wheels of justice grind slowly."

"How's it going on your new job?"

Levinson tipped his head back and raised his hand to within an inch of his nostrils. "I'm up to here in it."

"How come you changed precincts? I thought cops pretty much stayed in the territories they were familiar with."

"The twentieth had a bad year. Retirements, a few corruption charges, two undercovers killed in the line of duty. They were looking around for new blood and, with Rossimoff on sick leave, I was in temporary limbo at the eighteenth. My name came up, they interviewed me and I hit the street running."

"Heavy caseload?"

Levinson snorted. "I've got a backlog from here to eternity."

"Anything I could help you with?"

Levinson shook his head. "I can't have a civilian work any of my cases. My lieutenant would have my balls."

"It would be unofficial, of course. Think about it. You know what I can do. A fresh pair of eyes might give you a whole new perspective."

"What do *you* want?"

Crowe told him about Seth Greer's death at the Buddhist retreat, preceded by the fight with Dean Bishop, and followed by the evasive behavior of Kitti Poornchai. Now Bryan Abbott was behind bars, charged with murder and denied bail.

"I believe he's innocent, but the only way I can help him is to try and find out who really killed Greer. It's obviously not Bishop and probably not Poornchai, but there's something about the pair of them that piques my interest, and I mean that in the worst possible way. However, I need help to substantiate my suspicions."

"Specifically, how?"

"Background checks. Criminal record, citizenship, financials, litigation records, titles to property, business ownership, driving and vehicle records and anything else that turns up - drug tests, education, psych evaluations, military records."

Levinson pulled a face. "Sure. You want fries with that?"

"Come on. One of your analysts could probably pull this together in a few hours."

"More like a day."

"Whatever it takes, I'll match you."

"And what exactly are you going to do for me?"

"I know you can't let me participate in an active case. Other officers are involved, and your superior would be on top of it. But you probably have a few cold cases lying around. The older, the better. Anything that anyone considers a lost cause. Give me a couple and I'll see what I can do."

"Only a couple?"

"What do you expect for a day's work?"

"Who's doing who the big favor?" Levinson reminded him.

"Okay, give me what you've got and I'll see what I can do." Crowe shook his head. "Anyone ever accuse you of being a heartless S-O-B?"

Levinson pushed a pad across the desk. "Write down the names of those two people, plus whatever else you know about them - date of birth if you got it, address, occupation, nationality - in case there's more than one person out there with the same name. I'll put one of my guys on it this morning."

Crowe gave Levinson the photocopies from Abbott's files - Bishop's and Poornchai's application and registration forms.

Levinson went away and came back five minutes later with Crowe's originals, plus a stack of files under his arm. They went into one of the small conference rooms in a corner of the Homicide section. Levinson closed the door and dumped the files on the table.

"That's more than one case." Crowe counted eight blue files and one red file.

"No. It's just one case with several victims."

"A serial killer?"

"Looks like it."

"You didn't hand this over to the FBI? Aren't serial murders their area of expertise?"

"We tried, but they didn't have the resources to spare. Anyway, you've been watching too many TV shows. That's not the way it works in the real world. These days, the only time the NYPD gets active FBI assistance is in terrorism. Murders confined to city or state jurisdiction are ours alone. For this case, the feds gave us one analyst - a retiree - for two days. All he did was write a profile."

Crowe pulled the red file toward him. "This the general file?"

"Read it at your leisure, but I'll give you the big picture now. This is a series of eight rape-homicides going back twelve years. All the victims were Asian women, ranging in age from early twenties to mid-forties. The common elements are violent rape, death by strangulation, biting and sodomy.

Except for one, all victims were dumped in garbage bags along Riverside Drive. For lack of a better name, we've called it the Riverside Rapist file."

"I'll go through it all and see what I can find."

"I've got to run." Levinson left a card with his numbers and departed.

Crowe called his wealthy client Kevin Blaikie. After some pleasant banter and exchange of news, Crowe got down to business and asked Blaikie if he could arrange bail for his friend Bryan Abbott, explaining the circumstances in brief. Without hesitation, Blaikie agreed to try. Crowe gave him the number of Abbott's lawyer in St. Johnsbury, Vermont, and left it in his hands. Before signing off, Blaikie insisted they get together for lunch or dinner this week. Crowe said he'd call him back in a day or two.

Crowe turned his attention back to the files on the table. Each blue file had an individual case number, name of victim and date. He put them in order and began to read.

24

THE MURDERS HAD BEGUN in September 2000. The first victim was a 23-year-old Japanese girl on a student visa at NYU. She'd been reported missing by her roommate, September 4th, after failing to return to their West Village apartment. Her body was discovered Tuesday the 5th, duct-taped inside two black garbage bags, dumped at Riverside Drive and 80th Street. She'd been bitten, raped, sodomized and strangled. The coroner had estimated time of death in the early hours of Monday the 4th.

The second victim died in August 2002. She was Korean, a 31-year-old liquor store manager. Her husband had reported her missing when she didn't come home Wednesday night, August 14th. Her body was found Saturday the 17th, wrapped in garbage bags, at Riverside and 99th. Sexually assaulted and strangled like the first. Estimated time of death, forty-eight hours prior, probably Thursday the 15th.

The third murder was in July 2004. The victim was Chinese, a 27-year-old lawyer who didn't show up for work on Monday, July 26th. She'd disappeared somewhere between Chinatown, where she lived with mother and sister, and Beekman Street where she worked. Her bagged body was found next morning at Riverside and 85th. Raped and strangled. Time of death was assumed twelve hours earlier, late Monday afternoon or early evening, the day she'd disappeared.

The fourth victim, in July 2006, was known to the police, a 24-year-old Filipino hooker who worked Times Square. She'd vanished Thursday night, July 6th, but wasn't reported missing by the three other working girls with whom she shared an apartment. Her body was discovered the following Sunday afternoon at Riverside and 101st. She'd been bitten and strangled, but evidence of rape and sodomy was tenuous, given the regular nature of her work. The medical examiner estimated death forty-eight hours earlier, the morning of Friday the 7th.

The fifth murder took place in June 2008. A 32-year-old Vietnamese pharmacist at a Hell's Kitchen homeless clinic had finished her Sunday shift at nine PM but never made it home to the Lower West Side. Her husband had reported her missing at midnight. Her body was found the next day - assaulted, murdered and bagged like the others - at Riverside and 99th. The medical examiner estimated death about twelve hours earlier, late on Sunday June 15th.

The sixth victim, a 24-year-old Malaysian ticket clerk at the Port Authority Bus Terminal, was killed in December 2009. Her roommates said she'd gone out Sunday afternoon to meet a friend. He'd phoned an hour later to ask where she was. After repeated calls to her cell phone, they reported her missing at midnight. Her body was found during rush hour the next morning at Riverside and 88th. According to the autopsy, she'd been killed just a few hours earlier, likely around three AM, Monday December 14th.

The seventh murder occurred that same week. The victim was a 42-year-old Vietnamese woman, a curator at the Manhattan Museum of Asian Antiquities. Her body was discovered in her apartment the evening of Thursday, December 17th, by a co-worker concerned by the curator's three-day absence from work. She'd been dead for at least a couple of days. The medical examiner speculated she'd been killed sometime late Monday, or early Tuesday the 15th.

This seventh victim was an anomaly. Although she'd been sexually assaulted, there'd been no bite marks or sodomy. And whereas the other victims had been strangled, her neck was broken. She was also the oldest victim. And unlike the previous six, she hadn't been dumped in Riverside Park. But because she was Asian and her condo building was at Riverside and 77th, her case had been added to the Riverside Rapist file.

The eighth murder was in October 2011, the victim a 33-year old Cambodian translator at the UN. She'd gone out for drinks with friends Thursday night in Lower Manhattan, but never made it home to her Tribeca condo. Her husband had reported her missing the next morning. Her ravaged body wasn't discovered until early Monday morning at Riverside and 105th. The medical examiner estimated time of death three days earlier, possibly early hours of Friday October 28th.

The general file in the red folder had been created after the discovery of the third victim, when it was recognized that the rape, murder and disposal of these Asian women had a distinct pattern implying a serial killer at large. The file was a compilation of observations, statistics and theories about all eight cases treated as a group. It included memos from meetings among various investigators who'd handled the cases, as well as correspondence and input from the FBI's Behavioral Analysis Unit.

Forensic analysis had turned up little. Vaginal and anal swabs had found no trace of semen, so it was assumed the rapist used condoms in every case. Pubic hairs had been recovered from the Filipino prostitute but they'd come from two different men, identities unknown.

Strangulation marks on the victims' throats suggested a right-handed person of average stature. Bite marks on the buttocks, inner thighs and labia of most, but not all, victims had been made by teeth so regular there were no distinguishing features to allow a match against any known suspect, of which there were none.

The garbage bags and duct tape were popular household brands available at Walmart and other retailers. No fingerprints were found on either bags or tape, implying the perp may have used gloves to protect his identity.

Except for the curator, all the victims had been dumped on Riverside Drive between 80th and 105th. After the third murder, patrol units along Riverside had been asked to investigate any suspicious vehicles pulled to the curb, especially vans with side doors facilitating quick off-loading. Within the first month after each murder, patrol units zealously took names and license plates for investigators to follow up on. After a month, the zeal for this fruitless task lost its shine until the next murder, and then the cycle repeated itself. No valid suspect had ever been identified.

Riverside Drive had adequate surveillance: stationary cameras between 78th, 79th and 80th; a global camera between 93rd and 94th; four stationary cameras between 104th and 105th; another on the southeast corner of 109th. None of the dumps had occurred within camera range of these locations, implying either luck on the perp's part or, more ominously, knowledge of the camera network.

Although the victims were all Asian, the distribution of nationalities was so widespread as to seem calculated. Given the large Chinese population in New York, demographics should have dictated many more Chinese victims. Someone had printed a page from Wikipedia and extracted statistics:

According to the 2010 Census, New York City was home to more than one million Asian Americans. Of these, almost

660,000 were Chinese.

Chinese made up 6.0% of the city's population, Koreans 1.2%, Japanese 0.3%. Filipinos were the largest Southeast Asian ethnic group at 0.8%, followed by Vietnamese at only 0.2%. Indians were the largest South Asian group, comprising 2.4% of the city's population.

Based on these numbers, half of the eight victims should have been Chinese. But there was only one Chinese victim, but two Vietnamese, despite that nationality being one of the smallest ethnic groups.

The FBI profiler had floated the theory that the rapes and murders were the work of a racist white male, age 30-50, either acting alone or in concert with another perp of similar disposition.

The perp was assumed to be in reasonably good physical condition. Although most victims bore bruises suggesting a struggle with their attacker, none had suffered concussion from a blunt object, a typical failsafe resort for juveniles and older perps who couldn't handle sustained resistance.

An alternative theory suggested that, if the perp had been armed with a knife or gun, the threat of a weapon might have discouraged victims from struggling. The bruises could then be explained by the perp simply asserting his dominance over the victims.

All victims exhibited signs of vaginal bruising and tearing, indicating a rapist of some virility and aggression. Sodomy implied a misogynist, or someone who'd been raped in prison, perhaps both.

The victims' underwear - both panties and bras - had been taken. This implied a trophy collector or fetishist who relived his rapes by handling his victim's clothing. It also suggested confidence he wouldn't be caught with incriminating evidence.

Despite these cases having occurred long before his transfer to the 20th Precinct, Levinson and his new partner had re-interviewed the victims' families and friends. Except for the Filipino prostitute, none of the victims had experienced previous assaults, rapes or verbal threats. None had problems with boyfriends or unwanted attention from co-workers or customers. Despite a month of on-and-off canvasses, interviews and queries to follow up on thin leads, the Riverside Rapist case file remained a mystery and a frustration.

Crowe closed the red folder and pushed his chair away from the table. He felt heavy, like he'd just eaten a meal of uncooked rice and beans. This would take some time to digest. He returned the files to Levinson's desk and left the building.

25

CROWE BOUGHT A JUICE and a sandwich from a health food takeout and went to Theodore Roosevelt Park. As tourists walked past on their way to the American Museum of Natural History, he did a few yoga stretches and several minutes of deep breathing exercises. After absorbing some *prana,* the vital energy emitted by the vegetation around him, he sat on a bench and ate his lunch slowly and mindfully.

It was a sunny afternoon and the thought of returning to those case files made him feel like a schoolboy with nothing better than hooky on his mind. He phoned Levinson. As luck would have it, the detective was in his car and had time for a quick chat.

"When are you coming back to the office?" Crowe asked.

"Not until end of day. I've got back-to-back interviews to conduct all afternoon. What's up?"

"I read through all the files but now I need a break. I'm going to take a little time to run down a lead of my own."

They agreed to meet back at the precinct at six PM. Crowe headed south on Columbus Avenue. He wasn't running away from the puzzle, just trying to get a different perspective on it.

As always, he paid attention to street corners.

Intersections were like the knots in strings that formed nets where things became trapped - objects, feelings, even ideas. Guruji had taught Crowe that intersections were like portals between two different worlds - the phenomenal one in which we lived, and the paranormal one that operated on an entirely different level.

At Columbus and 80th he saw a phallic red letterbox in front of a café where an attractive young woman in a red dress stood watching pedestrians walk by. She smiled at Crowe as he passed. He wasn't sure if that was an omen or just a reminder that his libido hadn't been let off the leash for longer than he cared to think about.

At 77th a sign in front of a high school yard advertised a Flea Market on Sunday. Some wiseacre had used a marker to change it to "Plea Market." Crowe turned and headed west. The only plea he recalled having heard recently was Abbott's parting request before being led away in handcuffs.

I need you to figure out what happened at the quarry last night. Someone's trying to frame me for Greer's murder, but I have no idea who or why.

At 77th and Broadway, Crowe passed a store called the Bra Smyth whose front windows displayed multiple posters of over-flowing bras. He was reminded of the Riverside Rapist's *modus operandi*, taking underwear as souvenirs of his victims. Could he be a cross-dresser as well as a killer?

At 77th and Riverside, Crowe came to a halt in front of a four-story building with a rooftop terrace. This was where Thi Nguyen, the curator of the Manhattan Museum of Asian Antiquities, had lived. Crowe looked around him. Across the street was Riverside Park, beyond which was the Hudson River. People dreamed of living in such a neighborhood, adjacent a park in one of the world's most dynamic cities. But for Thi Nguyen, that dream had turned into a nightmare of violation and death. Why?

Crowe walked up Riverside Drive. Below 78th, a fence separated the curb from the park. Perhaps that was why no bodies had been dumped this far down, because the fence would have made it difficult to off-load a body from a parked van onto the grass.

At Riverside and 79th, an east-west street gave access to the Henry Hudson Parkway. Above 79th, a wide sidewalk and a low stone wall separated the curb from the park. North of that, a wrought-iron fence stood between the sidewalk and the park.

Crowe continued all the way up to 105th. Without having originally intended it, his walk to clear his mind had taken him past each of the locations where the victims of the Riverside Rapist had been found.

He opened up Google Maps and reviewed the locations where the victims had been dumped. All were on Riverside between 80th and 105th. Of seven bodies, five had been dumped on the west side adjacent Riverside Park. The pair dumped on the east side had been at 93rd and 102nd. There was no cross-street intersection at those locations because narrow parks separated the two-way Riverside Drive and a parallel one-way Riverside Drive hugging the residential buildings along the Upper West Side.

In all cases, the killer had been able to dump the bodies from the right-hand side of his vehicle, either onto a sidewalk or the grassy verge of a park. Most vans had a right-hand side door. That would have made it easy for quick off-loading without local residents witnessing anything.

At 79th and 96th, access roads led to the Henry Hudson Parkway. Was it a coincidence that so many victims had been dumped within a few blocks of either on-ramp? Crowe wondered if the killer might not be a local but a visitor, dumping the bodies just minutes before he got on the toll highway and left town. It might also explain the periodicity of the killings, whose average interval spanned almost two years.

Crowe was interrupted from his speculations by his phone's ringtone. It was Selena Greer. She'd just landed at LaGuardia. If he wanted to meet her at Greer's condo, she'd give him the address.

26

CROWE TOOK THE SUBWAY to SoHo, and a taxi to the Lower East Side. Somehow it seemed fitting that Seth Greer, who'd written for an alternative weekly, would live in this part of the city. But the once less-than-desirable neighborhood had enjoyed rapid and wide-sweeping gentrification in the past decade. Trendy new restaurants were springing up on Clinton Street every month.

Greer's condo was at Clinton and Stanton. It was a modern five-story construction of brick, aluminum and glass, with a few balconies overlooking the street. Crowe rang the buzzer and went up to the fifth floor apartment.

Selena Greer was an elegant woman in her early fifties, with a thick mane of black hair in which she'd allowed streaks of gray to appear. She wore stylish glasses and a pant suit in a dark check pattern. She shook his hand with a warm grip and accepted the card he offered as proof of who he said he was.

"His place was burglarized." She closed the door and locked it. "I arrived just a few minutes ago, so I haven't had time to determine what was taken. But someone completely ransacked his office."

The apartment was a two-bedroom furnished in a sleek Scandinavian style. A granite counter separated the kitchen from a small living room with a balcony overlooking the street. A wall unit held a flat screen TV and a sound system that also included a turntable, an uncommon item these days. There was a large collection of CDs, but also a hundred or more vinyl albums.

Down the hall were two other rooms - a bedroom and office. In the first, the double bed was unmade. A bicycle stood in the corner, a T-shirt hanging from the handlebars. The closet doors were open, as were the dresser drawers.

In the office, one wall was dominated by bookcases. Behind a desk were two filing cabinets in the corner. The drawers were open, file folders spilled across the floor. The closet had held half a dozen cardboard file boxes. Four had been pulled from the closet, their contents strewn on the floor, the other two gutted where they lay.

A flat-screen display and a keyboard stood on the desk. The desk drawers were open, papers dumped on the desk. Crowe looked under the desk and saw several loose cables but no computer.

They returned to the living room, where Crowe noticed a guitar case beneath the sofa. He took it out, feeling a twinge of envy when he saw the Martin name on the acoustic guitar. He sat on the sofa and played the opening lines of Eric Clapton's "Heaven". The tone was beautiful.

"In 2005, his grandmother left him an inheritance," Selena said. "It was a toss-up between that and a new car. He wouldn't tell me what he paid for it."

"It's probably worth ten grand or more." Crowe put the guitar back in the case. "You should get it appraised and insured. They're constantly going up in value."

"Funny the burglars didn't take it."

"I don't think they were here for anything like that. The guitar, sound system and CDs are all portable. It looks like the only thing they took was his computer."

"Why?"

"It might have had something to do with what he was working on." Crowe told her about what had happened at *The Village Voice*. "You said he'd received threats in the past. Were you aware of anything recent?"

"I need a drink." Selena searched the kitchen cabinets and found some liquor. She splashed some scotch into a glass. "Want something? He has rum, vodka, gin, tequila..."

"Water's fine."

She opened a can of club soda and poured him a glass. They sat on the sofa. She took a drink and sighed. "Now I need a cigarette."

"Can't help you there."

She looked around as if hoping to spot a pack of cigarettes lying nearby. "I moved to Florida six months ago.

We didn't talk much after that - just a few pragmatic things regarding joint property, investments, IRAs, that sort of thing. We stayed up-to-date on family news, but he didn't talk about work. I had no idea what he was currently writing, or what he was doing in Vermont."

"Did you talk to Lieutenant Lynch?"

"Yes. He called about an hour after you. He told me what'd happened in Vermont. I said I'd be handling Seth's affairs and he gave me the number for the coroner's office. I called Seth's parents in Albany. They're making arrangements with a local funeral home to transfer the body. I'll drive up there tomorrow to be with them. It's too bad Michael can't be there for the funeral but we have no way to get in touch with him in Peru. He's in the jungle."

"Did Lynch ask you if Seth had received any recent threats?"

"No. He seemed pretty confident they had a strong case against this guy Abbott."

Crowe puzzled over this. Lynch hadn't asked her to contact him if she found anything in Seth's effects that might assist his case. What made him so sure of Abbott's guilt?

Selena drained her glass. "Did you still want to look through his papers?"

"I might as well."

"Go ahead. I'm going out for cigarettes." She left the apartment and closed the door behind her.

Crowe went to the office and looked at the hillock of strewn files covering half the floor. Three-quarters of the folders were off-white, the others a mix of primary colors - red, blue, and yellow.

He sat for a moment in Greer's desk chair and surveyed the mess. What was he looking for? A clue as to what got Greer killed.

With too many file folders to look through, he decided to narrow his choices using ruling planets - the day lord, the ruler of the Moon sign, and the ascendant lord.

Monday was ruled by the Moon, whose color was white.

..hat was no help. There were too many off-white folders.

The Moon was in Taurus, ruled by Venus, whose color was blue. So blue folders might be relevant.

Leo was rising, ruled by the Sun, whose colors were golden. So a yellow folder might hold a clue.

Which color offered the best odds of revealing something - blue or yellow? Since Venus was currently in its own sign Taurus, that favored blue. Crowe scooped up all of the blue folders, about a dozen of them.

He sat at the desk and flipped through them, not really knowing what to look for, hoping something might catch his eye. The material was mundane - cronyism in New York State's college system, property insurance scams, disability pension abuses by civil servants, sexual misconduct of health-care professionals, food contamination cover-ups in soup kitchens...

Crowe heard the apartment door open and close. He held his breath. He heard the fridge open, the clink of ice cubes in a glass. Selena was back. After a few moments, Alice Coltrane's jazz harp floated out from the sound system.

Crowe set the blue files aside and had a quick look through the yellow files. None of them contained anything of interest either. Maybe he was barking up the wrong tree.

He opened his astrology app for a closer look at the chart of the moment. Documents were signified by the third house Libra. Its lord Venus was in Taurus with the Moon in the tenth house. Since that was a fixed sign, the files had to be nearby. But Saturn, which sometimes obscured things from sight, occupied the third house. Perhaps near a doorway, which the third house also ruled...

He went to the foyer. Selena was sitting on the balcony, having a cigarette. He looked in the hallway closet adjacent the entrance. Several jackets and coats hung on a rod. Near the back of the closet was a long black winter coat. Saturn in the third house: something stiff in the arms. He felt inside the coat and withdrew three blue file folders that had been rolled together and hidden inside the coat sleeve.

Each file was almost half an inch thick. He immediately got the sense this was what he'd been looking for. He opened them on the kitchen counter.

The *"Rogue Elephants"* folder contained notes on the Golden Triangle, the area of heroin production straddling Burma, Laos and Thailand. There appeared to be extensive documentation on the role of US military advisors smuggling heroin into the USA.

The second folder, *"Artful Dodger"*, was about counterfeit art, not just fake paintings but also sculptures and works of antiquity. Since skilled artisans understood the science behind curators' authenticity tests, the market was now awash in highly sophisticated forgeries. The file included a long list of art dealers and suspected forgers.

The third, *"Rancho Gomorrah"*, contained information on sex trafficking. Houston was a major hub where girls from all over the world were lured by promises of employment, but ended up in strip joints and brothels serving year-round conventions and sporting events.

Crowe checked his watch. There was too much material in the folders to do more than skim their contents. He joined Selena on the balcony where she sat with cigarette in one hand, scotch in the other.

"When I opened the balcony door, I noticed the lock was broken." She pointed overhead. The roof was only ten feet above them. "It must be how they broke in."

Crowe looked at the patio door. The metal jamb was deformed where someone had used a pry bar.

"Did you find anything in his files?" she asked.

"A couple of things piqued my curiosity. Would you mind if I took them away for a closer look?"

"The subject matter – is it personal or professional?"

"They appear to be investigative stories he was working on."

She fluttered her cigarette hand. "Be my guest."

Crowe looked at her. She was a study in grace under pressure, but she was suffering. "Do you have a friend you can call?"

"Yes, but I don't need anyone today, thank you. After I've come back from Albany, I'll get someone to come over, help me sort through his papers for anything I need to deal with."

"I should be going. I have an appointment uptown."

"I'll walk you out." She butted her cigarette in a saucer and drained her glass. She walked with exaggerated care from the balcony to the kitchen.

"If you hear from his brother, can you let me know right away?" Crowe picked up the files on his way to the door. "Or have him call me. My number's on the card I gave you."

"I'll do that."

27

CROWE HADN'T SURRENDERED his visitor's badge on leaving the 20th Precinct, and returned to the Homicide section unchallenged. Levinson stood at his desk looking at a handful of message notes, his suit jacket still on.

"How'd your interviews go?" Crowe asked.

"Better than I'd hoped. Went to check an alibi and came back with a confession. How was your day?"

"Not nearly as rewarding. But I do have some observations about your serial case."

"Great. Let me check with my people, see what they found for you." Levinson headed toward some cubicles in the far corner. "I'll meet you in the conference room."

Crowe retrieved the case files he'd stashed under Levinson's desk, and took them to the conference room with the folders from Greer's condo.

Levinson joined him and placed a small sheaf of papers on the table. "The background checks on the three people you asked about."

"Anything of interest?" Crowe said.

"Dean Bishop is former CIA. Served in covert ops in Burma, Cambodia, Laos, Thailand, Vietnam. Retired from the service nine years ago, now runs a security agency called Edgewater Risk Management. Clients are mostly Manhattan firms with off-shore manufacturing in Southeast Asia. Also has a few clients in Dallas and Fort Worth. Lives in Tribeca. Now single but was married in 2003, divorced in 2006. Has one son, age six, and pays regular child support to the ex as per court order. A couple of DUIs, but otherwise a clean record."

"And Greer?"

"Graduated Columbia School of Journalism, made his name with a book about the Freemasons a decade ago. Worked for some of the biggest newspapers in the country – *LA Times, Daily News, Chicago Tribune, Houston Chronicle*. Now a freelancer, mostly for *The Village Voice, LA Weekly* and *Houston Press*. Had a temporary restraining order filed against him five years ago to stop hounding prominent Wall Street lawyers he accused of stock market manipulation. Bit of a die-hard conspiracy theorist. Married, no kids."

"He was in the process of getting divorced."

Levinson shrugged. "Until it's legal, doesn't show up in the system."

"What about Poornchai?"

"Wait. There's more on Greer. A lot of his stories covered child labor, drug trade and sex trafficking in Southeast Asia. There's an obvious overlap with the geography covered by Bishop. Read between the lines, there's an immediate clash of values. Greer was obviously a social activist, while Bishop's clients include manufacturers who might be exploiting child labor in off-shore facilities."

"And Kitti Poornchai is a Thai national?"

"Landed immigrant status two years ago, green card pending. Arrested for facilitating prostitution last year, but the charges were dropped for no apparent reason."

"That's it?"

"Most of it." Levinson pushed the sheaf of paper across

the table. "You can read the rest of it on your own."

Crowe glanced at the sheet on Kitti Poornchai. On her green card application she'd listed her originating address - a unit and building number on Soi Pradit, Silom, Bangkok. Crowe had been to Bangkok. The notorious Patpong red light district was near Silom Road.

He set the background material aside. "Thanks for this."

Levinson nodded at the stack of files he'd given Crowe this morning. "Did you get through any of that?"

Crowe recapped his initial observations. "The location of the dumped bodies, all within a few blocks of access ramps to the Henry Hudson Parkway, makes me think of a visitor getting rid of his victims just before he leaves town."

"True. But many of these women were held - a few hours to a couple of days - which means he had a place to hold them captive without discovery or escape. Even if it was just a camper van, he still needed a place to park it while he did his dirty work. But it had to be relatively secluded to avoid the risk of anyone hearing screams, so that eliminates public parking lots. He may have had an accomplice who provided a secure place to abuse his victims."

Crowe agreed. "The interesting thing is the periodicity of the killings, averaging just under two years. Maybe something brought him here on a regular basis, like a conference or some scheduled association activity."

"We looked at convention schedules," Levinson said. "No matter whether they're political, business, or cultural, they tend to recur in the same month, or at least, the same season. But this guy's schedule drifts backwards through the year, which forced us to look at religious calendars, like the Islamic New Year and the Muslim holidays of Ramadan and Eid. As it turns out, they're all quite regular. Once you know one, you can calculate the next by moving it up two weeks earlier. Yet these murders are spaced out two years less a month or more, sometimes even less regular."

Crowe concluded his input. "Final observation, Thi Nguyen's murder doesn't fit with the others. She was the oldest victim, her body wasn't dumped in public, and her murder occurred the same week as another. It feels like a copycat killing, with only some of the signatures in place."

"I agree, but because of the common factors, we were obliged to include her with the rest."

"Are you getting a lot of heat on this?"

"Several Asian council members sit on the Committee for Community Affairs. They're giving the Deputy Commissioner regular grief about our failure to arrest a suspect."

"I noticed the absence of any strong suspects."

Levinson shrugged. "Despite all our interviews with victims' friends and family, we identified only a handful of people worth a look. Even the low-lifers associated with the Filipino hooker turned out to have air-tight alibis."

"Okay. I made notes of the key elements. I just need time to digest this." Crowe pushed the case files back across the table.

Levinson eyed the three blue folders Crowe had kept on his side of the table. "What are those?"

"Some files from Seth Greer's home office."

"Anything relevant?"

"Too soon to say." Crowe told him about the three files - Golden Triangle heroin, the forged art market, and sex trafficking. None of it pointed a finger at Bishop, but the overlap with Southeast Asia was something to explore further.

Levinson walked him to the elevator. "Good luck, and I mean that, for both our sakes."

"I'll be in touch."

Crowe surrendered his visitor's badge and left the building. He walked west on 82nd to Broadway, where a 15-story building topped with a tower commanded the corner. He looked up and saw a lone bird wheeling high above. By its size and shape, he guessed it was a peregrine falcon.

The bird triggered an association - the peregrine planet. Peregrine was a word of Latin origins meaning "alien" or "foreigner". Medieval astrologers considered a planet without dignity in a horoscope as being isolated from the other planets.

To be without dignity typically meant the planet wasn't in a sign it ruled, nor in a sign where it was exalted, nor in a house where it was strong.

Symbolically, therefore, a peregrine planet was a drifter without status in his current environment. Therefore, the planet, or person signified, might act out in ways contrary to core values.

This reinforced Crowe's idea that the Riverside Rapist was from out of town, a drifter with no stake in the community, thus emboldened to violate dharma.

Astrological theory said, a peregrine planet in the chart was sometimes the key to understanding a person's behavior.

Two other notions arose from the concept of the peregrine planet - outrider, and outlier. An outrider was a guide or forerunner. In statistics, an outlier was an anomaly, numerically distant from the rest of the data, deviating from other members of the sample in which it occurred.

In the case of the outrider, Crowe could only speculate - was the Riverside Rapist the harbinger of worse to come, or merely the tip of the iceberg for things that had already happened?

As for the outlier, his thoughts immediately returned to Thi Nguyen, the only victim who'd been discovered dead in her home. Her circumstances didn't fit the rest of the data set. And for that reason perhaps, her case deserved closer scrutiny.

Study the peregrine, solve the puzzle.

28

CROWE CALLED TRACEY to see if she was free this evening. She was apologetic, saying she'd just been notified there'd been a triple homicide in the theater district, evidence was being collected at the crime scene, and she'd been put on notice that material would be arriving at the lab within the hour.

"Depending on how much of a rush the detectives put on it, I could be looking at an all-nighter," she said. "But until the evidence arrives, I've got a little time to kill. Do you want to meet for coffee in the vicinity?"

They agreed to meet at Bagel Stix on Eighth Avenue. Crowe took the Broadway line to Columbus Circle and walked down to 53rd Street. Tracey was already there with a coffee in a corner booth. Crowe got a tea and sat opposite her.

He told her about Levinson's cold case files. She knew about the Riverside Rapist because one of his victims, the Filipino prostitute, had lived and worked in the jurisdiction of Midtown North. Although the hooker had been murdered a few years before Tracey joined the NYPD, the case had crossed her desk when sustained pressure from the Asian community had obliged the Deputy Commissioner to authorize overtime dedicated to the unsolved cases.

"I had to review all of the forensics - blood work, vaginal and anal swabs, bite marks, ligature marks - looking for a connection to any of the suspects they'd ever identified. Nothing matched."

"Tell me about the case. Do you remember anything out of the ordinary?"

"She had extensive bruising around the ankles. Of course I didn't see the body when it was originally processed, but the file photos tell a compelling story. I think she was hung upside down for quite a while. The ligature marks were deep behind the ankle, and the angle of the ligature around the rest of the ankle was consistent with the way a rope would cut into the skin if the person was suspended."

"Like an animal to be butchered."

"I never thought of it that way, but you're right."

"That'd require a relatively high ceiling."

"Yes."

"Not suspended inside a van or a truck."

"Certainly not a van, anyway. Why do you mention that?"

"The general file, which you may not have read, theorizes

that the Riverside Rapist may have been an itinerant. One theory is that he was operating out of a camper van or something like it."

"Maybe so, but this victim was suspended somewhere with an overhead clearance much higher than any moving van. Cube trucks, for example, have a vertical dimension of only six and half feet."

"That's not enough to hang a Filipino upside-down? They're not that tall."

"Four foot eleven."

"You remember that?"

"I remember she was average height for her ethnicity. I looked it up."

"So why couldn't she have been hung up in a moving van?"

"Because of the extensive bite marks all around her waist area – buttocks, inner thighs, pudendum."

"I noticed that in the file. What about them?"

"They were all inverted bites. Meaning the upper teeth marks were lower on her body than the lower teeth marks. You follow me?"

"Yes, I get it. But how does that tell you she was hung upside down and bitten? Why couldn't she have been bitten before or after she was hung upside down?"

"It's possible. But the clustering of the bites implies she was bitten while hanging upside down, in a place with a relatively high ceiling. The average American man is five foot ten. That places his average mouth at a height of five foot two, or 62 inches. The distance from foot to coccyx of the average Filipino woman is about 26 inches. So if you add those two, you get 88 inches, which is roughly the height between the biter's feet and the upside-down victim's feet."

"That's seven foot four."

"Right. And we haven't yet allowed for anything above that, like a hook, pulley, pipe or cross-beam from which the victim could have been suspended."

"So now we're talking about a ceiling eight to nine feet in

height."

"A lot bigger than a moving van or cube truck. Unless we're talking about one of those big moving trucks. But they're not allowed on Riverside Drive where the bodies were dumped."

"That means the Riverside Rapist, if indeed he was from out-of-town, had a place to do his dirty work. Which implies an accomplice, unwitting or not, who provided the place."

"Good luck with that."

He shrugged. "I guess there's nothing easy about a cold case."

Tracey's phone rang. She answered it, listened a few moments, and said she was just around the corner, she'd be back in a few minutes. She closed the phone and looked at him. "Duty calls."

29

BACK AT THE WASHINGTON SQUARE HOTEL, Crowe stripped to his underwear and did some yoga on the floor. He finished with *shavasana*, the corpse pose, which segued into a brief but refreshing nap. He shaved and showered, made some green tea and settled down to study the three files he'd taken from Greer's office.

The *Rancho Gomorrah* file contained excerpts from several studies done by the Attorney General and the Department of Justice. An estimated 15,000 people annually were trafficked illegally into the USA from Thailand, the Philippines, India, Mexico, the Caribbean and Central America. Half were under 18 years old, most destined for the sex trade. Trafficking proliferated in high-population areas and international travel hubs in California, New York, Texas and Florida.

Houston was a major player. Multiple sporting events, conventions and festivals made the city a prime location for trafficking. It had over 200 brothels, with two new openings each month. It surpassed Vegas in the number of strip clubs and massage parlors that served as fronts for sex trafficking. Pimps flocked to Houston to ply their trade.

The file included memos from several official sources - state legislators, district attorneys, vice detectives and social workers. It also included interviews from anonymous informants - madams, pimps, hookers, lap dancers and "coyotes" who smuggled people across the Mexican border.

Despite the focus on Houston, there was a local element. US Citizenship & Immigration Service officers in New York claimed sex trafficking brought as many as 3,000 girls a year from Thailand and the Philippines. Once here, they were absorbed into local brothels, massage parlors and strip clubs, or sold off to other sex-trade operators throughout New England.

Greer had started a handwritten list of Manhattan clubs and massage parlors where USCIS knew or suspected sex trafficking victims of being employed. The list ran two pages, with over three dozen names and addresses.

Crowe opened the *Rogue Elephants* file, whose subject was the Golden Triangle, an area overlapping the borders of Burma, Vietnam, Laos and Thailand. After Afghanistan, Burma was the world's second largest producer of illicit opium, a major player in the international drug trade since WW2. Opiate exports were worth as much as all legal exports. Drug money fueled every economic activity in Burma, and big foreign partners shielded money laundering.

Opium and heroin base produced in northeast Burma were transported by horse, donkey and elephant caravans to refineries along the Thai-Burmese border for conversion to heroin. Most finished product crossed the border into north Thailand and then to Bangkok for international distribution. Thai Chinese and Burmese Chinese traffickers in Bangkok controlled foreign sales and shipment from Thailand.

Southeast Asian heroin typically entered the USA via couriers, usually Thai and US nationals on commercial airlines. California and Hawaii were primary entry points, but traffic was rising in New York and Washington. Traffickers initially had difficulty arranging distribution, but with growing incarceration of Asians in American prisons, contacts between prisoners gave access to organized gangs selling street heroin.

Allegations of CIA involvement in the heroin trade persisted. This dated back to the 1950s when the CIA used one of their business fronts, Air America, to fly heroin from Bangkok to China to help support the anti-Communist regime of Chiang Kai-Shek. During the Vietnam War, Air America again transported heroin to help fund the secret war in Laos. During the Soviet occupation of Afghanistan, the CIA supported the *mujahideen* who were also drug lords.

Greer had interviewed a wide range of people during his research - district attorneys, DEA officers, NYPD narcs, former Air America pilots, couriers and street dealers. Again, New York was active, and Crowe noted the frequency of Thai names, either people suspected of being key players, or businesses that might be laundering heroin revenues.

The *Artful Dodger* file was about art forgery. A Wikipedia page listed known forgers and dealers in forged art. Among them was Hans Van Meegeren, a Dutchman who painted and sold fake Vermeers to the Nazis in WW2. Since the post-sixties explosion of the art market, a large number of fake masters had been discovered in the past five decades. Museums went on high alert, employing panels of experts to examine works of art with scientific tools.

But since highly skilled artisans also understood the science behind curators' analyses, forgery had become increasingly sophisticated. Forgers bought centuries-old framed canvases to paint over, using home-made pigments mixed from recipes of the masters. Sculpted marbles were mined from indigenous quarries, and cast bronzes were aged by years of earth burial.

In addition to the physical authenticity of art works, curators also had to verify provenance. Certificates of authenticity from dead experts could be forged, along with deeds of sale. There were sometimes elaborate accounts of how a particular work of art had changed hands in a transaction, just outside the law, during times of war.

As for antiquities, they were more likely stolen than forged. Spain had looted Central and South America. England and France had plundered the art treasures of India and Egypt. Napoleon's armies robbed Russia, and the Nazis pillaged Europe. During the Vietnam War, many Buddhist temples were looted. During the Iraq invasion, whole museum exhibits of ancient Mesopotamian art disappeared overnight.

As an example, the file contained a picture of a statue - a temple warrior whose sale by Sotheby's had been blocked by Cambodia's claim it was looted from the ruins of a Khmer temple at Koh Ker.

Greer had interviewed federal prosecutors, fraud detectives, museum directors, art curators, collectors and art dealers. Since it was a key player in the global the art market, New York was well represented in a list of art galleries and dealers who'd been known or suspected of trading in forged or stolen works of art.

Crowe closed the file and stared at the ceiling. The *Rancho Gomorrah* and *Rogue Elephants* files had some obvious overlaps - smuggling, trafficking, Thailand, organized crime - but the *Artful Dodger* file highlighted a criminal activity that almost seemed abstract. Or did it just seem so because it was a white-collar crime whose victims were faceless museums or countries, as opposed to the real human tragedy of prostitutes and drug addicts?

Crowe wondered what these three files had in common. Why had Greer concealed them from easy discovery? So close to the door of his condo, as if he might need to leave with them in a hurry...

30

IT WAS SEVEN O'CLOCK and Crowe hadn't eaten anything since a falafel sandwich at noon. He recalled Kevin Blaikie's offer to get together and decided that, despite the hour, he'd call Blaikie on the off chance he was free on short notice to go out for dinner.

First, however, he planned his outing so as to kill two birds with one stone. After reading about the many Thai connections in two of Greer's research files, he'd been reminded of Kitti Poornchai. Dean Bishop's companion at the Dharmapada ashram had disappeared as soon as the silent retreat was over. She'd refused Crowe's offer of a ride to New York, and been spirited away by Lieutenant Lynch to the bus station in White Junction.

Crowe pulled out his copy of Poornchai's registration sheet and checked to see what she'd given as phone and address. It was a 212 area code number with an address on Wall Street Court. Crowe shook his head. That didn't sound right. How could she afford to live in the heart of the Wall Street district?

He used his hotel phone to call the number. A man answered with a slight accent Crowe could only peg as Asian. "Thai High Restaurant."

"May I speak with Kitti Poornchai?"

There was a momentary pause. "I'm sorry, but she doesn't work here anymore."

"Do you know where I can reach her?"

"She didn't leave a forwarding address."

"What about a phone number?"

"Who's calling, please?"

"I'm a friend. We were on a retreat together last week in Vermont."

"What's your name, friend?"

"Dean Bishop."

There was a longer pause. "You are not Mr. Bishop."

"Why, because he's there? May I speak with him, please?"

A dial tone buzzed in Crowe's ear like an irritated wasp. He put the phone back on its cradle and stared at the registration sheet. Kitti had used the phone number and address of a restaurant as her contact information. Apparently she'd once worked there, but no longer did. What had happened to her?

Crowe phoned Kevin Blaikie. His longstanding client was a corporate lawyer for whom he sometimes traced hard-to-find witnesses and whistle-blowers in major cases of corporate malfeasance. Blaikie was also heir to a billion-dollar family fortune but you wouldn't know it from his modest manner. Last year Blaikie's sister Janis had been killed in what had appeared to be a mugging gone bad. Blaikie had appealed to Crowe for help and, after a week's sleuthing, Crowe had uncovered a three-way murder conspiracy. The phone rang only twice before it was picked up.

"Hello."

"Kevin, it's Axel. What are you up to this evening?"

"Not much. Playing chess with myself and sipping scotch."

"Who's winning?"

"Spassky. It's the opening game of the 1972 World Championship in Reykjavik. Fischer just made a dumb move."

"Have you eaten?"

"No, but I am getting hungry. Grandmaster chess is hard mental labor. My brain is starting to gnaw the inside of my skull."

"So let's take your frontal lobe out for dinner."

"Okay, but I'm buying."

Half an hour later, a midnight blue BMW 750 pulled up in front of the Washington Square Hotel. Having been alerted by cell phone that Blaikie was within a block, Crowe stepped out of the hotel and entered the car. The two men shook hands.

"Where do you want to eat?" Blaikie said. "It's a Monday night, so I can make a quick call and probably get a table at Le Bernardin."

"Do you know a place called Thai High on Wall Street Court?"

"No, but I've heard it's... interesting."

"Feel like broadening your taste buds' horizons?"

Blaikie put the car in gear and headed toward Broadway. Crowe explained the reason for his interest in Thai High, saying Kitti Poornchai had given the restaurant's phone and address as her New York residence.

"It's an historic building, a dozen stories or more," Blaikie said. "Even if the ground floor is occupied by the restaurant, she might have a condo on one of the upper floors."

"How much is a condo in the area worth?"

"Walking distance to the Exchange, home-away-from-home for thousands of testosterone-charged hedge fund managers...? Probably a million for a studio."

"You think such an owner would consent to an eight-hour milk run on a bus from Vermont to New York?"

"More likely take a limo."

"Exactly."

"Maybe she doesn't own. Maybe stays with a friend who lives there."

"Her friend lives in Tribeca." The background check by Levinson's people had confirmed Bishop's address.

"Is her friend wealthy? Some people park their spare cash in real estate. Despite occasional market corrections, Manhattan property keeps shooting for the moon. Just when you think it can't get any pricier, it does. And next quarter, it does it again."

As they continued toward the financial district, Crowe thanked Blaikie again for helping with Abbott's legal case. Blaikie was nonchalant about his contribution.

"I spoke to his lawyer. The circumstantial evidence against Abbott is substantial. The District Attorney's office made a strong case that he's a flight risk. The Canadian border is only an hour and a half away, and from Montreal you can fly to anywhere in the world. The DA asked for bail to be denied and the judge concurred."

"What substantial evidence?"

"The autopsy's been done. The shovel found near the victim was definitely the murder weapon. Abbott's prints are on it."

"No surprise, considering it was farm property. And I know Abbott does a bit of gardening. A good lawyer should be able to defuse that evidence. The killer could have stolen the shovel from the tool shed."

"It gets worse," Blaikie said. "Apparently the police returned to the property on Sunday and conducted a house search. They found Greer's laptop. They haven't finished going through it all, but apparently one of the files included research notes on spiritual organizations and money laundering."

"Man, that cop's like a dog with a bone." Crowe told Blaikie about his discussion with Magnusson, who'd said Lynch had jumped to conclusions as soon as he heard about some of Greer's open files.

"Or maybe he's just a sharp cop following a lead," Blaikie said. "Anyway, it's looking very serious, so legal representation is an issue. Abbott's lawyer doesn't even handle criminal cases but he recommended a few big firms in Burlington. I made a few calls and hired the best. Their top guy will be up to speed in a day."

"That was fast." Crowe knew Blaikie wouldn't allude to it, but money was a powerful incentive.

"Yeah, well, he's going to have his work cut out for him. Between the files on Greer's stolen laptop and Abbott's prints on the shovel, it's not looking good. The implication is that Abbott had something to hide, and killed Greer to keep it a secret."

31

BLAIKIE FOUND UNDERGROUND PARKING in the financial district. They walked to the nearby Thai High restaurant, located in a narrow wedge of a 15-story building that separated Pearl and Beaver streets, its front door facing Wall Street.

"This is the old Cocoa Exchange Building." Blaikie opened the door. "Used to be a sushi restaurant a year ago, but it changed hands."

A Thai hostess showed them a table. A line of potted bamboo trees separated the dining area from the bar. A bas-relief of a reclining golden Buddha spanned the wall behind the bar, striking Crowe as incongruous, since Buddha nature was the antithesis of intoxication. The floor was bamboo, the tables dark wood, the light from suspended globes muted. Between the windows looking onto Pearl and Beaver Streets were wall-mounted figurines of Thai dancers and *Kinnari,* the bird-woman deity.

Crowe recalled his dream in Montreal, the night before he'd received Abbott's call for help. Did the *kinnari*'s appearance mean something? In Thai mythology, the hybrid form of the deity symbolized her ability to fly between human and mystical worlds.

A waitress asked if they'd like a drink. She was beautiful, wearing high heels and a green silk dress slit to the hip, revealing a swath of flawless thigh. The dress was sleeved, but scooped at front and back, revealing just enough cleavage to provoke the imagination.

Blaikie ordered a glass of white wine, Crowe a mango juice.

"Have you gentlemen been here before?"

"No," Blaikie said. "What do you recommend?"

"That depends on what you and your friend are looking for."

Crowe, who'd already intuited where this might lead, said, "What every devotee of international cuisine seeks –

something to tease and delight the palate."

She turned her almond eyes on him. "We can satisfy all your cravings - depending on your appetite and the time to indulge - in a single meal."

"Sounds wonderful," Blaikie said. "It makes my mouth water just listening to you."

"That makes two of us." She smiled and dipped her torso as she turned his wine glass upright, giving him a better view down her dress. "There's a gentleman's lounge on the second floor where you can sample some appetizers, or private rooms on the third where you can order anything you want. If you like, I can be your personal tour guide."

Blaikie fanned himself with his menu. "Thank you, but for the moment, we'll just try the food."

"That's fine. We hope your Thai High experience is a memorable one. I'll be back in a minute with your drinks."

Blaikie and Crowe watched her walk away, the high heels making her hips swing hypnotically. After she'd passed through the bamboo grove to the bar, they turned back to their menus.

"What was that all about?" Blaikie said.

"We can speculate later," Crowe said. "Let's figure out what to eat."

The waitress returned with their drinks. "Ready to order, or did you want to go upstairs for an appetizer or two?"

"Roast duck in red curry," Blaikie said.

"Ginger shrimp for me," Crowe said. Although he was for the most part a vegetarian, he occasionally refreshed his memory of how good well-prepared seafood tasted.

She nodded and walked away without another word. Obviously, they weren't worth wasting any more of her charm.

"Did you know about this place?" Crowe said. "Not the restaurant, but the so-called gentleman's club and the private rooms upstairs?"

"No, but it wouldn't be the first place to offer a full-service business. In the nineties there was Caligula on the

Upper West Side, a swinger's club with restaurant and bar, rooms rented by the hour. Just before nine-eleven there was a place in SoHo called Kama Sutra, a restaurant and bar with private rooms for expanding your sexual consciousness."

"How were they?"

"I never went to either, but I know people who did. That whole love-for-hire business isn't for me. It smacks of desperation. I'd rather be celibate."

Their food arrived. They ate with gusto and caught up on news. Blaikie's parents were a concern these days. Since his sister's death last year, his already-frail mother had spiraled into Alzheimer's, while his father had developed mobility problems. Crowe was sympathetic, but the contrast with his younger and healthier parents made him grateful.

During their meal they noticed several men - singles, pairs and once a foursome - led by a hostess behind a bamboo wall near the bar, where they disappeared. Curious, Crowe visited the washroom and made a detour to look behind the bamboo wall. He saw an alcove with an elevator door and a numeric keypad. He pressed the elevator button but the door didn't open, possibly needing a code to access the upper floors.

"Find anything?" Blaikie asked when Crowe returned.

"Maybe the door to Pandora's Box."

"Want to take a peek?"

"My imagination can fill in the blanks."

"Isn't a picture worth a thousand words?"

Crowe laughed. "Maybe you just want an excuse to go."

"Just trying to help." Blaikie leaned forward. "If you think this might lead to something that could get your friend out of jail, we should check it out."

Crowe looked at his watch. Nine thirty. The ascendant had changed about ten minutes ago, from Libra to Scorpio. The Rahu-Ketu axis now lay along the horizon, inviting experimentation, novelty, the exotic, the forbidden. The Moon and Venus, both strong in Taurus, were still above the western horizon, suggesting a connection to be made via a woman.

And Mars was overhead, urging action...

"Okay, let's do it."

When the waitress removed their plates, Blaikie told her they'd take a *digestif* upstairs. A few minutes later, she returned with their bill. Blaikie glanced at it.

"The additional two hundred dollars...?"

"For the gentleman's lounge. The first drink is complimentary."

Blaikie gave her his credit card. She used a remote unit to complete the transaction, and gave him a receipt. She beckoned for them to follow.

In the alcove, the waitress pressed three numbers on the keypad to access the elevator. Crowe looked up and saw a tiny camera in the corner of the elevator car. The door opened on the floor above and they entered a lounge. It was carpeted, with shuttered windows, clusters of leather furniture separated by dividers. The ambient music featured oriental flute with jazzy inflection.

She led them past a bar where two female bartenders mixed drinks. Girls in sarongs and high heels - all Thai beauties - circulated among the patrons. Through a gap between dividers, Crowe saw a man getting a lap dance in a deep leather chair. Their waitress guided them into an enclosure with a love seat and two club chairs in red leather. Blaikie settled into a chair, Crowe in the love seat.

"What would you like to drink?" she asked.

Blaikie ordered two cognacs, knowing that if Crowe declined to drink, he'd have a double.

"Been here before?" she asked. "Anyone you'd like to see again?"

Now wasn't the time to mention Kitti Poornchai, but if Crowe followed the trail of the planets, he might find what he was looking for. With both Moon and Venus in Taurus, it was a young woman. He used a technique associating sounds with the signs of the zodiac.

"A friend told me about a girl here. I forget her name, but it began with 'ch'. Something like Chastity, Cherry, China...?"

"Chandra?"

"That's her!" Crowe felt like he'd won the lottery. Not only did the name begin with a phoneme associated with Taurus, but Chandra was literally the Sanskrit name for the Moon.

"Let me see if she's available."

A bar-girl brought their cognacs on a tray. Blaikie sampled his and nodded approval. Crowe left his untouched.

Five minutes later, a girl appeared. She was just what Crowe had anticipated - young, lush and slightly deranged. She wore a mini-sarong with high heels accentuating the line of her legs. Except for her breasts, she was slim, verging on anorexic. Her face was beautiful but the look in her eyes suggested poor sleep and nervous exhaustion. She smiled and looked from Blaikie to Crowe.

"You like another girl to join us?" she asked with an accent.

"You're all I want, Chandra." Crowe patted the love seat, beckoning her to sit beside him. "My friend is celibate."

Blaikie rolled his eyes and sipped his cognac.

Crowe took her right hand in his. She had a slim palm with long pliable fingers - a water hand - emotional and susceptible to influence. In Chandra's hand, where the head and heart lines normally were, a single line spanned her palm. The simian line. Nineteenth century palmists saw it as a sign of sub-standard intelligence, but the idea still carried weight in modern palmistry.

"You have warm hands," Chandra said.

"You have poor circulation," Crowe said.

"You saying I have a cold heart?"

"Not cold, just hurt."

She lowered her eyes. He scanned her palm for individuating features. Her little finger was short, crooked and askew. Sexual trauma, probably rape, possibly at the hands of a family member. In the heel of her palm was a horizontal mark called *visha rekha*. The poison line was a red flag for substance abuse. He looked in her eyes. The lighting was dim, and brown eyes hard to penetrate, but he saw flecks of gold in her iris and knew she had an addiction. These were the chains that bound her.

She withdrew her hand and placed it on his thigh. "You want to come upstairs with me?"

"Let me get to know you first." Crowe lifted her hand from his thigh and held it lightly, his fingers curled around her wrist. "Where are you from in Thailand?"

"Ko Lanta."

Crowe knew it, a large island in the south. "I was there a few years before the *tsunami*. Were you there when it happened?"

"Yes."

"Did you lose family?"

"My mother, two sisters and a brother."

"And everything changed after that." A world turned upside-down, left in the care of a father who'd lost his wife, his desperation a petri dish in which nasty things might have flourished...

She nodded.

"Do you know Kitti?"

She looked at him, expression frozen, lips parted but nothing coming out. Sometimes silence did speak volumes. Furthermore, the hop and skip of her pulse beneath his fingertips told him the answer.

"Is she here?"

She hesitated, and he gave her wrist a sharp squeeze. He hated to treat her like this, but she'd been conditioned to behave in certain ways, and without a stick or its threat, there'd be no response.

"No."

"Where can I find her?"

She shrugged. "Long Island."

"Long Island is big. What town?"

"Babylon."

"What's the address?"

"I don't remember. It's near the highway."

"Describe the house."

"Ordinary. Two stories, an attached garage."

"When did you see her last?"

She shook her head as if trying to clear her memory. "Two weeks ago."

Crowe released her wrist.

She looked at him. "You want to come upstairs with me?"

"No. I have to be home in bed by eleven."

She laughed. "You big boy. You should stay and play with me."

"We're not into the same games."

"I play everything. You have a special game? I learn fast."

"I'm sure you do." Crowe stood.

She turned to Blaikie. "What about you, mister? Upstairs I show you everything."

"Sorry, I'm his chauffeur. When he leaves, I go too." Blaikie took a few bills from his wallet and pressed them into her hand. "But thank you for the offer. You're a beautiful young woman."

"Maybe you prefer lady boy? She is busy right now but maybe in half an hour...?"

"Thank you, no trannies."

Blaikie was still shaking his head as he and Crowe descended in the elevator. They left the restaurant and returned to the car.

On the way back to Washington Square, Crowe said, "How can I find out who owns Thai High?"

"Business registry office. I know a guy. I'll make a call."

"I really appreciate it."

"I'm still trying to pay you back for Janis last year," Blaikie said. "And let's face it, my life is pretty boring. If it weren't for living vicariously through your adventures, I'd have nothing to contribute in cocktail hour conversations."

32

Tuesday, April 24

CROWE AWOKE NATURALLY at five AM, showered and shaved. He meditated for half an hour and did some yoga. He used his astrology app to calculate a chart for the day. He made some tea and drank it as he memorized the current planetary positions, a daily mental discipline he'd observed ever since Guruji had drilled it into him fifteen years ago.

An astrologer must develop a powerful memory, Guruji had said. *Knowledge without memory is like money locked in a vault. If he cannot remember his PIN, a millionaire is no more than a pauper.* Guruji was a man of his time. Although schooled in ancient ways, he had a knack for modern metaphors.

Crowe went for a walk around Washington Square Park. The birds were noisy in the trees and a flock of pigeons were pecking at a handful of sesame seeds scattered on the sidewalk. From one of the highest trees a lone crow cawed three times. Crowe was tempted to call back to a kindred spirit but there were dog-walkers nearby and he didn't want to look like a kook.

He walked over to Sheridan Square and ate breakfast in a small restaurant with a view of the gardens. He was still thinking about what he'd learned last night at Thai High, wondering how he could possibly find the house in Long Island that Chandra had told him about.

He returned to his hotel and killed some time browsing the complimentary newspaper left outside his door.

At seven thirty he walked to Cooper Square. The atmosphere at *The Village Voice* was less frenetic than yesterday, but he still had to undergo a body scan at the security desk before being issued a visitor's pass to visit Magnusson.

In his office the editor was pounding away at his computer keyboard like a piano player trying to catch up to a tune from half a bar behind. As Crowe appeared in the doorway, he paused typing just long enough to reach into his briefcase and hand over a sheaf of paper.

"Read it here." He gestured to a chair. "But no questions, I'm on a deadline."

Crowe sat and flipped through the sheaf in hand. The draft article was about twenty pages of double-spaced text. Appended were another ten pages of miscellaneous notes, some typed, some handwritten.

The story concerned stolen art and antiquities. Since the creation of the National Stolen Property Act, the US Attorney's Office had been empowered to prosecute art dealers, galleries and museums lacking air-tight provenance for art and antiquities found in their possession.

This had become a major issue for museums ever since 2011 when LA's Getty Museum, after failing to provide proof of legal acquisition, had been forced to return to Italy its statue of Aphrodite. The scandal ended the career of the museum's antiquities curator, and exposed how the Getty and other museums had added stolen property to their collections.

The US Attorney's Office had since gone after museums across the country. Because donations to museums generated tax deductions for donors, many museums had received gifts of art and antiquities worth millions. Although most wealthy patrons donated art out of sheer charity, some canny billionaires simply acquired art to donate in exchange for tax deductions.

The widespread practice had created a bubble market. Curators were often encouraged by donors to over-evaluate items, meanwhile under pressure not to investigate too aggressively the paperwork concerning provenance - dates of discovery, import/export records, authenticity certificates and deeds of ownership.

Under the NSPA, there was no statute of limitations. No matter when an item had been acquired, possession without proper provenance was a crime. The museum's curator and board of directors were all liable for prosecution, and the museum could be forced to forfeit its holding.

Over the past few years, federal agents had paid surprise visits to dozens of museums, demanding proof of provenance. If found lacking, they removed the items pending resolution of lawful ownership. Museum officials scrambled to protect themselves from prosecution.

Greer's story wove in two other elements. One was about local players in the world of art and antiquities, not only museums but also private collectors and galleries whose feeder networks supplied them. The other was the shadow-world of forgers, thieves and smugglers who supplied product to a market which, despite its legal risks, offered great financial incentive.

It was like the game of hot potato. When the music stopped, whoever was caught holding the objet d'art was guilty. Thieves and smugglers had the least to lose, because the items moved quickly through their hands. But once it ended up in a collection - private or public - it became a stationary target at risk for discovery and prosecution.

Greer's story was apparently incomplete, but from the volume of his notes and the appended list of contacts, it was clear he'd had intentions to flesh out the story. There was a list of museums, with names and phone numbers of directors and curators. There was a longer list of galleries and their directors, and a shorter list of collectors.

On a couple of these lists, Greer had penned a red arrow with the word "key" in the margin. One was a curator, Roxanne Morton at the Manhattan Museum of Asian Antiquities. Another was a collector named Arthur Phuket. A gallery in SoHo called The Bodhi Tree was also flagged.

Crowe took out his phone. Magnusson was still absorbed in his race to a looming deadline, his fingers dancing across the keyboard as if it were too hot to touch. Crowe took a picture of each contact list. He fastened the clip on the sheaf and put it back on Magnusson's desk.

The editor paused a moment and turned to look at Crowe, his eyes coming into focus as if he'd just realized someone else was in the office. "Anything useful?"

"I don't know, but it gives me some ideas. Thanks for letting me take a look."

"Glad I could help. Sorry I can't talk now, but if you want to grab a drink end of day, I'm generally thirsty. Give me a call."

Crowe nodded and left.

33

CROWE CHECKED HIS PHONE for Dean Bishop's address, which he'd copied from the registration sheet at Dharmapada. It was on Vestry Street in Tribeca. It was about a mile away so he decided to walk it. He set off down Bowery. En route, he called Blaikie.

"Morning." Blaikie's voice sounded hoarse.

"Rough night?"

"I didn't sleep that well."

"Dreams of Thai dancing girls?"

"More like a nightmare," Blaikie groaned. "I dreamed I was staying with friends in Florida. I went for a late-night swim in their pool and an alligator grabbed my leg. What do you make of that, Dr. Freud?"

"No more cognac for you at bedtime."

Blaikie chuckled. "Anyway, thanks for the wake-up call. I need to get on with my day."

"When you call your friend at the business registry to ask who owns Thai High, see if the same person owns any property in Babylon."

"That house in Long Island the girl talked about? What do you think, some sort of brothel?"

"Maybe."

"I'll see what I can do. Might take more than one call, but my guy will know how to go about it."

"Give me a buzz as soon as you know something."

"Be careful out there."

Crowe continued his walk. Half an hour later he was at the corner of Vestry and Greenwich. Bishop lived in a seven-story condo building, what had once been a port warehouse, judging by the faded paint lettering on the brick wall above the Greenwich Grill.

Crowe called the phone number given on Bishop's registration sheet. A voicemail message said: "You've reached Edgewater Risk Management. Business hours are Monday to Friday, nine to five. Please leave your name and number. Someone will contact you shortly."

Crowe left a message. "Good morning, Mr. Bishop. You don't know me but I work with Bryan Abbott. I'd like to get some feedback on your recent retreat experience." He left his number.

Crowe sat on the steps of the Greenwich Grill debating his next move. He wanted to confront Bishop about what had happened at the retreat on Friday, why he'd decked Greer. Although a straight answer was unlikely, even lies in response to the right questions might reveal something. But if Bishop didn't answer the phone, how could he ask him?

Crowe took out his phone and opened his astrology app. He asked himself, was Bishop at home, and when might he intercept him? The app calculated a chart for 08:08, using local GPS coordinates.

Taurus was rising in the sidereal zodiac. Venus and the Moon, both representing Bishop, were still together in fixed sign Taurus. Bishop was at home. Fourth lord Mars and twelfth lord Sun were in an exchange relationship, suggesting he was also hiding.

Venus was three-and-a-half degrees below the ascendant. Since the ascendant moved about one degree every four minutes, this meant Bishop could appear in roughly 15 minutes.

The Rahu-Ketu axis, a fault line for eclipses in the chart, ran across the horizon. Ketu was in the first house, debilitated in Taurus. That suggested some kind of poison - tobacco, alcohol, recreational drugs.

He looked for another weak planet. Mercury, ruling lungs, was debilitated in Pisces and afflicted by Mars, ruling fire. Kitti Poornchai smoked, perhaps Bishop did too. Maybe he'd go out for a pack of cigarettes.

Crowe walked to the corner of Vestry and Greenwich, from where he could see the entrance to Bishop's condo building. He could intercept him if he came this way, or follow him if he walked west on Vestry.

He checked the time. 8:20. He felt his body tensing up and gave it some attention, willing himself to shake out his arms, loosen his shoulders. He did the same with his legs, rotating his hips. He took a few deep breaths and exhaled slowly, letting the air drift out of him like invisible smoke.

A man emerged from the Vestry street entrance and headed toward the intersection. He wore some sort of basketball jacket, black with red sleeves. Crowe watched him from across the street. The timing was right on; this could be Bishop.

The man walked briskly, upper body tilted forward as if walking into a gale. Crowe kept pace from across the street. On the next block, the man entered a convenience store. Crowe crossed the street and entered. The man was at the counter, asking for three packs of Marlboro Reds. Crowe bought a bottle of water and followed him into the street.

The man paused a few doors down, tore the wrapper from a pack and tossed it to the curb. He lit a cigarette, took a deep puff and headed back toward his condo.

"Hey, Dean," Crowe called from a few steps back.

Bishop stopped and turned, thus confirming his identity. "Do I know you?"

Bishop was just under six feet, with a rangy physique. He had a narrow face beneath a shock of black hair, and prominent eyebrows with a deep vertical furrow between them. If he was a meditator, Crowe thought, he was doing it all wrong. Age notwithstanding, stress was etched in the lines of his face.

"I left a message on your phone twenty minutes ago."

"I don't have time for some bullshit survey. Why are you following me?" Bishop studied him a moment. "More importantly, *who* are you?"

"A friend of Abbott's."

"What do you want?"

"Did you know Seth Greer was dead?"

"I heard that, yeah."

"From whom?"

Bishop hesitated. "Lieutenant Lynch from the Vermont State Police. He called to ask where I was around midnight on Friday. But I was already back here in New York by that time. So if you're looking for whoever did him, it wasn't me."

"Last Friday you and Greer got into an argument. You knocked him down. What was that about?"

"Like I told Lynch, the guy made a dirty remark about the woman I was with."

"Kitti Poornchai? Is she your girlfriend?"

"Listen, pal. You're starting to irritate me. Persist, and you're going to be sorry."

"Is that what you told Greer before you hit him? Or didn't he get a warning?"

Bishop resumed his brisk walk toward his condo. Crowe kept pace.

"Have you talked to Kitti since she came back from Vermont?"

"No. And she's not my girlfriend."

"You went to the retreat together."

"She's more like a business associate."

"She works for you?"

"None of your business."

"Do you know where I can find her?"

"I think she's gone back to Thailand."

"How do you know? Did she tell you?"

"She'd been talking about it."

"Why did she leave? She in some kind of trouble?"

"She had some family stuff to take care of back home."

"Where's her family? Bangkok?"

"Why are you so interested in Kitti?"

"She may have seen something the night Greer died."

"Kitti doesn't know anything."

"How do you know, if you weren't there? You've already admitted you haven't talked to her since Friday."

They arrived at the condo entrance. Bishop dropped his cigarette butt and ground it beneath his heel. He squared off to face Crowe, the furrow between his eyebrows now so pronounced that it seemed like his face could split open at that fissure and something ugly - like a creature from *Alien* - might emerge to bite Crowe's head off.

"What's your name, pal? Who are you working for?"

"Axel Crowe. But I'm not working for anyone. I'm just trying to shed a little light on a murky situation."

"You know where you can stick your light," Bishop said as he opened the door to his condo.

"Eventually the truth comes out," Crowe called after him. "That's just the natural order of things."

34

AFTER THE HEATED EXCHANGE with Bishop, Crowe walked west on Vestry to clear his head. At the end of the street a single-story vehicle storage depot stuck out like a sore thumb, its faded yellow and blue paint scarcely hiding its dilapidated state. It was the real estate equivalent of a terminal patient waiting to die, after which a condo building would spring up in its place, given the unobstructed view of the Hudson River and its greenway park on the other side of West Street.

Crowe's phone rang. It was Blaikie. "It cost me a couple of tickets for *War Horse*, but I got what you wanted. Thai High's owned by a guy named Arthur Phuket."

"Phuket?" Crowe told Blaikie he'd seen the name on a list of Asian art collectors in Greer's research notes this morning.

"He also owns the penthouse apartment in the Cocoa Exchange Building, and a gallery in SoHo called The Bodhi Tree," Blaikie said. "Not to mention a handful of restaurants and bars scattered throughout Lower Manhattan, Tribeca, and the West Village."

"What about that house in Babylon?"

"Sorry. Nothing under his name."

"Then how about a couple of tickets to *War Horse*?"

Blaikie laughed. "You want to go, just ask. After I saw the show, I was so blown away, I bought a hundred tickets to give away to clients. I've got every Saturday night covered from now till Christmas."

"I might take you up on that." Crowe thanked Blaikie and signed off. He called Levinson and caught the detective in his office.

"What've you got for me?" Levinson said.

"Not much yet." Crowe told the detective about Tracey Lovegrove's theory of a high-ceiling hideaway in which the Riverside Rapist must have hung the Filipino prostitute upside-down for his bite attacks.

"Interesting," Levinson said, "since she's not the only one who was bitten that way. And although hers was the fourth murder in the series, chances are it's not a copycat. We took care to withhold those details. Anything else?"

"Not at the moment," Crowe said. "I'm actually calling about my case."

"For more help? You think the NYPD's a charitable foundation?"

"No charity. I'm prepared to pay with tickets to *War Horse*."

"No shit. For when?"

"Pick a Saturday, any Saturday."

"Who do I have to kill?"

"No killing, just information." Crowe asked Levinson if he could run a criminal check on Arthur Phuket. He gave the detective the names of Thai High and The Bodhi Tree as well, thinking they might be useful in a cross-reference search.

"Who is this guy?"

"I don't know, but his name popped up twice in this case I'm investigating. Whoever he is, he's up there in the food chain."

"That's it?"

"One more thing. You have any connections in Babylon, Long Island? Maybe Vice squad?"

"That'd be Suffolk County. Yeah, I know a detective there. Would you believe, those cops make twenty, thirty grand more than the NYPD?"

"Life's not fair. Why's that?"

"Suffolk and Nassau counties have the highest pay grades in the five boroughs. I guess they realized, you want the best police, you have to offer top salary. A lot of our guys have applied. I've considered it myself."

"Can you give me your friend's name?"

"Detective-Sergeant Joanne Trenton." Levinson gave Crowe her number.

"Can I check in with you later regarding Phuket's history?"

"End of day," Levinson said. "Good luck with Joanne. She's a pistol."

Crowe looked up the address for the Suffolk County Police Department. It was in Yaphank, halfway down Long Island. He called Det. Trenton, identified himself and gave Jake Levinson of the 20th as a character reference. He outlined his case and explained he was looking for a potential material witness, Kitti Poornchai, gone missing.

"What do you want from me?"

Crowe recapped his conversation last night with Chandra at Thai High, how she'd described a house near the highway in Babylon that might be a brothel.

"I think I know it," Trenton said. "It's actually in West Babylon."

"What's the address?"

"Sorry, not so fast. Come out here and show me some ID before I share more. For all I know, you're just looking for some action."

"You think I'm a john? Would I drive all the way to Babylon when I could just walk down Tenth Avenue?"

"Give me a call when you're in town."

"Yaphank's an hour and a half from Manhattan. Couldn't we meet in Babylon? Maybe buy you lunch somewhere nice?"

"Are you offering a bribe, or asking me on a date?" The playful tone in her voice made Crowe think she'd acted this out before.

"Neither. I have a strict moral code."

"That sounds boring, but it's a welcome change from the people I usually deal with. Are you on expenses?"

Crowe didn't like to take advantage of his friend's largesse but it was all for a good cause. And as Blaikie had said, it was a small price to pay for participating vicariously in Crowe's cases. "Wherever it is, I'll pick up the tab."

"Okay. I could meet you in Babylon at eleven. That work for you?"

"Yes."

"Okay." Trenton gave him directions to a restaurant in North Babylon.

"How will I recognize you?"

"I'm tall, blond and armed," Trenton said.

35

CROWE FOUND THE NEAREST CAR RENTAL – a Hertz at Canal and Church. He headed over there, rented a Nissan Sentra for the day and hit the road. After crossing the Williamsburg Bridge, he took the Long Island Expressway through Queens, and the Sunrise Highway to Babylon.

The address Trenton had given him was a Chinese

restaurant called The Imperial Orchid on Deer Park Avenue. The parking lot was occupied by only one other car, a black Ford Crown Vic parked with its rear to the building. Crowe pulled in nose-first beside it, bringing himself directly opposite the woman at the wheel. They rolled down their windows.

"Detective Trenton, I presume?"

"ID." She extended a hand. She was an attractive blonde with bright blue eyes and a light tan.

Crowe gave her his Ontario driver's license and New York State investigator's license.

She compared his appearance to the photos on his ID and used her onboard computer to enter his name. After a few moments, she handed his ID back. "Restaurant's not open yet, so let's take a drive."

Crowe locked the Nissan and joined her in the Ford. Sitting next to her, he now realized how tall she was. She wore designer jeans and a bulky green sweater that concealed her figure.

She headed down Deer Park Avenue to the Sunrise Highway. They were on the expressway just long enough to pass an uninhabited wooded area before she took the next exit, drove north one block and turned onto Neptune Avenue. She slowed the Ford to a crawl and pointed to a large house on the corner.

"There's your house."

Crowe looked. It was a large two-story, windows all curtained, yard not maintained. A two-door garage was attached. "Is it a brothel?"

"No. Originally we thought it was a drugstore, complaints from neighbors about street traffic at odd hours, suspicious characters coming and going. Surveillance ruled that out. Not a brothel either. Maybe there's some hanky-panky going on, but not the usual trade. More like some sort of halfway house."

"For what?"

"Recent immigrants."

"How do you know that?"

"Surveillance videos. Lots of young Asian women. Usually show up in pairs, stay a few weeks, then leave."

"Where do they go?"

"Who gives a shit?" Trenton laughed. "We advised Citizenship and Immigration. They dropped in for a surprise visit a few months ago, found half a dozen girls in residence, but apparently all had papers in order. No drugs or prostitution, so the place is off our radar. Ready to eat?"

"Sure."

Trenton drove through a run-down middle-class neighborhood and returned to the highway. Back at The Imperial Orchid, the parking lot now held a dozen cars. She parked adjacent his rental and they went inside.

The Chinese hostess greeted her as Miss Trenton and gave them a booth at the back of the restaurant. The place was a little rundown but it smelled good and there was a small crowd at the buffet bar.

"How do you know Jake?" Trenton asked after they were seated.

"I helped him out with a murder investigation last year. As it turns out, I'm now trying to develop some new insight on a serial murder case. Have you heard of the Riverside Rapist?"

"Who hasn't?" she said. "That house on Neptune Avenue got anything to do with it?"

"No, that's my case." Crowe gave her a brief outline of the Greer murder and his role in trying to learn something that could help his friend Abbott. "Why do you ask?"

"The Riverside Rapist's victims were all Asian, weren't they? Is that just a coincidence?"

"Sometimes it is," Crowe said. "I haven't made up my mind about this one yet." He could never forget Guruji's rule of three: One event is just a point; two connected events formed a trajectory; three connected events formed a pattern. So far all he had were unconnected dots.

A waitress came with a teapot and two small cups.

Trenton lifted the lid to see if the tea was steeped, then poured for each of them. Crowe raised his in salutation.

"How do *you* know Jake? Did you work together?"

"For a short while, until it got personal. But I changed precincts before we got engaged." Trenton tossed her head, sending her hair cascading over one shoulder. It had a calculated look to it, as if she'd practiced it in the mirror. She shrugged. "I thought I had him hooked, right up until he got away."

"Sorry. I really stepped in that one."

"No, it's okay. We weren't ready for it. At least he wasn't. Or maybe it was me, I really don't know." She stood. "Let's eat."

He followed her to the buffet table, where she loaded up on dumplings and a few other things. He took a bowl of miso soup, some tofu and a heap of stir-fry veggies. Back at the table, she sprinkled soy sauce on her dumplings and attacked them like a woman coming off a ten-day fruit fast.

"That house on Neptune Avenue," he said. "Who owns it?"

"Some guy in Manhattan. An odd name."

"Arthur Phuket?" He spelled the last name.

She laughed. "Is that how you pronounce it? *Poo-ket*? I thought it was *fuck-it*."

"There's a city called Phuket in southern Thailand. That's how they pronounce it there."

"How'd you know he was the owner?"

"Just a lucky guess."

"Don't give me that." She wiped her mouth with a napkin and studied him. "There's some connection here you're not telling me about."

"You're right." Crowe told her about the Thai High restaurant in the Wall Street district, and Phuket's name turning up on Seth Greer's list of Asian art collectors.

"Sounds like he collects more than art."

"When did you have the Neptune Avenue house under surveillance?" Crowe asked. "And for how long?"

"Before Christmas, lasting just a week. Once we realized there was no drug or sex trade, maybe just a way-station for illegal immigrants, we shared our videotape with CIS and they did their thing."

"Did you identify anyone, keep track of license plate numbers?"

"We have the names of the husband and wife who receive mail there. And the owner of another vehicle that was a regular visitor."

"Do you recall names?"

"I'm not good with foreign names. Like *fuck-it*." She laughed. "But I can call the office and get someone to pull the file."

"Would you?"

She made the call and wrote the details on a napkin. Joe and May Dalangvit, plus plate numbers for a Dodge Caravan. And plates for a Lincoln Navigator registered to a Cutter Benz with a SoHo address.

"Mind if I hang out in their neighborhood a bit, see what comes and goes?"

"Be my guest. I don't think there're any stake-outs in the vicinity, but I'll alert our guys just in case. Wouldn't want you getting scooped up in something you shouldn't."

"I appreciate it." Crowe looked at the bill the waitress had given them. "I'll get this and then head out."

"All business and no pleasure, huh?"

"Next time. But thanks for your help. I really do appreciate it."

He shook hands with her. Her grip was strong, warm and slow on the release. He speculated briefly what it'd be like to be caught in her embrace. If Levinson had indeed been the one that got away, it was only because she'd let him.

36

CROWE DROVE BACK TO NEPTUNE AVENUE and parked a few doors down the street from the halfway house. A burgundy Dodge Caravan was now parked in the driveway. He hadn't been there five minutes before a small Asian man emerged from the house and drove away.

Crowe went to the house and knocked at the side door where the man had exited. The door opened promptly. An Asian woman in a peach-colored pantsuit stood there with a puzzled frown on her face. Perhaps she'd thought the man in the Caravan had returned, and was surprised to see Crowe instead.

"No salesmen," she said.

"May Dalangvit?"

"What you want?"

He held his private investigator's license up to the gap in the door. She reached for it but he withdrew it before she could get her hands on it. "I'm investigating the disappearance of Kitti Poornchai. Do you know where she is?"

"She not here." The woman shook her head violently.

"When did you see her last?"

"Couple weeks ago."

"She came here?"

The woman nodded.

"May I come inside?"

She shook her head.

"Mrs. Dalangvit, I could call the police. You don't want to be thrown in jail, do you?" It was an outright bluff, but he hoped she wouldn't call him on it. He had no authority to call the police, never mind enter the house, but he wanted to see what was inside.

She began to close the door but he stepped into the gap and blocked it with his shoulder. As he forced his way inside, she retreated to the far side of a kitchen counter and picked up a cordless phone. She pressed speed-dial and in moments her voice rose in a frantic pitch to convince someone to do something urgently. The husband had been gone no more than five minutes, Crowe knew, so he might return as quickly.

In the living room three Thai women, all young and attractive, rose from the carpeted floor where they'd been watching MTV on a big flat-screen, and fled like sheep at the arrival of a tiger. They scampered upstairs to the second floor. Crowe followed.

Mrs. Dalangvit came after him screaming, "You no go upstairs. You stay away from girls."

He ignored her and climbed to the landing. The first bedroom had a queen-sized bed and a single cot against one wall. All three young women were huddled in the corner on the bed, their expressions terrified. Crowe looked under the bed, saw nothing, and opened the closet to find it packed with clothes and cheap luggage.

He went to the next bedroom. Four young women perched like birds atop two bunk beds. No one was hiding under the beds or in the closet. But again, the fear in the girls' faces made him wonder what had scared them so badly.

The third bedroom was more substantially furnished and decorated, but unoccupied. As he turned from checking the closet, Mrs. Dalangvit came at him with a flurry of clawed hands.

"You stay out of my closet. Pervert. Now *I* call police."

Crowe defended himself with a pillow. "Where is Kitti Poornchai?"

"She not here," the woman screamed.

"Where did she go?"

"Home."

"Back to Bangkok?"

The woman nodded her head but instantly seemed to regret it, her face adopting a lock-jawed expression that made the tendons stand out in her neck. Her eyes were dilated and she looked afraid, like she'd revealed something that could cost her life.

Crowe glanced outside and saw the burgundy Caravan

pull into the driveway. Taking the pillow with him, he bounded down the stairs two at a time. He latched the chain on the side door and looked for the basement stairs. He flicked the light on and went downstairs as the side door rattled and a man yelled something in a foreign language.

He had a quick look around the partially-finished basement. There was a single windowless room in the corner with a heavy door and a steel bolt. Inside it was a futon on the floor and a toilet with a sink behind a curtain. It didn't exactly scream home dungeon but something about it made him suspect it was a holding pen of sorts.

Crowe went back upstairs. The Dalangvits were in the kitchen, the missus with phone in her hand, the man with a butcher knife and a look of fury.

"Where's Kitti Poornchai?" Crowe said to the man. "You killed her, didn't you?"

"No, she gone away."

"Tell me where," Crowe shouted. "Tell me where or I call the police. They'll tear this house apart and throw you both in jail."

The man shook his head fiercely. "She gone home."

"Where is home?"

"Patpong."

Crowe knew the name. Patpong was Bangkok's notorious red light district. "How do I know she's alive? How can I get in touch with her?"

The man shook his head. "She gone. You cannot find her."

"Why did she leave? Is she in trouble?"

The man shook his head.

Crowe moved to the door. The Dalangvits didn't try to block his way. They seemed more frightened of him than the threat of the police. He opened the door, tossed the pillow at the man and walked briskly to his car.

The man followed him from the house. He now had a cell phone in his hand. He approached the rental car, taking pictures as he came. "I got you now, you fucker. Mr. Cutter, he going to fix you."

Crowe drove off, but when he looked in his mirror, he saw the man still standing in the street, taking pictures of his license plate.

37

ON THE WAY BACK TO MANHATTAN, Crowe passed within a few miles of Aqueduct. Under different circumstances, he might have spent the afternoon at the track, using astrology to make a few bucks on the horses. But the thought of Bryan Abbott still in jail reminded him of more important things to do. Besides, racetracks were closed on Tuesdays, rendering the whole thing moot.

Before he reached the Williamsburg Bridge, he pulled over and used his phone to find the address for the Manhattan Museum of Asian Antiquities. The museum's name had turned up twice in the past day.

Thi Nguyen, the murdered curator included in the Riverside Rapist file, had worked at the MMAA. The museum was also on Greer's list of those scrutinized by the US Attorney's Office under the National Stolen Property Act.

Coincidence or something more significant? Crowe was an astute observer of randomness in nature, but also believed many things happened as per some grand design, however subtle its logic might be.

He recalled a metaphor for karma. Discrete events were raindrops on a window pane. As time passed and more events occurred, droplets merged and acquired mass. When gravity's pull set them in motion, droplets became rivulets with a direction.

The MMAA now constituted the nucleus of such a rivulet. He phoned the museum and asked for the director. She was in meetings all day, her secretary said, but when he mentioned the NYPD and the US Attorney's Office in the same sentence, half an hour of the director's busy schedule suddenly became free.

Crowe took the FDR Drive all the way up to 79th. The museum was just off Park Avenue on 80th, a modern four-story building whose front terrace was occupied by a 6-foot statue of a gilded Buddha seated in meditation. Buddha's eyes were closed and his expression serene, despite the growl of nearby traffic and a pigeon atop his golden head.

Crowe entered a foyer whose atrium extended to the second floor. The ground floor displayed rows of sculpture and statuary, mostly featuring the Buddha and various Asian deities. Based on what he could see from below, the second floor offered paintings, tapestries and carvings.

A Japanese woman of indeterminate age was stuffing envelopes behind a reception desk. He gave his name. She checked her agenda and pointed him to the elevator.

The director's office on the fourth floor overlooked the street. Crowe tapped his knuckles on her door. The woman behind the desk closed a file and came around to greet him.

"Roxanne Morton, Director of the Museum." She was perhaps sixty years old, with strong features, dressed in a black skirt and purple silk blouse. "How can I be of assistance?"

Crowe showed his ID, explaining he was a private investigator consulting on behalf of the 20th Precinct in the murder of Thi Nguyen.

"Poor Thi. When I heard the news, my first thought was, didn't she experience enough tragedy already, did she have to die violently too?"

"I don't know her personal history." At her invitation, Crowe took a seat across the desk from Morton. "What can you tell me?"

"She was one of the boat people, just a child at the time, who escaped Vietnam after the fall of Saigon. Her father was a jeweler who bought passage to Thailand with several other families, but pirates intercepted their boat. Her mother was raped, her father beaten so badly he lost an eye. They spent a year in a Thai refugee camp. Her father concealed several precious gems throughout his captivity by swallowing and recycling them until his release.

"They settled in Bangkok and her father started a jewelry business. Thi learned the language, studied Fine Arts at Bangkok University and wrote a Master's thesis on religious statuary. She worked for the national museum until 1996 when her parents were killed in a home invasion. With no surviving family, she came to the USA in 1997 and worked for a few galleries until I hired her in 1999."

"I saw pictures of her," Crowe said. "She was an attractive woman. She never married?"

"Thi wasn't lucky in love. Her high school boyfriend was killed in a motorcycle accident. At university she had a relationship with a professor who turned out to be married. Here in New York, her heart was crushed by a man she'd met in the course of business."

"What were the circumstances?"

"This guy claimed to be a collector, but I think he was into collecting women more than art. I pegged him the minute I met him. You could tell by the way he eyeballed women, he was a player."

"What was his name?"

"Tom Jimson."

The name rang a bell, but Crowe couldn't put his finger on it. "What year was this?"

"Summer of two thousand and eight."

"What was the business that brought them together?"

"Jimson had a Buddha he wanted authenticated and evaluated. Or more accurately, he represented a client who wanted it done."

"What sort of Buddha?"

"Bring your chair around, I'll show you."

Crowe moved his chair to her side of her desk. She angled her computer screen, displaying a photo of a golden Buddha. It was seated in the classic meditation posture with hands cupped atop crossed legs. Crowe was no expert, but the Buddha's elongated earlobes and beaded bonnet looked like many he'd seen in Thailand.

In the photo, a carpenter's square lay propped immediately behind the Buddha. Gauged against the two arms of the square, the Buddha was about twelve inches high, nine inches across.

"I assume that's gilded?"

"Solid gold," Morton said. "At ten point eight kilograms, the gold alone is worth almost six hundred thousand dollars."

Crowe whistled. "What about its value as religious art?"

"As art, add another million or two. As an antiquity dating back to the Lanna Dynasty of Thailand, a few more million. When Thi authenticated it in 2008, she assigned a market value of seven million. By now, it could easily be worth ten million or more."

"Where is it now?"

"I have no idea. All I know is, not in any public collection. Probably back in the hands of the collector Jimson represented. Some of these people have deep pockets and long horizons. With the rise of China, there's increased interest in oriental antiquities. In another decade it could be worth twenty, thirty million. Appreciation like that makes other investments look anemic by comparison."

"Did Thi Nguyen handle its authentication and appraisal?"

"Yes. I'd hired her because of her specialization in Southeast Asian temple art. She came with glowing recommendations from the Bangkok National Museum. Since joining us in ninety-nine, she was often invited by other museums to verify the authenticity of major pieces."

"So there was no doubt regarding this Buddha's authenticity?"

"Thi traced it back to the Theravada school of Buddhism in Chiang Mai. Actual date of origin uncertain, but probably late Thirteenth Century."

"And ownership?"

"That's trickier. Ever since the National Stolen Property Act, the Attorney's Office has been all over museums like hyenas on a herd of sick antelope. Provenance is the order of the day."

"Did Thi handle that too?"

"Yes. Apparently Jimson had a bundle of documents. The temple had originally given the Buddha, one of many in its collection, to a wealthy devotee in exchange for funding the temple's expansion in the nineteen-thirties. After that, it changed hands a few more times between galleries and private collectors. It left the country in the seventies and ended up in America, after which it was sold twice more. Apparently, no one bothered to authenticate it until Jimson's client."

"I notice you used the word 'apparently' a couple of times," Crowe said. "Is it because you don't remember the details, or there's something missing from the file?"

"It's much worse than that," Morton said. "Half of the file is missing."

"What do you mean?"

"Well, the authentication documentation is thorough and complete. It's the chain-of-ownership documents that are missing. If the Buddha were in the museum's possession, we'd be in serious trouble to prove how we acquired it."

"What happened to the documents? Surely they weren't the originals?"

"Because they're so critical, Jimson would have kept the originals. But he'd have shown them to Thi so she could assess their authenticity, and she'd have made copies for the file. The only possible explanation for their absence is that she must have worked on the file at home, but misplaced her copies. This was a private assignment, and she was overworked at the time because we were in the process of making several acquisitions. Although Jimson approached the museum with his request, I was basically a broker, setting the fee for Thi's services, half of which I gave her as a bonus."

"Why your museum? I assume several others have the resources to provide authentication research?"

"The Met is renowned for its Asian art and antiquities collection but their fees are astronomical. Then there's the Rubin and the Brooklyn Museum... But it's a good question, why he chose us. We were getting good press at the time because of our acquisitions, so probably that's how Jimson heard of us."

"When did you discover the file was incomplete?"

"Only after Thi was murdered. When the police asked about her personal life, I told them about her love affair with Jimson that ended so badly."

"In what way?"

"He courted her for about nine months - the best restaurants, Broadway shows, weekends in the Bahamas. They had so many common interests. He said he loved her. She was on top of the world. After everything she'd been through, he was a dream come true. But he had a dark side - controlling and abusive. He tried to make her do things with other women - degrading things she refused to describe. She was alternately mesmerized and horrified by his dual nature."

"And in the end?"

"He broke it off the spring of two thousand and nine, said he didn't love her any more, they should stop seeing each other. It was sad to see her that summer, she was like a zombie. For a while I was afraid she might hurt herself. When I heard she was dead, my first thought was suicide."

"Did the police question Jimson?"

"They couldn't find him. By the time Thi died, he'd been out of her life for more than six months. It was like he'd dropped off the face of the earth."

"Where did he live in New York?"

"He wasn't a New Yorker. Said he was from Johannesburg. During the year he was around, he had an apartment on the Upper East Side, a beach house during the summer. Plus which, he traveled a lot."

"What did he look like?"

"He was in his fifties. Handsome man, if you enjoy the feral look. Thick black hair, lean as a runner, always a bit tanned. A guy who seemed to have a lot on his mind."

"Why do you say that?"

"He always had a strained expression, like he was trying to look through you. Do you know the writer Jerzy Kosinski?"

"Yes, I read everything by him when I was in college."

"Remember his face? As if a wolf could be reborn as a man? Jimson had that same look of perpetual hunger."

"Do you have any pictures of him?"

"No. The police asked me the same thing. I thought they'd have found something in her condo, but maybe she'd burned them all."

"Do you know a gallery called The Bodhi Tree in SoHo?"

"Yes." Morton leaned back in her chair.

"What can you tell me about it?"

Morton paused and steepled her fingers. "In the Asian collectibles market, the Bodhi Tree has a reputation for playing fast and loose. Every museum in town has turned away people wanting to donate art and antiquities in exchange for tax write-offs. It's a standard practice: multi-millionaire donates art, museum issues a receipt, donor claims a tax deduction. But ever since the National Stolen Property Act, museums have become cautious. Unless provenance is airtight, we risk prosecution and loss of the art."

"But the donor would also lose the tax deduction plus the original cost of acquisition."

"Yes, but The Bodhi Tree and other galleries like it are the winners, so long as they don't get caught in possession. They can't be prosecuted for what's passed through their hands. Meanwhile, they have "art experts" on retainer who evaluate at the top of the market curve, and "document specialists" who forge authenticity certificates, import/export records and bills of sale. They scam the millionaires who think they're legally acquiring a genuine work of art any museum would be happy to accept in return for a tax receipt. But the reality is, museums are running scared, and very wary about provenance."

"And The Bodhi Tree is known, in your circles, as being

party to this black market?"

"Known to us, and the US Attorney's Office."

"You'd think the feds would find a way to put them out of business."

"They've tried. Go visit The Bodhi Tree. You'll see a gallery stocked with Asian art, but of a commercial variety. Nothing there's worth more than fifty thousand, and most of it's far cheaper because it's contemporary, not antique. The Bodhi Tree is just a front. The really valuable stuff is elsewhere, but you'd have to spend enough time with them to prove you're really a millionaire and not a federal agent on a sting operation."

"Do you know who owns the gallery?"

"Yeah, a crook by the name of Arthur Phuket. A dealer in stolen and counterfeit art."

"By any chance, had Jimson's client acquired his Buddha via The Bodhi Tree?"

"Definitely not. If their name had appeared anywhere in the chain of ownership, Thi would have smelled a rat."

"Did she know all the rats in this business?"

"No, but I was educating her about the local players. I didn't want her to get hurt."

"Hurt? In what way?"

"Here's the irony," Morton said. "Some of our own government people have been involved in smuggling art and antiquities out of foreign countries. Military personnel, CIA, diplomatic personnel. As a general rule, I like to keep my distance from people who've been trained to lie, sabotage and kill for a living."

"How do you know about this?"

"Take my word for it, because I'm not going to say anything more. You think the art world is all aesthetic, glamorous and sophisticated? The black market is its shadow side. The people who own it are powerful and the people who run it are nasty. They're way out of your league."

38

THE BODHI TREE WAS IN SOHO, on Thompson just north of Spring Street. It occupied the ground floor of a six-floor building in white brick, adjacent to a tiny parking lot holding four vehicles. Crowe parked his rental on the next block and walked back to the gallery. He noticed a black Lincoln Navigator among the four vehicles in the adjacent lot. He took out the napkin on which Det. Joanne Trenton had written the plate numbers of frequent visitors to the house in West Babylon. The Navigator's plates were the same tags Trenton had provided. That couldn't be a good sign.

Across the street were a fenced playground and a basketball court. Crowe sat on a park bench in front of the court, took several deep breaths and closed his eyes. Over the sound of squealing kids in the playground, he heard a police siren in the distance, but that was too common an occurrence to be an omen.

He opened his eyes and looked across the street. The Bodhi Tree's entire façade - door, frame, awning - was in bright Chinese red, a hot color associated with Mars. A tree with heart-shaped leaves was painted in gold on the front window. Another hot color, associated with the Sun. The address was 90. Nine was the number of Mars - a warrior, fighter, cop, soldier. What had Roxanne Morton said about the people who did the dirty work in the black market for stolen art? Often they were military personnel and CIA.

Crowe recalled what Joe Dalangvit had yelled after him as he'd driven away from Neptune Avenue. *Mr. Cutter going to fix you.* The Navigator registered to Cutter Benz was parked here. Crowe debated the wisdom of entering a place where his face might be known. He wasn't afraid of a confrontation, but didn't want it to happen the moment he set foot in the gallery. He needed time to reconnoiter the place.

He walked to Spring Street and found a variety store where he bought a pair of sunglasses and a Boston Celtics cap.

He pulled the tags off, put both articles on and checked himself in the reflection of a store window. Not much of a disguise, but probably enough to deflect immediate recognition.

He returned to the gallery. As he entered the door, a bell tinkled overhead. He caught a whiff of good-quality incense. A middle-aged Asian woman sat behind the counter. "Good afternoon. Have you been to The Bodhi Tree before?"

"No."

"Looking for anything in particular?"

"No. Just down from Boston for a few days, thought I might pick up something for my wife."

"I'm sure you'll find something to suit her taste. We carry items from Southeast Asia - Thailand, Cambodia, Burma, Vietnam, Malaysia, Indonesia. Jewelry and smaller works of art are on this floor. Larger pieces of sculpture and carvings are downstairs."

"Any religious art? *Kinnari*, the female winged deity?"

"You've been to Thailand?"

"Many years ago. Beautiful country, wonderful people."

"Thank you."

"Do you have any nice Buddhas?"

"There are several in the back." She pointed into the corner diagonally opposite.

Crowe wandered down the aisles to the corner. There were several attractive Buddhas, but all in bronze, wood or resin. In a few moments, the clerk appeared at his side.

"See anything you like?"

"Yes, but I'm looking for something more authentic, more valuable. Do you have any Buddhas in silver or gold?"

"They're rarely rendered in silver. But we have access to a few private collections with small Buddhas in gold."

"Where can I see them?"

"You'd have to meet Mr. Phuket to discuss that."

"He's the private collector?"

"The owner. He acts as an agent for private collectors."

"When could I meet him?"

"Can you leave a phone number? How long are you in town?"

"I was planning to go home tomorrow. And I really wanted to get something for my wife."

"What's your budget?"

"A hundred thousand, give or take."

"I'm sure Mr. Phuket can find you something in that range. Let me make a phone call."

She returned to the front counter. Crowe lingered in the Buddha section while she spoke on the phone. He took out his phone and opened his astrology app.

Quarter past three. Mars in the first house. The sign exchange between Sun and Mars was still in operation, but now they occupied the first and ninth houses. Dharma, noble action. He was on the right path.

Moon, Venus and Ketu were in the tenth house. This was a business involving the arts, but entailed something murky, Ketu's spirituality surrendered to materialism.

The presence of Mars concerned Crowe. The red facade, the number nine, the rising planet - all sending the same message. It was like the opening bell of a boxing match.

No sooner had that thought crossed his mind, the bell at the door tinkled and a bulky man entered the gallery. He stood blocking the door, listening to the woman at the counter who spoke to him in a whisper.

Crowe looked around for a weapon. There were several swords on the nearest wall. He took one down and drew it partially from its scabbard, making sure it contained a blade. It was the real deal. He went to the front, carrying the scabbard in his left hand.

The woman put down the phone. "Mr. Phuket can see you. He has an office a few blocks away. Mr. Benz will drive you."

"I've changed my mind about a Buddha," Crowe said. "I'll just take this sword."

She hesitated a moment and glanced at the big man in the door. Crowe looked at him too, getting a measure of the guy.

There was something Asian in Benz's lineage but what he most looked like was a UFC fighter in slacks and a polo shirt. His shaven head sat atop a pair of trapezium that made his broad shoulders look modest, which they weren't. His biceps and forearms rippled with muscle. His stomach was flat and his legs were set like a tackle about to launch at a quarterback.

"Let me see the price tag," the woman said.

Crowe pulled the tag off and handed it to the woman, unwilling to relinquish the sword, and not for a moment taking his eyes off Mr. Benz. It was a good thing, because that's when Benz, moving faster than Crowe had anticipated, charged.

Crowe didn't try to draw the sword. In the time his right arm would cross his body to pull the blade from its scabbard, Benz might strike a disabling blow. Instead, Crowe swung the loaded scabbard with his left hand and caught Benz on the right ear.

The man yelped but snatched the scabbard from Crowe's hands. He bent the sword over his knee and made a grab for Crowe. Crowe took two steps back and gave Benz a Thai-boxing kick in the gut. Benz doubled over with a retching sound. Crowe stepped around him and went out the door.

Seconds later, Benz followed him into the street with the bent sword, bellowing like a Minotaur who'd got his breath back.

Crowe looked around. He was glad to be out of the gallery, where a struggle among so many glass showcases risked an injury that could put him in the hospital, if not the morgue. He was safer on the street but still had to be careful of shop windows and pedestrians. He didn't know which was more important to avoid - creating collateral damage or having someone witness his humiliation if he got his ass whipped. Or worse, killed.

He debated running for it, thinking he could easily outdistance the bowlegged Benz, but where was the dignity in that? He recalled Krishna's advice to Arjuna in the *Bhagavad Gita.* Arjuna confesses on the eve of battle that he's afraid, but

Krishna tells him, your cause is just, therefore act in faith like a warrior, knowing you cannot control the outcome. Just do your best and leave the results to God.

Crowe crossed the street and entered the basketball court via a door in the chain link fence. Two black kids were playing one-on-one in the half-court nearest Spring Street. "Heads up, guys, keep your distance," Crowe warned them.

Benz entered the basketball court and closed the fence door behind him, jamming the sword through a padlock hasp, and twisting the blade like a pretzel so it couldn't be withdrawn. So much for the exit.

As Benz came toward him, Crowe now knew what it felt like to be a Christian thrown to a lion. Or in this case, a gorilla.

Benz took a run at him. Crowe danced aside. After several replays, it began to feel like a bullfight, Benz coming at him in a snorting rush, arms out wide like a Texas longhorn, Crowe feinting and pirouetting aside each time. All that was missing was a barbecue fork to jab in Benz's butt each time he went by.

The black guys were getting a kick out of this. They'd suspended their ball game and squatted against the far fence. Was there a better way to chill, watching one white guy beat the shit out of another?

"Come on, man, get your hands on him," one of the basketball players called to Benz. "This shit's going nowhere."

Crowe and Benz faced each other ten feet apart in mid-court. Benz's chest heaved, his face beaded with sweat. Crowe's adrenaline was up, and his heart was thumping, but he wasn't really tired. He could probably do this for another hour, but he had better things to do. He needed to find a way to end it.

"Call 911," Crowe appealed to the two black guys.

"Why don't I call your mama," one of them laughed.

Crowe shrugged. So it was going to be like that...

Benz made another rush, but this time he feinted. By the time Crowe corrected for it and pirouetted the other way, Benz got his hands on Crowe's left arm. He yanked him close and got his other arm around Crowe's neck.

Before the choke-hold even started, Crowe snapped his head back and smashed Benz's nose. As the big man's grip loosened, Crowe dropped and turned, bunching his fist in such a way that his second knuckle protruded from the rest. He drove it into the space just below Benz's sternum. This *marma* point, a vital junction of nerves, was one of the targets Crowe had learned from Guruji in his teaching of Cobra Tantra Shastra.

Benz made a strangled squeak like a giant rodent upon which a rat trap had been sprung.

Crowe backed away. Benz dropped to the ground on all fours. Crowe felt like he was in another time and place. Should he put his foot on Benz's head and ask the Emperor whether to kill or spare the man? Instead, he walked to the door, scaled the ten-foot fence and went down the other side as gracefully as he could. The two black guys applauded.

The saleswoman stood watching from the gallery door. Crowe crossed the street. She stepped inside and locked the door. He'd only wanted to tell her he was no longer interested in buying a Buddha from Mr. Phuket, but she probably knew that already.

39

CROWE RETURNED HIS RENTAL to Hertz and took a taxi back to his hotel. Briefly, he considered taking Magnusson up on his offer for a drink at day's end, not because he thought the editor had more information to share, but because he'd never felt more like a drink.

Instead, he walked to Sheridan Square and bought a carrot juice with a squirt of wheat grass from a juice bar in the neighborhood. He sat on a bench in the late afternoon sun and gave thanks he was sitting here and not lying on a hospital gurney with life-threatening injuries.

What had triggered Benz's attack at The Bodhi Tree? Crowe assumed the obvious. His visit to the house in West Babylon had alarmed the occupants. Dalangvit had sent Cutter Benz pictures of him. When Crowe showed up at The Bodhi Tree, Benz had recognized him. Putting two and two together, Benz had assumed Crowe's inquiries were not in Phuket's best interests, and had taken matters into his own large hands.

Crowe remembered he was supposed to call Levinson at the end of the day. He entered the detective's number. He was getting ready to leave a message when Levinson picked up on the fifth ring.

"It's Crowe. Did you get a chance to run a background check on Arthur Phuket?"

"One of my guys ran it off. Just give me a minute to find it in my in-basket. Anything new at your end? Any more ideas about the Riverside Rapist?"

"I don't think Thi Nguyen was murdered by the same man who killed the other victims." Crowe told him about the missing provenance documents Roxanne Morton had discussed. "The more I learn about her, the more she doesn't belong with the other victims. Did you ever interview Tom Jimson?"

"The boyfriend for whom she did the authentication? We never found him. Obviously he used an alias, which is suspicious, but maybe it was to protect the identity of the Buddha's owner. We had nothing to go on – no photos, ID, social security number or forwarding address. *Nada*. Trying to pick up the trail six months after he'd dumped her was difficult for the original case detective. Two and a half years after her death, it's now virtually hopeless."

"Did you contact the art community in Johannesburg?"

"No. That whole story about his being a South African national was a fiction. The State Department had no record of Jimson entering the country. So without a passport photo, all I had was a description. You know how far you can get with that?"

"Pretty much nowhere."

"You got it," Levinson said. "But here's the poop on Arthur Phuket. Thai national, DOB May thirteenth, sixty-two, got his green card in the mid-eighties. Opened up a restaurant and a bar, then several more of each through the nineties. Citizenship papers in ninety-seven. First arrest was for facilitating prostitution in one of his bars. Charges dropped. Then a couple more arrests for the same thing, charges dropped again. After that, clean as a whistle. Opened up more restaurants and bars, an art gallery in SoHo, an import/export business, all nice and legit since the turn of the century."

"Seen the error of his ways and embraced the straight life?"

"More like, found a friendly cop or judge, if not both, to ward off trouble."

"Speaking out of cynicism, or personal knowledge of patronage?"

"The former, of course," Levinson snorted. "And it's not like he's been squeaky clean. The US Attorney's Office issued several warrants over the past few years, searching The Bodhi Tree for stolen art and antiquities. But absent any charges, I assume they came up empty. Like I say, the man must have guardian angels. What's your interest in him?"

Crowe told him Phuket owned the restaurant Thai High where beautiful Asian women were available for dessert. Kitti Poornchai had named it as her home address but now she'd disappeared. One of the Thai High girls had told Crowe about the house in West Babylon. Under pressure, the Dalangvits had admitted Kitti Poornchai had returned to Bangkok. They'd reported him to Cutter Benz, obviously muscle for Phuket, who'd caught up with Crowe at The Bodhi Tree.

"You've had a busy day."

"Not to mention a lovely lunch with your ex-fiancée, thank you very much."

"How'd she look?"

"A man could turn to criminal ways just to have her come after him in hot pursuit."

"Please. You're talking about the woman I used to love."

"She implied you left her at the altar."

"That's ironic, considering I'm the one with the broken heart."

"So it's a classic case of he-said, she-said. As a cop, you must hear that a lot. Who's to believe?"

"Did she come on to you?"

"No, she was a perfect lady."

"Was she wearing a ring?"

"No, but she had a stud in her belly button."

"Don't mess with me, Crowe."

"Sorry. You're so pathetic you make an easy target."

"What about my tickets to *War Horse*?"

"Give me a few dates and I'll see what's available."

Levinson named three consecutive Saturdays in June.

"That's a long way off," Crowe said. "You need to figure out who you can get a leg over in exchange for that?"

"Shut up."

"I'll call you."

Crowe laughed to himself, trying to picture two independent-minded cops like Levinson and Trenton as romantic partners. Although relationships took a lot of work, in the end it came down to compassion and compromise, but these weren't the first qualities you'd expect to find in a cop. He understood now why Guruji had chosen celibacy. It was sometimes easier to devote yourself to God than another person.

He thought of Tracey. What he liked most about her was her quick mind. She was a problem-solver like him. Yet beneath that pragmatic exterior was a playful nature, an adventurous spirit. He liked that in a woman.

He sighed and looked around. Forget Tracey. He had another woman on his mind. Kitti Poornchai, whom he still suspected of some involvement in Greer's death, had disappeared. According to the Dalangvits, she'd gone back to Thailand. But was that true?

Crowe closed his eyes and checked the air flow through

his nostrils. Guruji had taught him the *swara* technique. For questions requiring a simple yes or no, it was straightforward. Day and night, the dominant flow of air alternated between left and right nostrils, mimicking the body's nervous system, in which vital energy flowed up and down the left- and right-hand networks known as *ida* and *pingala*.

Had Kitti Poornchai returned to Thailand? Crowe checked his nostrils. The right flowed marginally stronger than the left. The right side was male and today was Tuesday, ruled by a male planet Mars. Concurrence said the answer was yes. She had returned to Thailand.

Crowe took out his phone and started his astrology app. The question now was, should I follow her there, and what would happen if I did?

Virgo was rising, its ruler Mercury in the seventh house Pisces. The first house was home, the seventh not-home, so that told Crowe to go. But Mercury debilitated in Pisces implied difficulty finding Kitti. Although he knew her original address from her green card application, Bangkok was a big city. If she was hiding, finding her would be an impossible task for someone with no contacts who didn't speak the language.

The picture for Kitti Poornchai was even less promising. She was indicated by Jupiter, seventh house lord. It was in the eighth house of dislocation, trauma and death. It was influenced by malefics, the Sun and Saturn. Twelfth lord Sun implied imprisonment, while Saturn was a classic indicator for restriction and bondage. But since Jupiter was flanked on either side by benefic planets, Crowe concluded Kitti was alive.

For how long? The Sun was approaching Jupiter. In thirteen days it would create total combustion, symbolically spelling death. More subtly, this could be read on a shorter time scale, and in thirteen *hours*, Kitti's situation could take a turn for the worse. Crowe needed to act quickly.

He called Blaikie and explained his situation. He wanted to arrange for a pair of *War Horse* tickets to reward Levinson for his help. Then he was heading for the airport to catch the next flight to Bangkok.

"Fine, but I'm picking up the tab," Blaikie said.

"That's not necessary."

"Yes, it is. I owe you for what you did regarding Janis last year. And like I said last night, I get a kick out of financing your adventures, so long as you share your stories with me. And really, the cost is petty cash."

"Thank you. You're a generous man."

"This'll show up on my account as good karma, right?" Blaikie joked.

"Do you want a receipt?" Crowe laughed.

"No. You have carte blanche. But call me as soon as you return. I'll want a full account. Remember what I said about vicarious living?"

"You want me to eat some green curry shrimp for you too?"

"No, but it's been a long while since I had turtle soup."

"No way. There's a limit to my adventures."

Blaikie laughed. "*Vaya con dios, amigo.*"

Crowe searched online and found a Bangkok flight leaving in three hours. It was tight but possible. He booked it and packed his bag.

40

CROWE CALLED TRACEY from the taxi en route to Newark International. She sounded tired. The crime scene from yesterday's triple homicide in Times Square had spawned a mass of physical evidence. She'd been in the lab till past midnight processing the most critical elements. After only four hours of sleep, she'd returned to work early this morning, hoping to wrap sometime tonight.

He brought her up to date on the Seth Greer case and

explained why he was going to Bangkok. She was disappointed they'd had so little time to hang out together before he had to leave. He promised to give her a call when he got back in two or three days, he wasn't really sure how long he'd be in Bangkok. She told him to be careful, to stay out of tough neighborhoods and stick with bottled water.

Feeling vaguely unsettled, he stared out at Jersey City's industrial sector as the taxi raced along the Pulaski Skyway.

His United flight was scheduled to depart at 8:30. After clearing security he wandered around Terminal C, looking for something to eat, until he found an Asian outlet called Wok & Roll, where he had a spring roll and a miso soup.

He called Levinson and told him he was going to Bangkok and would check in when he returned. As for *War Horse*, just see Blaikie's secretary to pick up the tickets for the Saturday he'd wanted.

The flight departed on time, and Crowe settled in for the 14-hour haul to New Delhi, grateful for a window seat and no one sitting next to him. He had *The Ramayana* to read, music on his phone, and the Riverside Rapist to think about. He popped two homeopathic pills for jet lag and drank some water. Dinner came around and he ate most of a pasta dish. He skipped coffee and drank more water.

Nothing in the movie listings piqued his interest. After a few pages of *The Ramayana*, he set it aside. Rama's epic battle to rescue his wife Sita from Ravana's abduction was gripping, but Crowe already knew the ending. It paled in comparison to the mystery on his mind.

He reviewed his notes from the Riverside Rapist case, still puzzled by the timing of the killings. If only he could make sense of that, it would be the first step in developing a killer profile. He listed the dates of the killings, and the span of time between subsequent murders.

Murder 1: September 4, 2000.

Murder 2: August 15, 2002 - 23.5 months later.

Murder 3: July 26, 2004 - 23.5 months later.

Murder 4: July 7, 2006 - 23.5 months later.

Murder 5: June 15, 2008 - 23.5 months later.

Murders 6 and 7: December 14 and 15, 2009 - 18 months later.

Murder 8: October 28, 2011 - 22.5 months since the previous two.

The average time between consecutive murders was roughly 22.5 months. Crowe and Levinson had already discussed this periodicity, and they'd ruled out conventions and religious holidays. What else could possibly dictate a two-year schedule?

Medical check-ups? Crowe thought of his father. Because the standards for flying a plane were rigorous, a private pilot was required to undergo a full physical every two years in order to maintain his license. Depending on personal circumstances, that could mean two years, possibly less, between physicals. And if a person had medical insurance, it wouldn't discourage him from shortening the two-year cycle, since his insurer would bear the cost.

As an astrologer, Crowe naturally thought of correlating the two-year cycle with planetary motion. The first thing that came to mind was Mars, whose orbital period was 687 days, or 23 months.

In planetary symbolism, Mars was a warrior. Many a murder scenario carried Mars' signature, provoking violence and all its unhappy consequences.

Crowe opened his astrology app and created eight murder charts, using dates the medical examiners had determined for each victim's death. He was astonished to discover that, in every chart, Mars occupied Cancer. This was where Mars was debilitated, exhibiting more faults than virtues - anger, cruelty, rage, aggression and violence.

Crowe thought about it. Maybe this was the killer's raw nerve. Psychologically, Mars in Cancer suggested repressed anger awaiting provocation to act out. Planetary transits could trigger violence. Depending on the person's disposition, the release of pent-up rage might then be a self-fulfilling destiny. Crowe recalled Guruji's observation: *Thoughts become actions, repeated actions become behaviors, ingrained behaviors become character, and character becomes fate.*

How could he test this theory? Examine the birth charts of every suspect to see if they had Mars in Cancer? But the NYPD had failed to come up with any strong suspects in the Riverside Rapist case. Yes, they'd looked at a handful of weak suspects, but they'd all had alibis. Crowe didn't see where he'd get any traction from this idea. It would have to wait until he returned to New York and reviewed with Levinson...

By now he was tired. It was going on eleven and they were somewhere mid-Atlantic. He turned off his light, pulled a blanket over himself and closed his eyes.

41

Wednesday, April 25

New Delhi, India

CROWE AWOKE SEVERAL HOURS LATER. His watch read 4:15 AM EST but it was midday outside. They'd been aloft eight hours, so it was another six to New Delhi. The day was cloudless with excellent visibility. He scanned a land mass below, trying to guess where he was, knowing the flight would pass over the top of Scandinavia. He went to the washroom, taking the opportunity to look out the other side of the plane. To the north he saw what looked like the Murmansk peninsula. Russia.

In the washroom he splashed water on his face. When he came out, he asked the galley attendant for some apple juice, drank a glass on the spot and took another back to his seat. He inserted earplugs to block out the chatter of passengers around him, and meditated for half an hour.

Thus refreshed, he returned to the puzzle with which he'd grappled last night. Who was the Riverside Rapist?

Crowe debated calculating a *prashna,* or horary chart, to give him some clues, but decided against it for now. Vedic tradition dictated that an astrologer should never answer questions in a moving vehicle. When asked about this, Guruji had said, *A man risks enough confusion already with planets whirling around inside his head. He needs to be grounded in order to think straight.* Crowe deferred the *prashna* until his layover in New Delhi.

He ate the meals that came around, read and dozed off and on until landing in New Delhi's Indira Gandhi International Airport shortly after eight in the evening. He wandered around Terminal 3 to get some circulation back in his legs and bought an expensive cup of *chai* in one of the lounges. When he'd first come to India in the eighties, the airport had been a sorry collection of second-rate restaurants and cheap gift shops. Since India's spectacular economic rise in the past decade, the country had since upgraded its infrastructure and services with admirable zeal. Terminal 3 now looked like a mall in any western city.

Crowe used an internet booth to make an online reservation for Bangkok's Crowne Plaza Hotel on Rama IV Road. He'd never stayed there before but knew it was within easy walking distance of both the Skytrain and the Patpong entertainment district. The address on Kitti Poornchai's green card application was on Soi Pradit, roughly the same neighborhood.

Once that was taken care of, Crowe returned to the case of the Riverside Rapist, asking himself the key question: Who was the killer?

He calculated a chart for local time, 9:03 PM, in New Delhi, India. Scorpio was rising, its lord Mars in tenth house Leo. Mars was the key significator of the subject. Since it occupied Leo, Crowe assumed the Riverside Rapist was a man of mature years, perhaps a retired engineer, doctor, or policeman. Because of its exchange with the Sun in the sixth house Aries, the man could be ill.

The Moon was in the seventh house Taurus, a fixed sign, with its ruler Venus and a debilitated Ketu. So the Riverside Rapist was married but his wife was dysfunctional or a "foreigner" of some kind - via ethnicity, nationality or religion.

The man's psychological stability was at risk. The lord of the fourth house was Saturn exalted in the twelfth, a place of loss. Perhaps some kind of technical genius who'd lost his mojo, Crowe mused, like John Nash in "A Beautiful Mind". The dark Moon, another indicator of the mind, lay on the Rahu-Ketu axis, implying derangement. If not literally insane, the guy had a mental disorder.

Where was the Riverside Rapist from? Ascendant lord in a fixed sign normally implied a local. But here, Mars in Leo exchanged signs with the Sun in Aries, a movable sign.

Western astrologers called it "mutual reception". In Vedic astrology this was *Parivartana Yoga,* a "travelling combination". Although not taken literally, it could indicate a frequent traveler, or someone who lived or worked in two places. Crowe assumed the Riverside Rapist was from out of town.

He recalled the peregrine falcon he'd seen the other day. The alien, the foreigner, the drifter. This resonated with something else in the chart. The Moon was in the seventh house - the place not-home - and its presence on the Rahu-Ketu axis suggested a rebel, an oddball, someone marching to the beat of a different drummer.

Crowe put away his notes. He bought some bottled water and popped another of the homeopathic tablets he'd been taking every two hours since New York. He stretched and went for a brisk walk around the terminal.

The boarding call for his Bangkok flight came shortly before eleven. This time Crowe didn't have the luxury of an empty seat adjacent. The Thai Airways plane was packed. His companion was a Chinese businessman frantically trying to finish off a text message on his phone.

The plane took off. As soon as they reached altitude, the Chinese guy downed a double scotch and went to sleep. Crowe closed his eyes and calmed his mind with a mantra. To each his own.

42

Thursday, April 26

Bangkok, Thailand

CROWE'S FLIGHT TOUCHED DOWN at Suvarnabhumi Airport at 5:30 AM. He re-set his watch to local time, reminding himself it was now Thursday. He changed some money and took a taxi downtown to the Crowne Plaza Hotel on Rama IV Road. At this hour of the morning, the lobby was empty except for a gaggle of half-asleep tourists and their luggage awaiting a shuttle bus to the airport.

He checked into his room. From the 12th floor, he could see Lumpini Park to the east and the sun rising over the dense sprawl of the city. He showered and checked his pulse. He felt good. On the opposite side of the world, it was evening in New York, but he figured he could handle several hours of activity before his own circadian clock became a tide against which it would become difficult to swim.

A tourist brochure lay on the desk. Its recommended local sights included the former house of Jim Thompson, an expatriate American who'd singlehandedly saved Thailand's silk industry from extinction back in the fifties. The name rang a bell. Tom Jimson was the broker who'd commissioned the Manhattan Museum of Asian Antiquities to evaluate his client's gold Buddha, and subsequently broken the curator's heart. Had he adopted an alias, reversing the name of the most famous American in Thailand?

Crowe checked his email. His inbox had accumulated several client requests since he'd got involved in Bryan Abbott's case. He answered them all and made commitments to phone once he was back state-side.

At eight AM he was ready to go looking for Kitti Poornchai. He retrieved the fact sheet from the NYPD's background check and jotted onto hotel stationery the address she'd given on her green card application. He picked up a few of the hotel's business cards in the lobby and went out onto the street where the humidity greeted him with a clammy embrace.

Crowe walked to nearby Silom Road and headed toward the river. Silom was a major street divided by a median whose massive concrete pillars supported the Skytrain, Bangkok's elevated transit system. Small shops and restaurants lined the street but walking beneath the Skytrain superstructure was unpleasant, like being stuck under a bridge for several blocks.

He came to Patpong, the street the area was named after. He walked up it, not because he was curious to see the epicenter of Bangkok's red light district but because it would be deserted this time of day. With the exception of a few street cleaners, a beer delivery truck and the odd Australian staggering back to his hotel after a night with bar-girls, it was quiet. For a few short blocks, the street was dense with shuttered bars whose marquees advertised *Goldfinger's*, *King's Castle*, *Lucifer*, *Nakedgirls*, and *Superpussy* before subsiding into a string of cheap restaurants.

Crowe turned the corner onto Surawong Road, a commercial street. The traffic was a mix of motorcycles, trucks and cars, plus lots of *tuk-tuks,* the three-wheeled vehicles operated both privately and for hire. When they weren't weaving all over the road, vehicles drove on the left, so Crowe looked both ways before he stepped off a curb.

Soi Pradit was a single-lane street lined with two- to four-story buildings, barricaded shops on the ground floor and apartments above. Cars were jammed into tiny parking spaces. Street vendor carts stood in rows like little wagon trains, display racks locked down, wheels roped together with snakes of padlocked chain. The street smelled of fried eggs, laundry detergent, spilled beer and rotting vegetables.

The address Crowe sought was an apartment building opposite a gold-domed temple. The apartment building had a world-weary look betrayed by its chipped stucco and fading paint. Its ground floor hosted four different shops. The balconies of the apartments above were closed in with heavy wire mesh. Crowe had seen such grilles in New Delhi, protection from the local monkeys. Here, he reckoned it was more a deterrent for burglars.

He found the building entrance and climbed to the third floor. The smell of cooking oil and fish was pervasive. He knocked on a door. It opened on a middle-aged woman in a yellow silk housecoat and high-heeled sandals.

She dipped her head to peer over her reading glasses. Seeing no one else in the hall, she studied his face and raised a cigarette to her lips.

"You look for girl?" Twin plumes of smoke came out of her nostrils. "Or boy?"

"Does Kitti Poornchai live here?"

"No Kitti here." The woman coughed, a rattle of phlegm that sounded like a lawn-mower engine in need of a new spark plug.

"This used to be her address. Are you her mother?"

The woman shook her head and began closing the door.

Crowe felt like a cheap thug putting his foot into the gap, but he hadn't come this far to be turned away by a lie. He'd seen the clench in her jaw when he mentioned Kitti's name. This woman knew her. More than that, she was afraid for her. Crowe had seen the frantic look in the woman's eyes as she'd tried to assess what danger Crowe presented.

"I know she's in trouble. I just want to help." Crowe leaned his weight against the open door, but didn't cross her threshold. "May I come in?"

The woman didn't have much leverage, in any sense of the word. She backed away from the door and he stepped inside. The living room was crowded with furniture - unmade day-bed, two mismatched club chairs, rattan coffee table scattered with magazines, and in the corner some colored plastic crates containing clothes, with a TV perched on top.

"My name is Axel Crowe." He showed his ID. "I'm not with the police but I'm trying to help a friend in America. Are you Kitti's mother?"

"Yes." She retreated behind a narrow counter that divided the living room from a kitchenette. She stubbed her cigarette in an ashtray and lit a fresh one from a pack on the counter.

Crowe stood still, not wanting to alarm her. Through the window, he saw an old woman wrapped in a shawl in a chair on the balcony. At the other end of the balcony, two yellow birds in a bamboo cage flitted from perch to perch. Crowe looked at the grille enclosing the balcony. Cages within cages.

"What's your name?"

"Fern."

Crowe pulled out a wad of 500-baht notes and laid a bill on the kitchen counter. "Where's Kitti?"

She shook her head, looking at the money. "Gone."

"She just arrived a few days ago. Where'd she go?" He peeled another note from the wad and fingered it.

"Two men come look for her. They say just need to talk, but I know their kind, they talk with their fists."

Crowe added the second bill to the one on the counter. "What happened?"

"She out when they come. I tell them she don't live here, but they search apartment and find luggage. They take her passport."

He peeled off another bill. "And Kitti?"

"I send my nephew find her, tell her what happen. He come back with message, she can't come home because maybe they waiting for her. She go stay with friend."

He added the third bill to the others. "Do you know who, or where?"

Fern shook her head. "Better not know."

"Have the men been back?"

"Couple times. Once, middle of night."

"Did they hurt you?"

"Little bit." She pulled back the sleeve of her housecoat. The bruise on her upper arm was massive, almost as yellow as the housecoat itself.

"If Kitti contacts you, please tell her to get in touch with me." Crowe gave Fern a hotel business card. "I can protect her from those men."

Fern made a sputtering laugh and shook her head. "You get in way, they cut you little pieces, make you food for worms."

"I don't think so."

She butted her cigarette, plucked the 1500 baht from the counter and slipped it into her housecoat pocket. It wasn't much money where he came from - only $50 - but it would probably make a difference for her.

"What you want?"

"A little information. To help Kitti."

She studied him for a few moments, then gestured toward the club chairs. "Make yourself homely."

43

FERN PREPARED A POT OF TEA, and placed it with two matching cups on the tiny rattan table between club chairs. She sat in the adjacent chair and lit another cigarette, this time offering him one, which he declined.

Although once upon a time he'd been an occasional social smoker, Crowe had been weaned of the habit by Guruji's advice: *What goes into the mouth will dirty what comes out of the mouth. If you want to speak the truth – to give good readings and make accurate predictions – don't let your diet make a liar of you.*

"Why did Kitti come back to Thailand?" Crowe asked.

"She need vacation."

"She'd just been on a ten-day silent retreat." Crowe told Fern about the Dharmapada ashram.

"She need vacation from America."

"Is life so bad there?"

"Not what she expect."

"What took her there?"

"She meet this guy many years ago. She fall crazy in love but I don't like him much. Jimmy Kertang. Pimp and drug dealer. No problem, we all need money. Sometimes I help tourists enjoy good time in Bangkok. Germans have money but drink too much, chase schoolgirls. I like Australians but some very tough, like American rednecks."

"This Jimmy Kertang," Crowe said, bringing her back on track. "He's a local?"

She shook her head. "From Chiang Rai."

Crowe knew of it. Chiang Rai was in northern Thailand, near the borders of Burma and Laos. After Afghanistan, the Golden Triangle was the world's biggest opium farm.

"A drug dealer?"

"He talk about many big deals, but long time gone. He say he millionaire, but I never believe him. Maybe million baht, not dollars."

"And Kitti?"

"She love him. She say he love her. I call him bad man but she say he good to her. He say he quit drug business ten years gone because army take over, and he no want getting killed. He switch to sex trade. He move to Chiang Mai and become big bird in little cage."

Crowe had been to Chiang Mai. The cultural capital of Thailand was also in the north, a relative oasis compared to Bangkok's density and frenetic activity.

"What did he do in the sex trade?"

"He call himself talent scout," Fern said. "He visit hill tribes up north, find pretty girls, buy them from parents. He give them job in Chiang Mai, fucking tourists. He also supply girls to Bangkok. Then he get idea shipping girls to America."

"Is that how he met Kitti?"

"He need somebody to be auntie for Bangkok girls, keep them healthy and working, maybe dream better life in America..." She gestured out the window, where the balcony grille portioned the sky in a grid of limited possibility.

"Who were his contacts in America?"

She shrugged. "No names. He say he work for movie

company."

"The film industry?"

"Sure. Many girl become big star in America." Fern made an "O" of her pursed lips and pumped her fist beneath them.

"Do you remember the name of the company?"

She went to a bedroom behind the kitchenette and returned with a business card. It was nicely designed, a beautiful Thai girl at the wheel of a red sports car, a movie camera coming in for a close-up. Patpong Pictures had a website address, *patpongpix.com*, a 212 area code number and a New York address with a 10002 zip code.

"Kitti helped Jimmy Kertang recruit girls to go to America? When was this?"

"Three, four years ago. Then she move to America."

"After those guys came looking for her, you think she might have gone to stay with Jimmy Kertang?"

"She don't say, but I hoping not. He is past, not good for future. People in drug business tough, very bad."

"Where can I find him?"

"Chiang Mai."

"Do you have an address? A phone number?"

"No need address. You ask for Jimmy Kertang, everybody in Chiang Mai know him. He the man. Big bird in little cage."

Crowe debated what to do. Bangkok was huge, a city of eight million. If Kitti's mother didn't know where she was, trying to find her would be like looking for a stolen motorbike. That's if Fern wasn't lying... Crowe wondered how he might test her.

"How old is Kitti?"

"Twenty-nine."

"How old are you?"

"Forty-six." Crowe did the math. Fern had been only seventeen when she had Kitti.

"How much do you weigh?"

Fern thought about it a moment. "Forty-five kilo."

He looked at her, doing the math, and decided a hundred

...s looked right. She appeared to be telling the truth about her age and weight, but was this getting anywhere?

Crowe switched to numerology. She'd given him three numbers. Together they added up to 120, which reduced to a three, the number of Jupiter. Today was Thursday, the day of Jupiter. Across the street was a temple, with which Jupiter was also associated. Everything seemed to suggest *dharma* - the right path. He decided to be transparent with her.

"Fern, I need to decide whether to go to Chiang Mai looking for Jimmy Kertang. My question is, will this help me find Kitti or assist the case I'm investigating back in America? Don't say anything, just listen. You must have some books. Can you go get one - any book - and bring it to me?"

He watched her as she stood and went to the bedroom. She came back with a Michelin travel guide to Thailand. She held it out to him. Several photos graced the front cover; the largest three - a Thai dancer, a Buddha, and a mountain temple - were all in gold.

He declined to take it from her hands. "Open it and tell me the first page number you see."

She opened the book in the middle. "One hundred and eleven."

Crowe knew now he should go to Chiang Mai. When Fern had gone to fetch the book, she'd taken that first step with her right foot. On the human body, the left was considered female and passive, the right male and active. She'd returned with a book whose illustrations were all in gold, the color of the Sun, a male planet. The page number 111 was an odd number - also male - and for bonus points, added up to a three, the number of Jupiter, another male planet.

Out of curiosity, he took the book from her and looked at where she'd opened it. The two facing pages - 110 and 111 - were dedicated to the *Wat Doi Suthep*, one of the most revered Buddhist shrines in northern Thailand. It was just 12 kilometers from Chiang Mai.

Crowe closed the book and handed it back to Fern.

"You have answer now?"

"Yes, thank you." He stood to leave.

Fern followed him to the door and tugged at his sleeve before he left. "You find her, please, but take back to America. I love her but not safe here."

"I'll do what I can."

Crowe descended to the street. Finding Kitti would be hard enough, but rescuing her from whatever trouble she was in might take good fortune more than effort. He crossed the street, removed his shoes and entered the temple. Incense drifted on the air. Dozens of people sat meditating on the floor. A large Buddha sat at the front of the temple. In alcoves along the walls were smaller Buddhas, both seated and standing. Crowe sat for awhile and set his mind adrift on the ocean of no-thinking. When he came out of it, he left 1000 baht in the donation box and headed back to the hotel.

44

Chiang Mai

THE CROWNE PLAZA'S TRAVEL CONCIERGE booked Crowe the next available flight to Chiang Mai and reserved a hotel near the city's night market. On vacation seven years ago he'd taken the 12-hour night train to Chiang Mai, but had no such time to waste on this trip.

He caught the airport shuttle and shortly past noon was on a Bangkok Airways flight headed north. He declined coffee and drank some mango juice. He tried to sleep but two people behind him chattered loudly the whole trip. He stared out the port window at a mountain range to the west, the frontier between Thailand and Burma.

By the time he rode an airport taxi into the city and checked into his hotel, it was half past two. Crowe had chosen Le Meridien for two reasons: it was a stone's throw from the night market, and had a symbolic street number, 108 Chang Khlan Road.

108 frequently occurred in Vedic numerology. There were 12 signs in the zodiac, each divided into ninths, for a total of 108 *navamsas*. The zodiac also consisted of 27 *nakshatras*, or star groups, each divided into quarters, for a total of 108 *padas*. For this reason, 108 recurred in many spiritual contexts - 108 beads in a mala, 108 steps in some temple entrances, 108 petals in the lotus of the heart, and so on.

Thus, Crowe felt he was now installed in the appropriate place from which to conduct his investigation. Checking in, he asked for a room on the 18th floor. The bellboy showed him to Room 1809, from whose windows he could see the mountains to the west. As he looked out over the city, Crowe reflected that Chiang Mai had been designed according to principles of *vastu*, literally "good space", a well-organized environment.

The city had been built on the eastern side of the mountains, giving a broad vista to the river and beyond. The original walled city had been laid out in a perfect square, the epitome of stability. Its walls were aligned on the axes of the compass and surrounded by a moat across which several bridges granted entry via the city gates.

Crowe closed the curtains, removed his shoes and lay on the king-size bed. The time zones had caught up to him. Back in New York, it was three AM. No wonder he felt tired. In minutes he was asleep.

He awoke at 4:30, showered and emerged with a ravenous hunger, having eaten nothing since his layover in New Delhi. He went down to the lobby and asked one of the staff to recommend a good restaurant. The desk clerk pointed across the street to the Red Lion English Pub & Restaurant. Crowe said he wanted a good Thai restaurant. The clerk apologized and pointed him up Chang Khlan Road. The Siam Café was very good.

"What about a girl?" Crowe said.

The clerk shrugged. "After dark, night market is full of girls."

"I don't want a street girl. I want a really nice girl - attractive and sophisticated - who speaks good English."

"All girls speak some English. First they say, pay now. Afterwards, thank you sir, come again." The clerk laughed, showing a gold tooth.

"Someone in Bangkok told me about a guy who runs the best escort service in Chiang Mai. Maybe you know him? Jimmy Kertang?"

The clerk frowned. "I know him, but not because he has best agency. Jimmy Kertang has many girls, but also bad reputation with police, mixed up in drugs and smuggling. You don't want to do business with him. He is big talker, and rip-off artist."

"We have a mutual friend. I'm sure he'll treat me fair."

"You are a *farang,*" the clerk said, using the Thai word for foreigner. "No one will treat you fair."

"You know how to get in touch with him?" Crowe took 500 baht from his pocket, folded the bill twice and offered it to the clerk.

"I will find out." The clerk plucked the bill from his hand. "When you come back from restaurant, I will have number for you."

Crowe walked up Chang Khlan Road to the Siam Café where he had a papaya salad and a bowl of sticky rice topped with sliced mango.

He returned to the hotel and found the clerk, who took him out to the pool area, showing him where to pick up his complimentary towel. He handed Crowe the hotel's business card, on the back of which was written a telephone number.

"You call him after six o'clock. He fix you up with nice girls, as many as you want."

"Thank you, I appreciate your help."

"No problem." The clerk winked. "Have a nice night."

Crowe returned to his room and changed into his bathing suit, which was always packed in his overnight bag. Although not a great swimmer, he favored hotels with pools whenever possible. He enjoyed moderate exercise but he easily overheated, so swimming was the best way to get a cardio workout without raising a sweat.

He put on the complimentary bathrobe and went down to the pool area. Late afternoon, the sun was halfway down the horizon. Picking up a towel, he selected a lounge chair distant from the other tourists. He did several laps of the pool, toweled off and absorbed some sun while reading *The Ramayana*.

He returned to his room and did some yoga, but it was difficult. He'd developed a stiff lower back on the flights from New York to Bangkok, and no amount of stretching alleviated it. If a night's sleep didn't resolve it, he'd have to get a massage.

At six PM Crowe phoned the number for Jimmy Kertang. A man answered. Crowe heard sounds of traffic and assumed the call was being taken from a moving vehicle.

"Mr. Jimmy, you don't know me, but we have a mutual acquaintance in Kitti Poornchai. You know who I'm talking about?"

There was a moment's hesitation. "I don't know any Kitti. I know lots of other girls, though. You looking for a good time?"

"No, I'm looking for Kitti. Can you help me?"

"Why her? She's old. I can fix you up with a young girl, beautiful like the Princess of Siam."

"*She's old*? You said you didn't know Kitti."

"I used to. But she moved to the US a few years ago. What do you want with her?"

"She's in trouble. I want to help her."

"Why? You her boyfriend?"

"No."

"A cop?"

"I'll tell you all about it when we meet. Trust me. I got your name from Kitti's mother. I just want to help her."

"Where are you staying?"

"The Meridien."

Kertang gave him an address on Loi Khor Road, a block east of the hotel. A shop called Deadheads. Be there at nine.

Crowe used his phone app to create a chart for when Kertang proposed they meet. Scorpio would be rising again, just like Monday night when he'd gone to the gentlemen's lounge in Thai High, looking for Kitti Poornchai. But now the Moon was in the 8th house.

The Moon had been in Taurus earlier this week, but had moved into Gemini during his flight from New York to Bangkok. Crowe did some mental math and realized the Moon had also changed *nakshatra* the moment his plane touched down in Chiang Mai.

Although the zodiac comprised the twelve signs familiar to everyone, Hindu astrology also divided the zodiac into 27 *nakshatras*. The Moon was now in Ardra, an asterism associated with intense emotions that could provoke tears. Its themes were betrayal, solitude, sadness and rage. Its people were abandoned children, conflicted parents and wounded lovers.

Crowe pondered the chart. He needed Kertang's help to locate Kitti but, based on the Gemini moon alone, he anticipated ambivalence and double-dealing. Furthermore, the Moon's dispositor was Mercury in Pisces, another indicator of duplicity and subterfuge. He would have to play this meeting shrewdly.

It was dark by quarter to seven. Crowe took advantage of the time zone and called Blaikie in New York, where it was going on seven AM.

"This won't become a bad habit, will it?" Blaikie said. "Giving me a wake-up call from Asia every morning?"

"You always said you were an early riser."

"Yes, but I was referring to my sexual readiness."

Crowe laughed. "Any news from Abbott's lawyer?"

"His appeal for bail was denied."

"Any chance I could call and get him on the phone?"

"No communication allowed except legal counsel."

"How's he holding up?"

"Apparently he's meditating a lot. Not much else to do with his time, I suppose."

"He knows I'm working on his case?"

"Yes. He's praying for your success. Anything you need?"

"Not at this point." Crowe briefed Blaikie on where he was at.

"You're meeting a guy who's a pimp and a former drug dealer, who may be a trafficker in underage prostitutes? Sounds like you need a bodyguard. Or your head examined."

"I'm actually quite confident this will be productive."

"Good luck. If you end up in jail or a hospital, call me. If I never hear from you again, thanks for everything, it's been fun knowing you."

Crowe hung up. He wasn't put off by Blaikie's gallows humor. He was reminded again of Arjuna in the Bhagavad Gita, apprehensive and self-doubting on the eve of battle. But as Krishna had assured him, *When the cause is just, good men prevail.*

45

AT EIGHT PM, CROWE WENT FOR A WALK on Chang Khlan Road, now crowded with pedestrians, both locals and tourists. Shops and stalls offered fruit and vegetables, household items, motorcycle parts, hill-tribe crafts, leather goods, clothing, silverware, knock-off watches, antiques of every kind.

Crowe wandered into an arcade filled with artists' stalls where he spent half an hour admiring the art work. The subject matter varied widely, landscapes and celebrities and devotional art, but it was all superbly rendered, as good as any art gallery back home, and all at bargain prices.

At nine, he headed down Loi Khor Road. Near the

intersection with Lane 6, several tiny bungalows stood bunched together like books on a crowded shelf. Among them was *Deadheads*, a head shop and tattoo parlor, with a window display of glass pipes, bongs and hookahs. Inside were posters of dead rock stars, a rack of CDs, catalogs of tattoo designs, and bales of T-shirts. A trio of Aussie backpackers were haggling over the price of something under the counter.

After they'd left, Crowe approached the shopkeeper. He was big and fleshy, more Chinese than Thai, his puffy eyelids looking like someone had used his head for a speed bag in the local gym.

"Jimmy Kertang?"

"Who you?" the man said.

"Axel Crowe. Jimmy told me to meet him here." Crowe knew as soon as Puffy spoke his two words of broken English that he wasn't Kertang.

"ID." Puffy waggled his fingers.

Crowe showed the man his driver's license.

Puffy examined it as carefully as a passport control officer, comparing Crowe's picture to the person standing at the counter.

"Why you want to talk to Jimmy?" Puffy said.

"He knows. I explained on the phone this afternoon." The shopkeeper was being nosy but Crowe didn't feel like indulging him.

Puffy came out from behind the counter and frisked him. Finding only a water bottle in Crowe's shoulder pack, he went outside and lit a cigarette. A few moments, he returned to his stool behind the counter and squinted at Crowe.

Crowe stared back. "Should I pull up a chair?"

Puffy picked up his cell phone and made a quick call, a dozen words in rapid-fire Thai. He jerked his chin toward the door.

"You go now. Mr. Jimmy waiting."

Crowe stepped outside. A blue Toyota Cruiser with a white roof sat idling in the lane. He descended to the curb and approached the vehicle.

The driver was a once-handsome man in his fifties gone to seed. He had long hair tied in a ponytail that hung over the collar of his green silk shirt. Although his skin looked like well-soaped leather with a few wrinkles around the eyes, he had good teeth, and his eyes were alert as Crowe came to his window.

"Jimmy Kertang?"

"Get in."

Crowe went around to the other side of the vehicle, glancing into the rear to check for hidden riders. He slid into the passenger seat but didn't bother to buckle up. The law was non-existent, and you never knew when you might need to bail on short notice.

Kertang headed east on Loi Khor Road, using his horn to drive a wedge through motorcycles and pedestrians. They hit a set of traffic lights at a main street, then continued several blocks to cross a bridge over the Ping River.

"I'll take you to a place the tourists don't know." Kertang drove along the river before turning east again. A few blocks later he parked in front of a restaurant whose only sign was in Thai.

A dozen tables sprawled around a bar in one corner. The walls were red, the ceiling mother-of-pearl. All of the tables were occupied by Thai except for one vacant table in an alcove, apparently awaiting their arrival. Kertang took the chair at the back. Crowe sat at right angles with a view of the entrance. Near the door to the kitchen was a table with a man and three women, one of whom had a visible baby bump.

A beautiful young Thai waitress in a slit dress brought Kertang a Heineken and what looked like a scotch on the rocks. She smiled at Crowe and asked, "Something to drink, mister?"

"Mango juice."

Kertang lit a Marlboro Light and swallowed some scotch. He pulled the ashtray within reach and set his cigarette on its rim. He had a broad palm but his fingers were long and slim, elegant rather than effeminate. His fingernails were also broad but his fingertips were slightly tapered.

In lieu of examining the lines of the hand, skin texture and the fingertip patterns, Crowe was forced to judge Kertang's hands a toss-up between an air and water type. Hybrids were common enough, and interpretations could straddle the two types.

Kertang was likely a shrewd and intelligent man. He'd like to tell stories, and could be quite a fabricator. He'd be well-informed, and inclined to assemble and analyze information before making decisions. But he had his emotional side too, and if one could appeal to his feelings, his gut instinct would sometimes over-rule his logic. Because of this internal struggle between thinking and feeling, he was restless and unsettled – a man living near the edge of a nervous meltdown, like a cliff-hanging house on the Malibu shore, hoping nothing would push him over. He probably depended heavily on alcohol and *bhang* to calm his nerves.

The girl returned with Crowe's juice and said something in Thai to Kertang. He answered and she went away. Kertang sipped his scotch and chased it with a little Heinie.

"How do you know Kitti?" Kertang asked.

Crowe wasn't a bridge player, but he believed in leading with a hand that obliged an opponent to step up or step down. A version of the truth was usually the quickest route to mutual respect and understanding.

He told Kertang about Seth Greer's death at the retreat attended by Kitti and Dean Bishop. When she'd fled New York, he'd tracked down her mother in Bangkok who'd said two men were looking for her.

"What did they look like?"

"She didn't say. Just that they were Thai."

"How is Fern these days?" Kertang asked.

"She sends her regards."

"Bullshit. She'd send me a letter bomb if she knew my address."

"Why's that?"

"Just bad chemistry, I guess. I was very good to Kitti,

helped her move up to a better life. Fern doesn't seem to recognize that."

In the back of his mind Crowe was still thinking about the current chart. Moon in the 8th house in the constellation of *Ardra*. It implied some sort of abandonment, a deep loss from which Kertang had perhaps never fully recovered.

"She was the love of your life, wasn't she?"

Kertang shrugged, but he dropped his eyes at the same time and toyed with his cigarette, brushing the ash on the rim of the ashtray.

Over at the table near the kitchen door, one of the three women knocked a teacup to the floor. It broke and the waitress hurried over to pick up the pieces. The man and the pregnant woman exchanged terse words. She got up and went to the washroom with one of her girlfriends.

"Something happened between the two of you," Crowe said, growing ever confident in his speculation. In the chart of the moment, the 5th house was occupied by the 8th lord, a debilitated Mercury. The 5th lord Jupiter was in the 6th. Both were signs of failed romance or children denied through abortion or miscarriage. "She was pregnant but she lost the baby. For some reason she blamed you. You argued. You said some things you regretted. She never really forgave you. For that matter, you probably never forgave yourself."

The color drained from Kertang's face as he tried to maintain his composure. He stubbed his cigarette out and swallowed the rest of his scotch with a grimace. When he lifted his eyes to look at Crowe again, the muscle in his jaw was tense.

"When did you last see Kitti?" Crowe asked.

"Three years ago, just before she moved to the US."

"Have you talked to her since?"

"We spoke on the phone a few months ago."

"Concerning what?"

"A private matter."

"Let me guess. She was sponsoring girls for immigration, ostensibly for modeling careers, but actually for strip joints and massage parlors. You were recruiting local talent who believed the great American dream, where a girl might make a lot of money, or at least marry a rich guy and start a family."

Kertang cleared his throat. "Could be."

"Who owns the company called Patpong Pictures?"

Kertang shrugged, the vague gesture making it unclear whether his ignorance extended only to its ownership, or the company itself. Or he simply refused to say.

The girl returned with a tray, from which she dispensed half a dozen dishes - ginger shrimp, green curry chicken, a small fish in a red sauce, mango salad, noodles with bean curd, and sticky rice in long funnel-like baskets. As soon as she'd gone, Kertang began transferring portions to his plate.

Thais considered it bad luck to eat alone, and rude for guests to refuse food, so even though he wasn't really hungry, Crowe took some mango salad, noodles with bean curd, and sticky rice, the latter of which was particularly delicious.

"Kitti hasn't contacted you since she returned to Bangkok?" Crowe asked.

"I didn't even know she was in the country."

"If she had to go into hiding, where do you think she'd be?"

"I don't know." Kertang chewed a mouthful of chicken, but seemed to have trouble getting it down. "If she were in trouble, I hope she would have asked for my help. I would have done anything for her, no questions asked."

"You really loved her, didn't you?"

Kertang nodded and blinked several times. His eyes were wet but he was too proud to acknowledge tears by wiping them away.

"Has anyone else asked about her lately?"

Kertang hesitated. "I did get a call from someone two days ago."

"Who?"

Kertang clenched his jaw and shook his head.

"You're afraid of that person," Crowe said.

Kertang drained his beer and tinkled the empty bottle

against the ashtray. The girl came immediately with a fresh Heineken.

"Why are you involved?" Kertang said. "You could get her killed. Maybe get yourself killed."

"My friend's in jail facing a murder charge. I know he didn't do it. And I think Kitti knows something that could exonerate him."

"You want to sacrifice her to save him?"

"I don't want to see anyone hurt. I just want to talk to her discreetly. The fact she's dropped out of sight, and someone's looking for her, tells me she knows something and she's in trouble. I'd like to help both my friend and Kitti."

Kertang lit a cigarette and looked at Crowe. "Man, you are bad news."

It was Crowe's turn to shrug. "You know what Napoleon Bonaparte said about bad news?"

"Tell me."

"Don't wake me up to tell me good news, because there's nothing urgent about it. But if you have bad news, wake me immediately, because then there's not a minute to be lost."

46

KERTANG DROPPED CROWE AT THE MERIDIEN, saying he'd contact some of Kitti's friends in Bangkok. Maybe she'd sought refuge with them, or they'd heard from her. Crowe thanked him for his help. Kertang said he'd call him tomorrow with any news of Kitti's whereabouts.

Back in his room, Crowe channel-surfed until he found BBC World News on TV. By eleven o'clock he still wasn't tired enough to sleep. He'd just started reading *The Ramayana* when someone knocked on the door.

Through the peep-hole he saw a young woman in the corridor holding up a card that read "Room Service". He hadn't ordered anything, but she aroused curiosity more than suspicion, so he opened the door.

Viewed without the distortion of the peep-hole lens, she now appeared larger than life, almost luminous in her presence. Everything about her was perfect - a glossy cascade of hair upon her shoulders, wide eyes with prominent eyebrows, lush mouth accented with lipstick, the explicit curves beneath her clothes.

"Good evening, Mr. Crowe," she said in unaccented English. She wore a blouse and skirt with a short matching jacket and high heels. Her lime-green blouse and shoes complemented her permanent tan.

"There must be some mistake. I didn't call room service."

"Compliments of Chiang Mai Tourist Bureau." She held up a small Thai Airways flight bag. "My name is Eve. May I come in?"

He looked up and down the hall. Not a creature was stirring, not even a houseboy. He beckoned her in, locking the door behind her.

She walked around the room, glancing into the bathroom, parting the curtains to admire the view of the old city. She set her bag on the dresser and removed her jacket.

"Who sent you?"

"Mr. Jimmy." She took from the bag a bottle of white wine, a baggie of weed, a small water bong and a bottle of massage oil. "I'm here to make your visit to Chiang Mai a memorable one." She handed him the wine. "Can you open this while I get some ice?"

"I don't drink."

"Do you mind if I do?"

"Take it home and share with friends. I'm not up for a party."

She looked dismayed. "If I leave now, Mr. Jimmy will be very angry. He'll beat me."

"I doubt that." Crowe couldn't imagine Kertang's elegant fingers closed in a fist. Ordering someone else to get rough, yes, but not doing it himself.

"You don't know him. He can be very cruel. Last year he had a girl's arm broken because she didn't follow orders."

Crowe sighed in exasperation. "You can stay half an hour, then you leave."

"An hour. Any less and there'll be trouble. Even if you don't want to party, he'll accuse me of not trying."

Crowe unlocked the door and watched her go down the hall with the ice bucket. The dispenser rattled and coughed up a load of cubes. She came back promptly, smiling as she re-entered the room.

She pulled the cork from the wine bottle, poured two glasses and handed one to him. She drank from hers; he set his aside.

The moment Eve appeared at his door, Crowe had thought of a *visha kanya,* a poison girl. According to Hindu lore, kings had used such girls, a form of human Trojan horse offered as a tribute, to destroy their enemies. The girls were made poisonous by exposing them to low-intensity toxins from a very young age. Although many died from such exposure, others developed immunity and survived, although their body fluids became so poisonous that sexual contact could be lethal. In some cases, the *visha kanya* developed psychic toxicity as well and could kill a person just by looking at them.

She sat on the edge of his bed. "You won't drink with me?"

He sat in one of the chairs facing the TV. "I have an allergic reaction to alcohol. It makes me act like a juvenile."

"Sometimes it's good to forget our age and be young again."

"How old are you?"

"Twenty-one."

Crowe doubted it. In their first phone chat, Kertang had offered to set him up with a young girl, a veritable Princess of Siam. This could be her. In Thailand, eighteen was the age of consent, but being on the right side of the law would change nothing for Crowe. In his eyes, she was a child.

"Would you like to smoke some pot?"

"I'm allergic to that too."

She smiled "Why? Does it make you act like an animal?"

"Quite the opposite." It had been fifteen years since Crowe had indulged. Back then, getting high always made him feel like doing yoga. He'd asked Guruji about that, and he'd said it was a *samskara*, a karmic remnant. Many *sadhus*, having renounced normal life to become devotees of God, smoked *bhang* to evoke semi-ecstatic trances in which they lost normal consciousness and saw deities. Since that had never happened to Crowe, what was the point?

"You don't look comfortable." She slipped off her heels and patted the bed beside her. "Come, lie down."

"Thanks, but I'm fine here."

"Your back hurts, doesn't it?"

He hesitated, knowing she'd put her finger on it. Ever since the long flight, he'd had an ache in his lower left back that radiated all the way up to his shoulder blade. None of his yoga exercises relieved the stiffness. More troubling than the physical discomfort was his sense that, with his left side somehow impaired, he couldn't access the intuition that resided there. He decided to go along with her. Maybe something good would come of it.

"How did you know?"

"As soon as you opened the door, I saw your left shoulder lower than your right. Your spine is out of alignment. Let me adjust it before it gets worse."

"How do you know so much about the body?"

"I studied at the International Training Massage School here in Chiang Mai. It's one of the best in the world, recognized by certification boards of massage therapy in Australia, Canada, UK and USA."

"I'm impressed."

Taking this as her cue, she got off the bed and moved behind his chair. She laid a forearm across his left trapezium, applied some weight and rolled it back and forth between neck and shoulder. After repeating this on the right, she gripped his left wrist, pulled his forearm up and behind his head, meanwhile applying her fingers to a pressure point adjacent his shoulder blade.

In a few minutes she had him on the floor, where she worked every back muscle from his neck down to his waist, applying pressure with hands, forearms, feet, knees or entire hip. Crowe understood why advocates said Thai massage was like yoga for lazy people. Instead of your doing the yoga, you relaxed and the therapist did it for you.

Finished, Eve climbed off him and refilled her wine glass. She took it, along with the water bong and weed, into the bathroom and closed the door.

Crowe rolled onto his back but continued lying on the carpet. He heard the bathroom fan humming. The toilet flushed. The sink tap ran briefly. When Eve came out again he caught a faint whiff of marijuana.

"Feeling better now?" she said.

He looked up at her. She was wearing only panties and a camisole, cream-white against her tan.

"Yes, thanks. That was very nice. You're very talented."

"You haven't seen anything yet." She stood astraddle him and lowered herself to a squat, until her buttocks were mere millimeters from his groin. He felt the heat pulsing off her. She drained her wine and set the glass aside.

He caught her wrists before she made her next move. He sat upright and swung her off to one side in a smooth movement that left her sitting on the carpet with her back against the bed.

He turned her right hand toward the bedside lamp. In the heel of her palm he saw the bold horizontal mark called *visha rehka,* the poison line. In the context of some hands, it spelled substance abuse. In her hand, the head line ran long and straight across the palm.

"You're smart," he told her. "You're good in science. You should go to university and study to become a pharmacist or an anesthesiologist."

"I'm saving my money. I want to go back to school."

She had an excellent health line in her palm, a minor line so bold it had the weight of a major line. Its configuration was unusual, the upper end connecting a relationship line under her pinkie, the lower end terminating right on the poison line.

"You're going to meet somebody at university, fall in love, get married and emigrate. Within seven years, your life will have completely changed for the better."

"Are you serious?" Her face was incredulous.

"Yes. It will happen."

Her lip trembled and she raised a hand to brush a tear from her eye. He stood up and put his shirt back on. He beckoned for her to get dressed. After a moment's hesitation, she hastened to put her clothes back on, seemingly embarrassed now by her circumstances.

He walked her down to the front entrance and waved to summon a *tuk-tuk* to take her home. A driver scooted up to the curb. Just before she climbed into the rear seat, she suddenly grabbed Crowe's hand and bowed to press her forehead against the back of his hand.

"Thank you."

He waved goodbye as she drove away.

Maybe she wasn't a *visha kanya,* a poison girl, but he couldn't afford to let her stay the night in his room. Maybe she wouldn't have tried to kill him, but she might have opened the door for someone who would. Now that his back felt better, Crowe intended to watch it.

47

Friday, April 27

CROWE ACCESSED THE HOTEL'S WiFi network next morning to visit the site of Patpong Pictures. Its front page banner displayed the same picture on the business card Fern had given him - the girl in the sports car smiling for the camera.

The site was minimalist, just two other pages. One listed opportunities for attractive young women in American movies, or as models and actors in commercials for American products. No mention of remuneration, but a vague promise of abundant work.

The other page gave Patpong Pictures' contact information - address, telephone, fax and email: *kitti@patpongpix.com*. Crowe used Google's street view to check out the address on Stanton Street on the Lower East Side. It looked like a novelty store, with colored wheels and wrenches all over its barred door and windows. Above the marquee, a biplane was painted on the wall, a protruding ceiling fan for a propeller. Painted footprints ran up the wall from the ground to the third floor windows.

Crowe was puzzled. Whatever this building housed, he doubted it was the office of an advertising and film agency. Nonetheless, he wrote Kitti a short email. Even if she were in hiding, she might have internet access. He said he was in Thailand and wanted to talk to her. He phoned the New York number, listened to a recorded message in a woman's voice, and left a brief voicemail.

He showered and went out for breakfast. When he returned, a voicemail from Kertang was waiting on the hotel phone. He called back.

"Good morning, Mr. Crowe. Did you sleep well?"

"Yes. Any luck locating our mutual friend?"

"No."

"Who did you talk to?"

"Let's discuss this later," Kertang said. "Maybe during your tour of Chiang Mai? You said you were interested in seeing the temples."

"Okay." Crowe decided to play along. Maybe Kertang suspected his phone was bugged, and didn't want to disclose anything that might put him in danger.

"When can you be ready?"

"I'm ready now."

"I'll pick you up in fifteen minutes."

Crowe went downstairs and sat on a bench at the hotel entrance. A shuttle bus arrived, disgorging a six-pack of sleepy Germans. The valets loaded their bags on the luggage wagon and followed them into the lobby. Kertang's Toyota showed up moments later.

"Sleep well?" Kertang gave Crowe a searching look as he seated himself.

"Yes. You asked me already, remember?"

"The Meridien has very good beds, I'm told."

"True." Crowe's back had made a complete recovery.

Kertang drove with one hand, the other on the windowsill with a cigarette. Occasionally he gripped the wheel with his cigarette hand and sipped from a stainless steel mug between his legs.

"Did you enjoy Eve's company?"

"Yes, a very nice girl. We had a lovely talk."

Kertang gave him a sideways glance. "I sent you the most beautiful girl in Chiang Mai, and all you did was talk?"

"She gave me the best back massage I've ever had." Crowe flexed his shoulders. "Yesterday I was so blocked I couldn't think straight. Today I feel wonderful."

"You want her again tonight?" Kertang drew from his cigarette and flicked the butt out the window. "She could work on your lower half."

"That's not necessary. I do my thinking with the big head, not the little one."

Kertang shrugged. He turned without signaling, crossed a bridge over the moat surrounding the old city and drove through a gate.

For the next hour, Kertang gave Crowe a tour of the old city, principally a drive-by of several excellent temples, accompanied by Kertang's travelogue.

"Although Bangkok is fifty times bigger than Chiang Mai, our city has almost as many *wats*. Most of these temples were built five or six hundred years ago, the city's most prosperous era. Chiang Mai is often called the "rose of the north", and was chosen in the 13th century by King Mengrai as the capital of his Lanna Kingdom."

"Under his rulership, didn't it also become a major centre for Theravada Buddhism?"

Kertang squinted at Crowe. "You've been here before?"

"We've all been here before," Crowe joked.

Kertang nodded but said nothing. He stared at Crowe, still waiting for a straight answer.

"Yes, I've been here before," Crowe said. "I'm also a student of Buddhism, remember? My friend runs a retreat dedicated to the practice of Vipassana."

"The retreat where you met Kitti..."

"You said last night you'd call some friends in Bangkok. Did you learn anything of her whereabouts?"

"No one's seen or heard from her. They didn't even know she was back in Bangkok."

"Had anyone else asked them about her?"

"They said no."

"Would they tell you if they had?"

"I don't know."

"Did anyone ask why you were trying to find her?"

Kertang hesitated. "An hour after I talked to my friends, I got a call from this guy, the one I told you about last night, asking me how I knew Kitti was back in town."

"What did you say?"

"I said I'd got a call from her mother, who was worried after she'd dropped out of sight."

Crowe nodded. It was a safe answer that made sense and didn't risk coming back to bite anyone on the ass. More importantly, his name hadn't been shared. "Who was this guy?"

Kertang hesitated. "His name is Qing Qroc."

"That doesn't sound like a Thai name."

"He's Burmese-Chinese. There are powerful triads in Bangkok, some of them in business ever since the Opium Wars in the nineteenth century."

"Is that his business - drugs?"

"Mostly. But he's got a hand in almost everything. Very big player, and a nasty motherfucker."

"How do you know him?"

"I used to coordinate, um, shipments out of Chiang Rai. You know, the Golden Triangle?"

"When was this?"

"Seventies and eighties, mostly."

"The seventies?" Crowe reassessed Kertang. "What were you, a teenager at the time?"

Kertang shrugged. "Practically."

"You're lucky you're still alive to talk about it."

"My father and two brothers were killed in the eighties during gang wars over the opium market. That's when I left Chiang Rai and moved to Bangkok. Out of the wok and into the fire. I tried to carve out a business, using family connections, but it was like swimming with crocodiles. One day on a trip up north to coordinate a shipment, I was picked up by the Army and beaten for twelve hours. Up there, the police and military have taken over the drug business. They have guns and they don't like sharing. I took their advice to get out of the business and switched to something less risky."

"Girls?"

Kertang nodded. "Not as much money to be made, but at least you can help someone have a little fun without turning them into an addict."

Crowe said nothing, but continued to watch in the side-view mirror a black Range Rover parked some fifty yards down the street. He'd noticed it shortly after Kertang had parked opposite the *Wat Phan Tao.*

"You find that ironic?" Kertang said. "A pimp with a moral conscience?"

"Not at all," Crowe said. "The Puranas, which are stories adapted from Vedic mythology, offer many anecdotes about criminals who saw the light and turned their lives around to become devotees."

"So there's hope for me yet?"

"Ask not what your karma can do for you, but what you can do for your karma."

Kertang laughed as he lit another cigarette. "That's good. Did you just make that up?"

"With a little help from JFK."

Kertang looked at his watch. "It's too early for lunch. Anything else you'd like to see in Chiang Mai?"

Crowe looked at the Range Rover in the mirror. "No, I think it's time we got out of Dodge."

"What do you mean?"

"Scram. Let's drive."

48

THEY LEFT THE CITY, driving west into the nearby mountains. Farmland gave way to forest as they rose in elevation. They passed a roadside temple, its surrounding trees wrapped with yellow and red banners. After fifteen minutes on a road that twisted and turned like a snake, they arrived at a tiny village of shops and restaurants near the summit of a mountain.

They joined a dozen cars and a tour bus in a parking lot. A long stairway climbed through the trees to *Wat Doi Suthep*. For the less athletic, a funicular provided easy transport to the summit. Flanking the foot of the stairway, vendors' booths offered soft drinks and water, cigarettes, gold leaf, incense, flowers and fruit.

Kertang paused at a stall operated by an old woman with

a cigar gripped in her gnarled mouth. He selected a bundle of incense sticks tied with yellow string, and a packet of gold leaf in a tiny booklet. He spoke to the woman in Thai. She coughed up a reply and thrust his money into a purse strapped across her chest.

Another woman in her thirties approached and tugged Crowe's sleeve. She held up a cage containing a small bird with a dark crest and white breast, yellow shoulders and black-banded throat. The cage was just a woven basket, two hemispheres hinged together with twine and locked with a peg in a loop.

"Set him free, good karma for you," the woman said. "One hundred baht."

Kertang turned and barked something at her in Thai. She recoiled under his words, wiped away a frown and replaced it with an apologetic smile. "Sorry for my English, mister. I mistake my numbers. Fifty baht."

"You know it's just a scam," Kertang told Crowe. "You set them free and tomorrow some guy nets them to put back in a cage, and it all goes around and around."

"Sounds just like life, doesn't it?"

Crowe held the cage up to eye level, admiring the colorful little bird trapped within. The prisoner fidgeted and chirped in shrill little squawks, obviously hating the scrutiny. The vendor inched closer, wringing her hands, hopeful Crowe would pay to set the bird free.

The situation presented him with a moral dilemma. He knew it was a scam, but it wasn't all black and white. If he paid to set the bird free, another bird would be caught to take its place, and the practice would continue. But that money might feed a hungry child, or buy medicine for a sick parent. Which was more important, birds or people?

He handed the cage to Kertang. "You should do this. If not for Kitti, then for yourself."

Kertang shook his head. "I don't believe in that shit."

"Consider it an act of faith," Crowe said. "Look at this bird. He's in a cage, but we're no less trapped. From the moment we're born, we're burdened with history and expectations, our life filled with regrets for the past and anxieties about the future. We're not as free as we think."

Kertang stared into the bamboo cage, unwilling to see himself trapped like a little bird.

"Come on, let yourself go," Crowe said. "You do it, and I'll do one too." Merit or not, it would earn them equal karma. He beckoned to the vendor to fetch another of the cages lined up on a nearby stone wall. She scurried to get one.

Crowe held the cage in his hands a moment and looked at the bird. He saw Bryan Abbott in a cage of his own. *For your freedom, my friend.* He unfastened the clasp and opened the basket. The bird spiraled up into the air and disappeared into the trees. Crowe looked at Kertang.

"I don't need liberating," Kertang protested.

"Yes, you do. You're so full of guilt it's practically coming out your ears. Maybe you fell into bad habits, but you deserve *moksha* as much as the next person. We're all just travelers on the same path."

Kertang shrugged, held the cage aloft and tugged free the peg that released the halves of the basket. The bird took off like a rocket.

"You see?" Crowe laughed. "You couldn't wait to get out of there."

Kertang gave the cage back to the bird vendor. He pulled a bill from his pocket and pressed it into her hand. After a look of astonishment, she fell to her knees and pressed her hands to his feet. Kertang turned and walked away.

"That was for Kitti, not me," he told Crowe.

The stairway to *Wat Doi Suthep* was ten feet wide, flanked by huge snake sculptures, their several heads adorned by spiny crests. The *Naga* were benign serpents who guarded against evil spirits. Revered throughout Asia as protectors of the Buddha, they were ever-present at holy sites and shrines, appearing in staircases, roofs, doors, gables and windows.

Crowe and Kertang climbed the stairway. On either side, the bodies of the twin serpents undulated up the hillside, their stone scales ornamented with paint. Crowe counted a hundred steps by the time they were only a third of the way up.

They met several people coming down - young monks with shaven heads in orange robes, tourists with cameras and day packs, local families with three generations on hand.

At the summit was a paved yard and a monument of a white elephant decorated with ornamental tassels and bells. From across the complex came a steady ringing of bells.

"When King Nu Na visited this area in the fourteenth century," Kertang said, "his elephant marched to the top of this mountain, turned three times and trumpeted. The King took it as an omen and built a temple in this very spot."

Crowe stood admiring the monument, paying homage to the wisdom of both the elephant and his king. Back then, when wisdom was valued more highly than power, kings were instructed by wise men to observe and interpret *nimitta*, or omens.

Kertang led the way around a courtyard with a low wall. Below the summit were several buildings that housed monks and grounds keepers. Over the trees they could see the sprawl of Chiang Mai to the southeast.

The temple complex was in a square compound accessible by either of four doorways. Along one wall was a row of twelve bells. This was the source of the constant ringing, as devotees, pilgrims and tourists took turns knocking the tasseled strikers inside the brass bells.

Crowe and Kertang removed their shoes and entered an inner courtyard tiled in polished marble. At its center stood a towering *chedi* in gold, at each corner of which a column bore a large parasol. Kertang peeled a square of gold leaf from the booklet he'd bought, wet it with his tongue and pasted it to the nearest column. Thousands of gold leaves had previously been applied by other devotees, and the floor around the column was glittery with gold particle.

Kertang handed the booklet to Crowe. They circled the

chedi and applied leaf to the four columns. Two temples stood at the east and west ends of the courtyard, while on the north and south sides were tiny chapels. Kertang led Crowe into the temple on the west side.

A dizzying array of Buddhist artifacts greeted them. The walls were painted with deities, kings, devotees and sacred animals, the floor inlaid with mother-of-pearl. Along the walls, small statuary in marble, brass and resin crowded low tables draped with gold cloth. Beneath a canopy, a huge gold Buddha sat flanked by a dozen smaller Buddhas. They were surrounded by mandalas, bells and pictures of politicians and benefactors.

In front of this dais stood a row of sand-filled ceramic pots in which several incense sticks were burning. Smoke drifted overhead. Kertang divided his bundle of incense and gave half to Crowe. They lit their bundles and thrust the sticks into the sand. Crowe said a prayer for Bryan Abbott's release.

They left the temple and walked toward the exit. A bell caught Crowe's attention, its frequency so high it almost went unheard among the other bells. He glanced into the tiny chapel and saw an old monk. The monk beckoned for him to enter. Crowe hesitated.

A young monk emerged from the chapel and said something to Kertang, who translated. "The *bhikṣu* wants to bless you. It's a great honor, you must go."

"Come with me," Crowe said to Kertang.

"No, I can't."

"Of course you can." Crowe took Kertang's arm and drew him into the chapel. If it weren't so beautiful, filled with religious art and statuary, it might have been claustrophobic, since it was barely larger than a garden shed.

The elder monk, an aged version of the Dalai Lama, beckoned them to sit on the floor before him. He chanted in a low sonorous voice. Crowe bowed his head and floated on the mantra, buoyed by a tide that had lapped these shores for thousands of years. The *bhikku* dipped a small whisk into a metal cup and flicked water onto their heads three times.

The young monk said something in Thai. Kertang pressed his palms together and bowed to the *bhikku* several times as he got up and backed out of the door. Crowe followed suit.

They recovered their shoes and headed down the stairs. Kertang said nothing, but when Crowe glanced at him, he saw the other man brush tears from his eyes.

Back in the parking lot, instead of heading straight for his Toyota, Kertang went to one of the vendors and examined a collection of postcards. Finding what he wanted, he bought a card and slipped it into his shirt pocket. He took his car keys from his pocket and aimed the remote at the Cruiser. Its lights flickered and the engine gunned into life.

As they exited the parking lot, Crowe caught a glimpse of a black Range Rover parked near the entrance. Its driver wore sunglasses, even though the day was overcast.

49

KERTANG DESCENDED THE MOUNTAIN road at a reckless pace. More than once, careening around a corner, Crowe wondered if they wouldn't end up in the ditch. A hundred yards ahead, an elephant appeared on the road.

"Jimmy, slow down!" Crowe barked.

The sight of the elephant brought Kertang back to his senses. He slowed to 20 mph. The elephant was carrying a massive load of bricks on a makeshift rack, guided by a man with a long bamboo cane. Crowe waved as they went by.

Kertang continued at a more leisurely pace. Ahead appeared the red-and-yellow-bannered trees surrounding the temple they'd seen on the way up. Kertang braked and left the road, coasting onto the temple grounds. The Toyota wove through the trees, stopping on a hillcrest overlooking Chiang Mai. Kertang turned off the engine.

"Are you all right?" Crowe said.

"No." There was a stricken look on Kertang's face.

"What's the matter?"

"I've done terrible things. I'll be punished the rest of my life."

"What are you talking about? Drug smuggling, prostitution? You quit one, you can quit the other. It's never too late to start a new life."

"There's no hope for me. Nothing will fix what I've done."

"What are you talking about?" Crowe didn't know why Kertang had suddenly adopted him as father confessor, but he suspected it had something to do with their blessing in the chapel of *Wat Doi Suthep*.

Kertang showed the postcard he'd bought from the vendor. It was a picture of the altar they'd seen in the temple, with the big gold Buddha under its canopy, surrounded by a dozen smaller Buddhas.

"See this one?" Kertang indicated one of the small Buddhas. "The original was seven hundred years old. It was stolen in ninety-two and replaced by a copy."

"How do you know this?"

Kertang propped the postcard on the dash and lit another cigarette. He blew smoke out the window, coughed and spat in the direction of Chiang Mai.

"During the Vietnam War, Thailand let the US military use their air bases to fly missions against North Vietnam. The biggest was in Udorn, up in the northeast. It was also the Asian base for Air America." Kertang looked at Crowe. "You've heard about it?"

"A small airline covertly owned by the CIA. They provided support for the secret war in Laos."

"In the early seventies my father went into business with two men from the US military in Udorn. Mr. Dean and Mr. Roger. I don't know what brought them to Chiang Rai but maybe it had something to do with neighboring Laos. Opium smugglers crossed that border, so maybe communists did too.

"Anyway, my father began supplying opium to Mr. Dean

and Mr. Roger. They came in with a DC-3 cargo plane every few months, flew down to Bangkok, then back to Udorn. This continued until the war ended in seventy-five, and the US was asked to close its bases in Thailand."

"In Bangkok, it was processed into heroin? Where'd it go after that?"

"The USA, I think, but I don't know how it was shipped."

"How much opium was leaving Chiang Rai each trip?"

"A few hundred kilos, sometimes as much as a thousand."

"How'd you know this?"

"My brothers and I worked for my father. My brothers dealt with the hill tribes, handled the drugs and money. I was younger, a messenger boy and lookout, and arranged for girls for Mr. Dean and Mr. Roger when they were in Chiang Rai."

"Dean and Roger… You never knew their last names?"

"Years later I learned Mr. Dean's full name. Dean Bishop."

Crowe saw it all coming together now. "Kitti was with Bishop at the retreat where the journalist was killed. Did she know Bishop's history?"

Kertang shrugged. "She met him through me in Bangkok about ten years ago. Later, when she went to New York, he gave her some work."

"Do you have any pictures of them together - Bishop and Mr. Roger?"

Kertang shook his head. "Once, when Mr. Dean and Mr. Roger were in Chiang Rai, I offered to take a picture of them together. Mr. Roger got very upset and said if I ever took a picture of him, he'd kill me."

"You think he meant it?"

"He was a bad man. One time in the hills, some tribesmen stopped our truck and asked for money. They weren't thieves, just very poor. No weapons, only the tools they used in the fields. Mr. Roger took out his gun and shot one in the groin. He said, 'Last time you fuck with anyone', and drove away."

Kertang fell silent. He lit another cigarette from the butt

of the other. He took out his cell phone and checked his text messages.

Crowe tried to make sense of this. Dean Bishop had been in Thailand during the Vietnam War, possibly working for the CIA. In partnership with Mr. Roger, he'd got involved in the opium trade. How and why had he ended up in Bryan Abbott's ashram on a silent retreat? And why had he taken Kitti with him, not only that time, but apparently several times before?

Kertang put his phone away and resumed his account.

"The US military pulled out of Thailand in seventy-six. We never saw Mr. Roger again. But Mr. Dean showed up every six months or so to take a shipment, a thousand kilos or more. This continued until the mid-eighties when my father and brothers were killed in a gang war."

"Why were you spared?"

"I wasn't in Chiang Rai at the time. In eighty-five, my father had sent me here to study accounting, to become a legitimate business man." Kertang wiped his eyes with the back of his hand. "After his death, I moved my mother and sister down here. Then I went to Bangkok, where Mr. Dean found me a few years later."

"The death of your father and brothers must have put a stop to his opium smuggling."

"He quit for a few years. When he tracked me down, he asked me to use my family connections to get things going again. I didn't want to, but he offered a lot of money. So I went back up north and renewed my old connections, but quietly on a small scale. In a few years, we were moving five hundred kilos every six months. I tried to get some legitimate business going in Bangkok, but I kept rubbing shoulders with the same people, all stuck on the wheel of drugs and prostitution.

"In ninety-two, during a buying trip to Chiang Rai, I got stopped in the hills by an Army patrol. They held me for twelve hours, used a car battery on my genitals and beat me so badly I couldn't walk. They told me to get out of the opium business or end up as fish food. I spent two weeks in a hospital with a punctured lung and a ruptured spleen. Mr. Dean found me and brought me back to Chiang Mai.

"He was very different that time. He'd shaved his head and wore a *mala* around his neck. He said he'd spent a lot of time in a monastery, was even thinking of taking vows to join an order. In the hospital, he sat beside my bed and chanted a mantra, in such a deep voice it didn't sound human. He'd become philosophical. He said it was a sign - my getting caught by the Army - that it was time to change my life, find a way to make a new living.

"One day, just before we left Chiang Mai, we drove up here to visit *Wat Doi Suthep*. It was cloudy, with thunder in the mountains. In the parking lot, some kid approached us with one of those karma birds. Mr. Dean gave the kid ten *baht* but when he opened the cage, the bird wouldn't fly out. The kid had to shake the cage until it fell out. Then we saw the bird had a broken wing, and it just hopped away into the bushes.

"We went up to the temple, saw all those gold Buddhas, just like in the postcard. As we were leaving, Mr. Dean saw a monk in the chapel, and he tried to enter, but the monk said something and his assistant closed the door.

"I told Mr. Dean the *bhikku* had solitary meditations, it was just bad luck we'd arrived when it was time for privacy, but he felt insulted and was pissed off. On the way back to Chiang Mai, he started asking me about security up there. Did they have guards at night, dogs on the grounds, any kind of alarm system?

"I said they locked the gates at night. Probably a watchman did the rounds every few hours, but no dogs, and probably no alarm system. I said, everyone in Thailand is a Buddhist, and no one would steal from a temple because of the terrible karma it would bring.

"He dropped me off at my mother's place where I'd been staying since I got out of the hospital. Usually we had dinner together at a restaurant, but that night he went back to his hotel, saying he needed to sleep, we had a long drive the next day.

"Next morning we drove down to Bangkok. He was quiet the whole trip, didn't talk much, said he wasn't feeling well. He dropped me off at my place in Bangkok. He was flying home the next day. We said goodbye and then I didn't see him again for another ten years.

"When I phoned my mother a few days later, she told me Chiang Mai was buzzing with a story that someone had stolen a gold Buddha from *Wat Doi Suthep*. They weren't sure what day, but sometime last week. The police had rounded up every thief in town and beaten them to get a confession or some information, but no one knew anything.

"Everybody said no Thai could have done such a thing, so it had to be a *farang*. The police assembled a list of foreigners who'd been in Chiang Mai that week, thousands of names. That's how I learned Mr. Dean's full name, because the hotel had photocopied his passport. The police tracked down every tourist still in the country and questioned them about the Buddha.

"A detective from the Bangkok police came to see me, asking about Dean Bishop, knowing he'd visited me in the hospital. I was afraid to be arrested and beaten again, so I told him Mr. Dean was a family friend who'd known my father during the Vietnam War. I said he was a spiritual man, a practicing Buddhist, and he would never steal from a temple."

Kertang's voice cracked and his shoulders shook as he openly wept, his breath rasping in muffled gasps. Crowe laid a hand on Jimmy's shoulder. After a while, Kertang got control of his emotions. He fumbled in his door compartment, found some tissue to wipe his eyes and blow his nose.

"I lied to protect myself," Kertang moaned, "and in doing so, I lied to protect him. I betrayed the *sangha*."

Crowe shook his head. A basic precept of Buddhism was that the seeker of truth could always take refuge in the *sangha*, the community of fellow believers, who would in turn provide protection through solidarity and support. To turn your back on the *sangha* was to choose a path of loneliness, where the pitfalls were infinite and deep.

"Do you think he stole the Buddha?"

"I don't know it, but I feel it in my heart."

"You saw him again ten years later. Did you ever confront him with your suspicions?"

"I was afraid to. I never saw him do anything as violent as Mr. Roger, but I believed he was capable."

50

BACK IN CHIANG MAI, Kertang insisted on taking Crowe someplace nice for lunch. It was mid-afternoon and Crowe was hungry, so he accepted. They stopped at a restaurant just outside the western city gates. From a terrace overlooking the moat, they watched children tossing rice to a flock of ducks.

Kertang ordered a scotch and told the waitress what dishes to bring. While the food was being prepared, Crowe used the restaurant's payphone to call his hotel's travel desk. The afternoon flights to Bangkok were fully booked, but she could get him on an evening flight. He asked her to book him another night at the Crowne Plaza as well.

Crowe returned to the table. Food had arrived - fish curry, vegetable pad thai, spicy bean curd with noodles, and sticky rice for dessert. Crowe had a pot of tea with his meal. Kertang finished his scotch and nursed a Heineken through the meal.

"After you got out of the hospital, you didn't see Dean Bishop for another decade," Crowe said. "Why'd he contact you again?"

"In 2003, he showed up again in Bangkok, said he was handling liaison for American companies with offshore manufacturing in Thailand. He said maybe we could work together again, I could help him with recruiting."

"Recruiting for what?"

"The companies he represented needed models and

actresses, sexy-looking girls who spoke good English."

"Is that where Patpong Pictures came in?"

"How do you know about that?"

Crowe showed the card Fern had given him. "Is this where Kitti got involved?"

Kertang shrugged. "Kitti and I worked together. At that time I owned two small bars in Nana Plaza and Soi Cowboy, and had shares in a larger one in Patpong where Kitti was the manager. We had an arrangement to circulate girls among the three bars, keep things fresh for the clientele. Then Kitti got the idea to expand the rotation to other bars in those neighborhoods. Before long, she had a huge network of bar girls."

"You didn't run afoul of other managers?"

"Most prostitution in Bangkok is run by the Piglet Gangs. We reached an understanding with them."

"Piglet Gangs?"

"It's what the Thai police call Chinese gangsters. You remember the name, Qing Qroc? He's the biggest pig of all."

"And the piglets are the girls?"

Kertang nodded. "They squeal, but they can't run away."

"Except for those you and Kitti exported."

"For our best girls, Kitti convinced them of a better life in America, which wasn't difficult. If the girls belonged to someone else, we bought them if the price was right."

"It didn't bother you, trafficking in human lives?"

"These girls are already prostitutes. You think their lives are better in Bangkok than New York?"

Crowe said nothing. The dark side of Buddhism was its acceptance of life's pain and suffering, and a general belief that human misery was an atonement for sins from previous lives. Under such a regime, many believed that life as a prostitute was an inevitable result of their karma.

"What happened? Why did you and Kitti leave Bangkok?"

Kertang lit a cigarette and blew a pair of smoke rings, one large, the other smaller and faster-moving, that caught up with and passed inside the first. "We got discouraged."

"Business wasn't good?"

"Business was very good. Someone discouraged us from continuing."

"The Piglet Gangs threatened you?"

Kertang nodded. "Not enough room at the trough."

"Bishop didn't get involved?"

"He knew he was out of his depth. He said it was time to go to Plan B. Kitti wanted to leave anyway, so he set her up state-side to manage everything. I moved back to Chiang Mai. No Chinese here, so I can do what I want."

"If it was so dangerous in Bangkok, why would Kitti go back?"

Kertang shrugged. "Maybe things got out of hand in New York. Maybe she just wanted to see her mother again. Or her grandmother before she dies."

"I think I saw her grandmother. Is she sick?"

"I don't know. But she's in her seventies."

"That's not so old."

"It is when you've spent half of it working on your back."

Crowe shook his head. At the moat's edge, the children had run out of rice and were now throwing stones at the ducks. The wheel of karma was in constant motion, sometimes lifting you up, other times dragging you down. The ducks fled out of range to the far side of the moat.

"Let's go back to Chiang Rai in the seventies," Crowe said. "Dean Bishop had a partner named Roger. Did Bishop ever mention him on any of his subsequent visits?"

"No."

"Did you ever ask?"

"Why would I? The guy had threatened to kill me if I took his picture. I wanted nothing to do with him again. He could be dead, for all I cared."

"What did he look like?"

"Built like a football player. Blond hair and a reddish complexion, like someone who was angry all the time."

"Any distinguishing characteristics?"

"The girls said he had a huge dick. So big it hurt."

"Scars, tattoos?"

Kertang closed his eyes and puffed his cigarette. "I remember now. A tattoo on his left arm. A crest in red and black ink."

"What was in the crest?"

"A bat or an owl, something with pointy ears, holding lightning in one of its claws."

"Any words or numbers?"

"Something about heaven and hell. Maybe the bird was some sort of demon." Kertang opened his eyes and butted his cigarette in the ashtray. "Mr. Roger was, anyway."

Crowe looked at his watch.

"What time is your flight this evening?"

"Quarter to nine."

"Anything else you want to do in Chiang Mai before you go?" Kertang cast a sly look at Crowe. "Eve?"

Crowe shook his head. "No, thanks."

"You're passing up a great piece of ass."

"That's not why I came to Chiang Mai."

"Why did you come?"

"To find you, I guess."

Kertang opened his arms. "Was it worth the trip?"

Crowe pondered this a moment. "Have you ever gone someplace exotic, and eaten a meal that's different from anything you've ever had?"

Kertang shook his head. "I've never been out of Thailand."

"Then take my word for it. In ayurveda, a proper meal seeks to stimulate all of the tastes - sweet, sour, salty, bitter, pungent and astringent. But even if the meal is savory, it's only after it's been digested that we can judge if it's been good for us or not."

"Anyone ever tell you that you should have been a politician?" Kertang signaled for the bill.

51

THEY DROVE THROUGH THE WESTERN GATES and turned south along the canal. At one point Crowe glanced in the rearview mirror and thought he saw a black Range Rover, but when he looked again, it had disappeared. They followed Bumrung Buri Road the width of the old city, and crossed the moat via one of the eastern gates. Kertang dropped Crowe at the Meridien, but offered to return at seven o'clock to take him to the airport.

Crowe enjoyed a swim in the hotel pool and took a power nap. When he awoke he replayed Kertang's account of Mr. Roger and Mr. Dean. Had they really been drug-running rogue CIA agents based in Thailand during the Vietnam War?

He used his tablet to google Udorn. Wikipedia elaborated on what Kertang had told him. Udorn Royal Thai Air Force Base had secretly been made available to the USA in 1961 as a bulwark against Communist forces waging civil war in neighboring Laos. After the Vietnam War started in 1964, Udorn became a front-line base for the US Air Force. It was also the Asian headquarters for Air America, supplying covert operations throughout Southeast Asia.

Under the command of the 13th Air Force, the 432nd Tactical Reconnaissance Wing was activated at Udorn in 1966. Its mission was to provide intelligence about hostile forces in neighboring Vietnam, and use its fighter elements to destroy targets.

The 432nd deployed aircraft for photo recon, daytime via conventional photography and night-time using infrared. Analysts then inspected the evidence to identify targets, after which tactical fighters made strikes.

Crowe clicked on a link that took him to a dedicated entry on the 432nd Wing. In the corner of the page was a red-and-black crest, the wing's emblem. It depicted a bat clutching two thunderbolts in a claw. The wing's official motto was *Victoria Per Scientiam – Victory Through Knowledge.* Its alternate motto was, *If you can't lower Heaven, raise hell.*

It matched Kertang's memory of Mr. Roger's tattoo - a pointy-eared creature with lightning and the words, heaven and hell.

So Mr. Roger had served under the 432nd at Udorn during the Vietnam War. As for Bishop, he might have been CIA, working with Air America in Udorn.

Crowe recalled Bishop's birth data from the ashram's application file. November 1948. He'd have been about twenty-seven in the mid-seventies when Kertang said he first appeared in Chiang Rai.

But what was an ex-CIA agent doing at a silent retreat? His application had said he'd spent a year as a monk in a Thai monastery. Fact or fiction? Kertang's story of their visit to *Wat Doi Suthep* and his suspicion that Bishop had stolen the gold Buddha didn't hang together very well.

Crowe recollected a line from Walt Whitman: *Do I contradict myself? Very well, then I contradict myself. I am large, I contain multitudes.*

He'd discussed this dilemma with Guruji in the context of interpreting horoscopes. How many times had he seen contradictory indications in a client's birth chart, and agonized over which way the interpretation should go?

A human life is like a tree, Guruji said. *We are seeds that fall upon certain soil, watered by both the actions of those who care for us, and a world oblivious to our needs. We grow, spread our limbs, sprout leaves, flower and grow fruit. Some fruit is sweet and juicy, some bitter and dry. Shake the tree and both will fall to the ground.*

In his oblique way, Guruji meant that reading a horoscope wasn't just tallying good versus bad, as if more of this would cancel less of that, to get a net effect. Good and bad would co-exist in a life. The challenge for the *jyotishi* in interpreting the science of light was to tell a story that made sense of it all.

Even in Guruji's life there'd been many contradictions. Although a mediocre student, he'd scored so high in the state qualification exams that he won a scholarship to a renowned university. He studied law and passed the bar but never practiced, turning his back on a law career in favor of wrestling. He played the horses to win handsome payouts but donated all his winnings to the poor. He became the most renowned astrologer in Calcutta, but left it behind to become an unknown in Toronto.

Crowe's life had demonstrated similar, if less spectacular, swings. He didn't care to dwell upon them, but a recurrent theme was sexuality. At one time or another, he'd been celibate and promiscuous, moral and profligate, virtuous and wicked. He'd been around the block so many times he'd met himself both coming and going.

Therefore, he accepted the notion that Dean Bishop could in one lifetime be both a devotee of Theravada Buddhism and a thief of temple statuary. Obviously, he was a good example of mixed karma, where the streams from two very different sources merged to form a single river.

Crowe copied the Wikipedia pages onto a memory stick and went down to the hotel's business center. He used their color printer to reproduce the page with the emblem of the 432nd Wing.

Crowe packed his luggage and waited in the lobby. Kertang arrived promptly at seven. They drove to the airport, where Kertang accompanied Crowe to the Thai Airways desk for check-in.

With time to spare, they sat in the bar lounge before Crowe went through security. Kertang ordered a whiskey. Crowe showed him the Wikipedia page on the 432nd Wing. "Is that what Mr. Roger's tattoo looked like?"

Kertang nodded as he studied the design. "We consider the bat a sign of good luck and prosperity."

"If you think about it, Mr. Roger and Mr. Dean made your father rich."

"They also got him killed."

Crowe recalled his earlier thoughts on the omnipresence

of good and evil, sometimes within the same person or situation. "Maybe that's just an example of synchronicity."

Kertang frowned at the unfamiliar word. "What's that?"

"When two seemingly unrelated events happen at the same time, as if there's an invisible connection that makes sense of it all."

"Like karma?"

The PA system announced the boarding call for another flight. Knowing Crowe's departure was imminent, they took this as the cue to exchange email addresses.

"Don't go back to Fern's place," Kertang told Crowe. "If those people are still looking for Kitti, you'll only draw attention to yourself."

"Give me the names and numbers of her friends. I'll be discreet."

"No. They won't talk to a *farang*. And if they did, they might tell someone else you're looking for her. If she's in hiding, leave her alone. Believe me, you don't want the Piglet Gangs to take an interest in you."

A few minutes later, the PA announced boarding for the Bangkok flight. Kertang drained his whiskey and stood. They shook hands and Crowe headed toward the security gate.

52

Bangkok

CROWE'S FLIGHT GOT IN AT TEN PM. With luggage in hand, he headed for the ground transportation area, intending to get a shuttle bus downtown to the Crowne Plaza. Although Kertang's warning about the Piglet Gangs had given him pause for thought, he still intended to visit Fern again. Maybe she'd had some news from her daughter, or knew where he might find Kitti.

Dozens of men, some wearing yellow-and-green jackets of taxi companies, formed a gauntlet, calling out offers to take him downtown to best hotel, best restaurant, best live show of beautiful girls. Halfway down the line, a young man in a sleek gray business suit held up a placard that read "Axel Crowe". Crowe stopped.

"Mr. Crowe?" The guy flashed a smile of incredibly white teeth. He was about thirty years old, with one of those beautiful Thai faces whose sexuality seemed capable of going either way, depending only on hair and makeup to bend the gender.

"Yes. Who are you?"

"My name is Koko. Mr. Jimmy asked me to meet you at the airport, make sure you get to your hotel safely. No girls, no drugs, just take you straight to your hotel, get a good night's sleep."

"You must be reading my mind."

"I hear that a lot from my clients. That's why I'm so popular." He extended his hand toward Crowe's luggage. "May I?"

Crowe allowed him to take his bag. Koko headed toward the exit as Crowe kept pace.

"Jimmy didn't tell me he was going to arrange this."

"He wanted to surprise you."

They stepped outside. It was muggy and Crowe only realized now how pleasant it had been up in Chiang Mai. They passed a line of cars and came to a late-model white Mercedes sedan. Koko put the luggage in the trunk and opened a door for Crowe. A traffic attendant in cap and blue shirt emerged from the shadows of the terminal building. Koko gave him some money and got behind the wheel.

Although it was ten-thirty at night, the highway into Bangkok was dense with cars, vans, *tuk-tuks* and motorcycles. Koko fiddled with the radio, looking for western music. He paused at one moment, listening to a radio announcer in Thai. Then he finally found some music, AC/DC of all things, probably a popular offering for the many Australian tourists.

They were on the highway only five minutes when the Mercedes took an exit. They were soon on a paved rural road, racing past large agricultural estates whose houses sat well back from the road.

"Where are we going?" Crowe said.

"Oh, sorry," Koko said. "They just said on the radio there's a huge accident on the highway. A bus and several cars, many people injured. Traffic will be stopped for an hour. I'm just taking a detour. We'll be back on the highway in ten minutes."

Crowe looked at the crescent moon just visible above the western horizon. It had been in Gemini the past two days he'd spent with Kertang. A Gemini moon often evoked fabrication and trickery, occasionally playing both sides against the middle. It now occupied the seventh house, and therefore represented other people - at this moment, Koko. Seventh lord Mercury was in Pisces, another mutable sign. Its symbol of the contrarian fish turning in circles hinted at dual allegiance and misrepresentation.

A clammy feeling came over Crowe, and it wasn't because the Mercedes lacked air conditioning. It was the feeling of someone who'd taken a wrong turn and knew the road ahead was washed out. Why hadn't he taken a moment when Koko first appeared in the airport, and asked himself if this felt right?

Koko braked abruptly and made a sharp turn through a set of gates. For a moment it seemed they'd entered a tunnel. Trees rushed by on either side. The Mercedes burst into an open yard and skidded to a halt within a compound.

Before Crowe could react, his door opened and a gorilla with massive hands dragged him from the car. Another big man gave him a karate chop to the neck. The right side of his body went numb, except for his nerves that went into electrical shock, blinding him with pain.

~~~
~~~

The two men dragged Crowe like a limp protester into the nearest building. They took him down a hallway into a windowless room with a large wooden table and a few chairs. Angled lamps threw ovals of light onto the upper walls and ceiling.

A third man sat in a shadowy corner. The two thugs propped Crowe in a wooden chair, securing his hands to the chair with plastic cable ties. Gorilla frisked him and gave his wallet and passport to the man in the corner.

Koko came in, placed Crowe's bag on the table, and left without a word. The second thug, whose left eye had apparently suffered an injury reducing it to a closed slit, opened the bag and dumped everything on the table. He pawed through it and said something in Thai to the man in the corner, who grunted a few words.

Gorilla and One-eye stationed themselves at the door. The man in the corner came out of the shadows and pulled a chair up in front of Crowe. He regarded him a few moments, as if studying some odd specimen that had inexplicably washed up on his shore.

Indeed, Crowe felt like a jellyfish, with no motor function to stand up to this man, never mind escape.

"You know who I am?" the man said.

Jabba the Hutt, Crowe was tempted to say, but self-preservation got in the way of being a smartass. The man's large amorphous head spilled, without a visible neck, onto his shoulders. He looked like a wax figurine of a Chinese Marlon Brando that had been left out in the sun too long. Although his tent-like shirt tried to disguise it, he must have weighed almost three hundred pounds.

"No," Crowe said.

"I'm Qing Qroc."

"Pleased to meet you." So this was the kingpin of the Piglet Gangs, the one Kertang had warned him about. The one Kertang had sold him out to, Crowe now realized.

"Who is your employer?"

"I'm self-employed."

"DEA? FBI?"

Crowe shook his head. "A private citizen. Nothing to do with the police."

Qroc's open hand delivered a stinging slap. "You lie. Your ID says you're a private investigator in Canada and the United States. Who do you work for?"

"My client is a friend accused of a murder he didn't commit. I'm seeking information that might secure his release."

"Who is this friend?"

Crowe told him about Greer's death on Abbott's ashram. And Dean Bishop, who'd thrown a punch at Greer just hours before his death.

"Why are you looking for Kitti Poornchai?"

"She might know something about Greer's death."

"What were you doing in Chiang Mai?"

"Looking for Kitti."

"You're looking for a drug connection?"

"This has nothing to do with drugs."

Another slap across the face. "You lie."

Qroc said something in Thai. Gorilla went away. A few minutes later, Crowe heard a woman's voice, shrill with complaints or curses, coming down the hall. Gorilla reappeared with Kitti Poornchai in tow, his big paw twisting her arm at an unnatural angle. He pulled a chair from the table and flung her into it. One-eye used cable ties to bind her.

Kitti was barefoot in a dress torn at the armpit. She had bruises on her arms and neck, bloody scratches on her knees. Her hair looked dirty and some of her fingernails were broken.

"They say women can take more pain than men," Qroc said to Crowe. "Is it true?"

"There's no need for that. I don't work for the DEA or the FBI. I don't know anything about the drug trade. I just want to help my friend."

"You should let me be your friend."

"Release us and I'll consider it."

"Tell me everything you know, or this friendship will go

nowhere."

Qroc put his hand up Kitti's dress and did something that made her scream. Gorilla laughed. Qroc waited until Kitti's gasping breath became normal again. He brushed the limp hair from her face and cupped her chin in his hand.

"Ready to cooperate?"

"Fuck you," she said. "You're going to kill me anyway, go ahead and get it over with."

"For many lives you've lived like a whore, and you'll die like a whore. That's your karma. Nothing can change it now."

She spat at him but he'd anticipated her. Qroc blocked it with his hand and wiped it on her dress. He stood and looked down at them.

"I'll leave you alone for awhile. Decide your own fates. I know the DEA and FBI want to destroy my operation in Bangkok and the Golden Triangle. I know they've infiltrated my organization. Give me the names of the spies in my organization, and I'll let you go. If not..." He snapped his fingers.

He left the room. Gorilla followed. One-eye regarded them a few moments longer, bringing his single eye to bear upon them with laser-like intensity, as if he had X-ray vision that could see confessions already bubbling up their throats. When they stared back, he felt perhaps out-numbered, four eyes to one, and left the room, closing the door behind him.

53

CROWE TESTED HIS WRISTS against the cable ties. They were sturdy and no amount of twisting would stretch or break them. Despair rose from the pit of his stomach, but he forced it down with sheer moral strength. However he was going to die, he had to face it with courage and grace.

"How did they find you?" he asked Kitti.

"They were watching my mother's place. The day you visited, I'd sent a friend to get some of my things. They followed her back to where I was staying. They brought me here, beat me, raped me..."

"What do they want?"

"Someone told Qroc I'd turned informant. He thinks I'm with the police, using my old network of girls to gather information on their drug organization."

"Who told him that?"

"I have no idea."

"Do Bishop and Qroc know each other?"

"Ever since the eighties when they first divided up the heroin exports, and agreed to stay out of each other's way. I think Qroc took the biggest share of the business, both Europe and Asia, but left the USA to Bishop because he had a pipeline worked out."

"Is Bishop still in the drug business?"

"No. He cashed out in the nineties when it got too dangerous."

"Do you think he betrayed you? I thought you were business associates, or something more than that."

"We were. We loved each other. I know he wouldn't turn on me. He had nothing to gain from it."

"Was it Bishop's idea for you to leave the country?"

"Yes. When you started making inquiries, he was afraid the police would become involved."

"What would they have discovered?"

"I don't know."

"Kitti, look around you. Is it possible for us to escape?"

She shook her head.

"Then stop lying. Stop trying to protect Bishop. Tell me what really happened up there at the ashram."

"I don't know as much as you think."

"You know more than me."

She shook her head again.

"Why did Bishop strike Greer? What was going on between them?"

"Greer was working on a story. He'd turned up something about Bishop's past. He threatened to reveal it, and Bishop went ballistic."

"What aspect of his past? CIA? The heroin smuggling?"

"I don't know. He wouldn't tell me."

"Why were you at the ashram? I know it wasn't the first time. You'd gone with him twice before. And don't tell me you were just there to meditate."

"He was looking for something. He thought it was buried under one of the cabins."

"Looking for what?"

"I don't know, but it must have been valuable, because he was intent on finding it. The reason he brought me with him was so he could have unrestricted access to two cabins during each retreat. He'd bought a metal detector. The first night there, he went out in the middle of the night and crawled under each of our cabins to scan the ground beneath them."

"Did he find what he was looking for?"

"No, but not for lack of trying. He went out for an hour every night that week, using the metal detector to scan the spaces between cabins while I acted as lookout to warn him in case anyone showed up."

"Was Greer's cabin nearby? Do you think he might have seen you? Is that why he confronted Bishop?"

"I don't know. Like I said, he wouldn't even tell me what he was looking for."

"Did he kill Greer?"

"You know that's impossible. He drove back to New York that evening."

"Why did you write that note to Greer?"

"What note?"

"Don't play dumb, Kitti. Someone slipped a note under Greer's door that evening, telling him they'd got mixed up in something scary but wanted out, offering to tell him about it if he could protect them. Was that note Bishop's idea, or yours?"

"He wrote the note."

Interesting, Crowe thought. Although printed, the

handwritten note had looked like a woman's hand. He wondered if Bishop had done that intentionally, to throw suspicion on Kitti rather than himself.

"When did he write it?"

"He gave it to me just before he left the ashram."

"Didn't you think it was odd, luring Greer out to the quarry at midnight? Who did you think would meet him there?"

"I never saw what the note said. He gave it to me in an envelope."

"Bishop must have told you something."

"He just told me to slip it under Greer's door as soon as I had a chance. He said it would talk some sense into him."

"You never thought it might get you into trouble?"

"It wasn't supposed to be found. Bishop had worked out a plan. I watched from my cabin that night. As soon as Greer left, I searched his cabin. When I couldn't find the note, I assumed he must have destroyed it."

"How did you get into Greer's cabin?"

"Bishop had somehow acquired a duplicate key."

This didn't surprise Crowe. Bishop was ex-CIA and had been to the ashram many times. He'd probably made impressions of the keys and got someone to produce a master. But Crowe was still puzzled over what had happened that night. "So up until the local police investigated, you must have suspected Bishop had killed Greer?"

She shook her head. "I knew he was upset, but not enough to kill someone. As it turned out, I was right. Once Lieutenant Lynch got in touch with him, Bishop proved he was back in New York by midnight."

"Do you believe that?"

"Why shouldn't I?"

"Well, if Bishop didn't kill Greer, an accomplice did it for him. Any idea who that was?"

"No, but the thought of it scared me. My fingerprints were on that envelope. I could have been considered an accessory. It was lucky for me the local cops discovered something crooked about Abbott that made him a better suspect."

"When Lieutenant Lynch drove you to the bus station in White Junction, did he ask you about your relationship with Bishop?"

Before she could answer, the door opened and the three men came back into the room.

"Ready to save your lives?" Qroc said. "Give me names."

"We don't know anything about any informants," Crowe said. "Either someone's trying to make trouble for Kitti, or it's a mistake. Either way, you should release us. Don't perpetuate bad karma for yourself."

Qroc laughed so hard he had to hold onto his quivering belly. "You stupid man. Do I look frightened by your talk of karma? I swallow whole villages and spit them out like chicken bones."

"Then it's just a question of time before you're destroyed."

Qroc hit him again, this time with his fist. Crowe's chair teetered but didn't fall over. He ran his tongue over his teeth and tasted blood.

Qroc barked something in Thai. Gorilla came behind their chairs and used a knife to cut away the cable ties. One-eye dragged Kitti by the hair toward the door. Gorilla twisted Crowe's right arm behind his back and brought him along too.

They emerged from a long corridor into a walled courtyard at the rear of the house. They passed through a gate into an open yard flanked by low sheds. A pair of late-model black Range Rovers sat parked beneath a large tree. Crowe recalled the Range Rover he'd seen in Chiang Mai. The distance was too great for someone to have driven down to Bangok this evening, but it could well have been someone else in Qroc's employ.

At the far end of the yard, a six-foot stone wall ran fifty yards in either direction, disappearing into the dark. Qroc used a key to unlock an iron gate. They entered a compound smelling of algae, musk and rot. Crowe's nostrils recoiled at the stench. Last time he'd smelled something like this had been in his teens, discovering a dead deer on a wooded trail, gut-shot and bloated, victim of a hunter's lousy shot.

The crescent moon hovered just above the trees at the compound's perimeter. As Crowe's eyes adjusted to the light he saw what appeared to be half a dozen large swimming pools. Hundreds of ridged objects floated like logs with gnarly bark, their bulk just beneath the water's surface. As he watched, a pair of jaws yawned skyward, and a deep bellow groaned across the water.

Kitti made a choking sound, a gasp of fear and despair.

The hair stood up all over Crowe's body, ready to take flight.

54

"LIKE MANY SUCCESSFUL BUSINESSMEN," Qroc said, "I have diversified investments. Bloomingdale's, Macy's and Neiman Marcus all carry luxury handbags, shoes and belts. Designed in Europe by Hermes, Pollini and Vecceli, but the raw material comes from Thailand. Do you know what I'm talking about?"

Crowe and Kitti said nothing as Qroc's thugs led them along a 10-foot walkway between pools.

"Each pool holds crocodiles of different ages and sizes. We have to keep them apart to prevent the larger ones from eating the smaller. They have little sense of kinship, but that's the nature of reptiles."

They reached the far end of the compound. In two adjacent pools were scores of mature crocodiles, some fifteen feet long.

Qroc foraged beneath a bench adjacent the outer wall and returned with a plastic bucket that he set at Crowe's feet. Crowe looked down and saw a putrid mass of intestines, interspersed with pig's ears, chicken feet and other indeterminate offal.

"Now it's time to spill your guts," Qroc said. "Isn't that still a popular American expression?"

Crowe grimaced.

"Give me names," Qroc said.

"I know nothing."

Qroc picked up the bucket and heaved the guts into the pool. It hit the water in a gelatinous mass, immediately swallowed by a crocodile. Cued into action, every other inmate woke up and surfaced. A mass of scaly bodies swarmed toward their end of the pool.

"Enjoying the show?" Qroc said.

Crowe stifled his fear. If this was the first act, he wasn't looking forward to the last.

Qroc went to the end of the bench, where a large cage stood. He fiddled with a hasp, opened its door and reached inside. A bird squawked in protest. Qroc came back swinging a chicken by its legs.

"Sometimes, after a thorough interrogation, the suspect sings like a bird," Qroc said. "Isn't that another American expression?"

Crowe looked at Kitti. Her head was inclined, hair twisted in One-eye's grip, but her expression was defiant.

Qroc addressed them both. "Give me the names of the spies in my organization. Tell me or follow this bird."

"We can't tell you what we don't know," Crowe said.

Qroc tossed the chicken out over the pool. The bird beat the air with frantic wings, losing altitude quickly. Before the chicken had cleared the pool, a crocodile surged vertically from the water and took it down in a snap of its jaws. The water churned as a dozen other crocs arrived too late for dinner. A few feathers fluttered to the agitated surface.

"Who wants to go next?"

"Fuck you." Kitti spat at Qroc, hitting her target before he could deflect it.

He wiped his cheek, looked in his hand and made a fist of it. As One-eye held her, Qroc struck her three times in the face.

When her knees buckled, Qroc grabbed her from One-eye and heaved her into the pool.

In an instant, two crocs seized her. Her shrill scream ended in a muted roar of bubbles as she went under. The water boiled in a mass of scaly legs and thrashing tails.

Gorilla tightened his grip on Crowe's arm, still twisted behind his back. One-eye seized Crowe's other arm.

Qroc stood in front of him and wiped his hand on Crowe's shirt. "We've reached the point of no return, my friend. Kitti has gone the way of all trash, but you're still alive. And I can always use someone on the inside, telling me what the police are up to, and when I should be careful. I pay well. In a year you could be a millionaire. Tonight will become just an unpleasant memory, like a nightmare that fades with time. Will you work with me?"

Crowe shook his head. "You're a murdering drug lord. I'd rather die with honor than stain my karma with your blood money."

"Suit yourself." Qroc stood aside and said to his men. "Show him where his karma lies."

Just as the two thugs got set to heave Crowe into the pool, he uncoiled like a wound-up spring. He turned toward One-eye, pivoted at the hip and drove his knee into the man's groin. One-eye doubled over and fell to his knees. Crowe planted a foot on One-eye's back, used it as a launch pad, and catapulted backwards over Gorilla's shoulder.

Until that moment, Gorilla's grip on Crowe's twisted arm had kept him nearly paralyzed with pain. But when he rolled over Gorilla's back, the arm twist turned the other way, giving instant relief. As he landed behind Gorilla, Crowe tore his arm loose and drove a powerful one-two punch into each of the man's kidneys. Gorilla bellowed and turned toward his tormentor. Crowe jabbed splayed fingers into Gorilla's eyes. The big man screamed and flailed his arms. Crowe lashed out with a kick to Gorilla's solar plexus.

Gorilla staggered backwards and fell over One-eye who was still on hands and knees. His head violently smacked the concrete, an arm flopping over the rim of the pool. A croc yanked him in. One-eye grabbed Gorilla's foot but his shoe came off in his hand. Another croc lunged from the water. One-eye tried to scramble away from the pool's edge but Crowe had his back, one foot firmly planted between his shoulder blades. Crowe kicked. One-eye went screaming head-first into a set of gaping jaws.

Seeing things going to hell in a hurry, Qroc made a run for the gate, the house, the probable protection of a gun. Crowe went after him, racing along the 10-foot walkway between two pools. It might have been comical, Crowe thought, chasing this fat-ass coward who'd caused so much suffering, if it weren't so terrifying.

Just before Qroc reached the end of the pool that held the biggest crocodiles, Crowe tackled him and brought him down in a skidding slide at the pool's edge. For the moment, most of the reptiles were massed at the other end, fighting over scraps of Gorilla and One-eye. But a couple of them had followed Crowe and Qroc down the length of the pool, and more were now coming this way.

Crowe climbed astraddle Qroc's back, drove his fingers into the fleshy blubber of the man's neck and found the *marma* point to immobilize him. Qroc screamed but could do no more. Crowe dismounted, crossed Qroc's legs one over the other, and used a fireman's technique to flip the obese man onto his back. He crouched beside him.

"Who told you to pick me up at the airport? Jimmy Kertang?"

Qroc shook his head.

"Dean Bishop?"

Qroc's eyes rolled, seeing something moving across the pool.

"Who?"

"Mr. Roger."

Crowe saw it from the corner of his eye. He had just enough time to jump away, putting Qroc between him and the crocodile. Crowe grabbed the big man's hand. If he'd been a normal weight, Crowe might have yanked him clear but he didn't have the strength or traction to pull three hundred pounds of negative karma.

The crocodile surged over the edge, seized one of Qroc's legs and pulled him into the pool. Man and reptile disappeared in a violent turbulence as more crocodiles fought to get a piece of the big man. Sickened, Crowe backed away as the water churned with blood.

55

CROWE RETREATED FROM THE POOL of adult crocodiles. The screams of the thugs and the smell of blood had aroused the hundreds of occupants in the other pools. Everywhere he looked the surface of the water was alive with ridged snouts and reptilian eyes looking his way. He hurried to the gate but found it locked.

Between the stench of the pools, and the shock from having seen so much close-up carnage, he was overcome with nausea. He doubled over and vomited his lunch at the foot of the wall. He coughed and spat until he cleared his throat enough to groan.

Without a key to unlock it, Crowe had to climb the gate to get out of the crocodile compound. Keeping to the shadows along the wall and sheds, he went to one of the Range Rovers and found its doors unlocked. The keys were already in the ignition, a GPS unit sitting on its dashboard. He experienced a brief flutter of relief, knowing that if he chose to, he could enter Suvarnabhumi Airport as a destination and drive away right now.

Knowing he had that option gave him more courage to explore others. But he'd feel better if he had some protection. He looked in the glove compartment but found nothing useful. Nothing under the seats either. He went to the other vehicle and checked its glove compartment. Jackpot!

He withdrew the automatic pistol he'd found and examined it under the glove compartment light. He ejected the magazine, thumbed out seven cartridges and reloaded them. He located the safety and confirmed with a trigger pull on an empty chamber that it was engaged. He reinserted the magazine, worked the slide to chamber a round, and disengaged the safety.

The gate to the courtyard was unlocked. He crossed the yard to the house, listened at the back door, and went inside. Within five tense minutes he confirmed the house was empty. He found a bathroom, washed his face and rinsed the bad taste from his mouth. In the room where he and Kitti had been questioned, he retrieved his wallet and passport. He repacked his luggage and left it standing by the back door.

He found where Kitti had been held in a room with a barred window - unmade bed, bloody sheets, a pile of tissue in the corner. Her purse and some jewelry lay on a dresser. He put the rings and bracelets in the purse and carried it with his luggage to the Range Rover.

Instinct told him to drive straight to the airport, ditch the Range Rover and take a taxi to the nearest hotel. He had to stay low and get out of the country before he was discovered, perhaps suspected of Kitti's or Qroc's disappearance. But the thought of a mother and grandmother never knowing what had become of Kitti was incentive to do something more honorable.

Crowe started the car and entered the Crowne Plaza's address into the GPS unit, not wanting to leave any further details in the unit's memory. The route came up in a moment and he put the car in gear. Although it was a warm night he drove with the windows open and the AC on, trying to have the best of both worlds - fresh air moderated by the cool vents. It was almost midnight by the time he got back downtown to Rama IV Road. But he didn't enter the Crowne Plaza's courtyard.

Although a room had been reserved for him, he had no intention of checking in. From the hotel he used his memory and sense of direction to drive to Soi Pradit.

He found a place to park the Range Rover in front of the temple. He looked up at Fern's apartment and saw a flickering light inside, probably a television. He took some coins from his pocket and tossed them at the grille enclosing her balcony. He heard a coin strike the apartment window. He kept tossing coins.

Fern's face appeared behind the grille. She hissed something in Thai.

"It's Axel Crowe," he said. "I found Kitti."

She beckoned for him to come up.

He climbed the darkened stairwell to her floor. She stood at her door, cigarette in one hand, a glass in the other.

"Where is she?"

"Dead. I'm sorry."

They sat together in the living room and he told her what had happened. He gave her Kitti's purse with her jewelry. She didn't cry or say anything, and he began to wonder at her lack of response, whether she didn't understand, or didn't care what had happened. Then Fern suddenly stood and hurried to the bathroom. From down the hall, Crowe heard her vomiting. He grimaced and stifled his own nausea, not wanting to join her. After several minutes she returned and sat again.

"Thank you for coming back to tell me." She reached out a hand and patted his arm.

"I'd like to say a prayer for Kitti," Crowe said.

Fern lit some incense. Crowe chanted the *Mahamritunjaya* mantra, an invocation to the gods in the name of courage, faith and longevity. It took him half an hour to complete 108 rounds of the lengthy mantra.

Fern fetched him a glass of water. Crowe stood to leave.

"I saw Jimmy Kertang in Chiang Mai," he told her at the door. "He sends his regards, and asks your forgiveness. He loved Kitti, and I know he did what he could to help me. Maybe you should be the one to tell him she's gone. If you ever need help, I think he'd do anything he could for you, in her memory."

He gave her the Meridien's business card with Kertang's number written on the back.

She shook her head. "I am still angry at him."

Crowe remembered something Guruji had told him many years ago: *Anger is like a red-hot coal held in your fist. The tighter you grip it, the more it burns.*

She brushed tears from her eyes, embraced him and closed the door.

Back in the Range Rover, Crowe entered Suvarnabhumi Airport as a new destination in the GPS. En route, he debated whether to report the night's events to the police, but decided against it. Even in America, this would have been very risky. For all he knew, Qing Qroc had friends and protectors within the police or the judiciary. If corruption was as widespread as Kertang had led him to believe, no telling what sort of quicksand might swallow him if he confessed his involvement.

The appropriate response to some situations was penance, but there'd be nothing productive about doing time in a Thai prison. Bad enough his friend Abbott was behind bars. Crowe had to get back to New York as quickly as he could.

At the airport he entered a parking compound, took a receipt from the automated control unit and found a remote corner. He set his phone alarm for five AM local and reclined the seat to horizontal. With the pistol lying within reach, he caught a few hours of half-sleep.

He awoke an hour before the alarm and decided to distance himself from the Range Rover before daylight. He wiped clean the steering wheel, gear shift, GPS, door handles, anything he remembered having touched. Likewise for the pistol, cartridges and all, and left it in the glove compartment. He opened the sun roof a crack and got out of the vehicle, taking his bag with him. He locked its doors, slipped the keys through the sun roof and walked to the terminal.

He went to a Delta desk and booked a flight with a brief stopover in Tokyo that would get him back in New York early afternoon.

Still shaken by the night's events, he went to a 24-hour bar and ordered a Virgin Mary. A stalk of celery in six ounces of tomato juice, to which the bartender added an ounce of freshly-ground ginger and a pinch of salt. Breakfast of survivors.

56

Saturday, April 28

Tokyo

AFTER HIS FLIGHT DEPARTED at six AM, Crowe slept for a couple of hours. When he awoke halfway to Tokyo, he reviewed what he'd learned in Thailand. Bishop had been with Air America, Mr. Roger with the 432nd Wing, both in Udorn during the Vietnam War. They'd used Kertang's father to buy opium and, after processing it in Bangkok, smuggled heroin into the USA.

Bishop and Qing Qroc knew each other since the eighties, supplying their respective markets with heroin. But when Thai Army officers gave Kertang a near-fatal beating, Bishop had retired from the business. He'd spent time in a Buddhist monastery, maybe taken vows as a monk. But something went awry and, on his last trip to Chiang Mai, he'd stolen a gold Buddha from *Wat Doi Suthep*.

Bishop had then formed a new venture with Kertang and Poornchai, probably using his connections to facilitate the immigration of young Thai women to supply New York strip clubs and massage parlors.

Crowe's plane touched down at Narita International Airport. The Tokyo stopover was brief. He walked around the terminal to stretch his legs and had a bowl of noodles before boarding his connecting flight.

On the homeward leg, he used his tablet to access the plane's WiFi and read all he could about US units at Udorn airbase during the Vietnam War. The 432nd Tactical Recon Wing had consisted of five squadrons - one recon, two tactical, and two for ground support.

The 14th Tactical Recon squadron, whose fighters were equipped with advanced cameras, conducted aerial surveillance to gather photo intelligence on targets throughout Southeast Asia.

The 13th "Panther Pack" and 555th "Triple Nickel" were tactical fighter squadrons whose Phantoms flew strikes over North Vietnam. The 7th Airborne Command and 4th Special Operations squadrons flew cargo planes converted to gunships for ground support in South Vietnam.

Crowe was puzzled. What did the Vietnam War have to do with Greer's death? The only link was Dean Bishop, but what role had he played, and for whose benefit?

Crowe looked down on a cloud-scattered Kamchatka Peninsula. If Qing Qroc's dying words were credible, it was Mr. Roger who'd warned the Piglet Gang about Crowe's presence in Thailand. Obviously, Mr. Roger had preferred Crowe dead than return to New York. But who was he, and what was he trying to hide?

His tattoo of the thunderbolt-wielding bat was Crowe's only clue to Roger's identity. But the 432nd Wing had been one of the largest units of its kind. Its personnel might have numbered several thousand.

Crowe did some time zone math. His flight had departed Tokyo at three PM an hour ago. It was two AM in New York. He couldn't phone anyone there for at least four hours. In lieu of that, he emailed Det. Levinson with a CC to Tracey, telling them what he'd learned about Bishop and Mr. Roger. Did the NYPD have contacts at the Department of Veterans Affairs? He needed a list of everyone who'd served with the 432nd in Thailand, from 1970 to 1975.

Having done all he could do for now, he closed his tablet. He tried to sleep but his mind was too agitated. He inserted earbuds to block cabin chatter and meditated for half an hour. Surfacing from that, he remembered he still had another case to work. Here he was, soliciting Levinson's help with Veterans Affairs, but hadn't made any real progress with the Riverside Rapist file.

He reviewed his notes. Perhaps with fresh eyes he'd see something new. Although not entirely logical, it was still framed by his awareness of the larger picture. Crowe had learned from Guruji that individual eyes brought individual consciousness to every act and circumstance. Where one saw only a grain of sand, another saw a world.

The birth chart is just a two-dimensional map of lines and symbols, Guruji used to say. *But for those with eyes to see, it is a person with body, heart and soul, moving through the third dimension of time. Many things are dead until our awareness brings them alive.*

Crowe returned to the *prashna* chart he'd calculated in New Delhi, knowing it contained clues to the Riverside Rapist's identity. He still thought the killer was from out of town, but where?

Ascendant lord in the tenth house implied the perp had done his dirty work south of where he lived. Moon in the seventh meant he'd gone west. If Crowe gave those equal weight, like force vectors in a physics problem, it meant the killer had travelled southwest from home. Therefore, he lived northeast of New York.

How far? Home was the fourth house Aquarius, its lord Saturn at one degree Libra. The killer was Mars at 10 degrees Leo. Mars had moved nine degrees beyond the degree of Saturn. Nine units of time. Days were unlikely, so nine hours of travel. If driving, that was 400-500 miles, perhaps Maine, New Brunswick or Quebec.

What kind of car? Vehicles were indicated by the fourth house and Venus. Fourth lord Saturn was exalted in Libra in the twelfth. Probably used but a quality make. Venus on the Rahu/Ketu axis suggested a foreign model, or high-tech add-ons like radar detector or CB radio. Saturn and Venus both occupied signs ruled by Venus, so blue was likely, with Saturn making it more like a midnight blue.

Model? Six planets occupied quadruped signs of Aries, Taurus and Leo. Crowe considered vehicles named after animals: Ford Bronco, Mercury Cougar, Chevrolet Impala, Jaguar, Ford Mustang, Ford Pinto, Dodge Ram, Buick Wildcat...

Crowe set the chart aside and turned his attention back to Abbott's case. What was the underlying connection between

Dharmapada and Thailand? Was it mere coincidence that Bishop, who'd served with Air America in Udorn, had brought a Thai woman to the retreat?

Crowe thought about the karma birds he'd seen at *Wat Doi Suthep*. He recalled Kitti's grandmother watching the street through a wire grille on Fern's apartment balcony. It reminded him of Bishop's friend Kinkelman, with a crippled wife and two owls in a cage.

Kinkelman said he'd served in the Vietnam war, providing aerial reconnaissance support. Had he been based with the 432nd Wing in Udorn too? Is that where he'd met Bishop?

Crowe briefly wondered if Kinkelman was Mr. Roger, but rejected the idea. Kertang had said Roger was built like a football player, big and red-faced. But Kinkelman weighed no more than one fifty. Could he have been sick and lost that much weight? Crowe doubted it.

He reflected on Kertang's story of Bishop and the stolen Buddha. The director at the Manhattan Museum of Asian Antiquities had shown Crowe a picture of an identical Buddha, whose provenance the museum's curator had researched.

Six months after the broker Tom Jimson jilted her and disappeared, Thi Nguyen had become a victim of the Riverside Rapist. A victim of many anomalies, Crowe reminded himself. So many things about her case didn't fit with the other victims. He wondered whether her murder was unrelated or critical to solving the larger puzzle.

Understand the peregrine planet, said medieval horoscopy, *and you understand the rest of the chart.*

57

New York

CROWE'S FLIGHT LANDED AT JFK shortly before two PM. He caught a shuttle into Manhattan, and a taxi to his hotel. By the time he set his luggage down, it was three PM. He called Tracey's apartment and cell. He left messages saying he had to go out for a while and would catch up with her end of day.

He phoned Levinson and identified himself. "I'm back."

"Did you find Kitti Poornchai?"

"Too late." Crowe told the detective about having literally escaped the jaws of death. "Did you get my email? Know anyone at Veterans Affairs?"

"I do, but it's a no-go. Only the Defense Department can access service records. Names of Vietnam servicemen are withheld for security reasons."

"Because the war was so unpopular?"

"As far as America's psyche is concerned, out of sight and out of mind. Nobody wants to dig up old skeletons."

"Even if it might solve a murder?"

"What's your theory?"

"I'm still working on it."

To date Crowe still had scant evidence. So what if Bishop and Mr. Roger had met in Thailand during the Vietnam War? Or if Kinkelman had served there too? Aside from Thailand, what did they have in common? And where did Greer fit in?

"How about my cold case file?"

"I'm still working on that too."

"Okay, keep me posted." Levinson was unimpressed. "I've got to go."

After 18 hours in flight, Crowe felt stiff as an octogenarian. He went for a walk around Washington Square Park and visited the chess players' corner. He'd no sooner arrived when he saw a player sacrifice his bishop to take a pawn. Three moves later, he'd forced his opponent into checkmate. Crowe wondered if there was a lesson here.

He considered word association. Both Abbott and Bishop had names related to the clergy. An abbot was the head of an abbey of monks. A bishop was in charge of a diocese. Abbott's freedom had been sacrificed, but for what, or whom? And Bishop...?

Crowe took a taxi to Tribeca, getting out at the corner of Greenwich and Vestry. He entered the lobby of Bishop's condo building and buzzed his apartment. No answer. He called Bishop's number and got an automated response from Edgewater Risk Management.

He scanned the building directory for the administration office. He called the number and a woman answered.

"I'm a friend of Dean Bishop in suite 604," he told her. "I've been trying to reach him but can't get any response by phone or doorbell. Have you seen him?"

"I'm only here two afternoons a week," she said, "and I'm actually not familiar with many of the tenants. How old is he?"

"Early sixties, but he's got a heart condition." Crowe fabricated a little but not much. In his opinion, Bishop had no heart, but of course the woman didn't get that. "He might have had a stroke. Can you open the door so we can check on him?"

"I can't do that without the resident's permission."

"If I call 911, the fire department will break the door down. Dean won't like that either, but I guess you can explain it to him... if he's still alive."

"You're in the lobby?"

"Yes."

A minute later, an overweight woman in an ill-fitting pantsuit arrived at the door breathing heavily. She opened it and beckoned him in.

"Hi, I'm Axel Crowe." He showed her some ID.

"Linda Cardinal." She entered the elevator and pressed a button. She glanced at him as they went up. "We both have family names of birds."

"Yours is more popular," he said. "They named a baseball team after you. I guess nobody wants to be called a crow."

They got off on the sixth floor. She pulled a ring of keys from her jacket pocket and opened the door a few inches. "Hello," she called. "Anyone home?"

No answer. She opened the door all the way. They looked down a short hallway, past a kitchen and into a bright living room.

"Dean, are you here?" Crowe called out.

No answer. Crowe stepped around Linda and entered the living room. Immediately he saw signs of disorder. Books lay scattered on the floor near a coffee table placed at an odd angle. A spilled ashtray lay among the books. A broken glass lay on the floor. The residue of some drink had left a matte splash on the shiny hardwood floor.

"Don't touch anything," he warned Linda.

Sensing something bad about to unfold, she stayed in the hallway, one hand on the kitchen counter. A bottle of scotch sat on the counter. She looked like she might need some.

Crowe entered the room adjacent the living room. File folders and their contents papered the floor of a ransacked office. A closet door stood open, revealing a shotgun, a rifle and three fishing poles. A tackle box lay upended, hooks and lures scattered on the floor.

He entered the corner bedroom whose balcony overlooked Vestry. A man lay on a king-size bed with a wrought-iron headboard. He wore only a polo shirt and jockey briefs. There was so much dried blood on the upper half of his face it was impossible to know if it was Bishop.

Crowe placed a finger on the man's neck. No pulse. The body was cold. Crowe was no pathologist but guessed he'd been dead for several hours.

He noticed two small rents - about six inches apart - in the polo shirt. Beneath it were two small puncture wounds in the man's chest, each surrounded by an angry welt that looked like the worst bee sting ever. Crowe recognized the tell-tale trace of Taser darts.

Crowe examined his wrists. They were both heavily bruised, the skin broken in places. He examined the headboard and saw metallic scuff marks on the corner posts. No stretch of the imagination to see that he'd been handcuffed to the headboard and tortured.

His bare legs looked like they'd been scalded, from his feet all the way up to his groin. Crowe touched the damp bedding. He circled the bed and saw an oven mitt and two blackened knives on the floor. The soles of the man's feet were cross-hatched with burn marks. The old hot-knife routine, blades probably heated on the stove and applied to the feet.

Crowe turned his attention to the man's face. His eyes were discolored and puffy, forehead gouged, ears and nose bloodied. Pistol-whipped? Yet the blood from these injuries, smearing the upper half of his face, had not crossed an invisible horizontal line beneath his nose. Crowe lowered his face to within six inches of the dead man's. He saw flecks of white adhesive and a single sticky gray fiber on the man's cheek. Duct tape? How else to silence the screams of a tortured man?

Tortured for what? Revenge? Information? Something valuable? The bedroom had been searched too. The drawers of a dresser hung open, T-shirts, socks, jeans and underwear scattered on the floor. The double closet doors were ajar. Clothes on the rack were jammed to one side.

"Is everything okay?" Linda's voice from the kitchen was wound tight, a jack-in-the-box primed to explode.

"He's been murdered," he told her. "Call nine-one-one."

While she did that, he took the elevator to the parking level. He inserted his frequent flyer card into the door jamb so the spring bolt wouldn't lock him out of the vestibule to the elevator and stairwell.

The garage had three dozen parking slots, numbered for each resident. The car in 604 was covered with a protective shroud. He peeled it back and saw a ruby-red late-model Jaguar.

Crowe recalled the profile he'd developed via the *prashna*

chart. The Riverside Rapist might have a vehicle named after a quadruped. A Jaguar fit the bill. But he'd also speculated that the killer was from out of town, and that didn't fit Bishop. Unless the Jag belonged to a friend…

He used a pen-light on his keychain to peer into the car's interior. The glove compartment hung open and stuff was spilled on the floor. He used his shirt sleeve to cover his fingers and tried the door handle. Locked. So was the rear trunk. He dropped the shroud back in place and returned to Bishop's apartment.

Linda Cardinal sat white-faced in the kitchen, her elbows on the counter, her hands clasped together like a penitent in prayer.

Two uniformed cops arrived, followed ten minutes later by plainclothes from the 1st Precinct. Detective Sullivan was in his fifties, with a nose like a wine cork and a nervous eye that twitched several times a minute. Menendez was a good-looking woman in her thirties, her evident vitality implying regular workouts. They had a look around the apartment, then called the coroner and a crime scene unit.

Menendez went with Cardinal to fetch whatever the administration had on Bishop. Sullivan and Crowe sat in the living room and the detective took out his notebook.

"You a friend of Bishop?"

"No. I was investigating him as a possible accessory to a murder in Vermont last week." Crowe showed his license and gave Sullivan the high-altitude view of that case.

"Can you account for your whereabouts in the last twenty-four?"

"I just got back from Thailand this afternoon." Crowe provided his itinerary. "You can talk to Detective Levinson at the Twentieth."

Levinson's name didn't trigger anything for Sullivan. "Vermont's a bit out of his jurisdiction, no?"

"I'm consulting on a series of cold cases."

"Which?"

"The Riverside Rapist murders."

Sullivan nodded. "All Asian women, right? That why you were in Thailand?"

"No, just a coincidence."

"So why'd you come here today?"

"I wanted to tell Bishop that Kitti Poornchai was dead."

Crowe told Sullivan how he'd persuaded Linda to unlock the door, and what he'd discovered in Bishop's apartment. And the Jaguar in the underground garage - maybe Bishop's, maybe someone else's...

"Why the interest in his ride?"

"Just wondering if whoever killed him also took his car. Last I heard, he was driving a BMW X6. You might want to check DMV, see if he has two vehicles registered. Either the killer took the X6, or it's still in the neighborhood. There's a vehicle storage compound just down the block, corner of Vestry and West."

"Why would he keep his Beemer off-site?"

"Most condos only get one parking slot. But if you had two cars, wouldn't you keep the more expensive one closer to home?"

"If I had two cars, I'd sell one and take the vacation I can't afford. But thanks for the tip." Sullivan closed his notepad and gave Crowe his card. "You can go, but don't leave town without talking to me first, okay?"

58

CROWE TOOK A TAXI to the Lower East Side. It was just after six PM when he arrived at the corner of Stanton and Eldridge. From across the street he studied the three-story building that supposedly housed Patpong Pictures, the talent agency Kitti Poornchai worked for. It looked like the street-level novelty store was closed for the day, its alcove entrance sealed by an iron gate.

He crossed the street. Immediately adjacent the store entrance was another alcove and door, probably access to the floors above. He tried its gate. To his surprise, it opened. He examined the lock and saw scraped paint and gouged metal. The lock had been jimmied.

He stepped into the alcove and tried the door. It didn't open but he saw the metal plate covering the bolt had been torn off, leaving a portion of the lock exposed. Crowe took a jackknife from his pocket, inserted it behind the tongue of the bolt and popped the lock.

He pulled the door closed behind him. The tampered lock engaged with a solid click. A bulb lighted the carpeted stairway. He went up to the second floor. A door stood slightly ajar. The door jamb was deeply gouged where someone had used a pry bar and broken the lock.

Inside were four rooms. A kitchen and bathroom occupied the rear. Overlooking the street was a small office - a computer desk and two flat-screen monitors, speakers and headphones. In the desk drawers he found a box of business cards for Patpong Pictures, same as the one Fern had given him, but nothing else of interest.

A shelving unit against one wall held over a hundred DVDs with lurid art work and titles. *Bangkok Bondage, Phuket Phantasy, Thailand Tease*. Porn.

A filing cabinet stood nearby, its lower drawer open. Crowe flipped through the folders, finding contact information and nude photos of hundreds of young Asian women. The other drawer contained warranties on cameras, microphones, video editing software. Other folders held one-page resumes of directors, cameramen, sound technicians, makeup artists, editors, even a few writers.

As he closed the drawer, one of the warranty folders stuck in the support rail. The label on the folder caught his eye. *Bounty Hunter*. He opened it and found user instructions for a Bounty Hunter TK4, a rugged metal detector for hunting treasure in extreme ground conditions. A sales slip from Amazon was made out to Patpong Pictures for one TK4, a pair of headphones, and a nylon carry bag.

Crowe replaced the folder in the cabinet. Why did a porn studio need a metal detector? Had Bishop owned an interest in Patpong Pictures? He recalled Kitti telling him that Bishop had used a metal detector to search among the ashram cabins. What had he been looking for?

The room next door had a sofa, chair and king-size bed. Curtains covered the windows. Three tripods stood nearby, one mounted with a video camera. A boom mic hung over the bed. From a hole in the baseboard, half a dozen cables from the adjacent room awaited hookup to equipment in this room.

Crowe went up to the third floor. Another busted door stood ajar. This apartment had two bedrooms, with a living room overlooking the street. A loveseat and lounge chair faced a 60-inch flat screen TV. The coffee table bore several men's magazines featuring women, guns and vehicles.

The front bedroom held only a double bed and a dresser. The closet was empty and the dresser drawers hung open, revealing T-shirts, men's underwear and socks. The other windowless bedroom had two bolts on the outside of the door. A double mattress lay on the floor, wrinkled sheets in a bunch, like a dog had made its bed there.

A bicycle hung from an overhead hook. Just below the ceiling, a six-foot section of two-by-six joist had been bolted into the wall. Two rugged hooks, plastic-coated to protect bicycle rims, were screwed into it. Crowe judged the ceiling height at nine feet, placing the hooks at the eight-foot level. Just the right height to accommodate Tracey's theory of the upside-down Filipino hooker.

Crowe went to the kitchen. The fridge held a six-pack of beer, a can of coffee and two frozen pizzas. A few cans of chili and ravioli occupied the cupboards. Under the sink was a garbage container with a used coffee filter and an empty cookie bag.

He returned to the living room. On a shelf beneath the flat screen was a TV cable box atop a DVD player. Almost out of sight behind them were a dozen hand-labeled DVDs in translucent cases of red, blue and green. The red ones were labeled with the letters "TV" and the years 2008 through 2011.

He inserted the 2008 disk in the DVD player. In the video, a young man sat on a bed with a girl. They were an odd couple, a nerd in Dockers and polo shirt, her in a mini-skirt and a tube top from which her enhanced breasts seemed eager to erupt. She kissed and fondled him, did a little strip-tease and then she was literally all over him.

Crowe checked the later red series. The girls changed but the nerd remained the same. Most of the girls were Asian. All were young and, except for their breasts, small. Every sequence started with her initiating things, but ended with him pummeling her, twisting her arms or holding her throat at the climax.

Crowe's phone rang. He paused the DVD before answering.

"Mr. Crowe? It's Selena Greer."

"How're you doing?"

"I'm okay." He heard her draw on a cigarette. "I've found something."

"What?"

"A memory stick. It was hidden in a coffee can in Seth's fridge."

"And you just happened to discover it?"

"I got a call from Berndt. Seth's editor at *The Voice*? He just received an email from Seth. It was composed over a week ago, but set for timed release today. We'd talked on the phone earlier this week and Berndt knew I was staying at Seth's place. But he's out on Staten Island, didn't want to come in on a Saturday. Seth's email said the drive contained information that should be shared in the event of his death."

"You're at the condo now?"

"Yes."

"I'll be there in half an hour."

Crowe sampled the other DVDs. The green series was tame stuff - telephoto video clips of girls in beach bikinis, occasionally a shot of one peeling her top off to bare her breasts for the sun and, unknowingly, the distant camera.

The blue series was a compilation of video clips, seemingly from hidden cameras in motel rooms, of various couples having sex, very few of whom were attractive enough to merit the attention.

Crowe turned off the TV and put the DVDs back where he'd found them. He left the apartment and pulled its broken door closed behind him.

59

IT TOOK CROWE LESS THAN TEN MINUTES to walk the seven blocks from Eldridge to Clinton. Was it a coincidence that the office for Patpong Pictures was so close to Greer's condo? He recalled Guruji's Rule of Three, frequently invoked when Guruji was teaching Crowe how to read a horoscope. *Don't get all worked up every time you see a unique combination in a chart,* Guruji would wag his finger. *The police do not convict, and you do not predict, on a single piece of evidence. One coincidence offers a spark, two might ignite a flame, but it takes three to make a real fire.*

Crowe reflected on what he'd discovered at the office of Patpong Pictures. The second floor apartment was obviously a production studio to record and edit videos. The room with warm-up sofa and wide-angle bed was where all the action happened.

As for the apartment above, it'd had a transient feel, too little food and clothes to imply more than a temporary base for someone who lived elsewhere. The windowless bedroom didn't exactly scream dungeon, but the hooks on the wall made him suspect something more than a bicycle had been hung there.

He rang the bell at Greer's condo and was buzzed in. Selena Greer met him at the door. "I thought you'd have gone back to Florida by now," he said.

"It's taking longer than expected to settle Seth's affairs. I've been to his bank so many times I know everyone by first name. You wouldn't believe the paperwork they're putting me through. As if my grief weren't enough, this bureaucratic shit makes me want to buy a gun and shoot some bankers."

Crowe sniffed the air. He looked around and saw the light on a coffee machine. He was starting to feel the jet lag. "That smells good."

She poured two cups from the carafe and added a shot of Kahlua to hers. "How's your investigation going?"

He shrugged. "I feel like a fox circling the barnyard. I've got a bunch of feathers up my nose, but no chicken."

She came out from behind the counter, standing near him, body turned slightly, looking at him across her shoulder. "Does it tickle? Getting something up your nose?"

He wondered if she was flirting with him, or just teasing. He sensed she was lonely. No matter what she'd said before, about the breakup of her marriage being the real tornado, and settling Seth's affairs merely the clean-up after the twister had passed, it had to be difficult.

"Aside from the bank, how are you handling this? You went up to Albany for his funeral on Thursday?"

She nodded. "His parents invited me to stay over but I drove back that evening. Actually, I didn't make it all the way. I stopped in Catskill for dinner and ended up taking a motel for the night."

Crowe's imagination filled in a picture. An *aperitif* before, a glass of wine with dinner, maybe a *digestif* to follow... At least she'd been prudent to stay off the road.

"Did you speak to his brother yet?"

"No, we assume he's still in Peru. We've all left messages on his phone, telling him about Seth's death, explaining that we had to conduct the burial without waiting for his return. He'll understand. He doesn't practice but he respects tradition."

"When's he getting back?"

"We're not sure. Maybe late tonight."

Crowe made a mental note to phone Michael Greer tomorrow. "Can you show me what you found?"

She opened a kitchen drawer and gave him a baggie, a few coffee grains caught in the folds of plastic. Inside was a small red memory stick the size of a fingertip.

"Do you know what's on it?"

"No. I thought I'd wait for you."

"Too bad the burglars took his computer. We have no way to check it out here."

"I have a netbook. It's on his desk."

Crowe went to Greer's office and found it plugged into a power bar. He brought the netbook out to the coffee table and inserted the memory stick into one of its USB ports. Selena joined him on the sofa.

The stick contained a single MPEG file. Crowe started the media player. Seth Greer appeared onscreen. The video had been shot in his office.

"It's Tuesday, April tenth," Greer said. "Tomorrow I'm driving up to Vermont to see if I can crash a Buddhist retreat. Since you're watching this, something's gone wrong. Either I'm missing, or dead. Either way, it was probably at the hands of Dean Bishop.

"I've been tracking him for over a year. Three different stories, but last month they all came together. There are drafts on my home PC and backups at work. I was worried about break-ins, so my source notes aren't in my filing cabinet, but hidden in the hall closet.

"*Rancho Gomorrah* is about sex trafficking, mostly young women from Southeast Asia. *Rogue Elephants* is about heroin smuggling, facilitated by Thai criminals and our own national security agencies. *Artful Dodger* is about counterfeit art and stolen artifacts.

"Dean Bishop's name turned up several times. After digging into his past, I'm convinced he's the mastermind of these ventures, the linchpin that holds them together or, if pulled, might cause their collapse.

"During the Vietnam War he worked for the CIA

gathering intelligence along Thailand's borders with Laos and Burma – in the Golden Triangle, one of the largest opium-growing regions in the world. And the CIA had links to Chinese triads in Bangkok who processed opium into heroin.

"Historians of that era allege that Air America transported heroin to support Laotian forces fighting Communism. And China White heroin started showing up state-side in quantity near the end of the Vietnam War.

"Bishop likely began smuggling in the mid-seventies. With the help of military police or attachés, he probably shipped heroin to the US east coast where he had contacts, via Norfolk naval base or Langley air force base in Virginia.

"After the war, Bishop was reassigned to Bangkok until Air America disbanded in mid-1976. He coordinated field work in Cambodia, visiting twice just before the fall of Phnom Penh. He was stationed in Bangkok seven years and made several visits a year to Chiang Mai.

"Bishop abruptly left Thailand in the mid-eighties. Maybe he feared investigation and shut down operations. Maybe he sold the business. He spent the next few years in Washington and New York as the CIA's liaison officer with the former Immigration and Naturalization Service.

"During that period he made several trips to Thailand and became acquainted with Arthur Phuket, a Bangkok businessman. He left the CIA in the early nineties and started a company with Phuket called Edgewater Risk Management.

"Edgewater is a consultancy that advises American corporations on off-shore manufacturing in Southeast Asia. They started in Thailand, but have since expanded to Cambodia, Malaysia, Indonesia and Vietnam."

"Can you pause that for a minute?" Selena said. "I need a smoke break."

Crowe sat on the balcony with her while she had a cigarette. The sun was below the skyline but the streetlights hadn't come on yet. "That stuff on the video, is any of it familiar to you?" he asked her.

She shook her head. "Most journalists like to discuss what

they're working on. Give them a drink and they're off and running. But Seth admired Hemingway. His rule was, never discuss work in progress for fear you'd rob it of its vitality."

"Hemingway was a primitive," Crowe said. "His writing was all machismo - sex, blood sports and survival of the fittest. But he was like a tribesman who won't let you take his picture for fear you'll steal his mojo. Irony was, when the macho lifestyle failed him, he killed himself to escape the despair of his own ego."

"Thanks for the analysis, professor." Selena stubbed her cigarette in the ashtray.

"No problem." Crowe knew she was teasing him but he was okay with it. Humor was a great deflator of ego.

But his comment about the tribesman reminded him of what Mr. Roger had told Kertang. *If you ever take a picture of me, I'll kill you.* That wasn't superstition, but something else. Self-protection? From what?

"Did you go through all of Seth's files?" he asked Selena.

"Yes. In case there was anything relevant to his estate. Why?"

"Come across any pictures?"

"An album of family photos, mostly him and me. It was touching. I didn't know he'd kept it."

"Anything else? Photos related to stories he worked on?"

"No."

Too bad, Crowe thought. Although he knew what Bishop looked like, he had no idea about Mr. Roger. Somehow he'd hoped Greer might have acquired a full name or a photo. "Let's watch the rest of that video," he said.

"You go ahead. I'm going to stay out here."

60

CROWE TAPPED THE PLAY ICON on the media player. Seth Greer resumed his monologue.

"Edgewater has extensive networks in Southeast Asia, legitimately for offshore manufacturing, not-so-legally for trafficking. Bishop has connections in the former INS. Phuket has family ties in Bangkok who are known criminals. The police suspect him of supplying girls from all over Southeast Asia into the US sex trade.

"In the nineties, Phuket started buying businesses in Manhattan - restaurants, nightclubs, massage parlors and escort services. Outside New York, he owns strip clubs and escort services in Houston, a major hub for the sex industry.

"Asian girls enter the USA on student visas but wind up employed in the sex trade. China White keeps showing up in DEA interdictions. Phuket's name has turned up in various investigations by Vice and Narcotics units but he has excellent legal counsel, and none of their charges have stuck.

"He also owns art galleries in New York, Washington and Houston. Under the National Stolen Property Act, the US Attorney's Office has issued his New York gallery subpoenas on four different occasions for records regarding the provenance of religious antiquities.

"All items originated in Southeast Asia. Several involved statuary from temples in Cambodia - Angkor Wat, Koh Ker and others - looted during the Khmer Rouge era. Despite the end of decades of conflict, temple looting has dramatically accelerated since the nineties.

"Here's where it gets interesting. Bishop was in Bangkok when Cambodia fell to the Khmer Rouge. CIA field operations were running throughout the region. He's been back to Thailand many times. Cambodia is right next door. Given his background, coordinating local mercenaries in a steal-to-order mission would have been a piece of cake.

"When I was researching stolen art, I talked to the city's

top museums - the Metropolitan, Rubin, Brooklyn Museum, and Manhattan Museum of Asian Antiquities - regarding their holdings of Southeast Asian art. The director of the MMAA told me about a broker who'd approached them the summer of 2008."

Greer recapped what Crowe already knew from Roxanne Morton, about Tom Jimson and the 700-year-old gold Buddha from Thailand - his romance with the curator Thi Nguyen, her authentication of the statue, their breakup, his disappearance, her murder...

"Were Tom Jimson and Dean Bishop one and the same?" Greer continued. "I shared my suspicions with the NYPD. But they seemed to regard Bishop as one of their own, didn't even want to bring him in for questioning. Turns out Bishop had an alibi. He'd been in Bangkok the week Nguyen was killed. The NYPD dumped her case back in the Riverside Rapist file.

"I still think Bishop's a criminal. As a CIA agent, he's been involved in drug smuggling, kidnapping, forcible confinement and probably torture. His familiarity with Southeast Asia facilitated sex trafficking and the theft of religious antiquities. His partnership with Phuket, whose business interests run parallel, suggests the two are thick as thieves.

"But Bishop's a complex guy - a spook *and* a devotee. He attends talks on Eastern philosophy. Every Sunday he participates in group meditation at a Buddhist temple in lower Manhattan. Through them I've learned he's attending a retreat in Vermont, which is why I'm going too.

"I'd like to see Bishop behind bars, but I've run out of ideas, so I'm going to confront him. If that doesn't pan out, give this to the police.

"One more thing. After some research and a bribe, I acquired a photo from the Air Force Historical Research Agency dating back to Bishop's service during the Vietnam War. I don't have the names of other people in the photo, but I'll bet Bishop's heroin-smuggling partner is among them.

"I scanned it onto my PC and saved a backup at work.

The physical copy's in the jacket sleeve of one of my Thelonious Monk albums."

The video ended. Crowe put the memory stick in his shirt pocket. He'd share this with the police, but doubted it would resolve the Nguyen case. If Greer was right, the detectives who'd handled it in 2009 had already confirmed Bishop's out-of-country alibi for the week she was murdered.

As for Greer's murder, Lieutenant Lynch of the Vermont State Police had also ruled out Bishop's hand in it, since he'd been back in Manhattan by the time Greer took his swan dive into the quarry.

Crowe went to the large bookcase in the living room. The lower shelf held more than a hundred vinyl albums. He flipped through them, and saw they were grouped by rock, blues and jazz. In the middle of the jazz section he found three Monk LPs: *Monk's Dream, Brilliant Corners* and *Solo Monk.*

The first two albums contained only a vinyl disk in a paper sleeve. The third, *Solo Monk,* showing Thelonious in an aviator's helmet, contained a disk with another sheet of paper inside the sleeve.

It was a high-quality photocopy of a black-and-white photograph showing a large group of men and a fighter plane. Crowe recognized a Phantom fighter, the mainstay aircraft of the Vietnam era. Twenty men sat on its wing. Another score were standing. Another twenty sat cross-legged on the ground. All wore fatigues and combat boots, either bare-chested or in T-shirts, and all had crew cuts.

Beneath the photo was a type-written caption: *14th Tactical Reconnaissance Squadron, Udorn, Thailand, April 1974.* Beneath that, someone had written in blue ballpoint: *Middle row, third from left, Dean Bishop (military intelligence).*

Crowe studied the photo. If he hadn't been shown, he mightn't have picked Bishop out from a 38-year-old picture. But as he studied the face, he saw Bishop's hatchet nose, thick eyebrows and angular jaw were still the same four decades later.

Crowe scanned the rest of the group. Halfway through

the seated row, he lingered over a face. Or rather, the ears flanking it. This guy had a crew cut like the rest, but his ears stuck out like Yoda's. Crowe recalled meeting Bill Kinkelman on his aerie overlooking the Gulf of Maine, thinking he had elf ears.

The photo brought something else into focus. Kinkelman said he'd been a technical analyst for aerial reconnaissance. Bishop had been military intelligence. Serving together in Udorn, they'd have literally rubbed elbows while analyzing aerial photos for targets.

Why had Kinkelman denied his war-time acquaintance with Bishop? Was it a secret that Bishop had worked for Air America? Or because the CIA had later tarnished its reputation in so many ways?

Crowe went over the rows of faces again. Too bad the caption line hadn't included their names. An intentional omission? Like Det. Levinson had said, the war had been unpopular with civilians and military alike, and no one wanted reminding of having been there.

Crowe used his phone camera to shoot three close-ups from slightly different angles. He emailed them to Jimmy Kertang, asking if he recognized anybody from back in the days of Dean Bishop.

He put the photocopy back in the album sleeve and laid the album on the kitchen counter. He returned the netbook to the office and went out onto the balcony. Selena was staring into space, cigarette in hand, empty glass at her side.

"Have you eaten?" she said. "There's food in the fridge. I should cook it or throw it out."

"I have to go."

"Are you meeting someone?"

"A friend."

"That's good. Everyone needs a friend." She looked at him meaningfully. "Sometimes you just need someone to hold you and tell you it's going to be all right."

"We all need that." He hesitated. "It won't be easy, and it may never be all right, but you will survive. You're a very strong woman."

She came inside and walked him to the door. He tucked the Monk album under his arm. "I'm borrowing this for a while."

"Be my guest. What will you do with the stick?"

"Show it to the police. I'll keep you informed."

"Thank you."

He gave her a hug, said goodnight and let himself out.

61

CROWE DESCENDED IN THE ELEVATOR and sat in the lobby of Greer's condo building. It was 9:30. He found the business card for the director of the Manhattan Museum of Asian Antiquities and called the cell number she'd printed on the back.

Roxanne Morton answered, sounds of a party in the background. It took her a few moments to find a quiet spot so she could hear why he was calling.

"Remember Tom Jimson?" he said. "I might have found a picture. I'd like you to confirm it's him."

"I'm at a dinner party in SoHo. Want to join us for dessert?"

"Thanks, but I don't have time. Could I email it to you?"

"Alright."

Crowe took the photo of the 14th Tactical Recon Squadron from the album sleeve, and used his phone to zoom in on Bishop. He took two pictures and sent them to Morton. She phoned him back immediately.

"It's him."

"You're sure? The guy with the golden Buddha?"

"He's much younger in that picture but it's definitely him. Seeing his face again makes me so angry. What a rat! He broke Thi's heart."

"His heart-breaking days are over." Crowe told her that Dean Bishop, AKA Tom Jimson, had been murdered, possibly in connection with the case that had brought Crowe to New York.

"I'm not sorry he's dead, but I'd have preferred he rotted in jail."

"Maybe so, but his death has left a lot of unknowns in its wake."

"This reminds me, I'd heard Bishop's name before. Last year I met a journalist researching the black market in art. I told him about Jimson and his Buddha, how they'd both vanished. A month later he called to say he'd asked the NYPD to consider Bishop as a suspect in Thi's death. He urged me to call them, to identify Bishop if he and Jimson were the same. The police never returned my calls. A week later, he called back to say it was a dead end, Bishop had an alibi."

"I assume that was Seth Greer?"

"Yes. How'd you know?"

Crowe told her about Greer's altercation with Bishop at the Vermont ashram, and his murder later that night. "Despite Bishop's alibi for the week of Nguyen's death, Greer still suspected him of some wrongdoing. He must have confronted Bishop with what he knew, but it didn't end well. Ironically, Bishop had an out-of-town alibi for that night too. But thanks for confirming his picture. It's a critical piece of the puzzle."

"Glad to help. Hey, I've got to go. Apparently I'm supposed to make a toast for someone's birthday."

Crowe thanked her again and said goodbye. He called Tracey, who'd just got home an hour ago after a very long day at work.

"Today was Saturday," he said. "What's with all the overtime?"

"In the city that never sleeps, those that can't sleep seem eager to kill, or at least make a stab at it. We have more work than we can handle in the nine-to-five."

"Have you had dinner?"

"Yes, but I could go for dessert."

~~~

They met at Café Mogador on St. Mark's Place. It was a busy place with a young crowd and a warm ambience - dark hardwood floors, flickering candlelight, painted brick walls, framed art everywhere. They got a table for two in the middle of the café. Crowe ordered a soup and a salad. Tracey opted for a piece of baklava.

"I got your email," she said. "You're looking for a roster of Vietnam vets? But Veterans Affairs only handles medical benefits. I have a contact at the VA Medical Center here in Manhattan, but that's it."

"Levinson already told me it was a lost cause. But I found something else that completes part of the puzzle."

"The Riverside Rapist case?"

"No. The journalist's death in Vermont."

"The one from *The Village Voice*? Did you hear what happened?"

"The break-in? Hacking their network? I was there the day after, the place was like a war zone."

"They found the guy who did it."

"Who found whom?"

"The NYPD computer crimes squad. They traced the hacking attack to a guy in Bangor. He's a computer science senior at the University of Maine, apparently something of a genius. But he claims someone hijacked his computer to launch the attack on *The Voice*."

"Nothing to do with the physical break-in?"

"Strictly digital fingerprints. Still no suspects for the break-in. Obviously the two are linked, but the student disavows any knowledge of that. He got a good lawyer and is already out on bail."

"Remember his name?"

"I'd have to look it up. We can go back to my place later, and I'll sign in from my home computer."

"Sounds good."

"How was Thailand?"
~~~

"Harrowing." He told her about almost ending up, genetically speaking, in a ladies' purse.

"No time for a little sex tourism?"

"No interest."

They walked back to her condo. Tracey put on some music, *Bitch's Brew* from Miles Davis' electric period. Crowe loved the album as much for John McLaughlin's guitar as Miles' trumpet.

He saw a scatter of books on her coffee table and picked one up. *The Encyclopedia of Palmistry* by Edward Campbell. "What's this?" he teased her. "Trying to muscle in on my franchise?"

"It has a good section on fingerprints," she said. "You never know, maybe it'll come in handy at work."

"What have you learned so far?"

"To keep my mouth shut when there's a detective nearby."

"That'll change after you get some experience. Are you reading hands?"

"Just a few of my friends so far. It really seems to work."

"Duh."

"Let me look at your fingerprints."

He gave her his hands. "Don't tell me I'm going to die," he joked. "I have too many things to do this week."

She peered at each of his fingertips. "Wow! You have whorl patterns on all ten of your fingerprints."

He played dumb. "What's that mean?"

"The way I think of it, whorls are like bulls-eyes," she said. "That means you're focused. Whorls are good for concentration, meditation and creativity. The whorls are high on the phalange, so that means you have intellectual, maybe spiritual, inclinations. But you're also very stubborn."

He withdrew his hands. "Not bad."

"Touched a nerve, did I?" she laughed. "Let me test the flexibility of your thumb."

Crowe shook his head. "Next thing I know, you'll be all over my Mount of Venus."

"Would that be such a bad thing?"

"You know I hardly ever mix business with pleasure."

"The business being…?"

"You were going to pull up some info on that hacker."

"You are such a tease." She punched him in the shoulder, hard enough for him to suspect there might be a bruise in the morning. But she used her computer to sign into the NYPD network and find the Bangor hacker's name.

"Thomas Vandenberg. DOB, August eighth, ninety-one. Address, 202 Greystone Trailer Park, Veazie, Maine. Charged with trespassing and destruction of commercial property. Maine State Police exercised the warrant on Thursday, seized his computer and took him into custody. Friday, released on bail of fifty thousand dollars, conditional to wearing an electronic monitoring device. Independent of criminal proceedings, *The Voice* is laying civil charges for theft and destruction of property valued in excess of one million."

"I'm not surprised. It'll cost a fortune to restore their network. You have a picture of this kid?"

Tracey showed Crowe the mug shots from Vandenberg's booking. Only 20 years old, already a college senior, a sallow-faced kid with a shag of unkempt dark hair, thick eyebrows and pale blue eyes. His profile revealed a pointed nose, stud earring and protruding Adam's apple. The face looked familiar but Crowe couldn't put his finger on it.

"Can you give me a printout?"

"What for?"

"Hopefully, to clear my friend of that bogus murder charge. This is related. I may go up to Maine and ask a few questions."

"Related how?" Tracey said.

"Consider the timeline. Greer was killed Friday midnight. That same night, someone also broke into his Manhattan condo, ransacked his filing cabinet and stole his computer. Twenty-four hours later, burglars broke into *The Voice* and took all of his physical files. The hacker deleted all of his digital files."

"This was all coordinated?"

"Coordinated by one, executed by a team. Greer was onto something Bishop wanted kept secret. Greer probably confronted Bishop at the ashram, demanded a confession or tried to blackmail him. Maybe that's why Bishop decked him."

"But if he left the ashram, Bishop couldn't have killed Greer."

"Right. He returned to New York that evening. But he could have broken into Greer's condo later that night. He was ex-CIA. He could have found out where Greer lived, got around building security."

"If Bishop didn't kill Greer, he had an accomplice in Vermont. Didn't Kitti Poornchai stay overnight at the ashram?"

"Greer was killed with a shovel," Crowe said. "Is that a woman's style?"

"No. We prefer guns or poison. But how'd the police eliminate her as a suspect?"

"Maybe Lieutenant Lynch jumped to the same conclusion as me."

"So if not her, Bishop had a male accomplice, maybe someone in the area," Tracey said.

"Yes to the first, not necessarily the second. In the time Bishop drove from Barnet to New York, an associate could have driven up from New York. They could have rendezvoused in Springfield where Bishop stopped for gas and a meal. He could have given his associate instructions on where to find Greer and what to do."

"What's Vandenberg got to do with this?"

"I don't know. But the detectives from the First Precinct will examine Bishop's phone records. Whoever he talked to in the twenty-four hours after he left the ashram are potential accomplices."

"A team effort?"

"The newspaper burglary was a professional job. *The Voice* had a good security system but someone was smart enough to breach it. There had to be a lookout and at least two people to search for and destroy files. But Bishop was ex-CIA. A mini-Watergate would have been a walk in the park for a guy with his experience."

"If he's so smart, how come he's dead?"

"Typical motives. Money, revenge, passion... Whoever killed Greer probably killed Bishop too."

"Maybe you should run that idea by Sullivan and Lynch."

"Sullivan, maybe. But Lynch already thinks Abbott killed Greer."

"You have an alternate theory...."

"To start his investigation all over again? You know cops. They just want to close cases."

"Why all this interest in Vandenberg? So you can do an end run around two police forces?"

"He's just a link in the chain," Crowe said. "But I ask myself, who's pulling the chain?"

"Maybe you just need to sleep on it."

"I do need to sleep," Crowe said. The jet lag had finally caught up to him and coffee would be no cure. "Can you give me that printout of Vandenberg's mug shot? I'm going to head back to my hotel."

She walked him to the door. They embraced. She kissed him. He hesitated, then kissed her in return. Eventually he got away.

62

Sunday, April 29

BETWEEN TIME ZONE CHANGES, air travel and the activity of the last few days, Crowe was exhausted and didn't wake up until nine AM. In no hurry to spring from bed, he lay there indulging himself in the illusion he had nothing better to do on a Sunday morning.

He recalled a line about firefighters - days of unremitting boredom punctuated by hours of terror. But in this case, something had been smoldering far too long to be complacent about the outcome. Where there was smoke, there was fire, and behind a suspicious fire there was an arsonist. His too-close brush with death on the edge of the crocodile pool had been his wake-up call. The people he was dealing with were ruthless and brutal.

Out of habit, he opened his astrology app and checked the planetary lineup. Gemini was in the ascendant and the only angular planet in the sky was debilitated Mercury. If ever there was a prescription for killing time, this was it.

After 10:50 AM, things would kick into gear. The Moon would rise in Cancer. The Sun and Jupiter would be overhead in Aries, with Saturn at the nadir in Libra. With three *sattvic* planets angular, and a powerful Saturn in play, he saw an echo of that initial *prashna* when Abbott had first called him eight days ago. More importantly, he also saw the promise of its resolution.

He used his tablet to check the Amtrak schedule. Express trains to Boston departed Penn Station at noon, two o'clock and four. He figured he needn't reserve on a Sunday, and could choose his departure time later today.

He took a shower and meditated for half an hour. He went for a walk around Washington Square Park, deserted at this hour, and bought tea and a muffin on Sixth Avenue to take back to his hotel.

At eleven he called Kevin Blaikie to give him an update. Blaikie was thrilled to hear he'd almost got laid by the Princess of Siam, and barely escaped being eaten by crocodiles.

"What's next for our hero?"

"Not sure. I'm making it up as I go along."

"Anything I can do?"

"What's the name of that Burlington lawyer you hired? I'm driving up there tomorrow to see Abbott."

Blaikie gave him the lawyer's name, phone, email and office address.

Crowe packed his things and called Levinson. The detective couldn't talk right now. Crowe heard giggling in the background. He told Levinson he was leaving for Boston this afternoon and wanted to download what he'd developed on the Riverside Rapist case. They agreed to meet in Penn Station at three o'clock.

Crowe checked out and phoned Selena Greer from the lobby. Her voice was gravelly but she was happy he'd called.

"Don't get your hopes up," he said, "but yesterday I learned something that may lead us to Seth's real killer." He told her about the University of Maine student who'd hacked into *The Voice*'s network. "Does the name Tommy Vandenberg mean anything to you?"

"No."

"I'm going up there tomorrow to talk to this kid. In the meantime, do you have anyone you can stay with?"

"I'm okay. I know you've seen me drinking, but I'm not an alcoholic. I'm just hurting. Although we'd separated, I always thought Seth and I would get back together. I'm just coming to terms with the fact that it's really over. But I'll be fine."

"Okay. You have my number."

"Thank you for calling. You're a kind man."

"I'll keep you posted."

Crowe checked his watch. It was going on noon. He retrieved Sullivan's business card and called the detective's mobile. Sullivan answered on the first ring.

Crowe identified himself, reminding Sullivan of his interest in the Bishop case. "You asked me to alert you if I intended to leave town. I'm taking the train to Boston this afternoon."

"Could you first come down to the precinct for a chat? We'd like to fingerprint you."

"Why?"

"To eliminate you as a suspect," Sullivan said, although the way it came out didn't sound very promising.

63

THE 1ST PRECINCT WAS AT THE CORNER of Ericsson Place and Varick. A dozen air conditioners hung precariously from the windows of the three-story building, threatening to fall on the police vehicles parked on the sidewalk below.

Det. Menendez met him at the desk sergeant's counter. She wore jeans and a zippered hoodie that read "NYU" on the left breast. They took the stairs to the third floor.

He tried to make small talk. "This how you stay in shape?"

"This is how Sullivan stays in shape," she said. "I run marathons."

The homicide office had four pairs of steel desks joined at the hip, the pairs separated by dividers. Menendez led Crowe into the far corner. Sullivan wore the same clothes as yesterday, dark slacks over Rockports, wrinkled white shirt and loose tie. Menendez pulled out a chair for Crowe. It didn't look like a hot seat but context was everything.

Crowe decided to lob the first question. "Did you find an extra computer in Bishop's condo? Maybe in his storage locker?"

"You're here to answer questions, not ask them," Sullivan said, but the clench of his jaw told Crowe that he'd made a correct assumption.

"Just trying to help. If you find an extra computer, chances are it belonged to Seth Greer, the journalist who was murdered. His condo was burglarized last week, his files ransacked and his computer stolen. I suspect Bishop was responsible."

"Why?"

Crowe sketched the bigger picture as he now understood it - Greer having discovered Bishop was a player in more than one of the stories he was investigating, and Bishop needing to silence him and eliminate anything Greer had documented on him.

"Bishop was mixed up in narcotics, sex trafficking and stolen antiquities?" Sullivan said. "You make him sound like an arch-criminal. Who else besides Greer knew this?"

"Kitti Poornchai knew at least some of it, but now she's dead. Bishop's accomplice, whoever killed Greer, probably knew too. Especially if that same person also killed Bishop."

Sullivan nodded. "Let's get you printed."

Menendez took Crowe to a basement office. A fingerprint technician entered his ID into a computer and led him to a Motorola console. She scanned his ten digits, both palms, and the edge of each palm where a note-writer's hand would contact a horizontal surface.

Menendez walked Crowe back upstairs. As they entered the homicide section, Sullivan was just hanging up the phone.

"Let me guess," Crowe said. "That was your fingerprint techie. In the time it took us to walk back up, AFIS found no match between my fingerprints and whatever you lifted from Bishop's Jag."

Sullivan shrugged. "Some people are smart enough to wear gloves."

"Did you find the BMW?"

"Storage depot, corner of Vestry and West, like you suggested."

"Had it been ransacked as well? Was the GPS unit missing from both cars?"

"How'd you know that?"

"Just a hunch, but here's my theory," Crowe said. "Whoever killed Bishop knew about his BMW off-site. So this wasn't a home invasion gone wrong. This was a falling-out between criminal associates. The killer tortured Bishop for information. Whatever he learned wasn't enough. The killer took Bishop's car keys and searched both vehicles. He probably didn't find what he was looking for. So he took both GPS units in order to retrace Bishop's movements."

"We've made a few inquires about Bishop," Sullivan said. "His service file is sealed. He's a spook with no known associates."

"That's not quite true," Crowe said. "He's partners with Arthur Phuket. Bishop ran Edgewater but Phuket owned it. You didn't know that, or were you encouraged to look the other way? I understand both Bishop and Phuket have pull."

"Hey." Sullivan rose from his seat, shifting his weight onto his fists and his blood pressure into his cheeks. "We go where we have to, and follow justice where it leads."

"That'd make a great inspirational poster," Crowe said.

Menendez stifled a chuckle. Sullivan took a deep breath and lowered himself back into his chair.

Crowe held up a hand. "For the record, I don't think Phuket had anything to do with this murder. For him, Bishop's death is probably a significant loss. In fact, Phuket's probably called your commander already, expressing his concern and offering to cooperate however he can, whatever it takes to find Bishop's killer. Am I right?"

Sullivan said nothing, but Crowe could see he was trying too hard to keep a poker face.

"I can imagine your frustration," Crowe said. "I know what I shouldn't know, and I don't know what you think I know. I really wish I could help you more, but I've answered all your questions and told you everything I can. May I go now?"

Sullivan opened a notepad and jabbed it with a pen. "Where can we find you if we need you?"

Crowe gave them his father's address and phone number, his Saab's license plates, and his proposed itinerary.

"Why are you going back to Vermont?"

"My friend's still in jail and I haven't spoken to him in a week. Besides, it's on my way home."

"Have a safe trip," Sullivan said, but it sounded more like good riddance and don't come back.

64

AT PENN STATION, a billboard above the main entrance announced upcoming events at Madison Square Garden - a home game for the New York Rangers, and another show on a North American tour for a sexagenarian rock band.

Inside the station concourse, Crowe found Det. Levinson at the Police desk beneath the electronic Departures board. They went to a nearby Starbucks for coffee.

"Sorry to spoil your day off," Crowe said.

"As we say in Homicide, when a murderer's day ends, ours begins. What've you got?"

Crowe reviewed the timeline of the Riverside Rapist murders, separated on average by periods of 22.5 months. His theory was that the killer was probably from out of town, his visits to New York keyed to a pattern of medical checkups every two years. His father, for example, needed a full medical every two years to maintain his pilot's license.

"Makes sense," Levinson said. "Trouble is, our only suspects were local guys."

"What about other aspects of the profile?" Crowe suggested the Riverside Rapist was a married man, formerly police or armed services. He had a psychological disorder, maybe some physical debility. He drove a dark blue second-hand vehicle, probably with distinctive upgrades and - still sticking to his theory - bearing out-of-state plates.

"Where's all this coming from?"

"The astrological signatures of the case." Crowe kept it vague, not wanting to say it was based on a single chart he'd calculated in the New Delhi airport. Levinson wouldn't understand how a well-intentioned question could elicit an informed answer no matter how far removed - in time or place - the astrologer was from the matter under investigation.

"I don't see the logic."

"Can you use your contacts at Veterans Affairs? Get the names of every non-resident who's used the Manhattan facility in the past twelve years. Narrow that list by looking at schedules within a week of the Riverside Rapist murders."

"You're suggesting this out-of-state veteran comes to New York every two years, less a month or so, for some routine medical examination. And while he's in town, instead of taking in a Broadway show, he rapes and kills Asian women?"

"Maybe."

"But there are VA facilities in every state. Why wouldn't he simply seek treatment in his vicinity?"

"There's an old saying: *It's a dirty bird that shits in its own nest*. Maybe he just wants to distance himself from his crime sprees."

"Maybe," Levinson nodded. "But the VA won't hand over any information without a subpoena, and I don't have probable cause to justify one."

"You have the periodicity of the killings."

"Nothing in our investigation points to a veteran, never mind one from out of town."

Crowe knew this wouldn't be easy. His leap of faith via astrology could only be followed by Levinson through paperwork. The legal system's checks and balances reduced the investigation to a maze the detective would have to negotiate on his own.

"Maybe I can give you a tentative connection."

Crowe told Levinson what he'd recently learned about Dean Bishop, AKA Tom Jimson: approaching the museum with a gold Buddha, romancing the curator until she'd authenticated it, dumping her nine months later.

"Nguyen was killed six months after that, deemed a victim of the Riverside Rapist based on her ethnicity, proximity to the park, and rape. But as you know, she was different from the other victims."

"True," Levinson said. "Although Asian, she was much older than the others. And her body was found in her condo while the others were dumped along Riverside Drive."

"I read all the files. There were other differences too."

"Yes. Nguyen bore no ligature marks like the others whose bruises suggested restraints. She had no bite marks. And she wasn't strangled, but had her neck broken, a relatively quick death."

"If she doesn't match the victim profile, she wasn't killed by the same man."

"But she was murdered within a day or two of the sixth victim."

"It could have been a copycat."

"If so, it was the only one."

"What does that tell us?"

"That the second killer isn't a nut job like the Riverside Rapist, but more controlled and calculating."

"Or he only needed to kill one person - Thi Nguyen - and the Riverside Rapist was a convenient scapegoat."

"Where's the connection to the out-of-town veteran?"

"Bishop was CIA since the Vietnam War, involved in covert ops throughout Southeast Asia. His whole career was spent rubbing shoulders with the military. His old boys' network would include veterans."

"You think the Riverside Rapist is one of his old pals?"

"Whether he knew or merely suspected his friend's activities, he may have taken advantage of his presence in town to tack an extra victim onto his series."

"How would he have known?"

"Maybe the friend talked about it. Maybe Bishop figured it out, noting the coincidence of his friend's visits and the deaths of Asian women."

"You think this has something to do with Vietnam? Some psycho's obsession with a third world country that bloodied America's nose and destroyed a Presidency?"

"You'd need a shrink to reveal the Riverside Rapist's motivations," Crowe said. "But for whoever killed Nguyen, the reasons were probably more pedestrian."

"The gold Buddha?"

"After Nguyen's death, the museum realized her notes on the Buddha had disappeared. They weren't in the office where they should have been, nor in Nguyen's condo. Although the director brought this to your predecessor's attention, Jimson had disappeared and the trail was cold."

"Now that Bishop's dead, it's colder still."

"Only with respect to Nguyen's murder. But Bishop died at the hands of someone he knew. It could have been the Riverside Rapist."

"You think the rapist finally learned - after all these years - that Bishop had killed Nguyen, trying to pin it on him?"

"Bishop didn't kill Nguyen. He was in Bangkok that week. Whoever killed Nguyen was likely Bishop's accomplice, but something happened to sever their loyalty."

"Your questions about the Buddha may have stirred him into action."

"Not just my questions. Greer had been investigating Bishop and knew a lot more than me."

"You think the Riverside Rapist killed Greer because he got too close to Bishop? Then killed Bishop before it led to him?"

Crowe held up his hands. "I don't have all the answers. I'm just sniffing a trail through the woods. What lies at the end remains to be seen."

65

AMTRAK'S ACELA EXPRESS departed Penn Station shortly after four PM. Half an hour out of Manhattan, Crowe called his father and asked if he could meet him at Westwood at 7:30.

"Are you going to eat on the train?"

"Probably not."

"Okay, I'll make something for dinner. See you in a few hours."

Crowe looked at his watch. 4:30 here, 1:30 in LA. No matter how late Michael Greer had got home last night, he'd had enough sleep by now. Crowe called his number.

"Hello?"

"Michael Greer?"

"Yes. Who's this?"

"Axel Crowe. Selena Greer gave me your number."

"Is this about Seth? Selena and my parents left messages. I just got off the phone with my father a few minutes ago. I can't believe Seth's dead."

"Did you listen to all of your messages?"

"Yes."

"Anything there from Seth? From last weekend?"

"Yes, but he scarcely had a chance to say anything before someone interrupted him..."

"Michael, can you play that message back for me?"

"Why? What do you know about Seth's death?"

Crowe explained why he was involved. "Seth was lured from his cabin late at night. Someone must have ambushed him right after he dialed your number. I need to hear what's on that message. It might offer a clue to the killer's identity."

"Shouldn't the police handle that?"

"We'll get a copy to them as soon as possible. First, I need to hear what was said."

"Call me back on my cell and I'll replay the land line message." Michael gave him the number.

"I didn't think you had a cell phone." Selena hadn't

mentioned it.

"I only turn it on when I go out, but I'm usually home. Everyone knows to call my land line first."

"Get your cell. I'll call you back in a minute."

Crowe hoped he wouldn't change his mind and refuse to play back the message. But when he called back, Seth's brother answered right away.

"Ready?" Michael said.

"Go ahead."

Michael played the message that had come from Seth's phone:

"Hey, Michael..." Presumably, this was Seth's voice.

In the background, the sound of feet crunching through underbrush.

Seth's voice again, now distant from the phone: "Where's Kitti?"

Another man's voice, deeper, further away: "She couldn't make it."

"You're not part of this group. Who are you?"

In the background, the sound of feet moving through grass.

"Just a guy who walks softly but carries a big stick."

"What do you want?"

"To shut your mouth, asshole. You stuck your nose into one too many places."

Another shuffle of feet in the grass. Then a brief cry and a heavy "thunk" as a blow struck home. A sharp gasp. A hushed pause. Then a brief squall of static, followed by dead silence.

Crowe asked Michael to play it again. This time Crowe painted a picture around the sound. Greer had waited up on the ridge where the prayer flags defined a safety perimeter at the quarry's edge. He'd probably just dialed Michael's number when the other man came out of the bushes. The voices were indistinct, even Greer's, perhaps because he'd hidden the forbidden phone behind his back. When the killer struck him with the shovel, Greer had stumbled through the line of prayer flags and fallen into the quarry. His phone had been flung free, but landed on the ledge where Crowe had found it, the case having cracked open and the battery ejected.

Crowe told Michael about Seth's research into Bishop's past, their confrontation at the ashram, and the likely reason for his murder by Bishop's accomplice.

"Did you recognize his voice on that playback?"

"No. But if the police identify a suspect, voice-analysis software can place him at the scene."

"They don't have a suspect?"

"They've arrested someone but he's not guilty. This recording will exonerate him. Do you have a good-quality recording device?"

"Of course. I'm a composer."

"Make a couple of high-quality recordings. Email copies to me and these two detectives." Crowe gave the email addresses for Levinson and Sullivan. "While you do that, I'll make a call to see how we should register this as evidence."

They broke off to handle their respective tasks. Crowe searched his directory for Liam Cobb, an FBI Special Agent in Albuquerque. Their paths had intersected last year when Crowe was running down leads in a three-way murder conspiracy case that had claimed Kevin Blaikie's sister as one of the victims.

After several rings, the FBI agent answered. "Lucky for you, Crowe, I'm on call this weekend. Plus, I recognized your name. What's up?"

"I need advice on how to handle a piece of evidence." Crowe described the situation - innocent accused in a Vermont jail, exonerating evidence on voicemail in LA, and two NYPD detectives with a stake in the case.

"It's an across-state-lines federal crime. Get your friend to call the LA field office." He gave Crowe a 310 area code number. "Their Criminal Investigations unit will assume responsibility for the evidence and its chain of custody."

When Crowe finished the call, he checked his email. He'd received a message from someone called *music_shaman*.

The email message read: *Copy #1 of voicemail received 12:15 AM EDST, April 21, from cell phone of Seth Greer to home phone of Michael Greer,* with a WAV file attachment, and CCs to

Levinson and Sullivan. In moments, copy #2 arrived in his inbox.

Crowe called Michael Greer and gave him the number for the FBI's LA office. "Call them right away."

"Anyone else we should tell about this?"

"Did you get calls from anyone else about Seth?"

"A cop named Lynch in St. Johnsbury, Vermont, left a message, apparently last weekend, saying Seth had been killed, offering condolences. He left a number but at the time I heard the message it was three AM on the East Coast, so I didn't call back. Since then, my father filled me in on the particulars."

"Can you hold off calling him back? I'm going to see him tomorrow, and I'll tell him about Seth's last voice-mail."

"What if he calls me?"

"Just don't answer any 802 area code calls."

"Why not? Isn't he in charge of the murder investigation?"

"He's also a redneck who runs his county like the sheriff of Dodge City. He arrested my friend on thin evidence and I don't want him knowing we've got exonerating evidence until I've spoken to his lawyer."

"I get it."

"You should call Selena, though." Crowe told him about her struggle with the paperwork involved in settling the estate, meanwhile trying to manage her grief.

"I'll do better than that," Michael said. "I'll catch the next flight to New York."

66

Boston

THE TRAIN ARRIVED at Westwood station at 7:30 PM. As Crowe crossed the platform, his father stood waiting in the station. They embraced and walked to the parking lot.

"Have a good time in New York?"

Good time didn't quite describe it. Crowe related the highlights of his investigation - running with homicide cops, ex-CIA agents, illegal immigrants, drug dealers, strong-arm goons, prostitutes and crocodiles.

"I hope you wore condoms," his father joked, not sure how much of his son's continent-ranging adventures to believe.

Back home, his father went to work in the kitchen. Half an hour later, they sat down to a dinner of fettuccine primavera and a spinach salad with walnuts. His father poured himself a glass of white wine. Crowe started in on the food. He hadn't eaten since breakfast.

"I was starving," he told his father, "but this is truly delicious."

His father beamed at the compliment. "There's more."

They'd just finished eating when Crowe's phone rang. It was Det. Sullivan.

"I just received Michael Greer's email. What am I supposed to make of this recording?"

"The voices are Seth Greer and his killer, probably Dean Bishop's accomplice. The same guy may have killed both of them."

"But you don't know who that is."

"Not a clue. Anything new at your end?"

"You know I can't discuss an active case with you."

"So much for quid pro quo."

Crowe closed his phone. His father raised an eyebrow. Crowe had just finished explaining when his phone pinged to announce a new email. He was expecting Levinson to acknowledge receipt of the WAV file that Michael Greer had sent him too. Instead, it was an email from *jimmy@siamescorts.com*.

Glad to hear you got home safe. Fern told me about Kitti and the piglet gang. Thank you.

I recognized Mr. Roger in the photo. And another guy who came just once to Chiang Rai with Dean Bishop and Mr. Roger. Good luck.

Crowe opened the attachment, the photo of the 14th Tactical Recon Squadron he'd found in Greer's jazz album. Jimmy had circled two men in red ink and added a caption below the photo.

Standing next to Bishop – Mr. Roger. Sitting – Yellowtail.

Crowe studied the man next to Bishop. He was a big guy, a few inches taller than Bishop, with a thick neck and broad shoulders. Like a football player, Jimmy'd said. Unlike most of the others in T-shirts, Mr. Roger wore a khaki shirt with sleeves rolled above the elbow. On his left sleeve was a black armband with white letters, of which only an "M" was visible.

He showed the photo to his father, who'd done his Navy tour of duty in Okinawa, safely distant from Vietnam. "What's that arm band?"

"Military Police."

Crowe expanded the picture and studied Mr. Roger's face. Despite the passage of thirty-eight years, some things hadn't changed. The eyes, the mouth, the set of the jaw.

He switched his attention to the man seated in the bottom row. The face Jimmy had circled was the same one Crowe had noticed when he first saw the photo at Greer's place. The protruding ears stuck out like a pair of bat's wings. Crowe puzzled over the caption. *Yellowtail*. What did it mean?

"Mind if I use your computer?"

"Go ahead. I'll clean up."

Crowe sat at the computer in his father's study. He opened the attachment from Kertang and printed a color version of the photo.

He googled "Vermont State Police", whose site informed him that the state was served by twelve barracks. The St. Johnsbury unit had jurisdiction over Caledonia and Essex counties, including the town of Barnet. There was a picture of local commander Lieutenant Roger Lynch.

Crowe compared it to the photo of the 14th Tactical Recon Squadron. Mr. Roger was Lieutenant Lynch.

He googled "yellowtail" and got hits for Australian wine and sushi. He added "Thailand" and "Vietnam" but got only spearfishing and seafood products. He gave up. Maybe it was some kind of nickname.

Crowe returned to the kitchen, where his father was cleaning up. "Dad, I've got to take off."

"What? It's almost nine. I thought you were staying tonight."

"I don't have time to explain." He could have taken the time, but he feared it wouldn't make sense. His father would think he was crazy, that he should call the police and let them handle whatever he thought he might accomplish on his own.

Crowe said a hasty goodbye, tossed his bag into his car, and hit the road. It was raining a torrent by the time he got onto the I-89.

He tried phoning Det. Sullivan again but his call went straight to voice-mail. He left a message that he now had a solid clue regarding Bishop's probable killer. But he didn't want to name a cop as his suspect, at least not until he could explain the circumstances.

He called Levinson and told him what was happening. Levinson was incredulous, but not in a nice way.

"Are you out of your fucking mind? If you're wrong, you could wind up in jail with your friend. If you're right, you could end up dead."

"How about some official back-up?"

"Who'll request the warrant? I don't have any jurisdiction in that case."

"I've already called Sullivan. His phone's turned off."

"Listen, you're way out of your league. Take a motel for the night, cool down and drive up there in the morning. Talk to your friend's lawyer, give him the voice-mail recording, and let due process take over. This cowboy bullshit will just get you in trouble."

"I'll take that under advisement."

Crowe drove on. It was still raining heavily. He stopped for gas in Lebanon, New Hampshire, and soon after switched from I-89 to I-91. Two hours down, another hour to Barnet.

It was eleven o'clock local, nine in Albuquerque. He called Special Agent Cobb again. He knew the FBI had a reputation for clean living, but hoped Cobb hadn't gone to bed already.

"Mr. Crowe." Cobb's tone was a few degrees north of irritated. "What do you want on a Sunday night?"

Crowe explained. Bishop and Lynch had smuggled heroin during the Vietnam War. Greer's research had uncovered Bishop's involvement in sex trafficking. When the journalist confronted Bishop, seeking a confession or a bribe, Bishop had enlisted Lynch to kill Greer.

Lynch had used his position as a state trooper to frame Abbott for the murder. When Crowe followed Kitti to Thailand, Lynch had asked the Piglet Gang to kill them both. Having failed in part, and now fearing discovery, Lynch tied up loose ends by killing Bishop.

"These are serious allegations," Cobb said. "Both men served our country. As a CIA agent, Bishop had certain security privileges. Lynch is a state law enforcement officer. In the absence of compelling evidence, their lawyers will mop the floor with your speculations."

"Does that mean the FBI can't help?"

"Nearest field office is Albany, a three- or four-hour drive from Barnet. No one's going to mobilize at midnight on the basis of what you've just told me."

"A helicopter could be there in less than an hour."

"Could, but won't."

"Give me their number."

"There'll be no one there this time of night except a duty officer."

"Maybe he'll be more receptive than you."

"Don't count on it." Cobb gave him the number anyway.

Crowe didn't call, only because it was raining too hard to fly, but he felt better having the number. By now he was only half an hour from Barnet. He wondered what he'd do when he got there.

67

Barnet, Vermont

IT WAS ALMOST MIDNIGHT when Crowe left the I-91. It had finally stopped raining. He took the Barnet exit and followed a rural road west to Dharmapada. He hoped Abbott's assistant Neville was still in the house, and could let him stay overnight. First thing in the morning he'd visit Abbott's lawyer and play Seth Greer's recorded message.

When he arrived at the property entrance, he saw a chain across the driveway with a brand new "No Trespassing" sign. The ditch beneath the culvert was swollen with water, tonight's heavy rain adding to the spring runoff. He inspected the chain and found no padlock. He unhooked it, drove through, replaced the chain and continued up the driveway.

The floodlight on the pole overlooking the parking lot was extinguished. He cut the engine and the car coasted under a line of trees separating the parking lot from the barn. It was a quarter moon tonight but the cloud cover was so thick it couldn't be seen. The house was in total darkness, although a light came from among the cabins on its far side.

Crowe got out. He heard an engine from the north side of the house. He went around the house to the side door. Parked adjacent the barn, out of sight from the parking lot, was a four-door Chevy Silverado with a Vermont State Police crest. Crowe looked inside and saw keys in the ignition. He removed them and tossed them under the vehicle.

The side door into the house was unlocked. He went through the dining room and climbed the stairs in the dark. He checked the office. It looked the same as when he'd seen it last. Down the hall, both bedroom doors were open, beds unoccupied. He went to the bathroom at the end of the hall and looked out at the guest cabins.

At the north end of the cabins, he saw a tractor whose front-end loader was illuminated by two headlights. It was trying to lift one corner of a cabin off its supports. Whatever was going on here, the midnight activity spelled covert.

Crowe left the house and walked through the wet grass, dodging from one cabin to another. He didn't worry about anyone hearing his approach. The tractor's engine was so loud it would mask anything short of a scream or a gunshot.

He hunkered down behind a neighboring cabin. The window on his side was shattered, the deck of the small porch splintered. He looked around him, seeing gouged sod and overturned construction blocks that had lain under each corner. The cabin had been shifted from its original foundation.

Crowe watched the tractor maneuver around the next cabin. The operator jammed its front-end scoop under a corner, raised it two feet and swung it ten feet north, pivoting the cabin on its opposite corner. Glass shattered as a window popped; wood creaked and splintered under the stress. The operator let the cabin down with a thud and maneuvered to raise another corner and swing it further north. Judging by the remaining construction blocks, the cabin was now shifted completely off its original footprint.

The operator cut the engine and climbed down, leaving the tractor headlights on to illuminate a patch of torn sod. Skirting the pool of light, he picked something up from the ground. When he walked back into the light again, Crowe saw a big man in a rain jacket carrying something - a metal arm with a large disk at one end.

Crowe recalled the shipping invoice he'd discovered in the office of Patpong Pictures, and an operating manual for a metal detector, the Bounty Hunter TK4.

The big man switched on the control unit and began sweeping the metal detector back and forth over the ground where the cabin had stood. The unit gave off a steady growl of static, then suddenly emitted an electronic squeal. The man swung the detector in a few short arcs along east-west and north-south axes, getting a fix on whatever was buried in the ground. He turned the detector off and laid it down to mark the spot where he'd received the strongest signal.

He went to the rear of the tractor and in a moment came back into the light with a round-mouthed shovel. He began to dig with slow and purposeful thrusts, almost as if he were respectful of the earth itself, not wanting to assault it too aggressively.

Crowe watched. The man had his back to him. Between that and the lighting, Crowe still hadn't got a good look at his face. The man continued digging and after ten minutes had removed two bushels of topsoil from the deepening hole. He continued another five minutes, now standing with one foot in the hole, before he took a break. Crowe could hear him panting.

The man walked over to where he'd moved the metal detector aside, peeled off his rain jacket and laid it on the ground. Crowe saw a pistol on his hip. The man stooped to pick something up from the ground. He pulled the tab off a can and raised it to his mouth. He gurgled, sighed and belched. He drained the can and tossed it into the grass.

As he turned back toward the hole, the tractor's headlights illuminated his face. It was Lieutenant Roger Lynch, Vermont State Police.

68

CROWE DEBATED HIS OPTIONS. He could slip away before he was noticed and call the police. But who'd respond to his 911 call - the Vermont State Police? And if he left, he might miss seeing whatever came out of that hole. So he had to stay.

But once Lynch had unearthed the cache, then what? Take pictures? Confront Lynch and record his admission of guilt? Or die trying?

Lynch had a gun. He'd used a shovel on Greer, and Tasered Bishop to death. He wouldn't hesitate to put a bullet through Crowe's head. Talk about a no-brainer. The grave was already dug. He'd only need to cover Crowe's body and push the cabin back into place.

Crowe looked around. Last time he'd been here, he'd seen brooms on some cabin verandahs. He found one in the grass nearby where it had fallen when the cabin was shifted. He hefted it, a traditional model with a thick wooden shaft and a weathered head of corn-stalk bristles.

Crowe's training with Guruji hadn't been just intellectual - astrology, palmistry, numerology and omens - but martial arts as well. In ancient India, there'd been a caste of astrologers called *Ganaka* who'd practiced both esoteric and martial arts. Guruji had been trained under a tradition called *kalaripayattu* - fighting school - and he'd passed it on to Crowe.

In the beginning Crowe had learned to dance - a repertoire of twirling, weaving, ducking and leaping. Then came long stick fighting, using broom handles just like this one. He remembered limping home after practice sessions with Guruji, nursing huge bruises as badges of his perseverance. Later came shorter sticks, using children's baseball bats, their shafts wrapped in electrical tape to blunt the blows. Still shorter weapons were made with hockey sticks trimmed to eighteen inches, most of it handle, but with a tapered heel at the business end.

Finally, it all came down to hands and feet. Guruji had

taught Crowe a range of holds, chokes, kicks and strikes, some with closed fist, others with open hands. *Varma ati* was the science of striking with weapons, feet or fists. *Marma ati,* utilizing only the fingers or one protruding knuckle, attacked the body's vital nerve points. These advanced techniques completed his training, but only after he'd learned from painful experience how much the basics could hurt.

Crowe assumed the proper grip on his broom and steadied himself with a few deep breaths.

Lynch had stopped shoveling and was now crouched in the hole, removing soil with his bare hands. In a moment he dragged from the hole something wrapped in a black garbage bag. He sat on the rim of the hole and opened it. Inside was an orange garbage bag. He peeled it away to reveal some documents in a zip-lock bag, and a bulky item covered in bubble wrap and electrical tape.

Lynch tore at the bubble wrap. The head of a gold Buddha emerged. As it caught the beam of the tractor's headlights, something like a golden flame appeared on the Buddha's crown.

Crowe sprang from his hiding place. In half a dozen quick strides, he was at Lynch's side and drove the tip of the broom into the *marma* point of his shoulder.

With the light in his eyes, the cop hadn't even seen Crowe coming out of the darkness. He screamed and clutched his left hand to his right shoulder, where the attacked nerve bundle had sent two shock waves - one of paralysis down his arm, the other of pain to his brain. The Buddha tumbled back into the hole.

Crowe snatched at the pistol on Lynch's hip. The holster strap came loose and he pulled the gun free. He didn't bother to determine whether it had a manual safety or how to disengage it. Simpler to just get rid of it. He threw it as far as he could into the darkness behind the tractor.

"Is that why you tortured Bishop?" Crowe said. "To learn where he'd hidden the Buddha? You helped him smuggle it into the country two decades ago, didn't you? You were partners in crime."

Lynch was startled by the specifics of the accusation. He raised his left hand to shield his eyes from the headlights' glare. From where he sat, he still couldn't distinguish Crowe's face. "Who are you?"

"The ghost of Seth Greer."

"This is private property. I could arrest you."

"Go ahead and try."

"This isn't your place, friend. You're interfering with police business."

"It's after midnight. You're in civilian clothes. What's the business?"

Lynch clambered from the hole and moved off to one side, out of the headlights' glare. He shook his right arm, getting some feeling back into it. "You're Abbott's friend, aren't you? I've got your name, Crowe. As soon as I return to my office, I'll have a dozen state troopers on you faster than a pack of dogs on a sick coon."

"You're not going anywhere. I already took the keys to your truck." Crowe went to the tractor and pulled its keys from the ignition, although the headlights stayed on. He hurled the keys off into the darkness. "Now your tractor's useless too."

Lynch retreated to the hole and picked up the round-mouthed shovel. He looked at the Buddha a moment as if debating what to do with it. Then he swung wide of the headlights' glare and came back toward Crowe, the shovel held in a two-fisted grip, its blade cocked over his shoulder.

Crowe readied himself for an attack torn from a page of the *kalaripayattu* textbook. Brute frontal assault with a heavy weapon.

Lynch rushed in, the cocked shovel telegraphing its only possible trajectory, thinking its weight and cutting edge would slash through whatever resistance it met - Crowe's broom, arm or head.

Crowe clearly saw the incoming shovel while Lynch, half-blinded by the headlights, could see only Crowe's outline.

Instead of trying to block or step back from it, Crowe dove inside the weapon's arc. He slammed a shoulder into Lynch's midriff and heard a pained expulsion of breath as Lynch doubled over. Crowe thrust the broom handle between Lynch's knees, pivoted in place and toppled him face-first onto the ground.

Crowe raised the broom and jabbed Lynch once in each shoulder blade. Lynch bellowed with pain. He tried to rise but couldn't lift himself with his arms. He rolled over, sat up and stood shakily. When he stooped to retrieve his shovel, he seemed to have lost his grip, and the tool slipped from his hands.

Lynch faced off against Crowe and made another lunge for him. Crowe danced aside and whacked Lynch's arms with the broom handle. Lynch yelped again and, grateful his legs still worked, ran away from Crowe and his broomstick. He retreated twenty yards, shaking his arms to get some sensation back into them.

"What do you want?" Lynch said.

"Surrender and confession."

"Fuck you."

"I've got all night."

Lynch stood looking at Crowe, chest heaving, head lowered as if ready for another charge. But having seen what Crowe could do with a broomstick, he was uncertain of what to do.

"You may have duped the District Attorney's office last week," Crowe said, "but tomorrow your involvement in this case will come under very close scrutiny."

"You don't know anything."

"Bishop asked you to silence Greer because he knew too much about him. You came here and borrowed a shovel from the tool shed. You killed Greer, broke into his car and stole his laptop. Later you added the research notes Bishop emailed from Greer's home computer, the story about money-laundering spiritual institutions. After Abbott's arrest you planted Greer's laptop in the house, and brought your officers back to conduct a search. You probably let Quaid find the laptop. The research notes appeared to have given Abbott a motive to kill Greer."

Lynch picked up the shovel with awkward hands. But rather than shoulder it again for a second assault, he used it as a walking stick. He came toward Crowe, pausing to glance at the hole where he'd dropped the Buddha.

"It's worth millions. We could share the money."

"Is that what Bishop told *you*? How'd that work out for him?"

"Bishop was a fool. He let too many people into our business."

"Kitti Poornchai?"

Lynch shook his head. "You've got your story, I've got mine. I got an anonymous tip regarding the Buddha and came out here looking for it. But you showed up and attacked me when I found it. You fabricated this elaborate plot in an attempt to get Abbott off the hook."

"So we each have a story. We'll see who the DA believes."

69

LYNCH WENT TO WHERE he'd set aside his jacket and metal detector. He retrieved a backpack and shoved the bubble-wrapped Buddha into it. He picked up the zip-locked documents and put them into the pack too.

"Are those the authentication documents?" Crowe said. "Thanks to Thi Nguyen, that stolen Buddha now has a false legitimacy. Bishop romanced her to make sure she'd set aside any doubts regarding its provenance. But she was a liability. A change of heart and she could have robbed you two of millions. You couldn't let that happen, so someone had to kill her."

Lynch looked at him but said nothing.

"Bishop was out of the country when Nguyen was murdered," Crowe continued. "You went to New York and killed her yourself, didn't you? Because of their relationship - knowing how much she'd loved him - he thought she'd never betray him. He didn't see the need to murder her. But you convinced him otherwise, didn't you?"

Lynch shook his head.

"But he balked when it came to killing Kitti. You wanted her dead because she knew you killed Greer. But Bishop cared for her, didn't he? More than he had for Thi Nguyen. Is that why you fought? He found out you'd arranged for the Piglet Gang to track her down in Bangkok and kill her."

"He fell in love with that bitch. It messed up his head."

"You know what your problem is? Arrogance."

"Fuck you." Lynch shouldered the backpack and cinched a buckle across his chest that held the two shoulder straps together.

Crowe recalled what Roxanne Morton had said about the Buddha. Almost twenty-four pounds of gold. Not a great weight for a big man like Lynch, but it would slow him down.

"Where do you think you're going?"

"I'm out of here." Lynch picked up the shovel. His arms seemed to be working again, and Crowe knew he'd attempt a second attack.

"Who's Yellowtail?"

Lynch cocked his head, not connecting the dots.

"The guy in the photo, with you and Bishop and the rest of the 14th Tactical Recon Squadron in Thailand."

"Where'd you see that?"

"At Greer's place. Somebody missed it when they ransacked his condo. Was that Bishop or one of his people?"

Lynch said nothing.

"Who burgled *The Voice*? And hacked their network? Friends of Bishop from back in the day when he was a spook?"

Lynch shrugged.

"Who's Thomas Vandenberg?"

"Never heard of him."

Lynch took a few steps forward, shifting his grip on the shovel. The numbness in his hands and arms seemed to have gone. Crowe figured the only reason Lynch was indulging in this dialogue was to wait for the right moment to attack.

"Who's Yellowtail?" Crowe repeated.

"Just some guy we knew in the service over there."

"Why the nickname?"

"Every fighter had a strip painted on its tail to identify its squadron. The 14th was the yellowtail squadron."

"But anyone in the unit could have had that nickname."

"This one was personal. Yellowtail referred to his fondness for gook pussy."

"Bill Kinkelman told me he'd contracted VD from some bar girl over there."

Lynch shook his head. "My god, you're a nosey motherfucker. Where'd you come across Bill?"

"Did he get into any other trouble over there?"

"Matter of fact, he killed a girl."

"The one who gave him VD?"

"That was another girl but, now you mention it, he had a grudge against them all. He'd got plastered one night, got into some rough sex with a whore and strangled her to death. Bishop got him out of there before the local police were called. As an MP, I investigated on behalf of the base, found evidence to blame it on some sorry gook bastard."

"And after that, you blackmailed Kinkelman?"

"What? No, I never liked the guy, and I never saw him again. I think he and Bishop stayed in touch, went moose-hunting every fall. Is that how you found out about him?"

Crowe took out his phone. "I'm phoning the FBI field office in Albany. They'll take you into custody and take your statement."

This time Lynch didn't telegraph his intentions by raising the shovel. He rushed Crowe, swinging the shovel low in an attempt to cut him off at the knees. Crowe's practice of *kalaripayattu* rewarded him with an immediate response. Jumping had seemed silly back then, but after getting smacked in the shins so many times with Guruji's broom handle, he'd learned to jump like a kangaroo on speed.

Crowe leaped high, pulling his heels up. The shovel blade whistled beneath him. Lynch dropped his shovel and lunged for him. Crowe raised his broom and jabbed its bristles in Lynch's eyes.

Lynch screamed and pulled a bloody bristle from one eye. He threw a right hook. Crowe stepped back from it and, reversing the broom, jabbed Lynch again with its tip, striking the *marma* point above his heart. Lynch staggered back with a gasp. As soon as he caught his breath, he turned and ran off into the field.

Crowe retrieved his fallen phone and called the FBI in Albany. He identified himself and told the duty officer he wanted to make a citizen's arrest. He named Lieutenant Roger Lynch as a suspect in two murders, saying NYPD detectives Levinson and Sullivan were familiar with the cases. He gave his location and requested assistance apprehending the fugitive. The duty officer said he'd pass it up the chain of command.

Crowe thrust the phone in his pocket and, broom in hand, went after his half-blinded quarry.

Lynch ran doggedly through the tall wet grass of the open field. He was doing well, considering the weight of the Buddha and the injuries Crowe had inflicted on him. He reached the dirt road used for walking meditation, and headed for the woods at the end of the property.

Without the handicap of burden or injury, Crowe caught up to Lynch, and trailed him from twenty yards back. He wondered where Lynch was headed. West Barnet Road was a quarter mile to the south, but dense woods lay between. Furthermore, the stream that Crowe had crossed on the way in was heavily swollen with spring runoff. Maybe Lynch thought that if he could cross it, Crowe couldn't follow.

Lynch disappeared into the trees. Crowe approached the tree line cautiously. Although Lynch had left the shovel behind, he might have something else he could use as a weapon. But as Crowe entered the woods, he heard Lynch ahead of him, stumbling through the underbrush. Without any moonlight, it was impossible to see more than a dozen feet ahead, but Crowe followed the sound. It struck him as ironic they'd been reduced to the state of animals.

The ground sloped beneath him. Evergreens on higher ground gave way to a thicket of alders bordering the stream. Crowe used the broom to protect his face from branches. Lynch was only a few yards ahead, breathing hard and cursing as he thrashed his way through the alders. Crowe heard the rush of water nearby.

Lynch plunged off the bank and began wading across the stream. Crowe arrived on the bank. The stream was only twenty feet wide but the water was rushing by at a furious rate. Lynch was now up to his waist but less than halfway across, leaning against the flow to stay upright.

"You can't do it," Crowe called after him. "The current's too strong."

Lynch took another step, staggered and almost went under. Crowe stepped into the water, one hand grasping an alder branch, the other hand extending the broom handle to Lynch.

"Come back."

Lynch grabbed the broom handle and jerked. Maybe he'd wanted to pull himself out, or maybe he'd wanted to pull Crowe in. Whatever his intention, he pulled so sharply that he yanked the broom out of Crowe's hands. Lynch lost his balance and took a step to right himself, a step that took him into chest-high water. The current knocked him down and he went under without a sound.

There was nothing Crowe could do. The current was so strong he couldn't risk going in after him. And the light was so poor he never saw whether Lynch surfaced again.

70

Monday, April 30

THE FBI ARRIVED SHORTLY AFTER SUNRISE. There were four agents - three men and Special-Agent-in-Charge Karen Willis. Crowe replayed the recording - the last minute of Seth Greer's life - that had been left on Michael Greer's voice-mail. Crowe told them everything he knew about Roger Lynch and Dean Bishop.

Most of it he'd figured out for himself, but some of it had been patched together by Captain Mack Loomis, whom he'd phoned after midnight. Loomis was Military Police, Kirtland Air Force Base in Albuquerque, and Crowe had met him last year while investigating the murder of Blaikie's sister. Loomis had been working graveyard shift this week, and was able to answer Crowe's late-night query. As an MP, he could access Air Force personnel files and thus track Lynch's career.

"During the Vietnam War, Lynch used his Military Police status to clear state-bound cargo," Crowe told the FBI team. "After the war, he secured a post at Langley Air Force Base inspecting inbound cargo, probably using his authority to clear shipments in which heroin was smuggled. That lasted until the mid-eighties, when competition in Thailand cut off the supply. In the mid-nineties, state-side DEA investigators started paying more attention to military bases. Probably fearing exposure by the DEA, Lynch retired and took a job with the Vermont State Police.

"In the early nineties, while still with the CIA, Bishop stole a gold Buddha from a Thai temple. This was just before Lynch retired, so getting it into the US might have been the last job he did for his partner. Bishop kept it under wraps for fifteen years until the National Stolen Property Act forced his hand. When the US Attorney's Office started investigating the provenance of antiquities, Bishop realized he'd never sell the Buddha without documentation.

"He posed as a broker for a private collector, provided forged ownership documents, and requested a certificate of authenticity. Once he had it, he dumped the curator he'd romanced for nine months, and disappeared.

"Fearing discovery and a property search, he brought the Buddha here and buried it under a cabin. It seems crazy, but maybe it felt right to him, hiding it on an ashram. In the meantime, he assumed Nguyen would never expose its dubious provenance since it would reflect badly on her. But Lynch wasn't so sure.

"Since Lynch had an interest in the Buddha too, he needed to protect himself. An investigation of Bishop could have implicated both of them in heroin smuggling. So they conspired. Bishop went to Bangkok for a week. Lynch went to New York and killed Nguyen to seal the deal."

Crowe led SAIC Willis and her men outside. They walked through the sprawl of cabins to the tractor. He showed them the metal detector, and pointed out the swath of field into which he'd thrown Lynch's pistol.

"When Bishop returned a year later, he found the original eighteen cabins rearranged in a different pattern and another nine added. He couldn't figure out where the Buddha was buried. So he bought a metal detector and started coming to every retreat, looking for it.

"This last time, he was confronted by Seth Greer, who'd built a file on him. When Bishop assaulted Greer, Abbott booted him off the retreat. Before leaving, Bishop wrote a note promising information in exchange for anonymity. Kitti slipped it under Greer's door. When Greer showed up for the midnight rendezvous, Lynch killed him.

"Back in New York that night, Bishop broke into Greer's condo. When he didn't find what he wanted, the next night some other guys, probably former spooks, broke into *The Village Voice* and stole Greer's office files. Thomas Vandenberg, whose connection with Bishop is unknown, hacked into *The Voice's* network and purged all of Greer's digital files."

Crowe led the agents out the dirt road where he'd

pursued Lynch last night. They followed a trail through the trees down to a swollen stream, its surface littered with clumps of leaves and branches.

"To protect her, Bishop sent Kitti back to Thailand. When I showed up asking questions, he probably told Lynch. Thinking Bishop had lost his objectivity, Lynch contacted their old Bangkok associates to find Kitti and kill her. When Bishop learned about it, he confronted Lynch and they fought. Lynch tortured Bishop to reveal the Buddha's location. He used Bishop's metal detector to find it, but I interrupted him. This is where he went into the water."

As they looked at the torrent of muddy water, impossible for anyone to cross, a dead raccoon swept past. One of the agents said, "Is that an omen or what?"

A phone rang. Agent Willis answered it, heard what the caller had to say and assured them she'd be there in half an hour.

"That was Sergeant Quaid in St. Johnsbury. Somebody discovered Lynch trapped in a mass of debris beneath the bridge in Barnet. They've taken him to the hospital. He's got a concussion and is suffering hypothermia, but he's alive."

"And the Buddha?" Crowe asked.

"No sign of it."

Willis left her people on site to process the scene and search for the backpack Lynch had probably been forced to jettison. Chances were, the Buddha was underwater but the stream was so swollen and murky that divers were pointless until the runoff subsided. The agents were discussing grappling poles and scoop nets when Crowe and Willis left in his car.

They drove to the Northeastern Vermont Regional Hospital in St. Johnsbury. Lynch was in the intensive care unit. SAIC Willis advised Sergeant Quaid that his former superior was a suspect in a double homicide and should be kept under armed guard to prevent his escape or suicide.

"What about my friend?" Crowe said. "Now that you have Lynch in hand, can you arrange for his release?"

"Where's Abbott being held?" Willis asked Quaid.

"County jail pending trial."

"Here's the name and number of Abbott's lawyer." Crowe copied the information onto one of his business cards and gave it to Willis.

"I'll need the name of the judge in charge of the district court," Willis told Quaid. She checked her watch. "In an hour or two, I'll make a few calls, see if the judge will allow his lawyer to make a fresh case for bail."

A doctor came out of Lynch's room. "He's conscious now. You can probably talk to him for a few minutes."

Willis took a digital recorder from her purse. "This'll take more than a few minutes, but I might as well get started."

"If you're done with me," Crowe said, "I'm going to head out."

"Where are you going?"

"Breakfast," Crowe said. "I'm hungry." This was true, but breakfast could actually wait. Ever since Lynch's admissions under duress last night, Crowe's appetite had been whetted - not for food, but truth.

71

Bangor, Maine

CROWE TOOK HIGHWAY US-2 TO MAINE. The sun rose above the White Mountains of New Hampshire. It was spring in the valleys, but the peaks still carried snow. And although the murders of Greer and Bishop could now be laid at Lynch's feet, Crowe hadn't got much warmer with those cold cases.

The Riverside Rapist crime scene photos floated up into his mind's eye - bruises and bites and strangulation marks. It bothered Crowe that he'd done no more than develop a profile of the killer. It was like a melody hook with no chord progression. It looped through his mind without the lyrics to tell a story.

He stopped halfway in Rumford for gas, food and a nature break. Fifteen minutes later he was back on the road, following its twists and turns though the woods. He didn't encounter any moose, and by noon he was in Bangor.

He retrieved Vandenberg's address from the printout Tracey had given him. Veazie was a small town on the Penobscot River, halfway between Bangor and Orono, home to the University of Maine. Stephen King lived around here somewhere, but Crowe didn't have time to look him up. He already had enough horror on his mind.

He followed State Street north along the river to Greystone Trailer Park. Vandenberg's unit was at the north end of the subdivision, a cream-colored trailer with fake green shutters and plastic door awning. An old yellow Ford pickup badly in need of a wash sat parked in front of the trailer.

He speculated whether this vehicle matched the profile he'd developed for the Riverside Rapist, but it was all wrong - color, manufacture and even its condition. In his hands astrology was never 100% correct, but neither was it so completely wrong.

Crowe rapped on the door. A gangly kid with a mass of spiky hair answered. He looked like someone had just given him shock therapy.

"Thomas Vandenberg?"

"Yeah. Who're you?" Vandenberg looked over Crowe's head to his Saab, regarding it with narrowed eyes. He scanned the immediate vicinity, as if expecting an ambush. "If you're with *Bangor Metro* or the *Daily News*, my lawyer's told me not to talk to you guys."

"I'm not a reporter." Crowe handed Vandenberg a business card. "I'm a private investigator."

Vandenberg crushed the card in his fist and threw it on the ground. "Then I've definitely got nothing to say to you."

"Has anyone told you Dean Bishop is dead?"

"What?" Vandenberg stared at him.

"Can I come in?" A raw wind blew off the nearby river, its humid fingers clawing at Crowe's exposed neck. "It's cold out here."

Vandenberg hesitated, then opened the door. Crowe entered a small living area with bench seating and a built-in table on which a laptop sat. On the opposite wall, a TV was tuned to CNN. They sat at the table. Vandenberg closed the laptop.

"I thought the police seized your computer," Crowe said.

"They did. But no one said I couldn't buy another. How'd you know about that?"

Crowe chose not to answer. "I know they're trying to prove you hacked into the network of *The Village Voice*."

"Like I said, my lawyer does all my talking for me."

"Can he protect you from whoever murdered Bishop?"

"Murder?" Vandenberg's throat made a noisy gulp. "What are you talking about?"

"He's already killed two men. Ten days ago, Seth Greer, the journalist whose files you destroyed. Two days ago, Dean Bishop himself. His killer tortured him before he killed him. You think he'll play nice with you?"

"What guy? Why me?" Vandenberg was shedding attitude by the minute. His original bluster verged on tipping over into a whine.

"You know too much. You're a loose end that needs to be tied down. Permanently." Although Lynch was now in custody and in no position to harm anyone, Vandenberg didn't need to know that.

"Fucking shit, man, I don't know anything."

"I'm sure he'll take your word for it. But you wouldn't believe what he did to Bishop. I wish I hadn't been the one to find the body." Crowe rubbed his face, as if trying to erase the memory. "Do you have a neighbor to check in now and again, make sure you're all right?"

"Knock it off. Why're you messing with me?"

"How well did you know Bishop?"

Vandenberg said nothing, but the way his jaw locked and

his eyes started looking for a place to hide, Crowe knew he was boxed in a corner from which there was no escape.

"I don't know him at all."

"Don't lie to me, Tommy. If you don't cooperate, I'm going to make life very difficult - not only for you, but for someone close to you."

Vandenberg couldn't resist asking, "Who's that?"

Crowe took out the group photo of the 14th Tactical Recon Squadron. He tapped one of the circled faces in the photo.

"This was almost forty years ago, but maybe you recognize Bishop?"

Vandenberg stared at the photo.

Crowe indicated the adjacent face. "This guy next to him? Roger Lynch, his killer. They used to be friends and partners. Ironic, but that's life, right?" Crowe recited a lyric from Frank Sinatra. "*Riding high in April, shot down in May.*"

Vandenberg looked at Crowe, the fear in his eyes now palpable. Maybe he was a computer genius, but at the end of the day he was still just a kid. He could play all the video games he wanted, slay legions in *Call of Duty* and *Gears of War*, but any goon with a contract to fill would break his arm off and beat him to death with it.

"What do you want?"

"Look at the third man in this picture, the one in the bottom row. Look familiar to you?"

Vandenberg stared. His Adam's apple turned over again, but no words came from his mouth.

"Looks a lot like you, doesn't he? A remarkable resemblance, I think you'll admit."

"Where'd you get this?"

"From the files of that journalist. It was taken in nineteen seventy-three during the Vietnam War at Udorn Air Force Base, Thailand. That's where Bishop and Lynch met your father."

Vandenberg's face twitched. He couldn't bring himself to look at Crowe, probably because he knew his eyes would inevitably give him away.

"Your dad and Bishop stayed in touch after the war," Crowe said. "Bishop came up to Maine every season to go hunting and fishing with your dad. Maybe you met him on one of those trips? If not, maybe you met him when your dad took you to New York. Between the two of them, they led you astray - in more ways than one - didn't they?"

72

VANDENBERG WAS RELUCTANT TO TALK, but in the end, Crowe teased enough out of him to understand the tenuous connections he'd intuited. He now believed Tommy was William Kinkelman's illegitimate son.

Tommy never knew his real father, and had been raised by his mother in a run-down sector of Bangor. When he was seven, his mother introduced him to "Uncle Bill" who lived in Bar Harbor. Uncle Bill visited occasionally, but always came alone because his wife Marta wasn't well. Tommy never met her or visited the house where Uncle Bill lived.

With his mother's encouragement, Tommy started going on regular outings with Uncle Bill - movies, bowling, games arcades. As he got older, they went fishing, whale-watching, and took day trips to Portland. Uncle Bill introduced Tommy to his extensive collection of techno-gadgets - sonar devices, high-powered binoculars, recording devices, spy cameras.

Uncle Bill gave Tommy his first camera when he was eight, a computer when he was ten. Tommy quickly mastered Office applications, simulation games, HTML code, and began earning money as a computer geek and troubleshooter for individuals and small businesses in Bangor.

Meanwhile, Uncle Bill's jaunts took them on a widening spiral of distance, adventure and risk. They went on weekend trips, camping in state parks, stalking birds and animals with cameras. At Old Orchard Beach, they stayed in a seaside motel, using telephotos lenses to shoot girls in bikinis.

When he was fourteen, Uncle Bill taught Tommy how to handle guns - shotguns, rifles and pistols - shooting beer cans in local gravel pits or targets at gun ranges.

Tommy had a genius for science, technology and computers. He excelled in school and skipped a grade. Uncle Bill paid his tuition to enter a Computer Sciences program at the University of Maine. He bought him a second-hand pickup and rented an apartment for him. Tommy never questioned why. Uncle Bill had no kids, but a heart as big as all outdoors.

Over the years Tommy had noticed their physical resemblance, their shared fascination for technology, their aptitude for science. They were both brooding introverts, mystified and mesmerized by the opposite sex.

At eighteen, Tommy started hacking. Just pranks at first, changing names or prices of articles on retail websites. He cracked a school board network to mess up the grades of some guys who'd bullied him. He hacked a local newspaper to insert an obscenity into a story published the next day. He was stealthy and never got caught.

That summer Uncle Bill took him to New York for a long weekend. They had lunch one day with Uncle Bill's friend, Dean Bishop. Uncle Bill boasted of Tommy's hacking skills. Bishop made some remark, how it was probably amateur-level stuff, and Tommy had blurted out exactly what he'd done. Bishop was intrigued and asked Tommy if he'd try his hand at something serious.

At first there were a few off-shore sites - manufacturing facilities in Indonesia, Malaysia and Taiwan - where he scooped data on production costs. Later came domestic sites of American companies, their off-shore facilities in particular. Bishop paid well and Tommy was able to buy a trailer unit.

Vandenberg refused to admit exactly what he'd done to warrant a police investigation, but it didn't take much imagination for Crowe to speculate. Ten days ago Bishop had called him with a rush job - to hack into *The Village Voice* network and destroy all of Seth Greer's files, plus every other document with his name on it.

Crowe debated telling Tommy about the home-made videos he'd found in the apartment above Patpong Pictures. He knew that Kinkelman had been charged with solicitation in Bangor. Given his photo-stalking adventures with Tommy, it wasn't a stretch to imagine they'd graduated to a shared brothel experience. Obviously Uncle Bill had recorded some of those adventures, showing Tommy in action with various young women. But for whose enjoyment?

Crowe decided to spare Tommy the agony of knowing he'd been betrayed by his own father. The kid had enough grief already, and Crowe didn't need to add to it. The NYPD's computer crimes squad had the forensic expertise to nail Vandenberg for hacking into *The Voice*'s network, and justice would run its course.

Crowe drove back into Bangor at two o'clock. He withdrew a wad of cash from a bank and browsed the web to find two strip joints and three massage parlors with suggestive names. He visited them all in the next few hours, struck up conversations with club managers and quizzed massage parlor madams. He showed his ID and put money on the table to grease the exchange of information.

His cover story was, he was working a civil case of identity theft, nothing to do with facilitating prostitution. He showed Vandenberg's mug shot from when Maine State Police had arrested him on the NYPD warrant. If they cooperated, he assured them, he'd keep their names out of it, and they wouldn't be called to testify.

Both strip club managers recognized Vandenberg. Crowe didn't have a current picture of Kinkelman but their description of Vandenberg's older pal matched. The most damning testimony came from a woman who ran a massage parlor called Asian Loving Touch. The establishment's specialty was *shiatsu* and Thai massage, and her clientele were mostly stressed businessmen, the occasional sports injury. Her staff were all Asian, a demographic novelty in this neck of the woods.

"Did they always come together?"

She laughed at the *double-entendre*. "They were a tag-team. The older guy would buy half-hour sessions for them both. Then they'd leave, come back a few hours later, reeking of beer, and take another two sessions, usually switching therapists. Like they were comparing notes."

"Your girls ever complain of rough stuff?"

"There were a few incidents. One girl was scared pretty bad. Wanted to quit on the spot."

"What happened?"

"The old guy started choking her. Lucky she knew more than Asian massage techniques. She karate-chopped him in the windpipe and ran down the hall."

"Anyone press charges?"

"Who needs the attention?" The woman shrugged, as if it was a regular hazard of the business. "Anyway, he was all apologetic, said he was drunk and got carried away. Gave me his credit card to ding him five hundred right then and there to make up for hurt feelings."

"How about the younger guy?"

"Very shy. The girls said he was a pussycat compared to his dad."

"You knew they were related?"

"I just assumed. They looked so much alike. Not the first time I've seen a father-and-son act."

"Really?"

"Rite of passage, isn't it? In some cultures, that's the way it's done."

Crowe returned to his car thinking about rites of passage. If the massage parlor had been just a way-station on the road, what had been the destination?

73

Mount Desert Island, Maine

IT WAS ALMOST SEVEN PM by the time Crowe arrived at Mount Desert Island. As he crossed the Trenton Bridge, he saw a few trawlers out in Western Bay, homeward bound in the last half hour of daylight. Their fishing day was finished, his not quite...

His phone rang. It was Levinson. He'd secured a subpoena first thing in the morning, requesting visitation records for the VA's Manhattan facility dating back to year 2000. The VA had sent the NYPD the electronic files mid-afternoon. One of Levinson's people went through it all, looking for any repetition of veterans within a week of the Riverside Rapist murders. It was inconclusive. There were over a dozen names on the short list. He read them off to Crowe, who recognized only one.

"William Kinkelman." Crowe told Levinson what he'd learned in the last eighteen hours. "Can you issue a warrant for his arrest?"

"Merely on suspicion he might be the Riverside Rapist? Based on an unsubstantiated story that he killed a bar-girl in Thailand during the Vietnam War? That he might have got carried away with some masseuse in Bangor several years ago?"

"It speaks to character. According to his police record, he was charged with solicitation. And the schedule of his New York visits is proof of opportunity. It confirms we're on the right track. If it smells like a skunk, it probably is. Let's follow where it leads."

Crowe didn't reveal that his hunch was largely based on the *prashna* chart he'd created during his stopover in New Delhi a few days ago. But he'd been trained by Guruji to follow his intuition. According to the chart, the Riverside Rapist was a married man from Maine and drove a dark blue second-hand vehicle. Formerly police or military, he had some physical debility and a severe psychological disorder.

Levinson finally agreed to write it up and request a warrant for Kinkelman's arrest on suspicion of rape and murder, citing his documented VA visits as proof of opportunity for seven of the eight victims. Even though Nguyen had been killed within a day of Kinkelman's sixth victim, Crowe now knew that Lynch had been responsible for the curator's death.

They signed off without Crowe having said exactly where he was. He continued up Tremont Road, took the turnoff at Dix Point and parked his car opposite the cluster of mailboxes at the entrance. Before showing up at Kinkelman's house, he wanted to arm himself with as much information as available. He called SAIC Willis and she picked up after a few rings.

"How's it going with Lynch?" he asked after identifying himself.

"No confession yet," she said, "but it's just a matter of time. He hasn't asked for a lawyer, and we've been accumulating evidence. After questioning him, I sent my recording to our guys in Quantico. They matched his voice to the killer's on Seth Greer's voicemail message to his brother."

"Nice work."

"It gets better. I spoke with Sullivan at the First Precinct, gave him tags for both Lynch's police vehicle and his personal car. Toll booth records from the Henry Hudson Bridge have him entering and leaving Manhattan six hours on either side of Bishop's death. And security cameras at Bishop's condo caught a guy matching Lynch's description in the underground garage that same day. It's just a question of time before he breaks under the weight of evidence."

Crowe closed the phone and drove to the end of Dix Point Road. He remembered the surveillance camera at the lane entrance, and saluted it with his free hand as he drove past. He parked in the yard. Dusk was imminent but the lights were still off in Kinkelman's house. The garage door was open, the Dodge Ram parked inside. Crowe took note - a vehicle named after a four-legged creature. Staying in his car for a few minutes, he rolled down the window. The smell of spring was in the air, the scent of loamy earth on the sea breeze coming up from Goose Cove.

He looked at the other camera mounted beneath the eaves of the house. If Kinkelman was home, he'd know he had a visitor. Crowe felt a dampness creep down his spine. Maybe he'd been crazy to come here alone. He probably should have enlisted the Bar Harbor Police. They knew Kinkelman's reputation. Willy the Kink, the bartender at the Lompoc Café had called him. Some of the local police might have agreed it was plausible he'd taken his sexual obsessions on a road trip - to Bangor, Portland, Boston, New York... But without a warrant in hand, would they have been willing to do anything?

Crowe looked at his watch. It was almost seven-thirty, and dusk was falling. The house was still dark. He got out of the car and stood there a moment. From any of the windows he'd make an easy target for a man with a rifle. But as vulnerable as he was, he didn't get the feeling he was standing in anyone's sights. The house had an unoccupied feel to it. Yet if Kinkelman wasn't here, where had he gone?

Crowe mounted the deck that bordered the east and south sides of the house. He rapped on the door. No answer. There was no doorbell. He looked through the window but saw nothing. He walked around to the south side and peered through a living room window. Was that someone sleeping on the sofa? He tapped on the pane. The person didn't budge.

Crowe returned to the door and tried the handle. It wasn't locked. "Hello. May I come in?" he called inside. No answer. He stepped into the foyer between kitchen and living room. Stairs led to the second floor. He called in their direction. "Mr. Kinkelman, are you here?" Silence.

Crowe hesitated to go further. Was he now trespassing? He might tarnish this case. Worse, he might get shot. But what if the occupants were in jeopardy?

He went into the living room. The only source of light was a television whose sound was turned off. Someone lay on the sofa facing the TV. Crowe sensed by the outline of the body beneath a comforter that it was a woman. A pillow lay over her face, another pillow propping up her head. He went closer. Her hands were folded over her stomach and Crowe saw from the small-boned fingers that it was indeed a woman. He lifted the pillow to reveal the stricken face of Marta Kinkelman, her jaw locked in an open-mouthed gasp. It didn't take a pathologist to see she'd been smothered. He felt her throat for a pulse but found none.

Crowe went through the rest of the house, seeing well enough without turning lights on that no one else was here. He stood for a few moments in a second floor office, looking at the array of computer equipment, cameras and telephoto lenses, camcorders and directional mics. A shelving unit held hundreds of DVDs. The room reminded him of the office of Patpong Pictures. He wondered if he'd find similar content within this extensive library of DVDs but, at the moment, he didn't have time to look.

He went back to the living room and called 911. He identified himself to the dispatcher, gave his address and said he'd discovered Marta Kinkelman dead. The dispatcher encouraged him to try mouth-to-mouth resuscitation while the ambulance was en route but he told her that he'd checked for a pulse and Marta was definitely dead. The dispatcher said the police and an ambulance were on their way.

Crowe debated whether to turn the lights on for the cops, but decided against it. From up on the lookout, the house was likely visible, and he didn't want to alert Kinkelman that someone was in the house. He went outside and climbed the trail through the woods to the point on the bluff.

74

FIFTY YARDS FROM THE SUMMIT, Crowe caught a whiff of cigarette smoke. He stepped off the trail and worked his way into the trees. He came up behind Kinkelman on his right side, and crouched a short distance from the big pine under which Kinkelman sat. Crowe could hear the crash of surf at the base of the cliff below.

Kinkelman was sitting in one of his Adirondack chairs, a bottle on the deck at his feet. He raised a cigarette and puffed. The smoke drifted into the trees. Crowe wondered what to do next. Maybe he should have used the house phone to speed-dial Kinkelman, talk him into surrendering to the police. Now it was too awkward for that.

Kinkelman flicked his cigarette butt toward the cliff. Its ember arced like a shooting star against the western sky. The butt hit the ground and skittered over the edge. He raised the bottle, drank heavily and sighed, almost a moan. Crowe smelled whiskey. Kinkelman set the bottle down and picked up a pistol that had been lying on the right arm of his chair.

He ejected the magazine, worked the breech block, put the gun to his head and pulled the trigger. The mechanism clicked on the empty chamber. He slapped the magazine back into the grip and laid the gun on the arm of the chair.

Crowe stood motionless. This was what he'd feared. Armed and desperate, Kinkelman was ready to take his own life. He'd obviously done his wife. But what had pushed him to this?

Crowe looked at his watch. The police would be here in ten minutes. As soon as Kinkelman knew discovery was imminent, he was likely to do something drastic.

Kinkelman lit another cigarette. He took a few drags, picked up the whiskey bottle and took another long swallow. He stood up, taking a few shaky steps toward the sea cliff, but stopped well short of the edge. Even in the face of suicide, the animal in man had an instinct for self-preservation.

Crowe knew this might be his only chance. He came out from hiding, mounted the deck and snatched the pistol from the arm of the chair. Kinkelman didn't even hear him until Crowe worked the breech block to get his attention.

Kinkelman turned around, stunned to see someone standing there. The moon was up in the eastern sky, but its light was insufficient to make out a man's face.

"Who the fuck are you?"

"Axel Crowe. I was here ten days ago. We talked about writing, remember?"

Kinkelman moved across the deck so he could get a closer look at Crowe. "You're not a writer. You're a private eye. You talked to my son. What the fuck are you doing here?"

"Perhaps I'm here to serve you." Crowe recalled a quote from Robert Louis Stevenson, the author of *Treasure Island*. *"In the end, every man sits down to a banquet of consequences."*

"I'm not hungry, just thirsty." Kinkelman raised the bottle and drank again. After a long swallow, his arm swung loose like a pendulum, his hand gripping the neck of the half-empty bottle.

Crowe indicated the chairs. "Why don't you sit down before you fall down?"

"I'd rather die on my feet than live on my knees."

"I'm not going to kill you."

"You already have. You talked to my son. You told him terrible lies about me."

"I didn't tell him anything, except your being friends with Bishop and Lynch. Whatever he said to you, he figured it out on his own. He's a smart kid. You should have known this might go sideways some day."

"I told him it's all a pack of lies."

"You can deny him the truth, but not me. I know where you've been and what you've done."

"You don't know dick."

"Bishop is dead."

"What?"

"Lynch killed him."

"Bullshit."

"Bishop stole a gold Buddha from a temple in Thailand two decades ago. Lynch helped him smuggle it into the country. Bishop probably used one of his old CIA buddies to forge some documentation needed for its legal sale, but he was waiting for the right time in the antiquities market to sell it. Lynch got tired of waiting and tortured Bishop to find where he'd stashed it."

"I don't believe it. They were buddies."

"You and Bishop were buddies. You think he didn't betray you?"

"No way!"

"You hinted about your escapades, or Bishop figured out what you did with your spare time in New York. Either way, he and Lynch conspired to kill a museum curator, and timed it to piggyback on your visitation schedule. The NYPD tossed it in the file with the rest of your killings. She was Vietnamese and lived on Riverside Drive. Ring a bell?"

Kinkelman shook his head, speechless more than denying what Crowe said.

"Lynch told me their nickname for you. *Yellowtail.* And the bar girl you killed in Thailand. You had a love-hate relationship with women, didn't you? You brought it back home from the war. And when Tommy was old enough, you introduced him to the same pleasures and abuses."

"No."

"Every now and again, you needed a fix. Bar Harbor was too close to home, so you went to Bangor. Then Portland or Boston once in a while. Strip joints and massage parlors, mostly Asian girls because that's who you hated. Still nursing the anger you brought home from the war, your country defeated by little men in straw hats and pajamas, your buddies killed, your paycheck taken by bar-girls who only pretended to love you."

"Shut the fuck up." Kinkelman shook the whiskey bottle at him.

"When screwing them and smacking them around wasn't

enough, you raised the bar. You started going to the Manhattan VA hospital to get the biannual medical for your pilot's license. But that was just an excuse to get out of Maine, act out your fantasies five hundred miles from home. You probably began with rapes, ever since you started going to New York in the early nineties."

Kinkelman stared at him.

"Yes, I'm familiar with your schedule. I'm working with an NYPD homicide detective. He has a bunch of cold cases dating back twelve years. Asian women, raped and murdered, their bodies dumped along Riverside Drive. He talked to the VA. We know those murders occurred within days of your being in town for your medical."

"You can't prove any of that."

"Not yet, but they'll take apart your house, your truck, your little hidey-hole apartment in the Lower East Village where Bishop let you stay when you came to town. All they need is one human hair, carpet fiber or fingerprint in a place that can't be explained away, and you're done for."

"You sonofabitch."

"You cooked this meal, now you can eat it."

"You had no right to talk to my son," Kinkelman screamed. "We had a good relationship. We were family, we loved each other. You destroyed that. He called me after you left, asked me what I'd done with all those videos. He was in tears. He said I was a monster."

"What did you tell him?"

"I told him I'd destroyed them years ago."

"You think he believed you?"

"He hung up on me."

They heard the wail of a siren coming out the road. Kinkelman turned in its direction.

"When I found your wife dead I called the police." Crowe let the statement sink in. "Why'd you kill her?"

From deep in Kinkelman's chest came a moan of despair and agony. "The woman I married died years ago. She had Alzheimer's. Without me, she'd be lost."

Crowe beckoned. "Let's go down to the house."

Kinkelman hurled himself at Crowe, the whiskey bottle swinging for his head. Crowe used the pistol like a steel stick and hit Kinkelman just below the wrist. The bottle flew from his hand and exploded on the rocks. Kinkelman fell crying to his knees as he cradled his broken wrist.

Kinkelman fell to his knees, crying with pain as he cupped his broken wrist with his other hand.

"Come on." Crowe grabbed Kinkelman's arm and pulled him upright. "The police will take you to the hospital."

"I can't go to jail." Kinkelman tore himself loose from Crowe's grip and ran toward the sea cliff. Without a moment's hesitation, he flung himself out into space, his arms flapping like a wounded bird.

Crowe went to the edge of the cliff. Down at the shoreline, where erosion had heaped a pile of jagged rocks, Kinkelman lay face down in the surf. Crowe felt sick to his stomach. He sat in one of the Adirondack chairs and set the pistol aside. The smell of whiskey was strong all around him.

He looked westward over the Gulf of Maine. Above the horizon was a bright pinprick of light. An evening star, what he knew in fact was Venus. In Mayan culture, the priests had worshipped Venus as an avatar of war. They'd pierce their tongues with a knife and draw a knotted string through the hole, flinging blood at Venus to appease her. Crowe hoped Kinkelman's death was sufficient to put an end to further sacrifice.

He heard a flutter of wings and a low-pitched hoot. He looked up at the owls' cage overhead. In his mission to confront Kinkelman, he'd completely forgotten the two birds that lived here.

He climbed atop the armrests of the Adirondack chair, raising his head to the level of the cage. He looked through the bars at the two owls. Big eyes in round faces stared back at him.

Kinkelman's last words reverberated in the silence. About his wife, *"Without me, she'd be lost."* And himself, *"I can't go to jail."*

Crowe fiddled with the latch and swung the cage door open. He got down from the chair and moved a few feet away.

After a few moments, one of the owls appeared in the doorway. It sat there a moment, claws gripping the frame, trying to decipher the unfathomable depth of open space that lay before it. Then it leaped into the air and rose into the sky. The other owl immediately followed, and joined its companion aloft. Together they circled and headed inland, into the trees, into the uncertainty that only true freedom could provide.

75

Tuesday, May 1

Barnet, Vermont

CROWE STOPPED FOR COFFEE twice on the five-hour drive back to Barnet. He'd been on the go - literally, around the world - for more than ten days without a pause. The last thing he needed now was to nod off at the wheel and end up in the ditch in the middle of nowhere. Coffee was his insurance that fatigue wouldn't catch up to him.

He'd been up late last night. After the police arrived, he'd pointed out Kinkelman's body on the shoreline and told them how he'd landed there. With both Kinkelmans dead, the circumstances were suspicious, but Crowe's account, including his 911 call to summon the police, held up from start to finish. In the end the Sheriff had declined to arrest him on suspicion of anything.

Instead, he'd fitted Crowe with a monitoring anklet and directed him to a local motel for the night. In the morning, the Sheriff had called the list of contacts Crowe provided - Bryan Abbott's criminal lawyer in Burlington, NYPD detectives Levinson and Sullivan, and FBI agents Cobb and Willis. Everyone had substantiated Crowe's claims - that he'd been retained to assist in the defense of Abbott's murder charge, that he was consulting for the NYPD on a cold case file, and that he'd helped the FBI apprehend a rogue state trooper who'd killed two men.

At noon, the Sheriff removed his monitoring anklet, shook Crowe's hand and sent him on his way. Crowe felt like one of those karma birds released at *Wat Doi Suthep*. Free again, but how long before the net of human circumstance descended upon him in another form of bondage? Best not to think about it, and drive while the driving was good.

He made several phone calls on the drive back.

To Tracey and his father, both of whom had been blindsided by his sudden departures, he offered his apologies. He brought them up to date and promised to call again once he was home in Toronto.

He summed up for Det. Levinson the key role of William Kinkelman in the Riverside Rapist cases. Levinson would send an NYPD forensics team up tomorrow to search Kinkelman's property and vehicle for evidence linking Willy the Kink to seven murders in Manhattan.

With Lynch's confession in the pipeline for the murders of Greer and Bishop, Crowe also told Levinson how Lynch had likely murdered Thi Nguyen in 2009 in order to protect his interests. Ironically, he and Bishop had subsequently quarreled about Lynch's brutal handling of Kitti Poornchai, and Lynch had killed his partner. Levinson and Sullivan would cooperate in putting that one to bed.

To Selena Greer and Michael Greer, who'd lost a companion and a brother, Crowe provided closure. He confirmed the police work to date, that Lynch had been apprehended and linked to Greer's murder.

He gave Kevin Blaikie a ballpark figure of how much money he'd spent in the past ten days. Blaikie was unconcerned but wanted to know what was happening in Abbott's case. Crowe had to cut it short when Blaikie was summoned to an urgent meeting. Blaikie insisted Crowe call back on the weekend to finish his story.

Shortly before six o'clock, Crowe turned off West Barnet Road and into the lane to Dharmapada. A hundred yards in, he came to the bridge over the stream. He parked the car and looked over the railing. The water level had dropped by more than two feet since Sunday night when Lynch had been swept away. The water no longer looked like chocolate milk, but was clear enough to see the stream bed. Crowe got back in his car and drove up to the house.

His friend Bryan came out to greet him. They embraced

warmly and Abbott thanked him again for rescuing him from spending the rest of his life in prison. Abbott insisted on carrying Crowe's luggage inside, saying he was just in time for dinner.

"It's great to be home again," Abbott said, "not only for me, but Neville too. The day after I was arrested, Lynch declared the entire property a crime scene and evicted Neville."

Crowe nodded. "Lynch needed some privacy to look for the Buddha."

Neville was just removing a lasagna from the oven. He embraced Crowe and patted him on the back with warm oven mittens he hadn't had a chance to remove.

Over a leisurely dinner, Crowe told his story once again for the benefit of these two whom he hadn't seen or spoken to in the last ten days.

"A classic case of greed and betrayal," Abbott observed. "Given Bishop's and Lynch's activities spanning almost four decades, their comeuppance was long overdue. But it's nothing short of amazing how you were able, with so little concrete evidence, to run them to ground."

"And all in a week's time," Neville joked.

"Even more remarkable," Abbott said, "was your identifying Kinkelman as a suspect in the Riverside Rapist murders. Yet he was just a bit player in the other business between Bishop and Lynch. How'd you single him out for the serial murders in Manhattan?"

"Kinkelman's chart indicated a disturbed mind," Crowe said. "Moon and Mars, lords of the fourth and twelfth houses, were debilitated in each other's sign. Moon in Scorpio for mental derangement, Mars in Cancer for uncontrollable rage. Mars with Saturn in the twelfth indicated sexual abuse, confinement, violence. Sadly, I didn't anticipate suicide."

"What about the timing of his killing sprees?"

"The Mars-Saturn complex was a pathological time bomb. Prior to killing in New York, he'd acted out in other ways. Once a month the transiting Moon triggered his Mars-

Saturn combo, prompting visits to massage parlors, or sexual assaults in New England.

"Something in year two thousand - maybe his wife's illness - sent Kinkelman off the rails. Depression and rage would be typical. He took advantage of his veteran's benefits to use the Manhattan VA clinic for his biannual medical. At the same time, transiting Mars passed over its natal position and he suffered a psychotic break.

"We'll never know why that first murder occurred, but it probably started out as a rape of opportunity, targeting a young Asian woman. Kinkelman had the use of an apartment Bishop made available to him. That's where he held his victim and sexually tortured her. But it got out of hand and he killed her.

"He dumped the body on Riverside Drive and went home to Maine. Time passed and no one came looking for him. He probably reverted to his old ways in Bangor and Portland. Two years later, when Mars made a full orbit and returned to its natal position in Cancer, he felt the urge again. He booked an appointment at the VA hospital in Manhattan and went back for more."

"What a monster," Abbott said.

"He'd harbored demons a long time," Crowe said. "No doubt he struggled with them, but eventually they got the better of him."

76

Wednesday, May 2

HAVING GONE TO BED EARLY in one of the cabins that hadn't been disturbed by Lynch, Crowe slept like a dead man and didn't wake up until seven. He splashed a little water on his face, folded a blanket on the floor and meditated for half an hour. When he emerged from the cabin, a crow called from the tree-line, *caw-caw-caw*.

Wednesday was ruled by Mercury, whose creatures were birds. *Pay attention to your namesake, Crowe. What's he trying to tell you?*

Crowe entered the house where he was greeted by the smell of oatmeal porridge on the stove. He sat with Bryan and Neville, enjoying one of life's simple pleasures - a healthy meal with agreeable companions - and for bonus points, maple syrup on his oatmeal.

At eight o'clock a black Ford Explorer came trundling through the parking lot, giving a brief toot on its horn before it passed the barn and headed out the dirt road toward the south end of the field.

"Guests?" Crowe said.

"The FBI left two agents here to find the Buddha. They were here all day Monday on their own. Yesterday they brought in two scuba divers from Portland who concentrated their search just downstream from where you saw Lynch go under."

"They haven't found it yet?"

"You'd think it would be close to where he went in. It weighed twenty-four pounds, didn't you say?"

"It was mostly covered in bubble-wrap," Crowe said. "That wouldn't have prevented it from sinking, but given a little buoyancy, the knapsack might have been carried quite a distance in that current."

"It's a mile and a half from here to the village bridge

where Lynch was found," Abbott said. "At the rate they're going, it'll take them weeks to search it all."

"There's a quicker way than that." Astrology had a strong tradition of locating lost objects via horary charts. Crowe opened his astrology app and asked himself, *Where is the Buddha*?

It was 8:03 AM Wednesday morning. The ascendant was Gemini, its lord Mercury in the tenth house Pisces. Mercury, primary indicator for the missing object, was in a watery sign to the south.

Gemini was associated with roads, railway lines, tunnels and bridges, anything that provided passage from one place to another. The first third of Gemini suggested a portal of some kind - in the old days, a city gate, the entrance to an estate, a drawbridge to a castle.

The Moon was in the third house, which echoed the indications of a roadway, tunnel or bridge. This reinforcement of themes gave Crowe an idea. He stood and pocketed his phone.

"Do you have anything we can use as a grappling hook?" he asked Abbott.

"I'll get something." Neville threw on a jacket and left the house.

When Crowe and Abbott stepped outside a few moments later, Neville emerged from the lecture hall carrying a long rod with a hook at one end. Crowe recognized the tool Neville had used to open the high louvered windows for air circulation.

They walked down the lane toward the highway. Halfway between the house and West Barnet Road was the wooden bridge upon which Crowe had paused yesterday evening. A hundred yards upstream, the two FBI agents stood on the bank while the scuba divers explored the tangled thickets along either side of the stream.

Crowe descended the embankment and peered under the bridge. A mass of debris was jammed into the wooden pilings on the south side of the bridge, although the north side was perfectly clear, where even a rowboat could have passed. He beckoned for Neville to pass him the pole. He used it to probe beneath the tangle of debris. Within moments, he hooked something weighty but movable, and pulled it to the surface.

Neville joined him, holding the pole so Crowe could seize the knapsack as soon as it emerged from the water, one of its straps caught by the pole's hook. He slung it onto his back and clambered up the embankment.

"We found it," Abbott shouted to the FBI agents. "We found the Buddha."

He and Crowe opened the knapsack, peeled away some of the bubble wrap and held it up for the agents to see. The agents gave a brief cheer and tugged on the safety lines, signaling their scuba divers to surface.

Crowe shouldered the knapsack and carried the Buddha back to the house. They took it into the lecture hall and removed the remaining bubble wrap. Neville fetched water and paper towels to wipe it clean.

They knew they couldn't keep it, that it had to go back to *Wat Doi Suthep*, but while it was briefly in their custody, they would honor it. They placed the Buddha on the altar. Abbott lit some incense.

The cloud cover broke and a ray of sun came through one of the upper windows, bathing the Buddha in light. The three of them dropped to their knees and assumed meditation postures, opening themselves to be transported, perhaps illuminated.

~ The End ~

The Author

Alan Annand is a writer of crime fiction, offering an intriguing blend of mystery, suspense, thriller and New Age *noir*. When he's not dreaming up ingenious ways to kill people and thrill readers, he occasionally finds therapy in writing humor, short stories and *faux* book reviews.

Before becoming a full-time novelist, he worked as a technical writer for the railway industry, a corporate writer for private and public sectors, a human resources manager and an underground surveyor.

Currently, he divides his time between writing in the AM, astrology in the PM, and meditation on the OM. For those who care, he's an Aries with a dash of Scorpio.

You can find him on Facebook, Goodreads and LinkedIn, or follow him on Pinterest, Tumblr and Twitter.

Crime fiction by Alan Annand:

Al-Quebeca
Harm's Way
Hide in Plain Sight

The New Age Noir series
#1, *Scorpio Rising*
#2, *Felonious Monk*
#3, *Soma County* (2015)

For more information, see his website *www.sextile.com*.

Printed in Great Britain
by Amazon

86678682R00188